DAYBREAK BIRDSONG ALWAYS WAKES HIM

The Lives of Billy the Kid

DAYBREAK BIRDSONG ALWAYS WAKES HIM

The Lives of Billy the Kid

Pamela Ryder

TUSCALOOSA

The University of Alabama Press
Tuscaloosa, Alabama 35487-0380

FC2 is an imprint of the University of Alabama Press

Book Design: Publications Unit, Department of English, Illinois State University; Director: Steve Halle, Production Interns: Grace Benefiel and Molly Oldenburg

Cover image: *Storm Front* by Moira Marti Geoffrion, oil on paper panel, 2024; courtesy of the artist and the Mark Sublett Medicine Man Gallery

Cover design: Terrell Harris

Typeface: Adobe Caslon Pro (text)

Library of Congress Cataloging-in-Publication Data is available from the Library of Congress.

Paper: 978-1-57366-215-4
Ebook: 978-1-57366-918-4

For Gordon Lish

Author's Note: Sunup

Sunup. A clear desert morning in spring. The month the Apache call the Moon of Waking Bears. Birdsong commencing before the world is sun enkindled and the hardpan begins to heat. The folds in the distant foothills are dark with piñon and ponderosa pine, but here where the land is level, the terrain is treeless but for a sparse scattering of juniper and a solitary tree in the courtyard, a cottonwood gone newly green. A pair of desert doves so perched. Apache plume in flower. Buds on the bigleaf sage. Billy the Kid sits captive and shackled and awaiting his hanging. The story is well known. His killings long remembered. The names of the dead and the circumstances of their deaths chronicled. Nonetheless, a true account of his life has been lacking and herein it will be told before forever lost to time and the scouring winds of the West. What has been overlooked or deemed irrelevant will be revealed: the details of his days written in his own hand, the documents previously considered inconsequential, and the specifics of his murder by the unrelenting lawman who hunted him down. Then let us begin on this morning in 1881, with the sun just above Las Montañas de Sacramento and the boulders in the gullies glowing. With the men carrying the slipknot noose tied and newly tallowed and their shadows drawn long and narrow before them. With the pair of desert doves taking flight as the rope is thrown over a limb of the cottonwood. And with Billy the Kid numbering his days. Seeking the sum. Taking stock. Finding contingencies fraught. Endeavors each of us best undertake.

Chapter 1
Preparation for a Hanging in the High Desert
Lincoln, New Mexico, Courthouse and Lockup
April 28, 1881 – The Moon of Waking Bears

At last apprehended in this the spring of his nineteenth year, the boy desperado sits ankle-shackled in his cell, hearing the sweep and sough of the high desert wind in the boughs of the courtyard cottonwood beyond the single barred window set high in the whitewashed wall of adobe brick now dappled with light, a sound that carries him back to fragments of his first spring in the world—a child wind-swayed on a limb of a persimmon tree, just a bit of a boy he was. *A tiny creature he is*, his Mam said at her first glimpse of him. And his Da calling him *Just a smidgen of a lad, this little Billy*, this tad of a boy bedded in a dangling basket and squinting at the spangling of light through the weave of leaf and bough around him. And now in his cell, though so confined, he can recall the boy he was—can see the boy he was—vigilant even then in his beginnings, watchful of all that passed before him, a child that some might call delicate being small and slight in the shoulders and pale as a dinner plate. A child not given to fuss or struggle. So easily had his mother wrapped him in a coverlet and tucked him into a wickerwork basket which, he now recalls, ever so slightly swung when the wind rose and the twigs clicked. Or so he seems to recall. Or does not recall but instead has assembled a memory from a mother's story. *Once more, please Mam. About you putting me up in a tree.* Or a father's familiar tale. *Tell it again, Da. Tell about you fetching me down.* Or is it that the entirety of a life does not play out at the moment of death as it is said to do but instead unravels in the hours or days before what we fear looms ahead.

He lies belly down in the wall-hung bed in this lockup, wrapped in the rough serape they have given him against the high-desert cold of the New Mexico night and morning, in this the month the Apache call the Moon of Waking Bears, the season of their stirring in the close and sheltered places after a winter of sleep. Their great lumbering forth from the rock-tumble dens. The windfallen tree hollows. The forested foothills of Las Montañas de Sacramento cloaked in daybreak shadows of cerulean blue.

The desert floor is cool in these very early hours. Stones and seams of alkali in the wash-bed banks seem to glow. Denizens of the hardpan head homeward—carrion bug, darkling beetle, piñon mouse spied by a ground owl who extends her feathered leg and without struggle or deceleration bears it aloft in the clutch of her taloned toes while the brood of motherless mouslets begin to die in their den.

Now come the sounds of the Chihuahuan desert morning: chatter and trill of pipit in the sage, of sparrow in the ocotillo, and wren in the smokewood. Awakenings in the coop at the rear of Pablito's Egg & Produce: soft clucking (though this small choir was diminished when just last evening a leghorn hen was snatched sleeping from her perch and spirited away so swiftly that her sisters roosting beside her slept soundly on during her departure, and presently she remains only as a single feather clinging to a fox's snout).

In the livery, early stirrings. The snorting horses, a bleating mule. A lone dun-coat dog trots past the storefronts and along the walkway boards but pausing once to sniff a pair of frayed bloomers that had been tossed from a second-story window of the Cards & Kinship, and once to water a patron of said establishment who is sleeping off the evening. In the rooms one flight up, the ladies rouse their stinking, half-dressed clientele who lie snoring in a rumple of dingy sheets damp with a night of sweat, spilled liquor, and whatever else has leaked out of them, most with their unbuttoned denims and unbuckled chaps bunched at the ankles—so hurried were they to service their peckers and spend the remainder of the night drooling into the mattress ticking.

The desk-clock chimes on the jailhouse desk. Deputy James Lee Bell jerks awake and tips his chair forward. His hand goes to his holster and his bright new pistol. Billy? he calls. You up Billyboy?

Yes he is up, Billyboy is. Daybreak birdsong always wakes him. He sits. He puts his feet on the floor. They have not taken his boots: low-rise ropers, square-heeled, scuffed and missing stitching at the vamp. But his hat, yes. They have taken the hat he claimed his father had given him: a black, brimmed drover, crown imploded. *Belonged to my Da*, he liked to say, though this was a fabrication. It had been appropriated, as the sheriff of Lincoln County called it, when he took Billy in and locked Billy up and set it on his desk atop a plaster bust of General Custer.

And the sheriff had taken his horse as well, a piebald Choctaw, an Indian pony. A breed known for endurance and clever ways. Billy had ridden it when he was a drover, a ranch hand, a wrangler, and a rustler, and ridden it through much of the Territory, high plains deserts, and piñon pine mountains. He had asked the sheriff: Who's looking after my horse? Where'd he get to? Sheriff Garrett smiled and scratched his head. Well now Billy, he said, I can't hardly think of a reason a feller in your predicament to be needing a horse anymore, can you?

A soft coo-cooing comes from somewhere. Billy looks to the window above him—the bars there solidly set into sandstone and adobe—and beyond the window of this second-floor cell is his view of a single cloud adrift, the ghost of a morning moon, and the top of the courtyard cottonwood where a twosome of desert doves the color of weathered wood roosts and calls.

A flycatcher arrives at the window ledge—all flit and fidget and dance, a wounded lacewing twitching in its mouth—then flies off nearly as soon as it is seen, and again he is remembering that summer day in the persimmon tree and the bird that lit on the basket's rim and he reached his hand to it as if to take it for his own, this marvel, this wonderment—birds being God's own seraphim—what his mother liked to say when she sang to herself—only to herself, and the song now comes back to him—what she called a Timoleague tune, though once in a tavern he asked a favor of a fiddle-man to play it, *my Mam she used to sing it*, but the fiddle-man said he did not know it though he be from County Cork himself, born and raised, but told him *sorry lad, not that one—never heard of it* and neither did any other Irishman Billy would ever meet in all his life and travels:

Feathered angels at my bed,
One to keep me safe from dread.
And when the final bell does toll,
One to bear away my soul

and he recalls that the seraph that lit on the basket's wicker rim crouched as if readying for flight when his hand went to it, but instead it raised its tail and shot a fetid stream upon the coverlet, while others flew over him branch to branch and out of reach.

And so the child did wait in his hanging basket, even as the day went cold as some summer days will do. The wind rose, a hiss of it setting the leaves to clattering on their leafstalks and turning out their silvery undersides, but no one came to fetch him in, not even with dusk and the arrival of a sparrow flock come to roost unafraid of the intruder in the tree. They huddled to their twiggy perches, hunched against coming dark. But no one comes to fetch him in, not even as a soft rain falls, not even as darkness awakens the lightning beetles and sets them airborne, these winged lights that glow ghostly and float all around him like stars escaped from their courses. And still the child waits. The sky clears so he can see the motions of a rising moon through the portals between the leaves, and his small face shines in its light, and then in shadow, then moonlight, then shadow until the moon has set and the sky is sprayed with constellations. The Great and Little Bears lumber over him and now Cygnus is rising, but unlike any swan of this world that follows the flow of a shining river trail, it sweeps along the spill of the Milky Way. And the child sleeps. Or something like sleep—the wary sleep of journeying cormorants and kittiwake gulls as they wing for weeks—months—above the open sea. Dawn now, with color in the east as the sun recommences its circuit. Daybreak birdsong waked him that morning and as it henceforth always will: warbler, catbird, sparrow, others. Warmer now. The child still waits. No one comes to fetch him in. Not even now as he pisses himself. And shits himself and pisses some more, soaked from below in it and from above with last night's rain that rises steaming from the coverlet and from the bright, wet leaves, the hanging drops. Little prisms, these. For the child to watch, to marvel.

At last there are voices below him—his Da—his father—shouting to his mother *Where Catherine? You be leaving him where? Up there?*—and there they are, down there and pointing up at him hanging there in his basket. *Jaysus woman you've lost your mind, you have*—that summer day in a persimmon tree, his Mam crying *No Paddy leave him be! Wait for the Wee Folk. He's not our Billy*, but his Da pushing her away and saying *Not our Billy, Catherine? Gone daft have you? You born him! You're his Mam. You!*

Oh please leave him Paddy! his mother is wailing. *One more night for the Wee Folk to be coming and they'll be taking him back, they will.*

And his Da bending the branch and reaching up and saying in a softer voice than anything he's ever said: *Ah there Billy, poor lad. Poor lad. Your Mother might near to kill you* and his Da's big hands around him: *Why you're cold as a clam*, toted down on his Da's shoulder, *Woo! And stinking to high heaven, your nappie full up but not so much as a peep from you*, the basket left hanging, *just a bit of a lad for now, that you may be but a doughty one for certain*, that summer day or was it some other day. Or some other seraph or bird. Though not the ones for watching over good boys, his mother said, but those for bad boys like Billy: the creatures fallen from grace and doomed by the devil to do the bidding of devious Wee Folk and Sprites and Fairies. That would be the sort of birdy creature for you to follow, for you to fly to Billy, she said. Or some other sort of flying creature or thing that lives in the air.

Billy sits shackled in his cell. He swings his legs upon the canvas cot and folds himself over waistwise, reaches past chain and shackle-cuff to his boot-heel, the well-worn sole bearing at its perimeter a line of cobbler's nails. One nailhead brightly galvanized, bigger than the rest, and loose in its footings, a pivot he lifts with a fingernail. He twists the heel and it swivels open: there in the hollow keep a paper scrap has been folded and refolded to matchbook size, pressed in place with a pencil stub set in crosswise. The nub is blunt. He scrapes it to point with short strokes along the sandstone wall. He carefully unfolds the scrap. It is a list—the writing miniscule, in his cramped but upright hand. *Bigger letters Billy!* What his mother had said, attempting to teach him. *And hold your pencil proper now*, she said. *Are you just an idjit natural born or was it Sprites switched my true Billy for an imbecile, which?* And he hears her still. Even now and so many years gone by he hears her as he grips the pencil stub, tongue mashed between his rabbity front teeth and protruding just a bit, and he adds to his list: *dusky flycatcher*. He blows away the graphite dust and replaces the paper and pencil stub into the hollow heel of his boot. Beyond the window, the crown of the cottonwood lifts and pitches in a gust of foothill wind—smell of dry juniper and blue sage. Palo verde. Somewhere the ocotillo is in bloom. Fleecewood is budding. Now sudden gunfire from somewhere near. A shudder in the treetop as twigs are shattered, leaves dispersed. Birdsong silenced. The doves rise and whistle away.

The song of the dusky flycatcher (Empidonax oberholseri) begins with a rising "perll-lit" followed by a raspy "perdrrt" and a final "psseet!" all over the course of just one second, as if its passage through life be brief.

—Birds of America and the Territories,
Chapter 51: Tyrant Flycatchers

Breakfast was to be whatever he wanted, as is the custom for the condemned—for who can say what sustenance is offered in the hereafter or who the chef may be. Or if oblivion even keeps a kitchen.

What'll it be Billyboy? says Deputy James Lee Bell. (How curious are the living to know on what the doomed would dine.) Sheriff Garrett, he says whatever you want since Millie—that's the sheriff's missus—she'll fix it. Seeing it's the last meal you choke down before the rope chokes you for good, see. Coulda been a beefsteak but too late now. Likely as not we fed the last of that to the posse that brung you in. But chicken-in-a-pie? Chicken, we always got chicken. Me I like my chicken-in-a-pie with okras mixed in but some folks get put off by the slime. On account of okras being second cousins to slugs. But cook 'em correctly and you cut down on the slime considerable. You best cook 'em whole and cut 'em later. That seals in the slime, see. Not entirely eliminated, mind you, but cuts it down considerable—and he stops and cocks his head the way a listening dog would do and he raises a finger.

There is a faint scrambling on the roof tiles, then a soft coo-cooing. He looks to the ceiling. Hear that? says Deputy Bell. Sure you do. Doves. Nesting soon somewhere around, likely that big cottonwood out front. Damn easy shooting too. Here Billyboy. Take a looky here. See this? Got me this here new Colt six-shooter. They call it the Peacemaker. Beauty, ain't she. Don't need no rifle for dove-shooting. It's fish in a barrel. Missed 'em this morning but I'll get 'em. Goddamn doves. Good eating, doves. Put 'em in a pie if you're scarce on chicken but you best watch out for the birdshot. Broke a tooth once not watching out. Millie won't fix 'em. Not no how. She says—you shoot 'em, James Lee—you dress 'em. That Millie she . . .

Billy is face down on the cot.

He mumbles into the canvas, Good God will you not shut your goddamn gob-hole.

What's that? says Deputy James Lee Bell. Say that again?

But Billy will not say. And Billy will not eat this morning, preferring to avoid releasing a pantsful of piss and shit dripping into his boot as he hangs noosed and dangling by the neck. So having no last request, providing no answer at all, he is served the same as any detainee be it fugitive or hooligan, cutthroat or drunkard: cornbread, cabbage, and posole served in a redware bowl covered with a red-checked cloth. Pewter spoon. Though Millie the sheriff's missus has kindly sent along a bottle of cherry pop. What she thinks a boy would want—this outlaw just a boy, after all. Or recently just a boy, and that was enough.

The sun lifts above Las Montañas Mescaleras. Bluffs aflame. The rising heat. Smaller forms know what is coming. Tracks in the sand close and delicate as rows of stitching—the tiny thoroughfares of nighttime travelers scuttling to their bits of shade in dens and crevices. The dung-ball beetle. The Jerusalem cricket. The doves whistle in, one trailing a strand of barn straw in its beak. One with none. They resume their perch, side by side in the cottonwood. Deputy, calls Billy. But softly. No sense in getting the jailer's gander up.

He stands. The chain clinks. The leg irons slide. They are shackles meant for a bigger limb. A bigger man. A man. His leg has gone raw and weeping where the shackle-cuff rubs the boot shaft and the chain attaches. An axe would be handy. Pick-axe. Or a farrier's hammer, that being big enough to split links. Or even, ever hopeful: the key. Deputy James Lee Bell keeps a ringful belt-looped and his pistol hardly ever holstered and has sometimes waved it about carelessly and cocked, though sometimes rightly pointed and he never turns his back on Billy. No, no key, not just yet, thinks Billy. He looks again to the window. Will it be that cottonwood that does me in? he wonders. High enough sure, by the look of it. Though high enough might have nothing to do with it, he knew. He remembers. Another memory, another tree. When just a boy his father had taken him to a hanging. What the lad needs to see, said his father, having toted him north from New York's Irish Town to Elmira, the upstate county seat sanctioning the event where outcry against public executions had not yet reached. Billy sat straddled on his father's shoulders, and the entire event—all of what he was brought to see—did not go well, no not so very well at all. *Watch now*, his father told him, pointing to the gaunt and downcast man—one Henry Gardiner—his hands bound up behind him as he is pushed through the crowd and as those in his path step aside to let him walk on to the place prepared for him under an old sycamore tree often utilized for such purposes. He faces the throng of onlookers. His name is announced, his crime recounted aloud: *whereby having been a soldier of the Twelfth Regiment of the Union Infantry, and brought to ruination by Godlessness, greed, and drink, did thereby beat and murder Amasa Mullock with the butt of his musket for the old man's watch and money thereby bringing shame upon his regiment, and therefore by subsequent trial and conviction, hereby to hang, hereby, therefore, hereby, thereby, whereby.* A horse waits. A newly-broke roan, skitterish. A crate is placed beside the horse. How about a hand here fellas, says the man who had been doing the pushing. Men in the crowd step forward and hoist, most clumsily, the bound-up man upon on the newly-broke roan. Go on, get on up there Gardiner, don't give us no trouble. He sits upright in the saddle and slightly rocking as the roan shifts leg to leg, impatient and pawing at the earth. The noose is placed. Adjusted. The rope is thrown over a big bough of the sycamore. Bits of bark fall. Sycamores well known to shed. The bound man on the newly-broke roan turns his head to look about as much as the noose will allow: there the boughs above him, the dangling seedballs of the tree, the nickering horse under him, the red earth road leading out of town and away, away to the green hills beyond, and then the crowd—he gazes out upon the crowd, and it is our Billy he spies among those other faces, our Billy on the shoulders of his father, higher than the rest. Billy, taking ahold of his father's hair to steady himself and raising his hand in hello at the bound-up man looking back at him.

Hidy, calls Billy.

Quiet now, says his father.

A black-suited man in a black wide-brimmed hat steps up upon the crate and produces a small gunnysack, frayed at the open end where it has been cut down to the size of a man's head. Attempts are made pull it over the head of the man astride the just-broke roan, but he thrashes, squirms. The black-suited man with the sack in his hands puts on a face of weary disgust and turns his head and spits. Come on now Gardiner, he says, let's just get this over and done with. But the writhing and the thrashing continues, and the black-suited man smacks the face of the condemned who is perched upon the just-broke roan. You better settle down now, he says. The man on the just-broke roan speaks. Or what? he says. And he does not settle down. He bobs and twists. Well goddamn you, says the man with the sack and he takes the open edge of the sack with his two hands and gives it an angry and final downward yank, and roughly stuffs the excess folds under the noose. He turns to the crowd laughing and shaking his head and telling the crowd, Ornery cuss ain't he? and stepping down from the crate. You go ahead, he says to a second man, the preacher man, standing by. I'm done with him, he says, so you go on and do whatever it is you do. The second man, hatless, steps up, a bible laid open in his hands. He looks into the crowd, waits for quiet, and it comes. He reads, not nearly loud enough, almost to only himself, so all lean bibleward to hear it and some do and some do not, but it is nothing no one in the crowd has not heard before: the felons that hung on their crosses beside Our Lord hung on his, the choice of repentance or eternal stewing in the lake of fire, etc., take your pick. And turning to the noosed and gunnysacked man on the just-broke roan, says again: You too Mr. Gardiner, take your pick. And then he waits, but with no response forthcoming he then reads on. The noosed and gunnysacked Gardiner sits silently in the saddle, shifts with the shift of the restless roan. The sack begins to move. Then somehow begins to shrink, and then to disappear. The crowd now murmuring. No one sure what they are seeing or could know what spectacle will come. The cloth gathers in small tight folds at the man's mouth-hole as he takes it in his teeth, taking it in, untucking it free of the noose, swallowing the sack bit by bit as it slides forward over his head, peeling down from his head, and now down over his eyes so he can look out upon the crowd once more, and there is that child again, perched upon his father's shoulders, that boy again waving to him again.

Mister! Here I am, cries Billy, holding tight to his father's head and his father's hair.

Quiet Billy, says his father.

Over here Mister! Says Billy.

Quit it now I say! his father says. Ow! Leave go I tell you, you little shite.

But Billy does not leave go. He is pulled down screaming and clutching a sizable tuft of his father's hair in his fist, later to be discovered by a crow picking through the food refuse of picnickers and be carried off to line a nest. Mother of God what is it Billy? his father told him. What's wrong with you lad? Is it the fits you're taking? says his father setting him down. Set him back up there or he'll miss it, someone says.

And although both the Chemung County magistrate and mob believed the sycamore bough to be quite sound, it unexpectedly did crack clear through when the doomed man was relieved of his seat on the saddle cinched to the newly-broke roan who snorted and reared, his eyes rolling back to white, and then prematurely bolted, being additionally spooked by the ignition of a packet of short-fuse pyrogenics expertly detonated by two schoolhouse truants crouched behind Smiley's Dry Goods, and resulting in a brief interval of midair suspension before both tree limb and felon were flung earthward, and despite the immediate attempts of those in attendance to pry open his mouth and dislodge the tote sack (though succeeding only in tearing out his tongue) and to unravel the rope (the knots made more knuckle-busting by the forward thrust of the frightened animal, combined with the increased tensile strength of hemp when wet—oh yes, it had started to rain), the cause of death according to the circuit coroner (officially summoned for executions characterized as "bungled") was listed as the "concomitant effects of cranial contusion caused by a bough bashing in the decedent's occiput and windpipe hindrance due to ingestion of a gunnysack" and further detailed in the headlines as a

SHOCKING SCENE AT GALLOWS!

> *Those gathered in Elmira to witness the hanging of convicted murderer Henry Gardiner were left aghast by a barbaric display as the condemned man attempted to consume his death hood, bled from a head wound, and twitched for almost twenty minutes before final pronouncement of death.*
>
> *The Chemung County Chronicle*
> *Evening Edition March 15, 1866*

And let us not forget the men who cut the rope away from the sycamore limb, and as they lifted the body into the buckboard with piss and shit dripping, one said: Whew, Hank. If I'm ever strung up for something remind me not to have breakfast.

No, it did not go well, not well at all.

The newly-broke and runaway roan would later be found in the lot behind Elmira Eats grazing in the green patch where the kitchen crew dumps their dish-wash water, the soil there wet and the flora lush.

So: Billy sits shackled with a view from his jail cell window. There the courtyard. The sparrows bathing in a dust wallow, crouched and fluttering. The cottonwood with its big limb ready for rope. There it stands. Too bad, thinks Billy. A public platform, even one slam-dash cut and hammered, would better serve to strangle me dead than an old cottonwood. But he'd heard no hammering. No rhythmic hruff hruff hruff of saw. And no mob looking for a lynching. No angry gaggle had come in the night hoisting torches. No crowd of the just curious had assembled. Perhaps a transfer was in the planning. Maybe they would haul him away in a traveling pokey heading out for Carrizozo, the county seat.

Or Ruidoso, a good bit bigger. After all, eventually some sort of crowd would gather, requiring a plaza to accommodate the ruck and rabble with space enough so spectators needn't be perching in the trees like crows. Space as well for picnics—tablecloths and counterpanes spread with what country folks tote to a necktie party: crumb-fried chicken, mayonnaise potatoes, lemonade pinked with sumac, hummingbird cake. Everyone arriving with their reasons. Some spouting eye-for-an-eye scripture. Some come to someday tell their offspring that they'd witnessed the string-up of a celebrated assassin, the boy desperado Billy the Kid. And some come to look upon a man about to die in preparation for the day their deeds would be judged. As if such preparation would be possible. Oh yes, Billy is certain that many will make the trip in from the territories and from districts afar to witness his demise, choked to death on this to be his last day on this earth.

A day so much the same as his first day in the world, newly born and so similarly noosed. A strangling child—a disturbing sight indeed, said the doctor who nineteen years prior had been summoned to the bedside of a laboring Irishwoman in the poorest of New York city tenements and there finding Billy nearly born, his neck encircled by the birth cord, an earlier noose than the one he presently awaits. Or so it had been told. Or so it has been said.

Billy turns his boot-heel on the pivot nail. He unfolds the paper and takes up his pencil stub. He adds one more bird to his list: *clay-colored sparrow.*

He looks again to the window. There the bright day. He sees that the cottonwood leaves are still spring green and the catkins have not yet gone to floss.

The ocotillo flowers are already in bloom.

Javelina and their young piglets have been seen rooting among the stones in the graveyard south of town.

Sparrows flitter in the courtyard dust.

The song of the clay-colored sparrow (Spizella pallida) is a curious "bzzz bzzz zza zza" sung from an open perch—a position that increases the defense of its territory, but its vulnerability as well.
—Birds of America and the Territories, Chapter 77: New World Sparrows, Juncos

Chapter 2
The Infant in Distress

Doctor Arthur Broadwater's Guide to Pregnancy and Birth Second Edition, 1890: Strangulation In The Womb

Myths regarding cord strangulation abound. There is no truth to the notion that it is caused by the pregnant woman wearing a daisy chain around her neck, by wringing the neck of barnyard fowl, or by raising her arms above her head and causing the umbilical cord to migrate upward. I have encountered such superstitions among many poor and foreign folk, the Irish only one among many.

The Strangled Infant is a sight disturbing to even the most experienced of physicians: the dusky cast to the features, the protrusion of the tongue, the bulging eyes, and the tiny lifeless hands still clutching at its neck in a futile attempt to free itself from the umbilical cord that has become a noose. With breathing restricted, death of the infant is imminent. However, if the strangling cord is promptly released, the child may not die, but the temporary hypoxia may hamper future growth and impede progression to a normal height.

In 1861, I was called to assist in a difficult delivery in the poor Irish district of New York. The infant was in urgent distress as the umbilical cord was tightly wrapped and tangled about his neck. I immediately set about releasing the choking cord as the baby emerged, thereby permitting spontaneous respiration and restoring circulation.

The infant, however was a puny one. And as fate would have it, I was fortunate to encounter the boy years later during his adolescence when I happened to attend to his consumptive mother, and thereby reassess his appearance.

The boy had indeed grown, but he remained of small stature and was frequently referred to as "The Kid."

Chapter 3
Speak, Whisper, Croak

Incantations of the Leech-Woman of County Dún Laoghaire
Midwife to the Birth of Senoll Uathach the Hideous, 1401
Translated 1801 from the Original Gaelic by Donnegal Céilechair

Strangulation in the womb can occur when the pregnant woman wrings the neck of a chicken, or raises her arms when reaching, or forces a demented person to swallow. Speak the incantation to ward off strangulation:

Oscail an scornach,	*Open the throat,*
Anáil agus ithe.	*Breathe and eat.*

A bird perched at an open window causes deformity of the infant's shoulder blades. Keep windows shut during pregnancy and whisper the incantation:

Dúnann mé an fhuinneog,	*I shut the window,*
Lúb an cnámh.	*Bend the bone.*

Misshapes of the mouth occur when skinning rabbits or dreaming of ravens during pregnancy. Avoid encounters with these creatures and croak the incantation nightly:

Fágann aislingí mo cheann,	*Dreams leave my head,*
Dorchadas a chur i mo shúile.	*Put darkness in my eyes.*

Chapter 4
The Mother-to-Be of Billy the Kid
Serves Tea (and Scones)
Irish Town, New York
May 4, 1861

Ms. Catherine McCarty is pouring tea into the blue willow cups. Ah, dearie, she tells Mrs. Marjorie Darcy. I've had two little lads gone now, don't you know. Living only a day or so and then with the angels. So I'm asking my Paddy if he's hoping for a little lass this time. A daughter might be more likely to go on living.

No need asking him, says Marjory Darcy. You know it be a lad he's wanting, what all of them be wanting and this one, don't we now be saying our prayers? And asking that this little one be the one to live past his first days and be keeping on, keeping on. And your Paddy is sure to be naming him Patrick after his own self.

No, he'll not be a Patrick, says Catherine McCarty. My two that died, we were naming them Patrick both. But not this one, no. This one the dear Lord willing we be calling him William Henry, after Paddy's little brother. William Henry McCarty. Just eight year he was when he went to falling into the beet-chopper.

I thought it was the slurry tank.

Ah, no. That was Patrick's Da, it was. His own Da was the one lost in the slurry tank. Up on the ladder he was and poking in with the big pole for breaking up the crust at the brim and the gasses come out and he goes in. Overcome they called it. No, William was his brother, the poor lad, the one they find in the chopper. Or the parts of him.

So this one coming is to be a William then. But you're sure to be calling him Billy, says Marjory Darcy.

A Billy he will be, and don't you just know my Paddy will be toting his tiny lad Billy on his shoulder off to the pubs and telling the pub-keep: A pint for me please and a short one for my little Billy here. And can't I be hearing him already? says Mrs. Catherine McCarty. He'll be telling his little Billy: I'll be drinking that one for you lad, I will. But now don't you go telling your Mam on me.

Go on with you then, says Mrs. Marjory Darcy. Don't have me laughing now, I'll be spitting out my tea through my nose, she says.

Both blow into the steaming cups. There are scones in a dish. Have yourself a scone there, says Mrs. Catherine McCarty.

A tasty scone, says Mrs. Marjory Darcy.

Well wasn't it you showing me? says Catherine McCarty.

Well wasn't it you baking it? says Mrs. Marjory Darcy. Currents these are or raisins?

Persimmons. Minced. But the buttermilk is what makes it, says Mrs. Catherine McCarty.

Buttermilk yes, if you can get it.

If you can get it.

Well.

So, shall we get to it? says Mrs. Catherine McCarty. She takes hold of the gold ring on her finger. Me knucks been swelling up on me, same as with the last two, she says and she twists it off. This trick, she says, is it always true?

Always true and always telling, says Mrs. Marjory Darcy. You remember Flanna Devlin down Gouverneur Slip. We had to be hanging her ring on the last bit of her hair, what hair she had left after the big fire someone set. A wretched sight, you remember—the poor woman carrying out her little Molly dead with the smoke and she scorched herself. And everyone in the street shouting out Bernie! Bernie! Looking high and low for that wag of a husband of hers. Everyone asking poor

Molly holding on to the dead one still in her arms, Was he with you? Is your Bernie still in the house?—thinking he'd be burning up. And when what was left standing is just chimneys and embers still steaming from the bucket brigade, were there not twenty men with their lanterns lit, my own Geoff among then, picking through the hot bricks with their pokers and not finding a trace of a burnt-up Bernard Devlin. But don't you know come morning it's Liam Quinn the pub-keep at the Plough & Plover finding Bernie under a table—soused enough he didn't come to till noon. Flanna—poor scarred-up thing—she lives to forgive the rotten sot. Scarred, and hairless or nearly so, but good enough for Bernie to keep on having a poke at her. And it's not hardly a half year gone by when Flanna comes asking me for a reading for the new life she's carrying. So I go on and do what I do. I loop her wedding ring on her last bit of her scorched-up hair and get it going. Get it swinging and back and forth it goes the way it would for a girl child, but then it goes spinning for a boy. We do it again and we do it again and it's the same. Give it up, she says. So we give it up. And eight months later what is it but twins, one of each. So. The trick did tell, it always does, and she names the girl Missy for her dead Molly and the other one Melvyn. Both of them dead that very spring. Missy—the quinsy. Melvyn—the flux. You remember. But enough. No more talk of dead little ones. Such talk might stick. Now pluck out a strand of your longest locks, dearie girl, and we'll soon know for sure what's coming.

Mrs. Catherine McCarty unfastens the stay-comb on the top of her head. The comb in her teeth. The twist of hair unfurls. Taking it by turns in her hands. Winding a strand twice, three times, around her pointing finger, and she gives a tug. Here you have it, she says, and please keep a good grip. I don't want to be yanking out another.

A pair of noisy starlings have taken up residence in a rot-hollow in the tree-of-heaven that grows in the alley.

A light rain has started. The shirts and sheets strung across the alleyway flap and billow and women rush to their windows. The pulley wheels squeak and chirp as the lines are reeled in and the sparrows answer back.

Chapter 5
Brass Wedding Ring

THE NEW YORK MUSEUM OF CITY HISTORY

Exhibit 42: Brass Wedding Ring of Catherine McCarty Antrim,

Mother of Wm. Henry McCarty, also known as Billy the Kid.

On loan from the estate of Marjory Darcy, friend of Catherine McCarty

A popular practice of the past century to determine the sex of an unborn child was the so-called Ring Predictor Method. The pregnant woman would place her gold wedding ring on a strand of her hair, suspend it over her gravid abdomen, and observe its movement. Catherine McCarty had summoned her friend, Marjory Darcy, to perform the test. Mrs. Darcy described the event in her journal and maintained that the ring did not move in the expected patterns, but broke free from the strand of hair that held it and "went flying around the room, so I throws the window open and out it goes." It was not until years later that the ring was recovered, long after Catherine McCarty had remarried and moved to Wichita with her young sons, Joseph and Billy. Marjory Darcy had been pinning laundry to the clothesline strung over the alley way near her kitchen window when she noticed the glimmer of the flyaway ring amid the trash there below. The ring remained in the Darcy family for generations. The story of the flying ring is implausible, but Catherine McCarty, as well as many country people, held to a number of naïve beliefs, including the existence of the Wee Folk or Fairy Folk. In her journal, Marjory Darcy provided her own explanation for the motions of the ring, stating that it was not pure gold (as is required for an accurate prediction of the infant's sex) but only brass.

Chapter 6
The Mother-to-Be of Billy the Kid Waits Up
Irish Town, New York City
June 5, 1861

Catherine McCarty sets her mister's dinner in the warmer bin and stirs the coals to glowing in the grate. The gravy has boiled down, gone thick in the coddle pot. She adds a ladleful of water. Though the potatoes have gone a tad soft and the onions unfurled. She sits herself back in the chair that faces the door. Wrapping her shawl tighter. That chill when one sits and waits in the dark until she hears it in her sleep: the creaking stairs, the rattling knob. Locked out, am I? he calls.

Is it you, Paddy?

Expecting someone else then?

She hurries to the door. There he is. He kicks the door shut behind him.

So many kick marks on that door. He roughly jostles a chair as if he means to break it and throws himself into it. He shucks off his shoes—there a crust of vomitus and some other unknown filth. Mrs. Catherine McCarty takes each in two fingers, and holding them out and away from her, sets them beside the grate.

No supper ready for a working man? says Paddy. Still in his coat and cap. As if he may not be staying. She wraps a rag for a handhold on the bail of the coddle pot, ladles potatoes and soft chunks of meat onto the plate. An onion cooked whole, now exploded. She slices yesterday's bread, all the while holding the cloth to cover her empty ring finger.

Pours him out a pint. Wipes the table of the crumbs and the drips where he has already sloshed. She smells him as he unbuttons his shirt, undoes his belt: beer, smoke, and a sweetish scent of something. Lavender? Roses? Something not hers. She has no bottles of such.

Paddy, she says, as he is shoveling it up with bread.

She uncovers her hand and puts it forth. I've lost it, she says.

He brings the bread up, then sets it back in the plate. Well then, he says. Another one gone. Sorry old girl, he says.

No, she says. The child is still here, she says, patting her abdomen. Moving as well, right fit it seems. My ring is what's lost. Gone.

Gone where? he says.

Well, she says. It just flies away on me.

Flies away, you say? I see. So you've been talking with that daft Marge Darcy. Either that or you've gone and pawned it off. Didn't get much though, did you now?

My gold ring, Paddy? Oh no I never would.

Gold? he says. Have you not been seeing your finger going green? And us with hardly a pot to do a piss, tell me Catherine: How in hell would I be getting my hands on gold?

A young rat emerges from a corner chink-hole and sniffs at the vomitus on Paddy McCarty's boot.

There is a skittering in the stovepipe. Catherine McCarty imagines bats. Or the evening stirring of the Wee Folk. She is not sure which. She imagines it may be both.

Chapter 7
Deformities

Doctor Arthur Broadwater's Guide to Pregnancy and Birth
Second Edition, 1890: Birth Abnormalities

Multiple deformities can occur in a single individual, as I had observed during a difficult delivery of a particular male infant who emerged at birth with the umbilical cord twisted about its neck. The abnormalities observed in this infant are three.

1st—Scapular Winging or so-called "Bird Back" is a deformity of the shoulder blades. A myth persists that this malformation results when a pregnant woman witnesses a hawk swooping in and sinking its talons into the back of a dove or dog, and carrying it off.

Upon my arrival at the boy's difficult birth, I observed that his right arm was fully extended from the womb and his tiny hand in a fist. This unnatural presentation undoubtedly caused disruption of scapulohumeral development, resulting in scapular winging.

When I encountered the boy in his adolescence, he presented with a slope-shouldered appearance, and on lateral view, appeared to be "winged."

2nd—Atapostasis or so-called "Bat Ears" refers to ears that are prominent and resemble those of the Leaf-Nosed Bat (*Hipposideros obscurus*). Protruding ears are passed down to offspring from ancestors and not caused by observation of a lunar eclipse during pregnancy (a belief of those who hold with the existence of vampires), nor are these children changelings or the offspring of the so-called "Wee Folk" (a notion favored by some Irish countyfolk.) The ears of the infant I delivered were decidedly protuberant at birth and had remained so in his adolescence and youth.

3rd—Undersized stature is prevalent in premature births. There is no truth to the belief that the baby will be small if the mother looks upon a circus dwarf during her pregnancy or inadvertently ingests an ant or mouse. This boy's mother stated that had no relatives of short stature, and she believed that the boy was not her own, but a tiny changeling child forced upon her by Fairy Folk.

Chapter 8
At Last a Lad Still Living
Irish Town, New York City
July 19, 1861

The new little lad was just two days old when Catherine sent word to Marjory Darcy: *Dear Marjory, the baby is born, please come visit*, sending her husband with the note, down the stairs and across the alley and up the stairs again to the home of Mr. and Mrs. Darcy. Catherine being too weak, too worn out to go herself. She still bled a bit and was not at all feeling up to taking the baby out, not just yet and certainly not along all those ups and downs, oh no. Still unsteady on her feet. To be expected. After all, it had only been a day. Or half a day? She had lost track while nursing him, sleeping on and off while he clung to her breast—the infant, the little lad they had named William but already calling him Billy. It being too soon for a name, she said. Too small for a name. He might not live, not this boy, not this time. This boy might be lost like the others last time. Each time. This the third time. All the prior concerns, grief, dread—all of it coming back to her, all of it all over again when the pains came on too early, and of course expecting him to be born small or born dead, as it was with two others who had come before him. They had arrived early as well, both of them too soon, too small. One born ashen and gasping and (so sad) lifting its little hand in goodbye after just one day of being in the world, and the other born pale as chalk and shriveled (puckered came to mind, as well as shrunken, as if it had been held too long in the bath, as if—and it shamed her to think it—as if it had been pickled within her.) The one who briefly lived was too weak to take her breast, too small to suck. That one she wrapped in the bright yellow new-bought blanket she had intended for a born-alive baby. And the one that was shriveled, the one that been long dead inside her—that one that was given its own new blanket, a soft green, the color of the new leaves on a persimmon tree. Both dead boys, a year apart, carefully swaddled just so. Both dead boys leaving her with her breasts still filling as she twice held the small still bundles in her arms the way a mother of the living would (still so precious, with its head positioned close to her heart and supported by her hand) as she walked with her husband, with Patrick (the father of the dead) to the weedy tract above Turtle Bay where such small specimens were frequently placed in graves just a bit bigger than the bundled bodies they would sequester. No box, no box. Twice then, she had stood beside her Patrick as he scraped out the holes with a coal shovel. She watched him place the first small bundle into the hole and start a bit by bit sprinkling in of soil with his fingers and then shovel in the rest and pat the mound with his hand. Good lad, he had said. And then the same, hardly a year later: dig, bundle, sprinkle, shovel, pat, good lad. For the first she had collected small round stones and placed them circling the mound, with one red stone right in the center. Like a heart, she told Patrick, who didn't understand, and who didn't ask what in God's name do you mean, Catherine? Just what in God's name. And then, with the second one buried, she knelt and brushed the dead leaves and twigs away from that first grave, and found the red heart stone. No other stones from the circle, but there the same red heart stone. Or one similar to the red stone she had placed. See Paddy? Do you remember this? It's our firstborn's stone, she said, and a comfort to me just to hold it now when we be putting his brother beside him.

Yes dear girl, he said, I remember it now my own self, he said. But of course he didn't remember. He was just wanting it over with. Two sons dead and let us be done with it, he told her as they stood in the weedy tract long used by mothers for the interment of the too early, the too small, the malformed and the stillborn, for the smothered and strangled and aborted.

But now, another year has gone by and now another child is just newly born, born alive and alive still with the day nearly done. No walk to the weedy tract above Turtle Bay is needed! No third hole to be dug, at least not yet. Not this new baby. This boy. This new baby Billy. He was hard in coming, he was. Her laboring had been long and hard. Catherine screaming all the night, pleas and curses spewed forth to her husband and spoken as a devil might speak. Patrick couldn't calm her, couldn't endure it a moment more, and finally, finally, fetched the doctor. The two of them, the father and the doctor then, running through the streets. Patrick cutting through alleys, the doctor hurrying along behind him. This way Dr. Broadwater, Patrick was calling over his shoulder. The alley, a shortcut, this way, follow me.

A difficult birth, the doctor had said. Complicated by the child coming early. Complicated by the cord noosed around its neck. The child not breathing. Manipulations ensued, maneuvers were performed, and the cord was untangled. There at last came the gasp, the first breath, the blessed wail. Well alright then, Dr. Broadwater said, the child can breathe now, we can all breathe now, he said as he straightened up and stepped back and wiped his hands. Dry your tears, Mrs. McCarty. Your boy's alive.

And now, with nearly three days done he was still living, and not only that, despite being small, able to nurse. Having the strength to take her breast and suck. Seemingly hungry when she held him to her, but never frantic for food as she had seen the babies of other mothers be. No squalling or screaming. This one—awake at sun-up, or as his mother said, up with the birdies tweeting in the trees. But quiet he stayed all the day, quiet as mice she said. His little hands flailing about, reaching up, taking ahold of his father's fingers. Scrappy and strong, said the father. Looky here Catherine. See that grip there? See how he hangs on, keeps right on with me. Up lad! the father said. It was then, in that lifted position, that she noticed the odd sloping of his shoulders, the prominence of his shoulder blades—a temporary situation (the doctor said, by way or reassurance) due to his incomplete development. A premature birth. Therefore a lack of musculature. Or perhaps his position inside of her, his emergence not head first into this world, but hand first. His arm protruding. Odd, said Dr. Arthur Broadwater, but not unheard of. But calm your fears, Mrs. McCarty. He's sure to fill in and fill out, the doctor told her. Well, said the father, he's a strange-looking wee one he is, but a tough little monkey. My boy, he's a scrapper just like his old Da, aren't you now? Aren't you now, my boy, my Billyboy? etc. etc. When she held him to her he put his little hands (like little red claws, she thought, not like a little monkey at all, more like the paws of a newborn squirrel or rat, or some creature similar, or something else) flat upon her white full breasts and she shivered with mild disgust, squeamish as he rooted there, sniffing and snorting, his slightly misshapen mouth exploring her flesh, the mandible (as the doctor had called the part) receding and thereby giving the maxilla (also the doctor) the look of protuberance. *Doctor, what's gone wrong with his mouth?—Ah, nothing to concern yourself with, Mrs. McCarty, but he might be a bit bucked in the tooth, mildly malocclusive it's called, but don't be bothering yourself with that now, no no not at all, you have a healthy boy this time.* But, and this was more concerning than the mouth, more concerning than the shoulder bones: with her nipple in his mouth he turned his head, twisting her breast to keep his hold and gazing up at her with a look that she found unsettling. As if the child did not know her. Yes, that was it. The stare of a stranger looking up at her. A cold and knowing look, but not knowing her. Unfamiliar. An unnatural child and not her own, perhaps? Not the baby just born! Oh, surely this was not something she could remark to the doctor, now was it? Oh dear doctor, please tell me: Is this my little lad for certain? Or be it a changeling child? Not mine—not born to me—but a relation to the Wee Folk who came and snatched my true little one away? Oh no, it was not something she could say. And no, she could not ask her Paddy. Why, he'd think her daft. Completely daft. No, she would ask Mrs. Marjory Darcy, she would. Marjory would know. Please Paddy, she told her husband, get to Marjory Darcy's flat and fetch her here. Ask her to come, to pay us a visit. And she wrote out the note, and down the stairs did he go, the father of the new little lad. Down the stairs and cross the alley and up the stairs again to the home of the Darcy's. Marjory Darcy heard him on the stair, and she was quick to open the door, quick to be asking him, Is he alive Patrick? Tell me it's so!

I'm a Da now I am, he told her as he delivered the note. *Dear Marjory the baby is born, please come visit.*

The redness around the child's neck—the mark of the noose—had begun to fade. Patrick McCarty at bedside, staying near. Putting a cool cloth to her head. Fetching her tea. Plenty of sugar, Catherine old girl. For getting you back on your feet, to be caring for our new fella here. Warming the remains of a week-old loaf. No butter, but there was still some of her persimmon jam. Making her a soup of mashed-down potato and water and with no milk about to thicken it, tossed in scraps of the bread. She ate what he gave her. And the boy nursed. He was small, yes. But he took her firmly in his mouth and hung on. By the second day, stronger. Even robust. He was wearing her out, the child was. I must sleep, she told Patrick. Here Paddy take him, get him away from me, get him off me, she said. And she tried to pull herself out of the child's mouth but he still hung on, held on. Enough, she cried, and gave him a little snack in his snout. A little flick of her finger, only that. And his mouth stopped. And he looked up at her, his eyes fixed and steady upon her. So fierce she thought, so cold, and then he turned her loose. She lifted him up and away from her, telling Patrick to take him, it was for the child's own good, that she feared sleeping beside him, that she feared she might toss about in the bed, she might roll this way and that, lie upon him, crush the tiny thing without knowing she'd done it, she said. What an awful thing that would be, wouldn't it now? Or she might kick the bedclothes to tangle it all up and then suffocate him, by mistake of course. And so he took the child from her. He watched it lie quietly in his arms. The wee man, he said. Already a wee man you are, said Patrick, and needing your mam's ninny but not so much as a peep, oh no. My Billyboy. My tough little fella. Wake yourself up, he called to Catherine. Wake up old girl. I'm fetching your old Bible, I am. It's high time we get his name writ.

She roused herself. Sat up. No Paddy, she said. Too soon for that. We could lose him yet. He can't be writ in the book, not yet.

It's three days gone, he said, and the lad is living and that be three days more than the other two be dead.

Oh Paddy no, she said. Do it and we'd be tempting the devil.

It be the Lord's book we be writing in and not the devil's, he said and he toted out her leather-bound Bible and touched the nib of his pen to a slurry of lampblack and then to the place under the frontispiece where the names of the Bonney Clan of Timoleague Town on Courmascherry Bay had been written. All her kin who'd come and gone, their births and weddings and deaths, the most recent entries those starved in the Great Blight and Famine. And he put his pen to the end of the list of the long dead and buried in the green hills of County Cork, and there he wrote:

William Henry McCarty born Jul 19, 1861. City of New York.

There it is Catherine, he said. Now he'll stay living.

Chapter 9
No Promising Leads

HISTORIC ARTIFACT TAKEN IN DARING ROBBERY

New York Metro News August 12, 2024

NEW YORK—A leather-bound Bible that once belonged to Catherine McCarty, mother of William Henry McCarty, also known as Billy Bonney, but best known as Billy the Kid, has been stolen from its display case in the New York Museum of City History. The item was discovered missing when museum security guard William "Poots" Pootrick returned from lunch yesterday. Museum curator Quinten "Van" Van Nortwick described the heist as "a smash-and-grab operation" and doubts that the Bible will be recovered as "there is a thriving market for original items pertaining to the Old West, especially those related to Billy."

The Bible has historical significance as it was once customary to list births, weddings, and deaths in a family Bible, where such notations were considered legal proof of important events. The McCarty family bible bore the only known and true record of the Billy's birth, that being July 19, 1861 and not 1859, as reported by the sheriff who shot him.

No arrests have been made and there are no promising leads. It appears that the theft was an inside job. Security footage shows the two men wearing ski masks and breaking into the case around 11 a.m. Wednesday. Police are working to identify the suspects.

The Security guard "Poots" Pootrick was originally assigned to the museum in a janitorial position through a Dept. of Corrections work-release program. He had been previously reprimanded for leaving his post unattended but had not been dismissed due to the support of his union, Local 979 Federation of Museum Workers. On the afternoon of the robbery, Mr. Pootrick had taken an unauthorized two-hour lunch break at "Bobo's Babes & Barbeque" one block south of the museum. He has been suspended without pay, pending further investigation, and was questioned by Police Chief Sean "Shawny" O'Shawnessy as to involvement in the theft. "He's not a suspect," the Chief stated.

"He's an idiot," said Mr. Van Nortwick.

Chapter 10
Family Bible

THE NEW YORK MUSEUM OF CITY HISTORY

*Exhibit 50: Family Bible of Catherine McCarty Antrim,
Mother of William Henry McCarty, also known as Billy the Kid.
Gift to the City of New York from the estate of Joseph McCarty.

Open to frontispiece engraving *The Flood Subsides* and inscription:

When the deluge was done but waters still covered the earth, Noah brought forth from the ark the raven and the dove and he set them loose in the air. The dove found no place to set her foot and returned to the ark. But the raven would not return and flew above the waters until he could fly no more.

Below the frontispiece, note the final hand-written entries:
William Henry McCarty born Jul 19, 1861. City of New York.
Joseph Callen McCarty born May 14, 1865. City of New York.

*Exhibit 50: Family Bible is currently unavailable for viewing. A reward is offered for information leading to its recovery. Contact Police Department, City of New York.

Chapter 11
Beware the Wee and Fairy Folk

A Caution to Mothers of the Newly Born
Attributed to Fainín of Balingarry, 1544
Translated 1802 from the Original Gaelic by Donnegal Céilechair

Beware the Wee and Fairy Folk that roam the green hills of Inis Fáil. They live by mischief and ill deeds, hiding in empty eggshells, dwelling within stones and pods of milkweed, in the woven nests of birds, and in the caves where bats hang and peep. In such places Wee and Fairy Folk bear their many babies, some fresh as flowers and bright as morning. But when their young be conceived by carnal relations with small animals of either fur or feather, these be born of paltry proportions and bearing the ears of bats, the mouths of rodents, or the vestiges of the bird wings protruding from their backs. These be creatures that the Wee and Fairy Folk will not raise nor nurture. Instead they will wait for the chance to snatch away a mother's unblemished newborn and leave one of their misshapen own behind, and those that they steal, they tithe to the devil. Here then be warnings best heeded by mothers all: keep a leaf of clover in your newborn's mouth at night and a thing of iron in its cradle, or you will find a changeling in its place, a malformed wretch that attaches to your teat as if you would be the one who born it, but who resembles not you nor any of your kin, nor any other kind of human form.

Chapter 12
A Dab on the Dummyteat
(Also Peppermint Tea)
Irish Town, New York City
July 22, 1861

Well now. Let's have us a look at you, Mr. William McCarty, says Marjory Darcy. She lifts the coverlet. Well hello little William. He's an angel true. Blue-eyed and hair golden as honey.

Three days old and already Paddy be calling him Billy, says Mrs. Catherine McCarty.

Then hello Billy. And aren't you a little one.

Piddling little. He come early, you know.

He'll be catching up, this Billy will. Won't you now. Yes you will. A dab of the iron drops on his dummyteat and he'll be catching up.

See that pinched little mouth of his? What a mouse would have for a mouth, it is. He gets his mouth on me and he sucks a devil's worth but there's noise in his throat, grunts and gurgles. The doctor telling me it be a touch torn up from near to strangling. Likely to die he was, if the doctor not come.

Doctor Arthur was it? says Marjory Darcy.

Himself, says Catherine McCarty. Who else to be tending to the poor Irish these parts but Arthur Broadwater. And even calling my Billy here a fine-looking lad, once he got him untangled and taking his first breaths. Fine-looking, what he said. Even with the cord marks still on his neck. And those ears. You see them, Marjory? See them ears on him?

A bit grand they are, says Marjory Darcy.

They're not my ears. Not Paddy's neither, says Catherine McCarty.

Then from someone in the family back aways. Big ears likely to skip a generation they say. Likely there's kin you're forgetting.

No one. Nor his chin.

Dimple on the chin and the devil be within, says Marjory Darcy. He'll be a feisty thing, this little one.

He's awake first thing with the birdies singing in the trees and peering all about. And farting first thing as well, same as his Da.

A touch of the colic is all it is. He'll be taking some peppermint tea tonight and stopping his squawking by morning.

Mostly he's quiet as mice, sleeping in the chifforobe. Fifth drawer up.

Wee Folk won't be getting him there. And be keeping a clover in his mouth, says Marjory Darcy.

Every night. And the knife I been setting beside him. Paddy is telling me don't bother—if the Wee Folk be wanting him then they'll just come taking him and there's no ways of stopping Fairy Folk, none.

Let Paddy say what he will say, Catherine. But never have I knowed a baby been switched with a clover in his mouth nor iron in his bed.

Maybe they already come switched him, Marjory. Maybe Biddy Doro should be coming by.

Biddy Doro? Now what would you be wanting with such a one as Biddy Doro?

Here, says Mrs. Catherine McCarty. Put your hand here. Feel that? Maybe it's wings he's growing.

You mean this? This here? says Marjory Darcy. Thems his shoulder bones, Catherine. Regular bones these, sure a tad more poking out than some, but he come early, now didn't he. He'll fill out soon enough. See now? Reaching for his mam, strong even for a piddling lad.

Sometimes I need to pry him off me, says Catherine McCarty.

Alright, back to your mamma now. There you go, Billyboy. Got him? Light as a bird this one. Don't you be flying away on us now, little one. Wings, Catherine? And Biddy Doro? Whatever are you thinking?

New moon. Oceans bulge. Water moves. The estuary of the East River slides toward the sea. Smell of salt, smell of mud where all along Kips Bay and Turtle Bay the oystercatchers walk and probe the little pools along the banks for smaller creatures left stranded in the wake of the tide.

Chapter 13
Biddy Doro Foraging Flora and Fauna (But Eschewing the Newt)
Irish Town, New York and Environs
September 17, 1861

Biddy Doro. Heading out this bright autumn day, dressed in britches of burlap sacking broadly stitched every which way and belted by a length of bittersweet creeper, and cloaked in a weave of rag strips and honeysuckle with big patch pockets of every color at her breasts. Currently her hat is fashioned of plaited ivy, though this varies with the red and yellow and green foliage of the season—in winter she wears a twist of juniper or hemlock fir around her head. Her shoes are woven spruce root, softly lined with cattail down and strapped to her feet with willow. At her hip rides her purse of peeled birch attached to a braided birchy strap slung over her shoulder. She emerges from her hut. Shuts the door and latch but does not throw the bolt. She stops to give a sniff to the botanicals she has hung to dry across Dingman's Alley—lavender and lemon balm more fragrant with desiccation, nightshade and catmint more potent.

Other citizens of old New York are out and about along these narrow thoroughfares crowded by commerce. The foot traffic moving in fits and starts is seen from the rooftops and the windows above the street as a flow of porkpies and hombergs, skullcaps and shtreimels; passage slowed by the comings and goings from intersecting alleyways, by pauses at shop windows, exchanges at pushcarts, arguments and bargaining—there a clot of bonnets gathered at the fruitseller's, there a cluster of bowlers and top hats at the door of the bank. Wagons. Horses. Pickpockets. Hawkers. Merchants. Mendicants. Altercations. Arrests. Bits of commentary as people brush past each other or avoid or collide. Excuse me sir. So sorry Ma'am. Out of the way boy. Step aside, please. Move yer ass. Watch it now. Fuck off then. That was my foot, sir. But Biddy Doro goes easily through the throng, keeping to her steady pace, her passage unobstructed as the crowd gives way before her. A man tips her his hat. Another just touches the brim. A woman nods hello. Another pauses to half-curtsy, causing a series of pedestrian collisions and a momentary disruption in crowd flow. Some citizens see her coming and cross the street. Some who come upon her too late to change course turn up their collars and hunch past. To one of that foolish number she murmurs: That's right Harvey Rafferty. You'd better be looking away—as Mr. Rafferty inexplicably loses his footing and goes tumbling to the gutter into a newly deposited pile of dung. She goes on.

Stopping now for a woman with a small boy in tow. The stream of passersby widens around them. Good day Miss Biddy, the mother says. The boy breaks free of his mother's hand and hugs Miss Biddy around her legs. Oooh Biddy Biddy Biddy, he says into the burlap.

Unhand me lad, says Miss Biddy, and digs into her birch purse bringing forth a sweet sucker loosely wrapped in a leaf.

Oooh, says the boy and he snatches it straightaway.

Now Charles, what do you say to Miss Biddy? the mother says.

Snakey, says the boy. Snakey Snakey Snakey please, he says.

No Charles, says the mother. No Snakey today. Let's let Miss Biddy get on her way.

All right, says Biddy Doro, but just a peek. She unbuttons the breast-pocket flap on her raggedy cloak and makes a show of squinting and looking there and then whispering to whatever lurks deep within: So slither ye forth and show yourself. The black smooth head emerges, the sleek serpentine body follows, curved, extended, slightly wavering. The flicker of its dark red double-pronged tongue. The boy Charles squeals. The mother has gone pale. Back you go, Biddy Doro tells her pet and it withdraws into her pocket with its nose tip and tongue protruding just a bit. She gives it a slight tap. All the way, she says. There you go. She rebuttons the flap.

Again! says the boy. Again, again!

Get away with you now you foul little creature, Biddy Doro tells the boy.

And she proceeds to the bank.

Just inside, she passes by a watchman dozing in his chair beside a potted palm. Conversations become whispers then trail off in silence, but the ticking of the wall clock seems to grow louder. Citizens already at a teller's conclude their business and slink toward the door. Those at the hightables decide that their transactions might best be done some other day and set down their chained pens. Two of the three tellers peering out from behind their grills spot her early. One lowers her shade slowly hoping to subdue the squeak of the roller. The other quietly sets out her *Next Window Please* placard, sinks down below counter level in her swivel chair, and in reverse rolls away on its casters into a back office. The third teller—likely newly hired—has been filing her nails and when she finally looks up there stands Biddy Doro. Good day, says Biddy Doro as she unflaps her birchbark purse. She removes a packet of papers tied up in vine and sets it on the ledge, then upturns the purse over the counter trough, spilling the contents out: an assortment of coins mixed with bits of tree bark and seeds both prickly and smooth, a clawed and shriveled animal paw, a number of small clean teeth and fleshless bones. She slides the coins one by one under the grate. For deposit, says Miss Biddy Doro.

Miss Biddy Doro, continuing along now to the district that bounds Turtle Bay, knowing by her calculations of the moon and the swell of blood within her that the river this day, this hour, would be low to its banks. Knowing the flora and fauna that lives in these precincts of marsh and meadow and places touched and untouched by the estuary tides and what persists in the shade of the undercliff and between the rocks. She unfolds the packet of notes and scraps, and thereby consults the correspondence from an assortment of citizens of old New York:

Dear Mistress Doro.
I catched the two of them at it again.
This time please give me something
to finish them both straight off for good.
Brigit McGaffigan. The Five Points.

Missy Biddy:
What reliable remedy have you for the quinsy?
Dwight Donner, Major 5th New York, Retired
East B'way.

Biddy you damn old shit-witch.
You ungodly demented turd.
Pizzle eater. Poon dripper.
I know it was you. I know it.
You don't scare me none.
Some folks sure, but not me.
(Unsigned)

Dear Miss Doro,
Little Moishe almost two but not talking.
Can you come see him?
Esther Goldfarb, Delancy Street

Hello Miss Biddy Doro.
I born the new baby.
This time this one lived.

My mister named him Billy and dotes.
But this child, he is not right.
A creature he is.
I am afeard of him.
I am afeared Sprites or the Wee Folk
switched him in the night. Please come.
Catherine McCarty, Irish Town

To B. Doro.
I seen you going overhead last night before the moon set.
Ask me I don't care but let that priest see you flying on a
Sunday and he'll be coming after you he will.
Callie says tell you her foot is better with the poke-leaf poultice.
Abigale Methue, Gouverneur Slip

Missy Biddy,
Zeke beat me and our doggie Ennis last night for the last time,
the poor wee creature.
I set your snail pie on the table and Zeke he sniffs.
I am thinking he suspects but no he doesn't.
He eats the whole of it and starts into howling, bug-eyed and
gone mad with thirst, and throwing hisself into Sheepshead Bay.
So thank you and much appreciated.
Trixie Berryworth
Tillary Street, Brooklyn

Biddy Doro folds the packet of papers back into her purse. A salty breeze is blowing in off the river. Gulls sail over. Meadow rue sways around her. A ruffle of petals—the filigree of hemlock flowers. Daisy fleabane's fringe-petal faces. Stalks of arrow weed. The pale inflorescence of wild licorice. She toes over a rock where the water seeps. There sits a newt, his tiny lidded eyes blinking in the sudden light. She always has need for newt, though this one she deems too young, not big enough. Oh but looky there: a snail at her foot. Two. She places them on her palm for closer examination—shells of pearly brown, plump spotted bodies. Their eyestalks wave and search. Ah, a perfect pair—one shell spirals right and one spirals left. Yes, they will do nicely, though these she will not prepare by her usual recipe: mashed raw into a rabbit and potato pie to be fed to the unsuspecting, thereby inducing the triad of pain, polydipsia, and proptosis. No, these two she will simply dry and pulverize—one powder to make babies come and one to make babies go—for there are those women who regularly seek such remedies. She plucks the snails from her palm. They cling for an instant, then come away with the faint sound of puckering suction and strings of slime. Come lads, she says. In you go. And she opens her birchbark purse.

Upriver where the water eddies black and glassy, cormorants perch and preen on a lime-spattered snag of river willow, their wings unfolded, outstretched, and their feathers displayed fanwise for drying in the midsummer sun. They turn their heads to watch her as she makes her way along the bank, her spruce-root shoes muddied with a misstep into the muck. They do not gather their wings back to their sleek wet bodies to drop and dive when she passes by. They do not lift away into the air when she stops beside them and bends to fetch up some small thing she needs, and goes on again, stepping stone to stone to stone.

Chapter 14
Parchment Note

THE NEW YORK MUSEUM OF CITY HISTORY
Biddy Doro writes Mrs. Catherine McCarty Antrim,
Mother of Billy the Kid, September 18, 1861
Document is of historic interest for its folkloric content.
Low Level Lighting in Use for Document Conservation

Mrs. Catherine, I received your note.
Do not bring your child to me. Nor will I visit.
Read this and leave me be.
Signs for Detection of a Changeling:
1st Ears of a bat. Mouth of a rabbit. Shoulder bones of a bird.
2nd Constant hunger without crying but peeps or mews.
3rd Small at birth and thereafter.
4th Sings like a robin and partial to earthworms.
Biddy Doro, Eighteenth Sept 1861

Chapter 15
Sprites of All Species

Recovery of the Abducted Infant
From the Epistle of the St. Adomnain,
Martyred beside the River Shannon 762 AD by Danish Vikings
Translated from the original Latin to Gaelic by Cú Cathbat 1702
and from Gaelic to English by Eogan O'Rahilly 1801.

It is ill-advised to leave human babies unattended, as Sprites of all species are eager to replace them with Changelings if their own offspring are afflicted with malformity. They will not abduct babies that have undergone the Sacrament of Baptism as baptized children will not engage in their Heathenish Practices. Conversely, if a Changeling has not been detected by its human parents and is baptized, Elves and other Fairy Folk will refuse to take it back in exchange for the original baby. It is therefore essential that parents present their newborn for baptism upon confirming it to be their own, and essential they avoid baptism if they suspect their child has been taken and a Changeling has been left in its place. Fairy Folk maintain their immortality by tithing human children to the devil, so all efforts should be made to recover the abducted child. Methods for effecting its return include placing the Changeling in a willow-rood basket and hanging it overnight in a persimmon tree, thereby enticing the Felonious Fairy to investigate or take it away. An alternative method involves forcing the Changeling to laugh by repeatedly stroking the genitals with a feather or hairy bindweed. If this does not summon the Fairy Progenitors, the Changeling can be made to scream by excoriating its limbs with holly-leaf or stinging nettle. Lastly, it is possible to encounter all species of Wee Folk and Sprites at the entrances of their abodes. They will use tree-hollows and empty eggshells as temporary shelters but take up permanent residence in solitary stones. Access to the interior of a solitary stone is a tight-fitting door without lintel, knob, or latch, and is impossible to detect until opened at dusk when a glimpse of their kind may be had. Be cautious in their presence, as they are easily offended, but are easily amused and enjoy discourse sprinkled with puns. In the course of conversation, do not complement them on their attire. Do not speak of cats, bears, or rainbows. Make no reference to the shape of the moon. Offerings of persimmon jam, butter, or butterflies are likely to initiate negotiation. As would a gift of small, soft leather shoes.

Chapter 16
Mrs. Catherine McCarty Hunts the Solitary Stone
(To Exchange a Changeling)
Irish Town and Environs, New York City
September 28, 1861

Catherine hurrying along in the early evening, the child—the baby—concealed in her shawl, well wrapped, nearly swaddled. This baby. This William Henry. Or Billy. Just Billy. She does not say his name aloud. He might awaken. He might free his little hands and push the shawl from his face and cry out. Though there has been hardly a peep as she travels these darkening parts of the city where the hustle of trade is done for the day. Shops shut. The fruit wagons and coal carts wait horseless, battened and tarped. Men have gathered around a barrel-fire, their upturned palms and sooty faces lit by flamelight, and she crosses the empty street, away from them. Passes the stoops where women sit with their petticoats showing and camisoles too much unbuttoned for such cool nights. She makes her way through Irish Town—her Irish Town—past the white clapboard boarding house, past the crockery shop with Utensils New & Used. Going past the Tea-Time Tearoom where the chairs are set seat-down on the tables. Now the empty window of the fishmonger, the metal trays clean and stacked but still glinting with a scattering of silvery scale. Hurrying past a short alleyway where a hay-thatched shack is set, built of bare boards to the front and rear of it, but its sides simply the brick walls of the bordering buildings and its single window but a tacked-down square of greased paper and in the dark, bright with the wavering glow of lantern-light from within. This

Catherine knows to be the habitation and haunt of Biddy Doro—purveyor of botanicals and consultant to arcane predicaments—though no signboard of such be posted; her wares tied in twine, hanging upside down by their stems in bunches across Dingman's alley—monkshood, bryony, henbane, poke—there for the taking yet untouched by passersby who know better. And now she goes on through the Italian Quarter, passing the windows of the darkened shops illuminated by streetlamps and the crescent moon. In the window of Tucci's Shoe Repair on the shoemaker's bench sits a lone brogan presumably left behind by a giant. Oh yes she had recently visited Tucci's Shoe Repair and there made a purchase—a pair of tiny shoes. Old shoes with soiled laces, the leather cracked and shabby. Left for repair but never claimed. Tucci refusing to sell it at first. The bambino he die, Signore Tucci had said when she asked him the price. No signora, he said. Sono maledetti. Cursed. But he sold them off anyway, and she paid but two pennies. And on now she goes, past Zanetti's Bakery where she sees the sloping glass showcase with an arrangement of yesterday's pastries—cannoli, bomboloni, and the biscotti presently being nibbled by the resident rodent which continues his meal unafraid when she taps the glass. Passing now the establishments of tailors, lawyers, upstanding citizens formerly of Sicily turned lender and importer, merchants of olive oil and capocollo and wine. Now passing through the settlement of Jews and under the hanging signs that slightly swing and creak in their brackets and in the lettering of the Israelites promote the sale of dry goods and necessary garments: kippah, teffilin, tallit with a linen lining in the color of your choice. She stops beneath a streetlamp to adjust her shawl, shift the burden, for he is that—a burden, by her telling.

Now on to the perimeter of the city where commerce disperses and becomes the enclaves of lawlessness and the encampments of the indigent where the thoroughfares are left uncobbled, some with a smattering of gravel, most down-packed dirt crossed by footpaths leading to a shantytown of squatters' shacks and cabins constructed from the rotting boards of wrecked barges long ago run aground on the riverbank. Outposts of pigpens and rabbit warrens and garden plots where the thin soil atop the bedrock of Manhattan schist yields undersized cabbages and rutabaga and spindly beans. A ways more now to weedy fields, a boggy meadow, the environs beyond Turtle Bay. The landscape brightened only by moonlight on the river and dispersed by the patchwork of clouds. As she goes she unfolds the shawl to see him—he has been so silent—does he still live? And she lifts the edge, the fringe that covers his head. No, not dead. He smiles up at her. His tweaked little face. He is almost always smiling. She wonders why he is. She slides the fringe down. Not a peep. He doesn't seem to mind being covered. Hidden. Being concealed. She goes on, hurrying along on this errand in need of completion in these few hours between sundown and dark, when they—those whom she seeks—might briefly be seen before their evening of mischief commences; glimpsed at the entrances of their unobtrusive abodes: knotholes in tree trunks or tiny doors tucked between the twisted roots of the oak and chinquapin they favor, or undetectable entrances in solitary stones. No, not stones in their usual gatherings, not in a flock—not stones asleep in a riverbed or thrown up along a road where a road had been cut; not stones roused from their rest by digging and piled up or cast about a ditch or the places where digging has been done or is being done—gardens, plowed fields, excavations for the foundations of houses or the consecration of bones. It is a solitary stone she seeks. You yourself have passed them many times in your lifetime, but you've not seen them, not likely. Have not considered that they are pieces of creation strewn about everywhere, here to take up in your hand and ponder the time when the earth was a furnace. Here for the holding, in plain sight, inconspicuous. Some sit in the middle of a thoroughfare. Some rest without their brothers in the grass. A solitary stone may turn up on a walkway, porch, or step. You've just not taken notice, but they are there, and some be the homes of the ones she seeks: those diminutives in human form, all of them tiny but troublesome and oh so many breeds of them. Sprites. Fairy Folk. Wee Folk. Elves. All of them kin to one another. All of them clever but godless. All of them friends of the devil and most of them wingless, moving through the air by wonderment or will. And some, a very few, winged like angels or dragonflies. And some who cannot not fly at all, but hitch passage on the backs of birds and fly through a nursery window to steal the most perfect of newly born humans who sleep unattended and unawares in their cradles or the lower drawers of chifforobes. These creatures that have followed the Celts in their travels since the ancient seafaring days—sailing with them from Donegal Harbor and Inishfree Bay. Stowing away in their luggage, bundles, trunks. And finally tumbling down the gangplanks with the crowds of their countrymen to take up residence in the tenements of Irish Town, and soon enough be up to their usual tricks: spoiling the milk, tangling the sewing thread, and chewing the candlewax. And worse: slipping into nurseries at nightfall to take the prettiest and most appealing of human babies from their cradles to raise them as their own in some uncharted, enchanted land or sell them to the devil and leaving in their places their undesirables—the malformed or ill-favored. She was still Catherine Bonney then, just turned twenty and fleeing the famine when she set off from Timoleague Town on Courmascherry Bay, bound for the port of New York, when shipboard—in steerage—the chicanery began. She knew they were at hand—the Wee Folk were—when she woke with her hair in tangles that very first morning at sea, and her shoes—which she always placed right and left at the foot of her bed—were there beside her sea-berth but switched left to right. But more than that—she has seen Sprites and Fairies, actually seen them, as most country folk have. The have been to her house. To her kitchen, to her cupboard on a cupboard shelf, skittering away in the shape of a mouse. To her windowsill in form of a pigeon peering in. And to her bed on summer nights, taking their most infinitesimal form, hovering in the air on their tiny transparent wings, their dangling limbs as delicate as eyelash, and humming strange tunes as they come and go—humming or buzzing so close to her ear. But nonbelievers? Woe to them! Woe to the ones who swat Fairy Folk as if they were mosquitos, who smash them to a bloody smear on the wall and thereby tempt the legions of their tiny, revengeful kin.

She hastens along, hoping there would be trees here at the edge of the city, but there are no trees in these parts. Perhaps a bit further. Perhaps just over the next slope, but she is losing sight of the road far ahead as the land dips and then rises, and the river flows not along these low, muddy banks but far below the cut of the cliff-face upriver where the river is white and churning with the devil's own spit and a cloud of steam from a hole to hell in the river bottom hangs above the water there in all weathers, and there the world is wild and wild things live. There are forests there, she has been told. Tall old trees. Oak. Beech. But it is far, too far, and where no one goes. She had hoped there would be trees past the edge of the city, trees with gnarled roots and hidey hollows, but there are no trees here. So it must be a stone, and as she goes she looks to the roadside for one that sits alone, and yes—some seem to appear in the gloom. But closer, and they are only clods, or mounds, or tangles of leaves. One, so seemingly a solitary stone is nothing but the droppings of a horse in a tidy mound. Another, once more so certainly, so absolutely a stone becomes a small rabbit—ears flat to its head, and so still at her approach, so still until she is nearly upon him, then gone as if sprung from a trap. A decoy it was, it must have been, placed to confuse her and lead her away. A deception from some Sprite close by. Or perhaps several of them in collaboration, a conspiracy of Sprites. It is all too much: the journey, the watching, the weight of the child—all of it has tired her out. And it is colder now, much of her shawl taken up in the wrapping of the child. She does not think of him there against her chest. No, she imagines this bundle to be something else she must carry: a cabbage perhaps, or a loaf of bread. She has only to think of him there against her chest and he will wake. Does he know when she thinks of him? Does he feel her heartbeat go sickly and faint when she remembers he is there, because it seems that he does, and yes, here it comes now. A peep. A whimper. She lifts the shawl just barely enough to look at him. Oh why must he gaze up at her? He is hungry; he must be. Though he will not make a fuss. He peeps and mews but hardly makes a fuss. But he kicks a bit, loosening the wrap of the shawl at his feet. There his scruffy tiny shoes she purchased for two pennies, a gift for the Wee Folk to trade him away.

The roadside slopes. There is a place for sitting. She sits. It has not rained today, but the earth is wet. The sky has clouded over. Now no moon. It is dark enough that she will not be noticed. She unfastens the buttons at her neck and on her chest. He must be hungry. He must be thirsty. But his kind—do they hunger and thirst the way true babies do? Must she feed him? Perhaps a little. Just enough to keep him small so he will not overtake her. The buttons undone, he reaches for her. His tiny hands. Dear God, are they claws? Or is it just a trick of the darkness, the lack of moonlight. But plain enough: that pinched face. Those dreadful ears. The devil's dimple on his chin. That small mouth. He eats and all the while he watches her. He is disgusting. He is a small animal, not hers, not hers. She hears the workings of that narrow mouth. The sound of his lips, his swallow. The slight movement of his ears—those ears—with every suck. How bats must nurse—oh the very thought of it. She looks away from him. She peers around. There is firelight in the shacks and cabins. The spaces between the boards are bright. From some comes singing. From some come shouts. Hovels though they may be, there are women there who rejoice in their children. This she knows. This too she had hoped. Or, now she thinks, she hadn't hoped—not for anything—at all. She had married and the babies had simply come along as babies do. Had come and gone. Two dead, and now this one. This one she carries. Must carry. A dog barks. The pigs snort in their anguished sleep. Rats stream single file along a wet ditch and in single file disappear down a hole in the road bank. Something dark and silent overhead drops and rises and lifts the last in the line—the straggler rat—into the air. She must get on. She pulls the child away from her chest, though she knows that he has hardly gotten his fill of her, but that is enough. Enough. She could pinch his nose closed with her fingers now and the same moment, stuff the shawl into his mouth. Oh yes that would do. That might do. Though he might snap at her like a turtle as she lifts the shawl to his mouth. And then, of course, he would know what she was about. And his knowing, what would that bring? Friends from other realms, perhaps. Or a chance at her when he is grown. No. She will not. She adjusts the shawl to cover him and cover what she can of herself. The muted hooting of geese comes from somewhere above her, and she looks for them—it is good luck to see geese in flight, to count geese in a flock, but they are flying above the cover of low, rolling clouds, and are not to be seen, and the sound flies away with them. A cat trots along the footpath with something small and dark squirming in her mouth. Faintly squealing. Then still. Then silent. The child too is still now, silent. Not a peep. Perhaps he has choked on her, suffocated himself dead. If she uncovered him, would he be dead but gazing up at her with dead eyes? Would he know she had wished him gone? No, she will not look. There is no reason to look. There is no sound. There is nothing in the road. There is no nighttime rush of wind, no flutter of leaves. There are no trees in these parts. They are long gone to fuel and firewood. There are no homes in knotholes or hollow trunks and no gnarled roots that hide small rooms. The sky has clouded over. There is no moon. There is no wind. There is no stone. And the shawl is not nearly warm enough.

Chapter 17
Parchment Letter

THE NEW YORK MUSEUM OF CITY HISTORY
Exhibit 162: Parchment Letter
Biddy Doro writes Mrs. Catherine McCarty Antrim,
Mother of Billy the Kid, October 31, 1861.
Low Level Lighting in Use for Document Conservation

Mrs. Catherine, I have seen you outside my door with Billy, the small child that troubles you. If he be a changeling child, you will be rid of him with this method: Under a new moon, wrap a root of byrony in a scrap of a dead-woman's winding-sheet. Bury it in a place you have seen a yellow dog deposit its feculence. Use a silver spoon for digging. Water the spot with pig's milk in which a bat fallen and drowned with its tiny bat-pups still clinging to her teats. Under the next new moon dig up the root. Boil it as tea. Give the child a single drop.

He will quickly disappear if he is a changeling.

If he remains, then he is a human child and he was born of your body.

Knock my door 3 hard and 2 soft.

I will give you the bryony root.

Do not try to look in my window.

4 dollars for a small byrony root.

I also sell silver spoons.

Do not bring the child to me, nor will I visit.

Biddy Doro, Thirtieth October 1861.

Chapter 18
A Little Monkey of a Lad
Irish Town, New York City
1861–1870

No resemblance, his mother Catherine had said, not this baby, this boy Billy, not to nobody ever was, she said. Not in this family. This boy—she said—was nothing like her own father—Billy's grandfather—or even her brothers, for that matter. Solid men they were, she said. All my brothers, every last one of them sturdy lads, she said. And the same of all your father's kin, she told Billy—all of your Da's brothers—all be fine strapping lads. Burly. Unlike this little William Henry McCarty, this little Billy named for his father's brother who died at eight in a beet-chopper. But, said Patrick McCarty, that brother of mine would have been a big one had he lived, had he growed. No, this boy, his supposed son—this little Billy—was definitely small—a small baby. Puny, Patrick McCarty called his infant son. Piddling, said his mother. She picked the child up, dangled him by the arms. See Paddy, she told her husband. He's got no weight to him, no not a bit. He'll be a small child, and a small man. If he lives, she said.

Patrick liked to give his wife a good-natured poke in the ribs regarding the circumstances of the boy's birth. He come two months early, he said with an exaggerated wink to anyone listening, thereby evoking the possibility of a baby misbegotten. And then there was the matter of his ears. Protuberant, pale. Remindful of those on a big-eared bat or the wings of a large moth. And too, the shape of his mouth. Somewhat pinched with teeth at a slight forward slant. Not quite rabbity. More suggestive of a smaller rodent—a mouse perhaps. Possibly a squirrel. Patrick McCarty held the child in his arms. A little monkey of a lad you may be, he said. But mine or no—he said with a disapproving glance to his wife—it's no matter little fellow—come the thick or thin of it, I be your Da.

Catherine McCarty flinched.

Inquiries were often and well-meant: Are you feeding the boy? Or is it he's just sickly then? asked the other mothers with their robust and muscular broods flocking around them, little ruffians in constant motion made strong and sturdy by city living and a heritage of what was referred to as good Irish stock, those babies happily squalling in their arms, suckling so hard that the women winced when their babies drooled at the sight or smell of a breast and clamped themselves on. Some mothers, it is said, will dote on their odd ones, cherish their small or strange ones. Some mothers. Catherine McCarty was not of this camp. She was most ashamed. She preferred to keep what she called the child's afflictions covered in his father's shirts and pants—old ones near tatters, headed for the rag bag—to disguise the jut of his shoulder blades (she believed to be rudimentary wings, ready to sprout), bunching the sleeve to his elbow bones, buttoning him up neckwise to give his shoulders more of a square; and trousers too big, but these rolled at the waist and belted to provide the illusion of bulk. And lastly a hat. Them ears, she said. Pull that hat down some to be keeping them covered.

My Da's, he told the other boys when they poked fun at his flyaway clothes and poked him with their sticks. My own Da he give me these, he said. Pants and shirt, both. Plenty times he lets me wear his hat.

The boys circled. Closed in. Big boys, all of them: Cleary, Bert, Miles, Declan. Ready to pummel. One boy bigger than the rest—Bert the self-chosen chief agitator—stepped to the front of this company of hooligans and heartily shoved. Billy wobbled but stayed standing. Get him brother, said Bert to Cleary, his second in command. Cleary, happy to oblige, took a run at Billy and pushed him over. He lay in the dirt. Get up, said the Bert the shover, fists clenched. Aye, said Cleary, egging him on. Up.

Billy got up. He grinned at them. That odd small and squirrely face. Those over-sized clothes. He dusted himself off with dramatic sweeping gestures up and down his shirtfront and sleeves. He turned his trouser pockets inside out, swatted off the lint and he stepped forward to this little band of idiots and brutes. He took ahold of the protruding pockets and flapped them about and danced an odd little dance. A jig of sorts interspersed with ridiculous capering, assorted grimaces, and as a finale, with a finger pushing behind those winged appendages on his head—ear flapping and immediate scratching behind in the way a dog would do. Woof woof, he said. Or meow meow, if you'd rather. Cleary the pusher shook his head. Bert the shover—perplexed—unclenched. Miles and Declan looked on.

And they all tumbled toward him, laughing.

And he prevailed. Playing along when playing along became a way of biding his time. Devil-may-care, he seemed, but ever watchful and cautious in all things, talking trouble away or keeping quiet when trouble struck, as his Da told him to do. And soon enough he was a favorite with the other boys, the bigger boys, but then again, they were all bigger boys. Friends to a few of them, feigning friendship with those he thought would turn on him. He was clever and resilient. He was good company, sought after—this boy slight of build who stood and smiled in uncertain circumstances, lips tight together to hide his incisors, the way his mother told him to do.

Come lad, said his father. What you need is a lesson in using your fists. How to take yourself in hand and know where you are. Always be knowing where you are, he said. Keep your gob shut and your eyes open and get them off guard. Then you clobber them.

They're bigger than me, said Billy. All of them, Da. Every one.

No matter, said his father. There's always someone being bigger than you be, and there's always a way. Let me show you how it's done, the father said. How to crack a head. Bust a nose. Come on now, lad. Show me what you've got. Let's have a go at your old Da.

They circle in the kitchen, knock the old furniture about, the father a natural leadfoot and after his evening pint or two, a stumbling lumbering Paddy. Billy reluctant. Come, lad. Pay attention. Give it all you got, says his Da. Let loose and let me have it, he tells the boy, tapping his finger to his jaw. Right here. That's a good lad. Land one. Make it a one-two. I won't break. Make it a good-night knockout. Won't says Billy. Oh you will, his father says. Mind yourself now lad, he says, taunting him with a jab, a soft little hook. Hoping for a counterpunch. But no, Billy won't. Da, says Billy, don't you make me. Billy ducks, stands up, shuffles around, shifts around in some sort of a dance, or whatever such motions may be called. Light on his feet, as the saying goes, and laughing when his father doesn't connect and flies forward off balance. Ah now Billy-boy, says his Da on the floor. That is one way to be fighting, I suppose. Dancing around until they go dizzy. So you just keep on doing what you do and you're sure to be wearing the other feller out.

Author's Note: Sunrise

Sunrise. A clear winter morning in Irish Town, New York. The first stirrings in this district of tenements and shacks tilting toward the river. Birdsong commencing. Red sky above Turtle Bay. Smoke-spew from the chimneys, soot-fall on the rags of old snow in the street. The boy Billy pokes sticks into the cold woodstove. The mother chops persimmons. Hoof strikes on the cobbled streets below. Creak of the pushcarts. Rumbling of the wagons. Toots from the ferry. Hiss and shriek of the factory whistles as their steam hangs briefly in the freezing air. The oven heats. The mother lifts in the pans of batter. Irish cakes, two for a nickel. The narrow sidewalks and the gutters are already lined with the early vendors. The clamoring throngs. Pushcarts are propped. Small pyramids of produce there displayed. Onions. Pears. Peaches. Green plums. Apples. Get 'em here, folks. Apples here. Crabs and Macs. Romes for baking. Well now Ma'am. Wouldn't the mister appreciate a pie? Penny a pound. Take your pick. Shouts now from the wagon drivers. Coal. Ice. Bricks. Beer. Coming through, ma'am. Please sir, let a poor horse pass. Shop grates are slid open. Bang and smash. Doorways lead to dim interiors. Merchandise is hauled out. Cutlery. Crockery. Cups and teapots threaded through their handles, suspended along storefronts. Clothing hung up in bunches. Bottles are rattling in their slotted crates. Milkcans are clanging. Fishmongers are calling. Fresh cod and herring, the catch of the day. Lamppost crows await the fins and heads and innards. Or a rotted pear. Or a moldy melon. Perhaps a cast-off pig head or trotter deemed too putrefied for purchase or human consumption. A flock of pigeons rises from a rooftop coop. They lift together above the chimneys, pitch and turn in unison and glide back again. Flap and murmur. The male birds puff and spin. Blackbirds peck about the horses' legs and amid the feedbag spills. River gulls call above the wake of the fishing boats. Sparrows peep among the dung-balls in the gutter. The boy Billy hears them all above the city din. Listens for them in the alleys, on the rooftops, over the river as they are heading out to sea. Hears them as dusk descends and again just before the daybreak light. Early birdsong always wakes him. Have you heard it, have you listened? When will it wake you? As it did on his first day. As it will on his very last.

Chapter 19
Mam Spits Blood
by William Henry McCarty
Irish Town, New York City
Spring, 1870

Up on our roof, it was just where we liked to go. My brother Joe and me. Him being born four summers after me, and being a regular boy, as Mam would say. The kind of a boy that she needed after me. Joe and me going slow up the stairs, the younger of us and slower. And then we are through the roof door and out on the roof to see all of the city and all of the sky and all of the birds going over and the tumbledown houses just like ours leaning out along the East River shore. In summer we could see bedsheets and shirts and things flapping on lines hung window to window across the alleys, and in winter the black stovepipes sticking up and blowing out white smoke and black smoke and the brick chimneys where the hot air from coal fires above them bent the sky like water and birds sat on the rims getting warm. In the fall we could look out across the East River to the trees on the banks of Astoria and Ravenswood and see the leaves fading from green to yellow to brown and dead and then gone loose and flying off. And if there was no fog or smoke we could see way upriver to the blue hills past Spuyten Duyvil, and back down again to the boats and skiffs on our Turtle Bay, then Kips Bay, and downriver to the ferryboats bound for Brooklyn and back, all blowing their horns low and mournful for folks to be getting on and getting off, and even further where the river goes wide, the tugs and barges heading to the sea. I never did get that far, not to the sea. This was in the city. This was in Irish Town, before our Da quit us, or died. What difference, our Mam said. Knowing your Da, lads, could be either one.

From our bed we could see right straight across the alley into the Darcys' kitchen—Missus Marjory Darcy leaning out her window pinning the washing to the line and Mister Darby Darcy at the kitchen table, his blue macaw parrot named Fergus perched on his chairback, or sitting out in the Darcy's petunie box, screeching at birds he sees pecking down in the alleyway or sitting on the laundry line or even just flying by—and all of them in the pictures in Mister Darcy's big birdy book *Birds of America and the Territories*, and not just the ones flying around these parts. More kinds of birds than I knew there was or ever could be. And two kinds of names for each one, easy names and very stranger names that I couldn't say. But all the birds anyhow, and each one with their easy name that helped me learn my letters by: C-R-O-W. D-O-V-E. And some like G-U-I-L-L-E-M-O-T not so easy, but me learning them myself since Mam couldn't bear it to teach me. She plunked me down hard in the little maple chair my Da made for just my size and she had me take hold of a stick of chalk and the slate board with the painted frame and the rhyme written on the wood. *ABCD As Good As Any Boy Can Be* is what it said. I tried to be as good as any boy could be, I did. But even then I was thinking I was not a real boy, but some kind of boy what she got stuck with. What my Mam said. Poor Mam. It made her sick and dizzy to sit with someone so dim as me, she said. Oh the terrible screams she would do while I tried making my alphabet letters. Chalk letters and pencil letters both. So I didn't trouble her no more with it, no. I learned myself by just looking at Mr. Darcy's birdie book and putting the letters of birdie names on a paper. P-I-P-I-T. N-I--G-H-T-I-N-G-A-L-E. R-E-N. Which is actually with a W for no good reason I could tell. *Birds of America and the Territories.* All of them.

A bit of a nutter, that Mister Darcy totting Fergus around all the town on his shoulder, showing him off—his chest yellow as the lemons I see stacked up on the pushcarts in the street and his back bright blue as the sky—a pretty thing for sure—but damn, didn't that parrot go for me if I tried to pet him, nearly taking away a piece of my finger once or twice, even with Mister Darcy telling me, Mind yourself now Billy! He's a muzzy one, he is, all these macaws is. But it's Mister Darby Darcy saying so when I'm already got to bleeding right there on the street. A beak sharp as razors, that bird. Talky, too. Mister Darcy always sitting and reading the paper out loud in his kitchen with is Fergus bird saying bits of this and that: Brooklyn! Brooklyn! Fergus is squawking, when the headlines Mister Darcy is reading in the *Herald* is about *BROOKLYN BRIDGE UNITES THE BOROUGHS* –and in the *New York Irish News* it's *FERRY FIRE IN TURTLE BAY!* And right then Fergus starts in with his squawking: Fire! Fire! Watch it lads! Fire!

Me and my brother Joe, sitting in our bed we could see straight out and we called window-to-window across the alleyway: Hidy you Darcys! we called and Mister Darcy gets to looking all around, up and down, and he is telling his missus: Hear that Marjory? Good Jaysus, but is there someone calling at us or is it I be going daft now?—Mister Darcy saying it just to set us laughing, just for Joe and me, and we be calling back, It's us Mister Darcy! Over here! It's us.

Oh hello lads, says Mister Darby Darcy. A rotten wicked bunch you be, the both of you. You got me again you did, he'd say.

As I said, a bit of a nutter, Mister Darcy, but kindly enough to me and my little brother Joe. This was Irish Town, when we had our Da still with us. When I had a brother. Mister Darcy always had a *hello lads* for us anywhere we see him with Fergus—in the street or on the stairs up to our flat or up to his or in the shops—though the shops didn't take kindly to a big old bird who'd likely be taking a shit on a stack of dry goods or the pickle barrel. Or we'd see him in the alleyway where Joe and me always be picking around and finding what fell out of windows or folks threw out of windows—the smashed-up mirror Mam kept on the chifforobe until Da tossed it out, and once a knife all bloodied up, and once a dead dog gone so wormy you could hardly tell it to be a dog, and once a penny. And once a piece of green bottleglass I could hold up to my eye and the trees across the river would look green, no matter if they were yellow or dying or dead. At the end of the alleyway where the sunlight come in was the tree we called the cinnamon tree. Brother Joe and me—we always said cinnamon just to rile our Da, just to hear him holler at us: It's persimmon, you little shites! He'd be pulling his hair out over that one, over and over again. Joe and me, we'd never let up on him. Mam told us that he'd not be sticking around anyway, so why not? Cinnamon, cinnamon cinnamon—we'd be screaming like wild Indians, or what Da said we were: like rebel armies on the run. Persimmon was what it really was, growing just where the alleyway led to the street we could not see, and then on to the big avenue paved with river stones, so we could hear the carts and horses clomping along and the coal seller shouting and the fruit seller swearing and the knife man grinding and the trains coming or going—whistles and rumbles and everything louder on rainy days or rainy nights. This was before Wichita Kansas and before Mam started spitting red and before the shuttered house. This was still in Irish Town, when Da was still there, or not there, or Ma said he was quitting on us but sometimes coming around, I never knew which. This was in the city when we had the persimmon tree. Mam made cakes with cut-up persimmons and one time Da came home and said, Somethings smelling good in here. I remember the day. He took off his cap and set it on the chifforobe with the broken mirror, and he sat down at the table with us and what he said was: Good cake. This was us in Irish Town—the three of us—Da, Mam, and my brother Joe. This was when I had a Da. This was before the man that our Mam called Mister Antrim was coming round for visits. This is when I had a Mam. This was when I had a brother—my little brother. That Joe, he was big for a little brother, so I called him Little Man. Joe being the better brother. Mam always said. Easier, she said, though I tried to be easy. Joe was better, but I was the first—the first one that lived—she told me. But what would it matter. I told Joe, what good is there in being the better brother when our Da left and left us both behind, not taking neither. We waited for our Da those nights. Joe and me sat in our bed and listened for the stair to creak and some nights it did and some nights it didn't. Which was better, for sure I didn't know—a row with Mam when Da came home or none when he didn't? It's you two, both of you that run him off, Mam said. So ha ha ha on poor poor me, she said, and boo hoo hoo and then goes tearing around, pulling at her hair—oh how she did go off that away. The same way she screamed herself sick when I couldn't learn my letters on the slate board. The same way when she puts a stick of chalk in my hand and tells me how to make the marks. *Hold it like so*, she said, starting out quiet with me, but I didn't hold it like I was supposed. The chalk just fell to little bits in my hand and then she starts louder since I'm pressing to the slate too hard or too soft and she snatches up the slate and pitches it away. *An idjit you are, Billy, who can't take ahold of a piece of chalk*, she says and she gives me paper and a pencil instead of the chalk and the slate board and we start over. Mam calm now. Or just calmer. And I take up the pencil like I see my Da take it and Mam says *What's wrong with you Billy? Take ahold of your pencil proper now. That's no way to be making your B. Stay in the lines, you little idjit! Have you gone stupid, Billy? Or did Wee Folk snatch my true-born from his bed and leave me with one witless? You're no child of mine, I'll tell you that and always been knowing it.* This was when she give up on me and I learned my letters from Mister Darcy's birdy book. This was before Wichita. Our Da was long gone before Wichita, long done with us, us meaning Joe and me. We run him off, Mam said. Joe and me we were too much, she said, us always needing minding or dinner or shoes. The two of you it was done it, she said. You two. But I am thinking maybe it was that man Mister Antrim who run Da off. Mister Antrim always coming by visiting our Mam. What's he wanting? I ask Mam, but she never says. So maybe him. Or maybe it was on account of our Da was tired of seeing the specks of red in the potatoes or on the pillow or in the bread when Mam's spit was going bloody. Too many beets, she said.

I tell her, it's blood Mam. Blood. I knew blood. I seen it on the horses' spit when the man driving the wagon is pulling too tight on the metal in their mouths. Or on their backsides when they get a whipping. Blood, I knew it. But she said no, that it was the beets, or the strawberries—even if we never did have strawberries—or it was the fluff coming off the red wool patches on the comforter she used to wrap me and my brother in when we were tiny lads, or that it was on account of the moon. Oh for certain now, she said, the cough be the worst when the moon was full, pulling on the blood within her she said, the same as it be told in her leather-covered Bible when God pulled on the water in a big red sea somewhere and made a road right in the middle for the Israelites to go riding through.

But the cough keeps on when it's any old moon and the blood keeps coming. Go fetch Biddy Doro, says Mam. And she sends me down to the hut on Dingman's Alley with a nickel and a note:

Dear Miss Biddy,
Here is Billy, I am sending him to you.
He is grown some but you can see he stays small and squirrely.
I am poorly with the cough, even walking weakens me.
Please come up to Irish Town.
Or send along your cohosh leaf and licorice root until you make a visit.
Bless your good heart till then dear Miss Biddy.
Billy has a nickel and a note in his pocket.
I tell you this so he can't say otherwise.
Catherine McCarty, Irish Town

So I go by way of Turtle Bay since I have seen Miss Biddy there when the river is low as she goes stepping on the river stones, picking little things from the mud and putting them in her pouch. But this time early morning the river is high and hardly any place to walk, and I know she must be home in her hut down Dingman's Alley. I been there before.

I never have to knock. I never have to call: Hello in there Miss Biddy. I just stand quiet by her door with my note in my hand and my nickel and out she comes. Just like I knew she would. She takes the note. She takes the nickel. She rubs her chin and some black coal soot what is on her hand goes on her chin, but I keep quiet about that, keep my gob shut up about her chin looking sooty. Then she looks me over and she takes me to the strings of things she has tied up across the alley—the stems with leaves and thorns and old faded flowers hardly the colors they once was, and some dried-up mice in bunches strung by their tails and dead bats in clumps pinned up by their papery wings, all with shreds of fur still sticking, and a few baldy looking birds dried out dead and hanging head down with bits of feathers, and some dry little fishes, them dead too but still silver and strung gill to gill. She picks a piece of this and a piece of that and folds the pieces up into the note. For your Mam, she says and I put the paper in my pants pocket, the one left where there still is stitching.

Now you my little one, says Miss Biddy. She pulls a leaf off what's hanging on a string and puts it under my nose for me to sniff. But anything what Miss Biddy has hanging in her alleyway is not something I want to be sniffing.

Come lad, she says. It won't be hurting you.

So I sniff. It smells very good. Like cake.

Like cake, I tell her.

Ah. That to some but something else if you are something else, she says. But you, I know what you are.

Oh Miss Biddy, I say. What am I?

Small, lad. You are small. But to be afeared of nothing, she says. Open your mouth then and make it so.

And I do. It's not cake. Not like any cake I ever had, though I hardly ever had any cake. My tongue goes tingly, like I ate something too hot. Or a sticker's in my mouth. Or something alive or wiggling, but I know it's not.

Good lad, she says. Now fly on home with you then, she says.

Mam is waiting. At the top of the stairs she is waiting. From just looking at her I know I am going to get a big fat whupping. Get your goddamn self up here, she screams, but it is hard for my tired legs to go. Stair, stair, stair, stair. She runs partway down and she grabs ahold of me by the shirt and I try to get loose of her but she's got me, dragging me up and along the way at two more flights up is where she hauls off and gives me a good whump or two or three and she says where in hell have you been, what was it you been doing all this time, and why, oh tell me that you little shite, oh sweet Jaysus tell me why you just now be coming to home in the dark? I tell her I don't know. I tell her how Miss Biddy she gives me a leaf to sniff and she sets it in my mouth but don't ask me what and she sends me home. I tell her how I went up Dingman's Alley and around the same way I came by way of the river but the river was low with the tide and the moon rising so I could walk aways along the bank but couldn't keep my feet on the ground no matter how hard I tried. And then I was up up up over the river. High up but I wasn't afeard of it, no. I was looking down and I could see the silver fishes down though the water. I could see the people in the ferryboat looking up and pointing and some of them waving their hats as I went over. I could see all of Turtle Bay and Irish Town and all the way to Brooklyn and past Brooklyn to whatever it's called after that to where before I never could ever see. There's cormorants flying to their night places on the tree snags, and I'm going with them through the little clouds rising from the river. And then I'm flying downriver with a line of geese until they turn for the harbor and leave me all alone and I turn myself around too, for home.

You lying little shite, says Mam. And evil too, she says, and she gives me a good whack. But there's no need for crying. It doesn't matter none. I know a birdy name. I know how to write. I can write it down. *Cormorant.*

For a while Mam's coughing goes better some. For a while the blood's not coming around. The man she calls Mister Antrim, he's coming around but not the blood, not for a while. But soon enough all the blood comes back again, starts up the same as before and she starts taking the cohosh and licorice, but everyone Mam knows tells her no—that there's no cohosh or licorice that's good for fixing cough blood. It's the city winters, everyone tells her. It's the damp from the river. Better off in the West, they say. West somewhere where it's warmer. The Territories maybe. Or Kansas, even, where the sun and the air is what grows all the corn. Mister Antrim who comes around when Da doesn't come around, even he tells her: Wichita Kansas. Come to Wichita. Even Mister Darby Darcy tells her so—it was his own brother going west to Wichita ten years before, and this brother of his never had a cough a single day while he was in Wichita, well not until the day he died, and true enough—he was coughing some blood that very day—but that was mainly on account of a bullet getting caught in his chest while stealing somebody's horse.

So then it would be Wichita, Mam says. But she won't say when and she won't say how. Only that there's a train to be coming and taking us away to Wichita.

The eggs of the cormorant (Phalacrocorax auratus) are a chalky blue
—Birds of America and the Territories, Chapter 11: Cormorants

Chapter 20
We Take the Train to Wichita
by William Henry McCarty
Summer, 1870

We put what we had in bundles made of blankets and set them by the door. The bed was bare, but we left the mattress so we wouldn't mind the slats. I itched and twisted all night with the straw poking at me though the ticking. We slept in our clothes so we wouldn't be cold. Mam coughed from time to time. Like she does. Joseph cried in his sleep. Like he does. Mam held him like she does but he always cries anyway. All night long I listened for Da on the stairs. I heard Mam get up in the dark and sweep the floor.

In the morning Mam puts her Bible and licorice root and spit rags in her big purse.

In the morning the Darcys—Missus Marjory Darcy and her Mister Darby Darcey and Fergus—they come by. Marjory Darcy put her arms around Mam and kissed her, and kissed Joe and next she came after me and kissed me the same. I wiped it off when she wasn't watching, but I didn't mind. And she gives Mam a going-away handkerchief with a trim of yellow stitching and *CBM* stitched in. Mister Darcy gives Joe a penny. I've something for you too lad, says Mister Darcy, so you'll be knowing the name of all the birds where you be going, he says and he hands me his book. It's the one I learned my letters from, the book he's always let me be reading, *Birds of America and the Territories.* See, lad? he says. All the birds wherever you are and then some. You can read them in the book and you can put them on a list, if they be flying or swimming or singing or whatnot. Then you'll know what you see and you'll know what you didn't. Off you go then, he says and he shakes my hand goodbye, and I am feeling more than mournful now. I don't care a whit if Fergus wants to take a swipe at me. And then I am even hoping he would take a swipe at me, take a piece of me, a chunk off my finger in his beak and chew a piece of me up and send me down in his belly and it will be there forever. I put my hand out but Fergus doesn't go for me the way he always did. No, he sits hunkered on Mr. Darcy's shoulder, and the birdy shit there was different than the usual birdy shit—all green this time it was—with pieces of it dried up and stuck to his bottom. Poor Fergus, says Mister Darby Darcy, Fergus is poorly of late. So I give him a little tug on one of his long blue tail-feathers just to get him going a bit, but it comes off in my hand. A long blue feather. Fergus opens his mouth and I think now he'll get me, but he just says: Poorly, in a croaky voice, not even opening his beady little birdy eyes. Poor Fergus is poorly, he says, and I know I will be keeping the feather for always.

Mam writes out a paper and folds it over and puts it on a nail on our door. In case your Da comes by, she says. I tell her: But Da quit us, didn't he? Or died, didn't he? But Mam says to hush now. So maybe he didn't quit us. Not yet. Maybe if I worked on it, if took myself in hand, then I could be the better brother. I could write being better in a note and put the note on a nail on our door. I could tell him:

Da, we are gone. Look for us in Wichita. The Darcys know where.
Da, I have your hat.
Da, it was Mam made me go.
Da, here is a list of what you wanted me to do and I am doing it:
I am taking myself in hand.
I am catching them off guard. Then clobbering,
I am shutting my gob-hole when it needs shutting.
All of it, I am Da. I truly am. All of it, Da.
Your boy Billy.

Now we are in the station.

We are waiting for our train.

It is dim in the station except for the light from the big clock shining big and white the way a rising moon looks over Turtle Bay and except for the sun slanting down some through the big windows in the roof it seems something like the beginning of nighttime. We can see right into the train where people already on board are looking out at us from the train windows, sitting in their seats or fussing with their bundles, and the light inside the train is the same golden color the kitchen would be when Da came home late and got a fire going in the grate. That kind of golden. We are waiting for the train beside a green iron pillar with the big moonface clock. I can hear the clock. Trains come chugging in and go screeching to a stop, and whistles are blowing all around and folks are shouting and waving goodbye to people on the train and every other sort of hollering, but I can still hear the clock. I look up and when the minute hand is ready to go the gears inside it go click but it does not move ahead right off. No, it clicks backwards as if it wants a running start on the next notch, the next minute, and then the gears go grinding and the arrow goes click, jumps back and notches ahead, notches ahead, to one minute more, or is it one minute less.

Here comes a train.

Not ours, says Mam.

The clock grinds, clicks.

Trains come and go, but not ours, not ours, no not ours, says Mam.

She gets up to look and says, I think that one is our one, but then she says, No not ours.

Pigeons are flying right in and out of the station, landing on the big roof bars and making soft noises and dropping shit down on the people. Pigeons. I see 'em. I will make a list of every bird I see and maybe all of them in the birdy book. I tell Joe, see Joe? See the birdies? And I tell him to look but Joe won't.

A lady is holding a little dog. I'd like to go pet the dog but Mam says no.

A man is selling wieners from a shiny tin box on his chest with a strap around his neck. Like Da's belt. Hot wieners, enjoy a hot wiener, he says. Mam buys us three of them, and right there the wiener-man rolls them up in paper and puts them in a paper sack. I could smell the wieners. But Mam said not now, for later because there's no supper on the train. We are waiting for the train. For our train. I am holding onto Joe's hand and looking at all the legs passing close by to see if any of them is Da's legs, Da come to see us off. Or come along. I could be seeing more if I was up the way Da would tote me on his shoulders but it was Da I was looking for and I am calling out Da Da just in case he was there, come to see us off, but Mam says: Enough. But no matter. He wouldn't hear me anyway, not little me for all the hollering I could do with the screeching of trains stopping and the whistles of the trains starting up and the steam in clouds all around and folks shouting and Ma with her coughing and looking worn out, even worse lately and even worse with us waiting for the train. And Mam sits herself down on our tied-up bundle.

Mam, I say. Get yourself up.

Mam.

But here is the wiener-man. He drops shut the lid of the tin box on his chest and works the strap around to his shoulder. May I, says the wiener-man and he takes the tickets out of Mam's hand. He looks down at me and says, And what might be your name, me lad? Billy, I tell him. Billy McCarty. And he says, Well hello Mister McCarty and help yer little brother there—take his hand, there's a good lad, he says, and when he says that, that's when I wish the wiener-man would come along on this train with us, or maybe I could stay behind, not go on the train, but stay right here in the station and stay with the wiener-man. The wiener-man might could use a boy such as me to help him sell wieners. I shout: Wieners! Enjoy a hot wiener! He looks down at me and laughs a bit. Well now, he says, will you listen to this. Smart lad you've got there, he says to Mam. Then he puts his hand under Mam's elbow and he says, Madam permit me. And he helps her stand herself up. He takes our bundles. He takes us to where you go to get on. He hands over our bundles to the trainman and tells him: For these folks. Mam goes up the step. The wiener-man picks up Joe by under his arms and tells Joe: Up you go—and swings him up beside Mam. He turns back to me and tells me, You're next young Mister McCarty. No need to lift a lad like you. Go on now—you'll make that step. I make the step. We go with the trainman. He puts the bundles in the rack. I get the window seat. I should be happy to get the window seat before Joe gets it but I am not. I don't know why but I am not. I am almost set to tell Joe take the window seat if you want to, but of course I don't say it and anyway the train makes a loud and long shhhhh, so I shush. I look out the window. There are people waving at the train and I am looking out for our Da and I am looking out for the wiener-man. He would have his wiener-box on this chest and he would be calling Hot Wieners Come Get 'Em Hot, but I can't hear the wiener-man calling. I can't hear the grinding of the big green-and-white moonface clock, or the people in the station with their hands cupped around their mouths and shouting things to the people they see in the windows on the train, people like us on the train.

I am watching out the window for the wiener-man, and I hear: Madam, is this seat occupied? and just for a clock-tick-tock I am thinking that the wiener-man has come back to us, or maybe it is our Da. But it is not the wiener-man. It is not our Da. It is some other man we don't know. Ma takes Joe from the aisle seat and sets him on her lap. The man sits. He has a small black hat with a brim all around. He has a gold watch that comes out of his pocket on a gold chain and he looks out the window at the big moonface clock and the train whistle goes off and he looks back at his watch and holds it to his ear and as the train heaves we pitch frontwise in our seats and the people still standing stagger around and fall into their seats and we are off, we are moving now with clouds of train smoke coming up all around the window, all around the people in the station, all waving us goodbye out of the clouds with slices of dusty light slanting down on them, and now we are passing the big green and white clock. The big arrow on the moonface jerks forward to one minute after two o'clock and I know—now I know that this is the last time for me in this city, this will be the last time on this train that's leaving this city, this is the last time it will be one minute after two o'clock today, and this is the last time it will ever be today.

Something goes bright in the crowd—a flash, a gleam—the kind of bright I would make with a piece of the mirror glass—the one Ma used to keep atop the chifforobe until Da smashed it up and I found the piece in the alleyway and I aimed it at the sun. And then there it is, the same bright flash in the crowd, but comes just quick, then gone quick too, then back again, that kind of light. And there again, a light in the crowd again and that is when I see him. I see the wiener-man. He is standing in the dusty bolt of sun coming down through the big windows, and I see the lid of the wiener-box go glinty when he opens it and then go dark when he drops it shut. I see the wiener-man but he doesn't see me. He is busy selling wieners. I holler Hidy Hidy and I hit the window with my knucks, hit and hit, and Ma says: Enough now. But it is not enough—it is not. And now we are moving away from the wiener-man, we are rolling out of the station and into the bright light of this sunny day, of this afternoon, of the one minute after two o'clock sunlight, all of us tottering the same in our seats, swaying sideways in our seats as the train rounds the bed going past the avenue with the riverstone cobbles, and there goes the top of the cinnamon tree, and then the back of the houses, and clothes lines the same as Missus Darcy has and some people sitting on their back steps and some standing in doorways wave and there is a dog tied to a post and there is someone in a yard throwing feed at chickens and someone flinging water from a bucket and someone throwing trash in a creek and birds in a row on a telegraph wire and the church tower bell swinging without any sound and the churchyard where two men are digging and earth is flying off their shovels and then we are faster, we are faster and then too fast if I look straight out, but I can see things if I snap my head back and forth to catch what is going by and then even with that it is all too fast to see.

Joe tells Mam, Where's all the corn? since she said we'd see how Wichita is far away from the city and all growing with corn. But Mam says, Corn? and then she remembers. It's not yet, she says.

I can smell the wieners wrapped in their papers in the paper sack, but Mam says: Not yet, wieners is for later.

Here comes the drink-man coming down the aisle. He is not shouting, like the wiener-man. I can hardly hear the drink-man: Drinks we got drinks, pop and sasperelly and coffee and tea. I tell Ma I need a drink. Please Ma. And I poke my brother and he says, Me too. Mam. Please Mam.

She is too worn out with the train and the coughing and with me and Joe, and no Da, and she gives in and me and Joe we get ourselves two bottles of cherry pop.

There, says Mam. Now you'll not be pestering me for a while.

Mam, I say.

No more out of you I tell you. Sit quiet. Read your birdy book. Or look out the window and pay attention to what's passing by.

But I am looking. I am paying attention. The way Da was always telling me: Keep your gob shut when it needs shutting. And pay attention. All the time. I am. I am looking all around. I have my book. I open my book and look for pigeon. *Rock dove* it says. The real name for a pigeon. I have a new bird name to write. I write it on my list.

When captured by a predator, the rock dove, or pigeon (Columbia liva) will release bunches of its fluffy body feathers into the attacker's mouth, assisting in its escape.

—Birds of America and the Territories, Chapter 39: Pigeons, Doves

Chapter 21
Finn Along the River Road
by William Henry McCarty
Summer, 1870

He came with a horse and buckboard and he took us—me and Joe and Mam—to the shuttered house and there we kept on for a while. This was in Wichita, in the house Mister Antrim said was his house.

He was there at the Wichita station, waiting for us. Ah Catherine, he says and he takes hold of Mam the way I never did see him take hold of her when he came around back home in Irish Town. And here be the lads, he says.

Mam says, You remember Mister Antrim? Come visiting after your Da died? She looks at me. She looks at Joe. Sure you do, she says. But I make a face like I don't. And Joe neither from the way he is hiding behind our Mam.

Hello there Joe, says Mister Antrim, and he reaches round her and gives my little brother's head a pat.

The way I used to give Fergus a pat.

The way my Da used to give me a pat. Or I think he did.

What a big boy you're getting to be, Mister Antrim tells Joe. How old are you my man, he says to Joe.

I don't know, Joe says, and now I'm almost in stitches since that little shite brother of mine damn well knows how old he is.

Mam says, He's just five.

Well you're sure a big one for just five, he tells Joe. And then this

Mister Antrim looks me over and next he's coming at me. And you, lad. You the big brother. How old might you be now?

I could tell him I don't know either, but I don't. Nine, I tell him. Ten come July.

Nine, eh? Is that so. Well now. What we have here's a little brother right big for five and a big brother too little for nine.

Billy come early, Mam says. He never did catch up.

We'll just have to feed you some of our good Kansas corn, we will. You and them cows they be herding down the pike, he says. And he starts coming at me and I dodge the pat on the head I know is coming too and I'm thinking I may give him a nice hard pinch with my teeth the way Ferus used to do me, but I don't do it. But it'll be no head patting for me, no sir. I stick out my hand right firm and proper the way I see men do. William McCarty, I tell him. Happy to see you.

Well will you look at this now, says Mister Antrim, and he does give my hand a shake but all the time he's looking over at Mam with a smile on his mug as if I am some sort of soft-headed ninny. So it's now William is it? And a small William at that, he says all the while gripping my hand so it's hurting some but just a little, not enough to say anything about it and even if it was hurting more than just a little I wouldn't and then he pulls me right to him and leans down and says in my ear very quiet, quieter even than the drink-man: I be a William as well.

And then he turns me loose.

Now let me tell you this—that I am feeling the same kind of uneasy the day my pals first set upon me back in Irish Town. Scared but getting madder and it goes rolling around inside me in my head and comes out the way I know it will without me even trying and I tell this Mister Antrim: I go by Billy, mostly. Folks mostly call me Billy. What do folks call you? Would it might be Willie?

Willie? he says.

If you've got a small one.

A small one? says Mister Antrim.

A small pisser, I say.

Billy, says Mam.

Mister Antrim gives me a little shove to my shoulder and tells Mam, It's all right, Catherine. We'll get this one straightened out soon enough. He's just been needing a man around the house regular.

We set our bundles in the buckboard and I tuck my *Birds of America* book in between. What's this now? says Mister Antrim, and he snatches it up.

It's mine, I tell him.

He's always reading it, says Mam. Keeps him quiet, she says.

I want to snatch it back, but I don't. I stand quite while he's thumbing through and rough with it. So you're a smart one then, he says. Well, good for you, clever lad. Whatever keeps you quiet, he says and he hands it back, and I don't say thank you, why should I.

Up you go, he says and he lifts Joe into the back of the buckboard, and he makes a move for me but I scramble up quick before he can lay a hand on me, and I am back there with Joe, and Mam goes up beside Mister William Antrim. The horse is a pretty one, brown all over with white socks, not like the poor old things in Irish Town, dragging market wagons up and down the cobbled avenue. He turns his head and looks right at me. White stripe. Hidy, old boy, I tell him.

We'll take the Arkansas River road, says Mister William Antrim. On with you Finn, and he gives the reins a flap. And a cluck cluck.

The road goes beside a river broad and blue as the sky is. There's skiffs rowing close to the shore and farther out grand paddleboats flags flying on the masts, steam stacks spouting steam, horns blowing to each other: Watch out we're coming through. There's none like the flats of Irish Town stacked five high, not here. Here are barns painted red and houses with yards and here's some red chickens and one white one walking nearly in the road. Muggy Owens' hens, says Mister William Antrim. Muggy just can't keep 'em fenced in, he says. Oughta run 'em over, he says. And now shacks with pens and there's two black pigs peeking through the slats. Ed Mueller's place, says Mister William Antrim, just down from us, one farm over. Those his pigs, those black-spot hogs. Sammy and Hammy, he says. And on we go past a row of painted houses with porches perched out along the river shore and folks there fishing. Lads, like fishing? says Mister William Antrim, shouting to us over his shoulder.

Mam tells him, They never been fishing.

Well then, he says. We'll have to be giving it a go, won't we?

And we go on.

Decent duck shooting, too. See there, says Mister Antrim.

I see them, but they don't look like any ducks I ever did see in Turtle Bay—these with orange feathers sprouting on their heads, and looking around and around right nervous, and sure enough something spooks them and they give a little leap up on the water and go head first under. Diving ducks.

Joe is gone fast asleep with the joggling of the buckboard. But me, I'm awake. I'm paying attention. I am always paying attention. The horse Finn is fast along this river road. We pass trees along the banks. Willows the same as some along Turtle Bay with branches draped down and swinging.

And there's more kinds of ducks, white-backed ones, whole rafts of them sitting and bobbing and then set to squawking and flapping like thunder when we get close, and next they all be lifting together, tilting in the air the same and settling again aways upriver.

And here's a hawk the kind I never did see, this one with wings wide and staying still as a kite over the water, then folding itself up and dropping himself like a stone, feet first. Diving hawks. Diving ducks. All them I'll remember. All of them with names that I'll be knowing from my book. *Birds of America and the Territories.* And there's crows, too. Crows of course. The same as the Irish Town crows going over us and over the big fields of bright leaves growing as far as you can see and rattling in the wind, and I think to be asking: Is that there the corn?—since never did I see corn growing, never did see corn at all except what the vegetable man kept on his cart with the potatoes and the onions, though I never saw onions and potatoes growing neither. Nothing was growing back in Irish Town, except what Mam called Tree of Heaven that sprung up in empty places, even some in gutters, and our persimmon tree, and the petunies Missus Marjory Darcy kept in a box by her window—except when that big old Fergus bird stepped out the window, grabbing them up by the bunches in his foot-claws and tearing them to bits with that deadly sharp mouth of his and all gone, every one. But I don't feel to be asking about the corn. If I do, this Mister William Antrim might be thinking me dim for sure. So I don't. I remember my Da telling me I got to keep my gob shut and pay attention. So I do. But no matter. I am here with Joe in the back of the buckboard rumbling along and our Mam sitting up front with Mister Antrim and maybe it's going to be all right here. There's a river. There's birds that go diving. There's fishing. There's Finn. From where I'm sitting I can see the muscles in his big rump and his tail swinging back and forth, and he is going along strong and steady.

I am thinking it might all be fine here. Yes it might.

The long hair along Finn's neck is black and blowing as we round a bend turning away from the river and into the wind and now the wind is in our faces. Finn shakes his head and snorts at whatever it is he is smelling coming in.

Finn slows, then stops. Stamps. He twists his head around. His nose is twitching and he blows hard. Same place every time, says Mister William Antrim. We get to right here, to this same spot and he don't want to go, he says and he flaps the reins to Finn's rump. Get on with you Finn, he says.

We get on.

I don't smell it. Not right off. And then it comes on stronger, bad and strong. It's the smell of blood that comes with Mam coughing and something gone rotten like the wormy dog in the alleyway. Mam puts her handkerchief on her face, and I think now she'll be having a coughing spell and the wind will be flying those red specks out of her mouth and right back on me.

It's blowing this way in from the yards, Mister William Antrim tells her. The Trail goes right through here.

Trail? says Mam.

The Chisolm Trail taking herds to the stockyards, he says. Right across this here Arkansas River the cows get herded on up to Abilene, then trains east. Chicago. And some—well, some won't be going nowhere from here.

He gives the reins another flap.

We'll be moving on past it soon enough, says Mister William Antrim. You'll see it—by the birds, he says.

And then I hear it, hardly hear it at first: a far-off sort of hum. And soon louder and louder still, and I am thinking it must be from the big boats on the river, the low sad horns the way the Ferry boats headed for Brooklyn and back would do when they were coming in or going off. Something like that sound. But no. Not that sound. And then it comes full on, and—how can I tell it—the most terrible awful cries a body might hear. Moans, I tell you, screams and moans and louder still so I'm not hearing Mister William Antrim talking to Mam next to him, and not the tweeting of the birds in the trees, and not the rattling rows of bright green leaves of corn or whatever the hell it is growing and not even the clop clop of Finn in the road. And it comes into view across the river between the passing trees—cows and cows and cows packed in tight together inside long roads of fences, flowing in one great brown crowd of cows with no end to them, not that I can see, with no space between them but holding their heads and ears and horns above the clouds of dirt-brown dust, and I can only see their heads and not the rest of them so packed in they be. We are too far off to see their faces, but I do. I see their faces. I see their round eyes and black noses and some with their tongues swell-up and hanging out, and I don't know how it is that I can see them but I do, I do, on and on until the lines of cows ten cows wide flow together into one big sea of cows, and they are crashing against the fences, and some climbing up the boards to get out, but there is nowhere to get out, nowhere else to go, and men sitting on the boards kicking and swinging bats at the cows trying to get away by climbing up the boards and the cows that won't go, oh I wouldn't go if I didn't have to, if she didn't make me, but I had to, had to go, our Da was gone and Mam spitting blood and there was nowhere else to go, and we go on, on, Mister William Antrim flapping the reins telling Finn to keep on cluck cluck keep on now, and Finn taking us along the road where the sea of cows flows into pen and pen and pen, a city of pens and a shed as big as all of Turtle Bay, and above it—birds—hundreds, a swarm of them, so much blacker and bigger than crows are, and turning in a big slow circle over the pens, teetering as if they may fall from the sky, but they are not falling, they will not fall, their dark wings spread for flying but nary a flap.

Buzzards, says Mister William Antrim. Damn them.

I watch them as we go. Buzzards. I will remember the name for them. I will. For my list. And for me to stay remembering. And then we are past the pens.

Past the big shed.

The horrible noise going away now. Nearly gone now. Gone to just a hum, then gone.

Finn takes a turn in the road and the river comes back to us, back into view with the boats and the flags and the skiffs but here the river isn't running the color the sky is—not here. Here where we are along the river are more birds, more of the same, but not circling here. Here they are sitting all along a big pipe jutting out from the bank, big as the shit-sewer that spits the shit downriver from Turtle Bay—and it is here at this hole where the cows spill out: heads and hoofs and the ropes of innards and some other parts I can't tell what. And here they squat, those big buzzard birds, hunched-shouldered and crowding wing to wing, pulling on the pieces of cows coming out the big pipe, holding the shreds of cows fast with their feet, their heads bald of all their feathers as if they'd been scalped, and red, the same red as what they be tearing up. We ride on just past, where the picked-over parts puddle-up and don't slide downriver but stay circling in a pool the river current misses, swirling around in the same sort of eddy when the tide sucked the river out of Turtle Bay and left the little pools where I would sometimes see Miss Biddy Doro picking up the little critters and weeds and greens, and where I used to muck around in. Where I could walk some on mornings when the moon was still up and the river ran faster out to the sea than the seawater coming in. Where I seen birdies walking in the shallows with legs and beaks long as broom-straws. But that's not how it is here. Here in this part of the river, pieces of cows are making circles in the eddy, and buzzard-birds are making circles above then and there's one of them buzzard-birds sitting on the bank. One off by himself. He turns that baldy head of his and he looks at me over his high-shoulder wings. Turning to see me as we go by. Setting his black bead of an eye upon me. I know who he is, this one. This bird. He stays out of the thick of it just keeping watch from where he is on the riverbank, waiting for the pieces no one wants, the parts picked over and left behind, but it is no matter, no matter one bit. The leftover parts will keep him flying and getting him to wherever he has to go same as the good parts would. But we are here now, me and Mam and Joe here in Wichita, on our way to the shuttered house with the man whose house it is. And here, downriver of the living cows and the giant shed and the dead pieces of cows and the hunch-shouldered birds, this river is not the color it was upriver. Not the color that the sky is. Not the color of our old Turtle Bay. And this river does not smell like our old Turtle Bay, not even when the sea-tide sucked it out and the banks went mucky slick and you could see whatever died or sank or stuck in the mud. This river here where it goes back on itself smells like rot and runs red.

The turkey vulture or buzzard (Cathartes aura) can detect the slightest scent of decay in even newly dead animals, including those well hidden under vegetation or the forest canopy.

—Birds of America and the Territories, Chapter 14: New World Vultures, Condors

Both the male and female mergansers (Mergus merganser) display an orange crest of headfeathers, which they shake dry after a dive.

Chapter 13: Swans, Geese, Ducks, Mergansers

The osprey (Pandion haliaetus) or fish hawk can see fish in the water 120 feet below him, and will hover above the prey, fold its wings, and drop into the water feet first.

Chapter 16: Ospreys

Canvasback ducks (Aythya valisineria), so named for their white backs, can be seen floating on rivers in large, tight flocks. They are able to dive by depressing their feathers, squeezing out air trapped within their plumage, thereby making their bodies less buoyant.

Chapter 13: Swans, Geese, Ducks, Mergansers

Chapter 22
The Shuttered House
Wichita, Kansas
Summer, 1870

Won't have it, says William Antrim, the man whose shuttered house it is, whose horse it is, whose barn and shed and jake-shack it is. If he was mine natural born, well then maybe I'd be naming him my name. But he ain't, so no. Can't be. Altogether a different story. No, Catherine. I won't have it.

The mother of the boys was in agreement. After all, here she was a widow-woman, or somewhat so, or so she said, but truly with no visible means of support as is said and two young 'uns in tow. So, as is also said, her prospects were grim. How could she not help but acquiesce. Yes, William, I agree. Completely. Two Williams living under one roof is just one too many. I might call: William come to supper!—and who would know to come? she said.

I would, said Billy. I would know.

Someone else might not, she said.

I could stay Billy, said Billy. I been Billy.

You haven't been, said the mother. Not where it's been writ, and what's writ is more what is, she said, and she toted out her leather-bound Bible, showed him the frontispiece page and there the quaint engraving—old Noah starboard, above him the rain clouds dispersing, his hands uplifted in release of a bird—palm-size, feathered sleek and smooth and pale—(Billy wondered: Vireo? Auk or dove?)—its errand, according to the inscription: *to see if the water hath receded from the face of the land*; and below this there are the entries, the lists of births and baptisms, weddings and the deaths of those now disintegrated in the depths of the face of the land but no longer flooded over and long since high and dry. Events there in recorded, penned with goose-wing quill and nib, in watered stove-soot and pencil-lead and Punjab black. Look here now, said his mother. Look and read, I know you can.

And there are the very last entries to the list, made in a slurry of lampblack ink:

William Henry McCarty born Jul 17, 1861. City of New York.

Joseph Callen McCarty born May 14, 1865. City of New York.

See, she told him. First one born is William. Then your brother Joe. Nobody been named Billy. Not you. Not no one.

I'll have me a talk with the lad, said Mr. William Antrim, the other William. He'll learn, has to. And he'll be answering to Henry from here on in.

And answer Billy did, though less and less, his silence smoldering as a silence will do while the heart disintegrates beat by beat, and wherein the space it once did dwell desolation finds its foothold. And so began the days of solitude and of solace taken in small things—and these the mother found on wash day, stowed in his pockets: stones and twigs, feathers and bone. A burdock stuck with hair he had combed from the fetlock of the horse Finn. A small skull, rat or bird. And once a turd-sized package of fur from which protruded a yellowish claw and three tiny vertebrae. The mother shrieked. Mr. William Antrim was summoned. The boy was interrogated but his explanation of a falcon's vomitus was far too farfetched. He showed them both his book, in *Birds of America and the Territories*, and he read aloud *avian pellets being the undigested parts of a bird's meal, including the fur, bones, and feathers of rodents and smaller birds, regurgitated from the gizzard. Birds of America and the Territories, Chapter 1, Avian Anatomy.*

See? said Billy. All about the birds, he said.

You think you're clever telling stories then, said Mr. William Antrim. But lies, them I won't abide, he said and gave him a whack.

Catherine, however, suspected the contents of Billy's pockets to be artifacts of conjury—the bits of bone and hair what he used in spells and the spine parts to be those of slain elfin foe. She found other signs of wickedness around the shuttered house as well. A toad sitting in the path (immediately dispatched by her foot). A piece of kindling in the shape of a mole (immediately thrown into the stove). And finally, stuck between the pages of *Birds of America and the Territories*, she found the folded paper note bearing the words of devilish incantations penciled in Billy's diminutive script:

Common crow (Corvus brachyrhynchos)
Wood duck (Aix sponsa)
and more.

Them words! said Catherine. All spells and hocus pocus, said Catherine.

Just the names of birds, said Billy.

I hate to think of the sort of a spell you'd be needing crows for, she said.

It's my list. All the birds I know, said Billy.

And these their witch names? she said. You'd be knowing them as well now, wouldn't you. She turned the book open and over and the paper scraps fluttered down. No more of this. No more now, she said and she opened the door of the stove. She gathered them up into one tight ball and tossed them in, then stepped back expecting sparks or a small explosion, but there was none.

A sprite that flies is what bring you to this world, she said, and ever since you've been wanting one of them to fly you back out of it.

If I could, said Billy.

When might you be flying away? she asked Billy, those times he was disobedient, bothersome. When he wouldn't listen or made some sort of mischief. Small things. Boy things. Acorns in Mr. William Antrim's hat. Pinecones in her mother's bed. Fetch in four potatoes, she told him. No eyes. And he did: three nice fist-sized purple potatoes and one no bigger than a pebble. He washed them clean of garden soil at the pump bucket and set them wet and glistening on the kitchen table, lined up, size order. He pulled his brother into the kitchen to show him. Joe laughed and hugged him, and laughed until he fell to the floor, but they knew trouble was coming. You stay away from him, Catherine McCarty Antrim told Joe. He's not your brother. Never was. That Billy, the one I born—he's gone—and again came the stories of Sprites and thieving Wee Folk who snatch natural-born babies and replace them with their own defectives—the witless, the deformed, the ones who put red potatoes in a row, the ones with animal features—yes, that would be Billy-not-Billy with his squirrely face and batty ears and jutting shoulder blades that she knew to be wings just under his skin, waiting to sprout.

You're not no boy I born, she said, but you'll still be minding me just the same. Or else Mr. Antrim will see to you, she said, shaking her head.

Oh, I shall see to him, said William Antrim, shaking a stick. He'll learn, this one. This Henry, he said. Won't you Henry? Yes you, he told Billy

But my Joe, said Mrs. Catherine McCarty Antrim. My Joe I'm knowing to be mine the minute being born. Spittin' image of my own dead Da he is, she said and held him to her, but Joseph wiggled away, learned from his brother to sidestep trouble. Joe oh my Joe, she said crying after him. Has he tainted you as well?

The shuttered house sat on ample land. The farm—as Mr. William Antrim called it—consisting of a bare-wood barn with simple implements of agriculture leaning in its corners and going to rust and a box stall with cribbed boards where a saddle was slung, long gone stiff and etched with mold and notched with the chewing of mice, and an assortment of tangled tack hanging on a hook. The rest of the acreage held several outbuildings with storm-wrecked roofs or no roofs at all, though the tilting jake-shack was still intact, and fields bordered by old rock walls and cultivated in weeds and brambles, and a small pond partly marsh and fed by a brook, an orchard of twisted old trees, a meadow seeped with springs, a stand of ash and oak, and finally a paddock beside the barn for the horse Finn. Finn. He was balky at first, as he had always been a hitching horse and never ridden, never saddled. Billy sat on the paddock fence with the old saddle he had newly soaped, oiled, restitched, and set it on the rail waiting for Finn to notice, Billy talking softly when he came close enough and telling him . . . telling him something that set the horse nickering and joyfully rollicking. Catherine McCarty Antrim watched it all from the kitchen window. What sort of witchery do you put on that horse? she said. What spell are you saying? she asked Billy. What witchy words do you tell him?

Good boy, said Billy. That's all I tell him.

And when Finn finally sidled up to the rail and stayed put, Billy set the blanket and the saddle on him, then fastened the girth, slipped the bridle over. Finn stamped, but stood. Billy set his foot into the stirrup and lightly slung himself down. Finn still stood. Stamped. Billy sat. Sat some more. Finn stood, rocking. Good boy, Billy told him again, now giddy-up you go, and they dashed away through the paddock and into the field, and that is what he told him every day when he came to the barn with apples from the old orchard and carrots from the garden plot, one specimen with a divided root that branched into what looked to be hairy feet, and at the neck of it below the leafy top—the protrusion of two nubs, rudimentary arms. Billy dressed this odd root in calico scraps from his mother's mending basket. Stuck in peppercorns for eyes. Carved in a tiny mouth with a miniscule shred of crimson yarn pushed therein. Piece of toothpick protruding there for a cheroot. He presented it to Joe, and Joe held it dear. Catherine was afraid to touch it—any artifact of Billy's making must certainly be an effigy of bewitchment, though she made one attempt to snatch it away. Give it here Joe, she said. No Mam, cried Joe. It's mine, Mam. Billy give me. No! And he commenced to howl and hold it hard to himself, his arms crossed against his chest. Catherine tugged and attempted to unbend the boy but he fell over blue and frothing like someone hanged and taking her down with him. And so she gave it up, figuring the carrot would rot, go soft, and fall to pieces, or Joe would tire of it. But instead it just dried out, almost mummified, and the face on it became one of an old man, cheroot tooth pick and all. Joe carried it with care, keeping it with him under his shirt or clutched even in sleep. He set it just out of sight but close beside him mealtimes. Gave it bits to eat, as children with their dolls will do. A bean. A raisin from the rice pudding. A pecan from the pie. Plenty of food kept on coming to that table, coming from somewhere, but certainly not from doings on that farm. Mr. William Antrim toted all of it home—staples of sugar, butter, flour, salt, and baskets of eggs, hard cheese, fine cuts of meat, sometimes sarsaparilla, and sometimes spirits, and in the pockets of his fine frockcoat—handfuls of paper money. Crumpled currency he spread out on the kitchen table beside his vest-pocket derringer. Once he was gone for nearly a month, returning bedraggled but with the usual loot and a story about a friendly wager gone bad aboard the riverboat *Topeka Queen*, and his hasty escape over the starboard rail and into the river and hightailing it home. Then shutting himself and Catherine up in the room with the big iron bed. She emerged at suppertime to lay the table and to cook, and with William Antrim to preside over his little family and eat.

Billy set about his chores, what chores there were to do on a farm that stayed unfarmed. City-boy Billy sent up a ladder to patch the roof, but finding no nails, no hammer, no boards in the yard that were without rot, covered the hole with a thatch of haygrass and rope. City-boy Billy, sent out to split wood but clumsy with axe and spike on account of an injury to his wrist during his infancy in Irish Town, New York. Barely the age of one he was, or thereabouts. Little Billy had been left unattended—who knew he had already learned to walk?—when he climbed the rails of his baby bed, made his way out the door of the flat and into the corridor, worked himself slowly ass-backward down the tenement steps one-by-one (four flights) and went toddling through the filthy alleyway over shards and garbage and the remains of a long-dead dog, and finally falling halfway up his climb into a persimmon tree, the very one when just weeks old his mother had tucked him into a basket and left him to hang there on a limb for a day and a night. So, city-boy Billy, sent out for chopping and hauling—both a sort of torment for a boy so formed: the off-kilter wrist, the congenital narrowing of the shoulders, the general smallness of his size for a boy his age. But he was sprightly nonetheless, quick to muck out the stall or tend the garden or gather kindling or sweep the floors clean in the shuttered house. Our Billy agile and light on his feet, avoiding the stepfather's big fast hand. Dodging the stick. The slap. The mealtime poke with a fork. Sit up there boy. You're near to sliding under the table. Let's fetch this little runt a higher seat.

There was food enough for them all, paid for somehow: corn off the cob baked with cheese, chicken in a stew and topped with peppered biscuits. Buttered beans. Peach pie. Coffee. Milk for the boys. Billy asks for coffee. Joe asks for a second piece of pie. Mr. William Antrim is always the first one done. He pushes away his plate. Produces a deck of playing cards. Performs a dovetail shuffle and series of flourishes. Cuts the deck. A little demonstration for the lads, he says. Palming, bottom dealing, false cuts, crimps. Executes a bit of sleight of hand for Catherine, accompanied by smooth talk and friendly patter. Artifice, says Mr. William Antrim. He shows Joe and Billy how it's done. But Billy already knows, won't say. See? says Mr. William Antrim, turning his hands over, splaying the cards on the table. Simple subterfuge, he says. He squares the deck and slides it away. Well then, he says. He kisses Catherine. Goodbye, Dearest. Joe, be a good lad. Henry, don't you be due for a whooping when I get back, he tells Billy. You hear me? Yes you Henry. Then gone. Catherine clears away the graniteware plates and her blue willow cups—the pair she carried away from the famine in Timoleague, surviving that travel though both were slightly chipped. And one with a fine dark line through the glazing, though you'd hardly notice—so much like part of the blue branch of the stylized willow beside the fabled footbridge where two hunted lovers were chased by a madman Mandarin and transformed by the gods into swallows to live on in this maudlin legend, set forever in blue and white chinoiserie. She washes and dries the cups with care. Sets them on their special shelf. She has her mending to do.

Joe has his carrot doll.

Billy has his bird list and his book.

Every evening there is oil enough for the lamps for as long as anyone wants them lit.

Billy is on the porch watching the shapes of tree swallows as they dip and dive in silhouette against the luminescent blue that lingers just past dusk and later when it is nearly too dark to see, listening to the strange cries of what hunts on the wing. He reads of what is common to these parts—*common to upland deciduous forests, fields, and farmland*—and what is not—*an uncommon visitor more frequent in early spring or fall*—and finally what is termed rare—*rarely sighted, possibly escaped specimen, off-course individual, migration straggler or procrastinator.*

Stragglers fly into an open window, get trapped in the kitchen, in the bedroom. They fly skyward, but there is no sky, and they perch in the curtains, beat themselves bruised against walls and windows and fall exhausted. His mother has her broom. She has her husband's big boot. She knows how to wield and how to whack. She sweeps the small corpse into a corner, pokes at it with the broom stick. Sweet Jaysus, she says, this one with horns! Was it kin to you? she asks Billy. Could it be a Wee Folk or Sprite you sent for? Or conjured up? Take it out of here, she tells Billy. Pick it up and take it way far, she says. And do whatever it is you do with dead things.

Billy, out behind the barn, notes the head unhinged. The tiny prong of a single feather above each eye. He will find its name in his book. Horned lark. He will remember the claws, clutching nothing and curled in a tiny fist.

The horned lark (Eremophila alpestris) is so named for the "horns" or pair of tiny headfeathers displayed by the summer male. Its song is a short series of chips and a melodic ascending trill voiced only in flight.

—Birds of America and the Territories, Chapter 52: Larks

Tree swallows (Tachycineta bicolor) bathe by skimming the surface of ponds midflight at moonrise or in the deepening dusk.

Chapter 53: Swallows, Martins, Saw-Wings

Billy and Joe sharing their bed. Joe sleeps. Billy is awake and listening.

There are sounds in the dark outside the shuttered house. Insects buzz and chant and whistle. Cogged wings are scraped each to each. Membranes are snapped and drummed. The creak and rasp of a cricket. The ratcheting of a Kansas katydid.

Billy hears the tree peepers start their trilling and the sound of a sawblade being drawn along a whetstone.

And then the woodcocks calling peent, peent, peent, snouting worms in the thickets.

The eyes of the woodcock (Scolopax minor) are on the sides of its head, providing the bird with 360° of vision.

—Birds of America and the Territories, Chapter 33: Sandpipers

The nocturnal call of the saw-whet owl (Aegolius acadicus) is akin to the sound of a saw being sharpened on a whetstone.

Chapter 42: True Owls

And there are sounds inside the shuttered house. The scamper of mice in the pantry. The wing-hush of swifts in the sitting room chimney. The rhythmic squeal of the bedsprings where the mother—the mother of the boys—sleeps with the man who came round in Irish Town, who has the name of William and takes Billy's name away, not wanting two Williams under the roof of his shuttered house.

Most nights Billy is winged, perched on the bedstead rail, watching the night sky through the open window, ready to leave the shuttered house, ready for flight and a shift of wind and then the wind comes and it comes carrying the scent of earth, grass, river, ruffling his feathers and swinging the shutters wide, and at last he is through them, carried forth by the reach of his wings, swooping away over the yard, the barn where the horse Finn hears Billy in equine dreams—Good boy, good boy—and now over the roof of the jake-shed, now the paddock and the spring-soaked meadow where the grasses lay silvery wet. Soaring now above the fields where mouse and shrew and vole travel the thoroughfares they have made in the folds and pleats of pasture-grass and sedge. Gliding spread-winged now above the stand of oak and ash where deer are bedded, skimming the tops of the tamarack where the saw-whet owl waits, and at last above the riverbank where the spadefoot toad backs rump first into his burrow, and now following the shine of the river as birds leaving a season behind will do. Tailwind now. Wingbeats. Beat, beat. Will do. Will do.

A whisper: Will do.

Chapter 23
As Blades Are Honed
Late Summer into Fall in Wichita, Kansas
1870

Now nearing dawn, first birds. Billy is awake with the birds and watching what pecks in the yard, what scratches in the dirt, or spiral creeping up the tree trunks. He sees what nests in the eaves, in the old beams in the ceilings of the barn. What perches on telegraph poles and the wires strung post to post.

Soon enough there will be skim-ice along the river shore. Soon enough will come the clatter of dry leaves on the last of the standing corn and the hiss of whetstones spinning as blades are honed: pig sticker, throat slicer, belly gutter. At Ed Muller's place, one farm over on the river road, the two black-spot hogs Sammy and Hammy hear their names called for the last time and at the rattle of the slop bucket bail they bound forth with simple porcine joy to the gate where the carnage will commence. Cudgel to the head. Bash. Throes. Hoists, ropes, hooks. Buckets positioned for the blood. Two black-spot hogs hung from the largest of tree limbs snout-down. Sammy in the oak and Hammy in the maple, though which is which who can tell with their skins pulled down like jackets inside out. The Muller children climb aboard the carcasses thus suspended and swing. Was this one Sammy? calls little Clara Muller, trying to keep a foot hold on the swaying corpse, slippery with hog fat and blood-slime. In a few hours the buzzards arrive for the cast-off innards, a slow-going spiral of them so high they seem not birds at all but bits of soot flown away from a fire. Mr. Mueller loads his Remington and takes a shot and their circling continues unchanged as they rise unperturbed into the clouds. Everywhere the smell of rot, salt, hickory smoke. William Antrim brings home packages wrapped in white paper seeping pink: Sammy and Hammy turned into tenderloin, trotter, chop, hocks. A ham to salt and cure. Crabby apples for Catherine to spice in cinnamon and put by. Pippins and Winesaps from what the old trees still bear, wormy parts pared out and cooked down to apple butter. Pumpkins to be tucked away in straw for the cellar, a cold corner-shelf safe from rats. Catherine, we're all looking forward to your pies. Ain't we now, Joe? There are yams to mash and a cabbage to shred and salt in the stoneware crock. Should be good with that tenderloin, Dearest. Ain't that right, boys? Billy leans in the doorway, listening. The time of year children are told the fable of the lazy grasshopper and the industrious ant, but that both will meet the selfsame fate is never a part of that telling.

Too soon comes the autumn season with the arc of the sun diminished, the clouds hanging in battened folds by day but the nights blown clear and with constellations anew and the water in the tilted dipper nearly frozen over but for the weep of stars that fall from the lip. A flock of robins roost in the apple trees late afternoons. Time to git, Billy tells them. Nearly past time, he says. This too, the season of geese. Do you not listen as they pass above you? Do you not hope to know what they say to each other in the air along the wavering lines of them on the wake of their own making, and do you not know that should you fail to be filled with dread or desire or dark longing at the sound of their talk that surely you must be dead? This season of smoke. Sweet butter. Johnny cakes. Persimmon jam. Acorn squash. Mrs. Catherine McCarty Antrim will roast it and stuff it with buttered crumbs the way William Antrim likes it. Blueberry buckle spooned out in the blue willow cups. There the crack. The chip. The blue willow lovers turned into doves. There always is food in the shuttered house. Mr. William Antrim fetches it home in a leather-lipped tote: pickles and pears in jars, snickerdoodles in a tin imprinted with *Destruction of the Merrimac* by Currier and Ives. Molasses, cornmeal, coffee. There is a slide-box of dominos for Billy, ivory and ebony. There is a red caboose for Joe. Catherine had asked for licorice and arrowroot—what a witch-woman named Biddy Doro in Irish Town gave her for her fever and bloody cough—and these he brings her, and sometimes baubles: a locket that opens to a tiny clover on one side and the other an empty space for her to put his picture in, strung on a chain he tells her is gold—a thousand carats of gold, he says, from a deep goldmine in the dark of Africa. And the one gift he thought was lost from the chest pocket of his frock coat that had been torn loose during an altercation over unfounded accusations of double-dealing—lost he thought, but no! Thank goodness, not lost at all but snagged there on a bit of ripped stitching: a comb for her hair, set with a row of clear stones he tells her are diamonds, and the red ones rubies, and the blue ones just blue.

He tells her how lovely she looks with her hair swept up from her face and secured by the comb but he does not tell her that her face so uncovered has a careworn and wasted look and that her features are severe and peaky with fever. No, instead he tells her that soon he will be gone again, soon to skedaddle and as he likes to say, to drum up some dough. There's plenty enough suckers in Sioux City, he says. I'll be coming back soon, I will. Dearest Catherine. You'll hardly have time to be missing me. You'll hardly know I've been gone.

He was gone six weeks and returned with the leather-lipped tote packed with loot and a small wire cage in which sat a nearly-dead canary—what he'd won, he said, at Five-O Poker, and had traveled home with him two days by train, one day by stage. For you, Catherine dear, he said and set it on the kitchen table. Eye level for Joe. Billy keeping his distance; no sense, he knew, in appearing interested. Catherine standing over. Just one more thing needing tending to, she said.

It hardly needs tending at all, says Mr. William Antrim. He'll sing and keep you company, he says. The bird sat drooping on a dowel-stick set between the bars, the cage itself not nearly wide enough for its wing spread. There was a slot for sprinkling its feed into a tray and a thimble wired-in for water. The bird uttered a weak whistle. He's singing, says Joe. That's not singing, says Billy, who knows that *Canaries (Crithagra flaviventril) seen in the wild are those escaped from captivity, and their song is a warbled zee-zeree-chereeo.* Come on then you, says Catherine rattling the cage. The bird is startled, struggles upright, then slides from the dowel-stick and weakly flaps in the shit at the bottom. Catherine covers the cage with a pillowcase and sets it away on a shelf. It'll shush now, she says.

But there comes another soft whistle from under the cloth.

He's sick, says Billy.

He's not, says Mr. William Antrim. Just don't feed him, that will have him singing for his supper.

There are more presents for the boys. For Joe: a pocket knife and a foldable Jacob's ladder.

And for Billy: a gun. Here you go Henry, he tells Billy, handing over a Collier flintlock by the barrel end. You're old enough to be owning a gun and you're puny enough to be needing it.

Billy takes the gun by the grip of checkered walnut set with a silver eight-point star, the barrel engraved in an old English script.

Mind where you're pointing it little lad, says William Antrim. Give it here, he says. See, some rust on the cylinder. It'd be an old one, but fine for whatever it is you'd be wanting a gun for. He hands it back to Billy.

You won't go shooting me now will you? says William Antrim. A lad the likes of you, who knows?—You're that sort of a lad to be watching out for.

Distant cries in the air. A cloud of snow geese is passing over, a thousand birds tilting together and together descending to Dark Lake.

Flocks of snow geese (Anser caerulescens) winter on lakes and waterways until their spring departure to northern timberlines and the tundra.

—Birds of America and the Territories, Chapter 13: Swans, Geese, Ducks, Mergansers

Although the yellow canary (Crithagra flaviventril) is not native to North America, it is listed here because it is sometimes sighted in the wild. Though it is often kept as a musical decoration, it sings not for joy, but as an instinctual defense of its tiny territory of confinement. It will attempt escape from its cage at any opportunity, beating itself against a window until released.

Chapter 79: Escaped Species

Chapter 24
Tribulations
Wichita, Kansas
November 1, 1871

Now the brink of the coldest season.

The tribulations of a winter in Wichita foretold in the autumn arguments of crows, in the industry of ants and the devil-may-care of grasshoppers, in the fields lately emptied of corn, and in the autumn mishaps of the harvest. Suffocation in a grain silo. Skewering on the tines of a hay tedder. Emerson Sweet decides to give the barn a good mucking-out before the first snow obliterates the path to the manure pit but is kicked in the head by one of his Holsteins, stumbles into the shit-trench, and succumbs to pit gas. Calvin Newcomb, while peening a dull scythe, misjudges the hammer-strike and slices his thumb and the cut goes clear through to the bone. The harvest done, farm folk set aside the implements of agriculture and ready their firearms while the forest trails are still snowless. The trees are bare, the underbrush reduced to leafless sticks and brambles. The woods are open. The hunted are revealed. The sound of gunshot and rifle fire is heard day and night. Mayhem ensues. Bloodshed on both sides, as it has been since antiquity. Misadventures at the very outset. Deke McGraw at the log pile sets down his axe to give his nose a good honk or two and has it blown off by Maddie Wellworth mistaking his white handkerchief for the rump of a buck. Ellie Vonderstone misplaces her spectacles and takes her husband Nuggie for a turkey. Zeke Oxenard cleans his gun and for no good reason peers down the wrong end of the barrel. Men talk of rut, points, racks. In the same trees where recently hung the family hogs to be rendered for human consumption, mule deer now hang by their hoofs. So begins the sharpening of saws, axes, hatchets. The deer decapitations for later display. Dangling tongues replaced with plaster and painted. The lashed and luminous eyes to be replaced with glass; the moist black noses to be shellacked over. The amputation of hoofs to be turned to hat-racks. Mrs. Hooper at the back-porch door hollers *Suppertime Bailey!* to Mr. Hooper on the upswing of his axe just as he is bracing the foreleg of a doe with his foot, and in turning his head ever-so-slightly to shout back *Coming dear* loses all five toes midfoot on the downswing. Whetstones, grindstones, sparks. Lester Findleman spies a rusted hatchet that has been hanging on his toolshed door for the past twenty years at least and for no good reason decides to set it sharp and on the first spin of the granite grindstone takes out his left eye with a sizable chip. Lymon James takes Little Lymon ice fishing out on scenic Lake Dark and chops a hole and drops his hook and line where last winter he pulled up a twelve-pound pike. A beautiful spot directly across from a stand of spruce bordering the shoreline and a cluster of white boulders on the bank. Easy to remember, easy to find, when the men come out with grappling hooks and ask Little Lymon to show them just where it was his father went under. The hole and surrounding crack and crater being refrozen and requiring additional axing; the men with the grappling hooks leaving the scene without the corpse of Lymon James, though they did pull up a nice-sized pike where Lymon James had dropped his line. The Arkansas River still flows, but ice has formed stone to stone along the banks and further out at gravelbars set sideways to the current where the backflow and the ice jams make ponds and small lakes. Martin Otis tells little sister Molly Jean how safe it is to walk on the ice if you slide your feet along like skaters do instead of taking steps. The cattle drive to the slaughterhouse on the Arkansas River brings the same moans and mooing as the animals are whooped and whipped along the boards and down the chute, now in winter and in every season, and the heat of their breathing and their bodies forms clouds above the rumbling throngs of them, and the cast-off pieces of cows not heading on to Abilene keep on flowing from the big pipe even as the pieces freeze and the ice turns a watery pink. The birds—the buzzards—are there, some tugging at what pokes up from the ice, some hunched on overhanging limbs or riverbank rocks and considering what choice parts to pluck from Molly Jean Otis who turns dreamily in the eddy with the pieces of cast-off cow, and blanched though she may be, the bovine blood around her lends her a rosy hue. There are storms to the west. The West. Suffering herds. Drovers on the plains deep in snow. Move 'em along before starvation sets in. And just overnight, Kansas is transformed into a wonderment, a misery. If hell be a caldera of roasting penitents, anyone awakening to a morning of midwestern winter would consider trading his soul for a stint in the brimstone pit. This Wichita winter is not what the family of McCartys had known in New York, where the snow first comes as a dusting—the ethereal fall of confectionary sugar when Mr. Tucci would sift it down on his fresh-made cannoli or the little clouds of flour raised when Catherine McCarty would beat the batter for her persimmon cake. In New York at the start of ferocious cold there would be warning enough for all those with sense to take heed and haul out their coats and cloaks and odd hats and for the poorest of Irish Town to cover themselves with all the clothes they own in wait for winter storms. Geese would go in their unravelling rows above the East River, headed for the open water below the spill of Spuyten Duvil, that arm of the sea where it is said that a fissure to hell in the riverbed keeps it from freezing and where boatmen fear to go. The Irish Town crows would grow bolder in winter and walk among the crowds to peck through the refuse of the marketplace—maggot-bored meat, rotted fruit, the frozen tangle of slimed innards the fishmongers toss into the snowy street. Pathways and walkways emerge, made by the mass of citizenry on foot, city folk trampling, shoveling, coming, going with the city inclination to move, get out, go out, go forth even in the worst of it, even if there be no reason to go. But what mostly moves in winter in Wichita is the snow, taken by the wind and set yonder and yonder still, leaving the empty cornfields thinly white and marked by undulating rows of stubble, laying the earth bare windward of boulders and fences, and scouring whole tracts of land right down to the frozen loam. Try to dig and at the first strike your shovel recoils, sparks, rings like a bell, but in certain corridors drifts go knee high or shoulder high or grows in great hanging crests high to the eaves, burying paths, blocking doors. City-boy Billy is sent to shovel it out, scatter cinders for the family's foothold, tamp it down. A boy after all—still a boy—hauling water from the spring house to the barn, to the horse, to the kitchen—a slip-slide struggle, water sloshing from the cumbersome pails smacking his legs with every step, encasing his shoes in ice, palms deeply creased by the wire bail, hands clawed with cold. Billy off-balance and stumbling along under the shifting weight. He stops to hear the hollow hooting of snow geese, a cloud of them tilting down for their wintering at the east end of Lake Dark where the stream comes in and the water stays open. Billy hears them still when he is climbing the ladder to the loft in his clumsy ice-slicked shoes. Pitching down the hay. Prying wood from the frozen pile, arm loads braced to his chest and chin and snow slipping into his sleeves. He brings in kindling and logs roughly split. He shows Joe how to feed the fire, stick after stick steaming before catching a flame. There is no coal. This is not New York's Irish Town where Billy—being the smallest—was always the one to squeeze himself down a cellar coal chute and pitch up pieces to Cleary and Bert while the other little criminals, Miles and Declan, stood look-out on the street or poked the wagon load with broomsticks while Billy occupied the coal-seller with questions regarding the mechanism by which coal burns or inquiries as to discerning a horse's age by the examination of its teeth. But this is not New York. There is no coal here, no long slow burn, only wood dusted with snow, smoking and cold, slow to catch in fireplaces and in cast-iron cookstoves. Catherine McCarty Antrim coughs, bedded. Billy cooks. Dark jars of peas and pears and pinto beans are toted up from the cellar, wiped of dust, and set on a kitchen shelf. There is food enough. Mr. William Antrim has seen to it and sends money for more, *for whatever it is you need* he says in a letter from Mississippi. Louisiana.

December 8, 1871
Dearest Catherine,
Will be leaving the Mississippi.
The river trade getting risky.
The California Rush is pretty much over but I am
considering Pikes Peak or the Comstock Lode.
Banknote enclosed. Use for whatever it is you need.
Love to you and the lads.
Your loving husband,
William

Snow devils spin through the barren fields. Buzzards tilt above the river in the high white sky and skulk along on the banks. The room where Catherine McCarty Antrim sleeps sitting up or sits and rocks in her bed smells like sweat and blood. She lifts her damp hair in a handful off her neck. You shut that stove, you hear me Henry? she tells Billy. This house feels like summer, she says. Shut it, she says.

Billy reaches to touch her forehead. You keep away, she says. I know what you are.

It's me. It's Billy, he says. I'm just Billy.

First of all you're Henry.

All right, says Billy.

And second of all is you've never been mine ever. My true boy was just new born, he was, when they took him and left me you, she says. Boo hoo. Poor poor poor me. Boo hoooooo. Her voice is a howl, a whine. Her pale lips pink with spit and fissure.

Billy brings water in the blue willow cup. She eyes it sideways.

Drink, Mam.

A potion, she says. A poison.

Water, he says.

You first, she says, and so he drinks—delicious and clear is the spring house water, faintly ferric, smooth in the mouth and smooth going down he thinks, but he does not say. She would think any comment to be part of a ruse. Now you, he says.

But she holds her head away. Water water everywhere, she says.

No Mam, not everywhere. This here, he says.

You listen now, she says. Water water everywhere but not a drop to drink. Are you listening Henry? she asks Billy. Do you know what that means? she says. You'll be telling me the answer then if you're not too dim to. Come on, she says. It's a song everyone sings and everyone would be knowing.

Well Mam, he says. It could mean the river, that place where there's blood in the water.

No, she says. Not it.

Or when it rained in Irish Town, says Billy. Those puddles in the street, plenty of bad water in the gutters.

No, she says. Not it either. What it means is you're stuck in a boat and you're thirsty, you are. But the boat is on the sea.

Alright, says Billy.

You wouldn't know, she says. You never been on a boat. You and your kind don't need to drink. I hardly nursed you. Hardly at all but you kept on living anyway.

Billy carries the pail of grain along the path to the paddock. The chipping sparrows peck and scratch at the spilled bits and barn mice venture forth and dine. Stamped there into the fresh snow is the little drama of a meal interrupted: the imprint of raptor wings, deeper at the upward bow. A plunge, a skirmish, the surface marked with disorder.

Snow scuffed about, feathery bits, flecks of blood.
Stains on Catherine's pillow.

The chipping sparrow (Spizella passerine) feeds by foraging in weedy places for seeds and spiders. As with most small ground-feeding birds, it is preyed upon by hawks that swoop in and take them away.

—Birds of America and the Territories, Chapter 77: New World Sparrows, Juncos

Chapter 25
The Ride to Gifford Trade & Grain
Wichita, Kansas
December 2, 1871

Billy makes a list of medicinals—what a witch-woman in Irish Town once gave his mother:

cohosh
arrow weed
licorice root

And a list of sundries:

soap
oats
salt
baking soda
cornmeal
wheat flour
potatoes
carrots
onions
black tea
coffee
molasses
butter
honey.

A bright winter day.

Billy setting forth to town, wrapped in double coats, a strip of blanket torn longwise, fitted over his hat and tied under his chin. He turns the horse from the stall and out from the dark barn, both blinking in the winter shimmer of sky and snow. Hold still Finn, he says. He sets the harness. Positions the crupper. Pulls the staves and adjust the traces. He climbs onto the buckboard seat and lets the straps give just a touch to its rump. Go giddy-up now Finn. And they take to the river road, wind-stripped clear of snow down to the frozen ruts, great wedges of earth heaved up. Hoofs ring on earth gone hard as stone. Trees sway and creak to the fife song of wind down the corridor of the river. Snow hilled up high against the stands of birch and buffer pine. Both horse and boy breathe clouds.

Frost on Finn's muzzle, ice crystals on his whiskers.

Rime on Billy's scarf around his mouth.

Finn shies at a procession of wild turkeys crossing a turn in the road, single file to the opposite field. They glean the meager ground, necks outstretched, stepping along in placid containment and seemingly untroubled by the grievous cold, their heads to the ground in solemn pecking, their feathers in every color of brown laid smooth over their bodies and backs—nearly opalescent and lustrous as the carapace of turtles. The tom purrs to the hens. Soft squeaks and gobbles, come along, come along. They travel without haste along the rows of blackened stems and clinging gray bits of wind-shredded leaf that were last season's sorghum and soybeans, then disappearing one by one into a rocky hedgerow and appearing again at the same pace on the other side, and climbing again, single file, up the next frozen slope.

Finn snorts. Turkeys, Billy tells the horse. All over out here, saw it my book. Never saw a one in Irish Town except it was hooked upside down in the market and swinging from its feet.

Alright Finn, says Billy. We seen them, says Billy. Let's be getting on. Gifford's might be closing early and there's more weather coming.

A wild turkey (Meleagris gallopavo) will vigorously defend its brood of fledglings, often fighting to its death to protect them.
—Birds of America and the Territories, Chapter 19: Turkeys

Billy drops the reins over the rail and steps onto the ice-coated porch that crackles with his weight. Drifts are windswept along the door sill. He tries the thumb-latch but it is frozen over. He gives it a tug and a jiggle. The shopkeeper's bell on the jamb-post rings. Hold on there, calls Mr. Gifford, the proprietor of the Gifford Trade & Grain, coming around from behind the wainscoted counter. Damn thing seizes up first frost, he says. Get yourself on in here boy, he says. You're letting out the heat.

Though it is hardly a sight warmer within—the proprietor himself dressed and booted as if for an arctic expedition. Wind gusts through the gaps in the chinking, dispersing the steam of their breathing and flapping a stack of paper scraps skewered on the receipt spike. The proprietor of Gifford Trade & Grain keeps a small fire going in the iron-wrought stove and has carefully set its four clawed feet on bricks to spare the floor planks, but there is hardly the need—so paltry the heat that a mackerel-coated cat sits warming herself atop the cookplate. Took the river road, did you? says Mr. Gifford.

Yes sir, says Billy. Finn and me.

Finn? Says Mr. Gifford.

Outside, says Billy.

He looks outside. Your buggy horse. I see.

I ride him mostly, says Billy.

And he's no trouble in the traces then?

No sir, says Billy. He pulls a paper from under his hat. His list.

Hmmm, says Mr. Gifford, list in hand. Hmmm. Well then. Sure.

Yes. Some items still waiting on delivery. The Smokey River's ice-jammed clear to Abilene. Butter no. Just won't keep no how. Flour, some. Soap, might be I still have soap. Green soap only. Will that do? And no on the honey. Never none this time of year. And these, he says tapping the list of medicinals. These for your Ma? Been a while since she's been in.

Yes sir, said Billy. My Mam.

Don't stock these neither, said the proprietor. Never do. I've got plain tonic she might rather try.

Alright, says Billy.

And some birch elixir. She might like that.

She might, says Billy.

Fine, says the proprietor. These for your Ma, then. Let's see what we can do.

I thank you, says Billy.

Glad to, says the proprietor. He shades his eyes with his hand and squints upward at the shelf as if he keeps his wares upon a mountaintop, and begins reaching up and turning back and forth to the counter to check the list at each turn. Coffee, he calls over his shoulder. Comes two pounds or five. Same with the salt.

Five please, says Billy.

Five it is, says the proprietor. He stops and looks Billy over. You be the older boy, that right? he says.

I'm the older boy. Older to my brother Joe.

Joe. Yes. He's been in. With your Ma. And you'd be Henry, that right?

Henry. Or Billy. I go by both, says Billy. But mainly Billy. Just plain Billy.

And your Pa these days, asks the proprietor of Gifford Trade & Grain. How's he? Where's he been at?

He's not, said Billy.

Heading home in the arriving dusk.

No wind now. No sound but their own. Rumbling of the buckboard. Squeak of the seat spring. Crack of the windowpanes of ice that cover the ruts. Finn goes strong and steady home, hoofs at a clopping trot in time to the Timoleague tune Billy sings to himself. Finn keeps on but turns an ear. Go on Finn. It's just what Mam used to sing until she quit singing, Billy tells him. The moon in nimbus, bright enough to cast the shadows of them riding beside them, long and blue beside them and curving in accommodation of roadside knolls and dips. Now a single star. Two. Three, Billy counts out loud. More than me could stand counting, he says. But what are stars, anyway? Birdshot through whatever the sky is—a big cup overturned and set smackdown to the edges of the land and the sea and keeping the sea from spilling over. Some say. And the moon. Well that too. What is the moon? Some nights it's rising round and clouded as the walleye of an old cow and some nights thin and sharp as rib. And some nights none. No moon at all. Where does it go Finn, don't you wonder? How could it be, or it might could be that there is no cup of sky, no edge for the sea to spill. Could be that the sky is nothing but air or not even air but nothing at all and the stars are just fires far away and burning slow the way coal fires do. Somehow nightly stoked. Or burning something what never needs a stoking. But tell me then, who is there doing the stoking? Well. Damn if I know, says Billy. Finn slows the way he does where the eddy is open and smells like rot. Giddy-up Finn. Go on. Get by there now. Good boy. Go on.

Overhead a nighthawk goes swift as any crossbow bolt but wondrously fletched as if by wizardry, sent straight and true on a single wingstroke then banking, turning without hesitation nor variation in velocity and crying peent peent peent at one last tilt and spinning away and away in silhouette against a sky of grotto blue but fading fast to indigo.

The common nighthawk (Chordeiles minor) has small, ineffectual feet unsuited for walking, and spends most of its life in the air. Its distinctive zigzag flight is similar to that of bats.

—Birds of America and the Territories, Chapter 43: Goatsuckers, Nightjars

Chapter 26
Freeze and Thaw
Wichita, Kansas
March, 1872

Winter wore on.

March brought a thaw that might have suggested spring to some, but in these parts everyone knew better and disbelieved the brief spell of melting, which was followed by another freeze and another snow, followed by a flurry of letters:

March 1, 1872
Dearest Catherine,
Enclosed banknote.
Hope this will hold you.
Home soon. Hellos to the lads.
Your loving husband,
William

A glazing rain falls, Wichita frozen and transformed. Every limb and twig, slope and stone, thorn and evergreen needle is plated in silver.

March 7,1872
Dearest Catherine,
Enclosed banknote.
Hope this will hold you.
If not, cut back where you can.

Home sooner than later.
Your loving husband,
William

A flock of wing-frayed and faded robins arrive early from the warmer districts where they had wintered and now sit hunched in the old orchard. Most would have starved if not for last year's fallen apples gone to mush, and those birds that are able peck through the snow and pull at the soft pulp and eat—those will live, though some of their numbers are so debilitated by the great distances they had traveled that they do not, and these freeze fast to their perches.

The robin (Turdus migratorius) is the first bird to sing at dawn and the last to sing at dusk.

—Birds of America and the Territories, Chapter 63: Thrushes, Solitaires, Bluebirds

And there they stay, robins ice-plated and glittering until the arc of the sun crosses the celestial equator from south to north along the ecliptic and the rivers begin again to swell with snowmelt, and the gilled and scaled inhabitants therein awaken, and the vernal equinox drifts into the constellation of the fish.

March 20, 1872
Dearest Catherine,
Recent run of bad luck.
Enclosed banknote.
Hope this will hold you.
Home shortly or sooner.
Your loving husband,
William

Branches crack under the freight of ice. Trunks split as if lightning struck. The birch beside the barn bows to nearly horizontal until the top sweeps the snow and those treetop buds are now in easy reach. A buck and a half-dozen does come to feed, pulling at the twigs, their long mouths working, grinding side to side. The ice shards ring down. A doe scratches her ear with her hind foot. The buck is vigilant, ready to bolt. Billy sets down his pail and whistles. A jay calls in alarm. The buck snorts. A muzzle of smoke. Billy snorts back. The buck undaunted takes a step toward Billy and stomps his foreleg, but he does not run.

Grass will begin to sprout between patches of snow in the field one field up from the paddock, and new clover too and stray shoots of flyaway sorghum blown in last fall from some other farm somewhere, and there will be bright bits of cress and blue-eyed grass among the stones where the springs surface and seep.

Freeze and thaw. Water finds its way. The flue in the sitting-room fireplace cracks. Bits of mortar and pieces of brick fall into the fireplace. Above the roof, small dusky birds chitter and spin in and out of the old chimney. Billy has his book, *Birds of America and the Territories.* He adds to his list: *chimney swift.*

Chimney swifts (Chaetura pelagica) rest only by clinging to the walls inside chimneys where they build a cupped nest of twigs glued to the brick with their saliva. They are unable to land on the earth, and feed upon flying insects and airborne spiders that drift on their lines of spun silk.

—Birds of America and the Territories, Chapter 44: Swifts

Billy does not fix the flue. He does not reset the bricks. A fire is never lit in the sitting room hearth.

March 31, 1872
Dearest Catherine,
Headed for New Mexico.
Lode gold in Pinos Altos!
Banknote enclosed.

I hope this will hold you.
If not, sell the horse.
Your loving husband,
William

Chapter 27
The Kid's First Kill
Wichita, Kansas
May, 1872

Spring settles in for certain with the first warm rain, and overnight the field above the paddock is overgrown with Kansas grasses—bluestem and timothy and sedge. And then the pretty poisons sprout: buttercup, poke, pimpernel. But Billy, city-boy Billy. New York born and new to such Midwestern expanses. What would he know of weeds and wildflowers and what a horse will eat? What would he know of bloat or strangles or colic or tainted hay? Or how the lush waves of Kansas grass—after a winter of hay and oats—would rupture its gut. Billy finds the horse Finn down on his side, moaning, belly distended, spewing a bloody shit. Eyes rolling back to the whites the way a china doll's would with its lead-weighted rockers broken. Billy, city-boy Billy. He has seen horses teeter and drop in the streets of Irish Town, shot down in the streets of Irish Town. A collision at the train crossing: the wagon immobile with a rear wheelrim jammed between bolt-head and rail, the wagon-driver shouting git damn it, pull goddamn you, and pummeling the horse that strains in its traces, and not a thought to setting the animal loose by freeing the reins and unfixing the tug-chains, and with the locomotive upon them, the driver jumping away, the wagon shattered and dragged, the horse still in harness skinned along the tracks, limbs still attached but at unnatural angles. A crowd then, always a crowd. All passengers will please remain on board the train. All passengers avail yourselves of the dining car until we are again underway, thank you. Eventually a pistol arrives, pointed, fired. Bone bespatters the cross-ties. The knacker arrives unbidden. And yes, Billy has seen old horses drop and die during a whipping, such old souls they are, past caring, past able, deciding better to go to their knees for the final blows, a pole between the ears, a rump nearly flayed open. A crowd again then, always a crowd. Please step back, ladies and gentlemen. Once again the pistol, pressed against the head. Fired. Brain flung this time into the gutter. He has seen the eyes still open. Staying so. Tongue bloodied between the worn and broken teeth. Alright folks, move along then, just a horse, nothing to see, folks. Nothing to see. City-boy Billy, he has a gun. Of course he does. He has seen a gun so positioned. Fired. He has seen the way it is done. And now here is the horse Finn, thrashing, wailing, eyes rolling, twisting its neck as if raising its head for one last look. Witchery, cries Mrs. Catherine McCarty from the kitchen window. Billy lifts his pistol. The Collier flintlock. *You're old enough to be owning a gun and you're puny enough to be needing it.*

That you shooting? calls Ed Mueller now, coming from one farm over, heading under the spruces and loading his Remington as he passes through the gloom, so dim there any time of day that nothing grows from the floor of fallen needles except the ghost pipes that have no need of light.

There the gunshot horse in the grass. The leak of blood from the mouth drying in clots in the morning sun. The day already warming. Well now, says Ed Muller, will you look at that. The bloat was it? he says.

Don't know, says Billy. Likely something I done, he says.

I'll fetch the lye, says Ed Muller. Got plenty.

Any day now larkspur will be blooming at the roadside.

Then penstemon in the fields.

Then jewelweed by the brook.

Turkey vultures have already begun their vigil. Three of them sit hunched on the roof of the barn. One spreads a wing and feathers fanwise and peers over the edge of its primaries.

Not so sure you got that hole dug deep enough, says Ed Muller with his sack of lye.

The sun sets. At dusk the tree peepers begin their trilling. Tiny bells in tremolo from everywhere. And it is just dark when Billy is tamping the last shovelful of earth on the trench.

Was it a spell you put onto him? asks Mrs. Catherine McCarty. Is that what you did? It bleeding and moaning, is it that what you learned from the Wee Folk?

Billy leans the shovel to the porch post.

No Mam, says Billy. I never did learn it. Didn't need to learn it. It just come to me natural.

Soil still clings to the shovel blade and bright silvery chips along the edge where stones have been struck.

Any day now there will be purple loosestrife in the marsh.

Then chicory in the ditches.

In the morning, mists rise from the river.

A dabbling duck comes into view through the smoke.

Deer have been seen basking on a south-facing slope.

A solitary grebe dives and rides away unseen downstream.

The pied-billed grebe (Podilymbus podiceps) does lift off the water when threatened, but dives and resurfaces at a distance in a sheltered location.

—Birds of America and the Territories, Chapter 3: Grebes

Chapter 28
Foreclosed and Going
Wichita, Kansas
August, 1872

Billy had taken to keeping the Collier flintlock handy.

There had been lawlessness in town, incidents.

A robbery at Gifford Trade & Grain of ten pounds of sugar and a big bag of cocoa, though Mr. Gifford admitted it might have been an error of inventory. (Local folks suspected Mattie McGraw who brought three sugar cakes to the charity supper, not the usual two. And a tray of fudge.)

A holdup at Wichita Savings and Loan, though the bandit be none other than Bailey Hooper telling the teller to stick 'em up but for only enough to forestall foreclosure on his farm, Bailey having been too poorly to keep the place going since he inadvertently chopped off a fair portion of his left foot and it still festering. (Bailey was let off, however, seeing that while in custody his went feverish and died of blackfoot.)

A disappearance of the Minister Vollman's wife as reported by the Minister who told the oft-told tale of a wife gone East to visit her sister, though he had no explanation for a severed finger found in the baptismal font.

A theft of three nice hams hung to cure in Lester Fidelman's smokehouse, though his coonhounds Dewdrop and Dink were likely suspects.

Suspicious strangers entering the post office, reading the notices and wanted posters, then leaving without mailing a letter or purchasing stamps or bidding so much as a how-de-do to postmistress Selma Pegg who is friendly and helpful to everyone.

Suspicious strangers trying on Stetsons and bowlers in the Horowitz Haberdashery (referred to by some unfriendly locals as Hebe Hats) but leaving without a purchase, which said locals didn't consider one bit suspicious, considering the prices.

Secretive strangers sighted in the woods and described by townsfolk as leering and lurking or skulking and loitering and such persons reportedly wearing either overalls or hunting jackets or rags or raggedy uniforms (Confederate deserters, some said, unaware the war was long over) or shabby suits. Some wore hats. Some went bareheaded. All had beards, all were shaggy-haired, all had beady eyes, all had never been seen in these parts before. All were armed and toting pistols or rifles or both. One had an axe, bloodied and stuck with bits of hair.

Gunshots in the wee hours were heard coming from the vicinity of Dark Lake, as well as from behind the hardware store, or from the woods behind the livery, or perhaps from the schoolhouse, or maybe from barns and root cellars and jake-shacks.

Silas Thomason discovered the barn door left open and he was almost certain he had left it shut, but when he searched the hayloft he found a distinct depression of someone who had obviously spent the night.

Hiram Stone found muddy footprints on the porch. Though Mrs. Stone believed they might have been Hiram's since he often forgets to wipe his feet.

Sukey Rachety was awakened before dawn when someone rang the gate bell out front. Though she admitted that it could have been the bell on the cat. Or a dream.

Jacob Cornelisse spied a one-armed burglar attempting to jimmy open his bedroom window. Jacob fired a shot through the window pane and he saw the intruder run off, though he admits it may have been a rabbit or a whistle pig. Or the moon.

Ed Muller spied something moving in the spruces and took a blind shot, but it being so dim there under the criss-cross of boughs he couldn't say exactly what it was. Betcha coyotes, he said. Skeedaddled same way coyotes do, he said.

And lastly, Mrs. Catherine McCarty spied Wee Folk cavorting on her windowsill and to her surprise they inquired as to what had become of Billy, asking her: Had he lived? Had he died? Had his shoulder bones finally grown into wings? And by the way, Mrs. Catherine McCarty, we are grateful for your raising of a misshapen changeling. And also by the way: Would you kindly inform us of his whereabouts? Where might that Billy be?

Where might that Billy be.

At daybreak Billy might be at the kitchen table reading his book, a tattered *Birds of America and the Territories*, reading what he has read and somewhat memorized so many times before: songs, calls, habits, coloration, habits of foraging, names, nests.

At dusk Billy might be on the porch of the shuttered house, sitting in a kitchen chair, Collier flintlock laid across his lap. He rests his heels along the rail, legs outstretched, pencil in hand, and his list against his knee. He watches for geese heading to Dark Lake to spend the night on the water. He hears for the sounds of night birds now awakening, and he adds them to his list: heron, poorwill, barn owl. He knows them by their patterns of flight—the poorwill in his low and unbroken going over the fields, the barn owl gliding out of the hayloft hole where she nests—or by their shapes moving along the moon-glittered water of the pond—the plover hunting in the shallows, the night heron stalking in the marsh.

*The common poorwill (*Phalaenoptilus nuttallii*) nests in a slight depression on the ground, shielded by brush or grass. When disturbed, it will pitch itself off of the nest, hissing like a snake.*

—Birds of America and the Territories, Chapter 43: Goatsuckers, Nightjars

The wing feathers of the barn owl (Tyto alba) are fringed so that its flight is silent.

Chapter 41: Barn Owls

The black-crowned night heron (Nycticorax nycticorax) lures fish within its striking range by flinging bits of debris into the water.

Chapter 22: Herons, Bitterns

Gray plovers (Pluvialis squatarola) flock before impending rain.

Chapter 32: Plovers, Surfbirds, Turnstones

Other sounds come in the night. Catherine coughing. Catherine singing her Timoleague tune. Pump-handle squeak. The kettle set to the stove plate. Clunk and crack, Joe fixing the stove wood and kindling. Billy can hear the river on very still nights, windless nights when the water is high. Or he thinks he can. And when a fog has settled in and sound travels far he can hear the ceaseless low moaning of the beasts where the Chisolm Trail splits and the thunder of their hoofs as they stumble down the chute. Or he thinks he can. And this night, a nearby bark. Thinking it must be the hounds, those coon dogs Fidelman keeps but then it comes from too close by. And then again quiet. And then again, barks and yips. Closer. Yes, likely those hounds on the loose again, tearing around and trailing the scent of raccoon or rabbit. But now the dark shapes enter the yard, dog shapes on the run, but it is not the careless bounding of hounds, not their gangling lope, hooting and howling as hounds will do, but coming on with a silent stealth and swiftness as if they are hardly touching the ground, then crossing past the barn, slipping under the paddock fence without hesitation, moving as if they are not dogs at all but the shadows of dogs or the essence of dogs or the origins of all dogs and no not dogs at all. Coyotes. They stop and sniff the trench with its smell of meat and lime, and start their furious excavation as their forepaws send sprays of soil behind them, this coyote pair upturning the trench, tearing at the horse and taking its torn parts in their teeth. Hock, fetlock, lip. Bolting parts whole. Thrusting with each swallow. Billy has his flintlock. He fires first into the air. Then takes aim. A second shot: misses. The coyote pair heading away now, shapes receding, over the ridge. Billy picks up a piece of the horse and flings it away. There, take what you want. Take it, he says. It was a horse, he says. Now it's meat.

Sun up.

The fire is still going in the iron-wrought stove. The kettle is hot, the water nearly boiled away. Catherine still in her bed. Joe sweeps the porch. Clematis there, winding up the post and beginning to bloom.

A smell of lingering rot rises from the dug-up trench. Buzzards perch along the roof. Billy finds a vireo outside the bedroom window, broken at the neck, the reflection of sky and cloud in the glass so easily mistaken for a way away. And leaving of itself a vestige of its final flight—bits of feather on the window where bird and its specter met.

Squirrels often raid the nests of the blue-headed vireo (Vireo solitarius) and eat the fledglings. To prevent squirrel attacks, the vireo will build its nest close to a nesting hawk, which does not prey on vireos, but consistently hunts and eats squirrels.

—Birds of America and the Territories, Chapter 62: Catbirds, Mockingbirds, Thrashers

William Antrim returned. As he said he would. He had sent word:

September 5, 1872
Dearest Catherine,
I am departing Pinos Altos under uncertain circumstances.

Home a week Wednesday next.
Your loving husband,
William

Come Wednesday next he came walking in from the road and turned down the path to the shuttered house.

He found Billy sitting on the porch with the Collier flintlock his lap. He took off his hat. It was a warm day, spring nearly finished, the doorstep of summer. He wiped his forehead with the sleeve of his frock coat and replaced his hat. Protecting the property, lad? he said. Or just your way of a welcome home?

Both, said Billy.

I see, said William Antrim. Been shooting?

Some, said Billy.

Become right chatty, have you? he said, and walked past and proceeded to survey the place.

He found pieces of the roof beside the house. Shingles, old boards.

He found a roof hole had been hay-thatched and it seemed to be holding nicely.

He found no horse in the paddock, neither in the stall.

He found the tamped-down earth over the trench in the field one field up, grown over with new wind-sown grass and bordered by stones evenly spaced.

He found the younger brother Joe much grown in that nearly a year he'd been gone. Almost caught up to your big brother, he told Joe. Though he'd hardly be a benchmark, now would he? This lad been behaving Catherine? asked Mr. William Antrim.

Joe always been my best boy, said Catherine McCarty Antrim.

That so? Mr. Antrim asked Joseph.

No. Ain't so, said Joseph. I'm not.

Well to be sure he is, said Mrs. Catherine McCarty Antrim. He's always looking out for his Mam.

And this one, said Mr. William Antrim now looking Billy over. What about your Henry here?

He's does what his kind will do, said Catherine McCarty Antrim.

His kind, says William Antrim.

He was born in other worlds, he was. Dark places where his kind comes from, she says. He knows their ways. Spells and tricks. Did you see, William? Did you see he fixed our roof the way the witches do, said Catherine McCarty Antrim. The Biddy witch I used to know. Her house.

Well now, said William Antrim. Is that what you've been up to, Henry?

It's Billy, said Billy.

Oh it's Billy is it? Seems to me we've been all through that when I took you in. You and your brother and your Mam. Seems to me you being Billy is done and over with is what we said back then.

What you said, Billy tells him. I never said. I never held to it.

Why Catherine, said William Antrim, would you listen to this now? Big talk from the small one. You been feeding this boy Catherine? he says with a wink. He turned to Billy. And you Henry me lad, eleven year you are, and a peewee still—that's likely all the growing you'll ever do.

He's not meaning to grow, said Catherine. Not his kind. Hisself being kin to smaller folk.

And if William Antrim found his Catherine diminished by winter, he himself was much the worse for wear and his frock coat more forlorn, the lining being slit, stuffed with greenbacks, and basted back up. Best I be laying a bit low a while, he said. Staying off the river. Staying off the roads. Maybe we'll be having a go at this farm, he said. Something easy. Say, Beets. Beets maybe. Or potatoes might do. Just what we Irish are supposed to know. The red ones again. They sprout eyes just looking at them.

And soon enough they'll be looking right back at you, said Billy.

Catherine shuddered. You hear him now? she told her husband. Now are you knowing his kind?

News arrives from New Mexico: All the gold is gone in Pinos Altos, including the lode, but that Mr. William Antrim already knew, having been there with the last wave of prospectors and all of them too, too late. But now the news was silver. And silver was a whole other story, he said. Silver enough to call it Silver City and silver coming every way that silver comes—nuggets, ore, veins, and lodes, all for the taking, said William Antrim. As for the farm, it is already too late for starting potatoes or beets or starting most anything in Wichita anyway. But not too late for us, he said, since we're going to Silver City.

But the house? says Catherine.

Ah. Foreclosed, says William Antrim. And the land. All of it. No matter, Dearest. I brought you here, but if I had the doing of it over, I wouldn't. Kansas is too damp for your lungs to mend. But New Mexico, there's the dry air and the heat you need and the hunks of silver. We'd be killing two birds, he says. One stone.

Gray catbirds had been seen building a nest in the orchard. Four eggs just as blue as the blue sky of a midsummer morning were laid and just one day later all four were pecked dead and carried off by crows. And later in the season, when the pair had recovered from their grief, the catbirds rebuilt their nest a good ways out beyond the orchard in the hedgerow brambles. Four eggs the same blue laid and just eleven days later all four were hatched. Billy adds to his list: *catbird*, and watches the them fly in and out of the bramble bringing in mouthfuls of blackberries and beetles and writhing inchworms for their hatchlings. And when the young birds are tufted with down and then when they are fully feathered, Billy watches them sit on the rim of the nest and he hopes to see them grow and finally fly off long before the farm would be sold and before Mr. William Antrim would take him and Mam and Joseph far and away southwest to Silver City, and this he hoped until the crows came again and carried off the four fledglings one by one just as the summer nights turned cool, just as the trees in the orchard had begun to set their apples, just as the grass on the grave-trench in the field one field up was finally as high and as lush as it had been before the digging.

Just as the ants and grasshoppers begin to sense the coming season.

Just as the fireflies are flashing furiously before their final dimming.

Just as the blue skies of the midsummer mornings are fading. And just as the fledglings of other birds—now feathered, ready—are poised for flight.

The fields now take on a faded look.

The last of the honeybees find goldenrod roadside and the final blooms of pasture rose along the fence.

The maples on the river set loose their winged seeds and the milkweed pods spring open and release their cotton.

Hoar frost on the grass.

Skim ice at the edges of the pond.

While most songbirds sing from treetops, protruding branches, or prominent places, the gray catbird (Dumetella carolinensis) sings while concealed within the foliage of bramble or shrub. Its call resembles the cry of an infant or the mewing of a cat.

—Birds of America and the Territories, Chapter 62: Catbirds, Mockingbirds, Thrashers

Chapter 29
We Start Again in Silver City, New Mexico
by William Henry McCarty Antrim
September 3, 1873

To the north we could see the Los Pinos Altos, the mountains of the tall pines and the new snow on the rocks and ledges where the pines did not like to grow, though the lower slopes were thick and dark with pines—a dark green almost gone to black when the shadow of the clouds went over, and lower still the piñon pines scattered throughout the plain and all the way down to the waters of the Arroyo San Vicente that went winding through the foothills, just a thread of a river twisting bright in the big light of these parts that seemed to come not just from where the sun was sitting in the sky but from everywhere, from all of the sky and lighting everything in a way that had you wondering if what you were seeing was a dream or was it real but clearer than you ever did see anything before. You could hold out your hand to the light and turn your hand over and look at it every which way and wonder if it really was your hand and then know, finally, that it was, and it was you and you were alive—that bright, that clear.

And to the south we could see the desert—the hardpan plain pale as bone and the rock of the cliffs and the mesas the color of copper and iron going to rust. Far off or near it didn't matter—you could see every little thing there was—pebbles and prickles on the plants and cracks in the rocks and every feather on the wings of the broad-winged hawks going over, and all of it true and clear as if it were right in front of you because of the light. And here and there lining along the dried-up riverbeds were the trees they call tamarack and cottonwood and mesquite and green stick. *Palo verde,* Jacinta told me. Green stick. And tall spikes of ocotillo with red flowers in the shape of birds. *Las flores rojas en forma de pájaritos,* Jacinta said. Jacinta the little señorita who sold the corn cakes and chilaquiles that set a person's mouth to fire. This was in Silver City, where we got to when we left Wichita on the very day the leaves on the bent-over birch beside the barn—the one that used to be our horse Finn's barn—turn from green to yellow. The same day no birds were singing to wake me at sunup like they do since they decided overnight that it be time to head somewhere to the south for wintering. And that day we went south too—same as the birds—but I wished I was going with them instead of with Mr. William Antrim or with Mam or even Joe. Just me flying away on those wings Mam said I'd been hiding, and me finding a flock to go with, ones that would have me. But no. Mr. William Antrim took us away from Wichita and we went south to Silver City. Silver City, where we stayed awhile before our Mam would keep on coughing blood. Where our Mam would die after Mr. William Antrim took us away from Wichita. Me and Mam and Joe. Good Joe, the good one—Mam always said. I tried it for a while. Being good. But there was no use in that for ones like me. Not my kind. But what would it matter anyway, good or bad. Want to know what it was I would tell Joe when Mam died? Here's what: See Little Man? See how it is? Da dead and gone and now Mam. And soon Mr. William Antrim would be leaving us too. So see? No difference in being the good one, is there? This was when we left the shuttered house in Wichita far behind us and took up in a log house for lease on White Hog Lane beside a dry arroyo, and so small it was it hardly could hold us. One room was all. Two beds. One for me and Joe, though that one was so small that you'd hardly call it a bed, and one for Mr. William Antrim and our Mam. Our Mam. She was supposed to be better here in Silver City but the nights were cold and she kept right on coughing and all that fall and winter we kept a fire going in the stove. And so we kept on for a while in the log house in Silver City.

What a place this was, this Silver City—just a few cabins for folks decided on staying but mainly what sprung up after the silver strike, with one rutted road leading to the diggings and lined with a jumble of flappy and tattered-up tents—hundreds of them—and stands and stores built overnight of new pine boards with their signs nailed on and their burlap banners hung or their painted placard set out saying

Expert Gunsmith, Firepins Replaced

and

City Livery
Horse Feed and Boarding

and

Dentist, Painless Procedures

and

Silver City Sentinel

and

Arthur L. Broadwater MD. All Ailments

and

Crowley's Trousers ~ Cotton & Wool

cobbled together from sticks and boards and pieces of shingles patched up every which way, some with signs for Miners Accommodations or Clean Beds Hot Baths but they were shacks all the same and barely holding together no matter what you wanted to call them. All day long the wagons kept on coming—young men driving with their wives and little ones sitting up beside them, and old men with long gray beards chucking the reins over their swaybacked horses, and their weary-looking wives wincing but without a word for every rut and stone they bounced over, and you just knew they'd been forty-niners and had done this all before at Sutter's Creek and Eureka and likely the Comstock, and what could an old gal do but on keep coming along with her man. Some came solitary rocking along in their broken-down buckboards and some riding in on their ponies or mules and some walking beside their sweet little burros and some just plain walking. Every other day the stage was rolling in and climbing out came men in smart city clothes for sure not come all this way for getting their suits dirty in a mine shaft nor their hands neither, and some that came were what you'd call sporting women wearing big skirts with frilly underpants poking out from under and feathered hats and right off heading for the Half Moon Dance Hall—though they didn't do much dancing, no sir—not from the time their feet touched the street and likely not never. Every month there was a new saloon with clever names—Rafferty's Barroom and the Tiltin Timbers and the Cave-In Café and Bedrock Bath & Spirits, and there were folks enough to fill all of them. Everywhere everyone was talking silver and which hill was worth a digging and which not, though most of it blarney and no better than what you'd call bunko. Deals being made or unmade, claims being bought or sold or won or lost at cards or claims just jumped. Cons and dupers on every corner. And fights, of course. Most started with drinking and cussing, and then came the shoving, followed by the shooting and the killing. But for some not shot-up enough to be dead, Dr. Arthur Broadwater was fetched from his medicine tent and he pokes around for the lead and gives the man a swallow of his *Broadwater's Bodily Rejuvenator*, and some went on living a while, and some longer, but most were too far gone for fixing. It was daily that a dead man was loaded and roped to a sled and dragged away and delivered to the boneyard at the south end of Silver City. Some folks ending up at south end of town died natural, keeling over during the nightly revival in the big canvas tent that's roped and pegged-down just off the thoroughfare, them having fits or fever or such. And these poor sick folks got collected by the congregation and carried out right under the banner that says *Come In And Be Healed.* Either way the next to be fetched was the undertaker who boxed up the body and billed the town five dollars, and next after that comes the preacher who stands graveside with his Bible in his hands and bills the town ten just for talking. He starts out quiet and calm about God in his infinite wisdom calling a broken body home and such and then gets into it good and loud about sprouting wings and heading up to heaven or being cast into a scorching pit, and he says what preachers say: heaven or hellfire, take your pick.

Come nightfall when the graves of the day had been filled in and patted down, the ruckus along the thoroughfare kept on, lit by woodpile fires set dab in the center of the road and by the kerosene torches stuck up on posts and sometimes even the posts were smoking and sparking and lighting up the table displays and what folks were selling right out the backs of their wagons—hardware and harnesses and every kind of comestible—bags of beans and cracked corn stacked up on barrels and bushels of apples and potatoes and onions. Some selling cider in jars and stoneware jugs and some selling plain water hauled in from Cat-bath Creek in big spigot-barrels at a dollar a cup, and folks paying that price with flakes of gold. There was meat sellers aplenty too—farmers and ranchers from all around the county with slabs of fatback and salt pork for sale, and chickens—live ones clucking low and quiet in cages while they watched the blood dripping down from their headless kin. Some days there'd be Indians. Apache. Choctaw. The squaws were the ones doing all the selling: chunks of blue stone and parched corn and red beans and yellow beans in baskets, and little drawstring pouches of plant powders for curing sickness, while the men—mostly old men with gray braids stuck in with little feathers—sat straight and stern on their horses—and the horses, all of them beauties: piebalds and paints of all colors and duns of every shade. Sometimes some of them were pure Choctaw ponies, and them the prettiest, with quick eyes and quick little ears, and never getting spooked by any ruckus in the street. And then there were the men come down from the mountains with burrs in their beards and their hair gone long and tied behind like horses' tails. Big men, all of them, in fringed buckskins with the furs of little beasts wound round their heads and draped over their shoulders, and some selling skinned elk shank and mule-deer rump swinging from poles and some upside-down rabbits with their thumpers tied in twine, some furred, some skinned. And there were bird hunters too, selling all sorts of birds and some I seen only in my book. There were bushels of passenger pigeons and quail keel-cut and gutted but the same ones I saw in the brambles and I write them down with the others on my list. One bird-seller had his birds in a bloody stack and I knew I'd seen them before and knew they must be ducks by their pintails, even with their paddlers axed.

The long neck of the pintail duck (Anas acuta)allows it to forage in deeper waters where it upsends and feeds on submerged plants that are beyond the reach of other floating ducks.

—Birds of America and the Territories, Chapter 13: Swans, Geese, Ducks, Mergansers

To escape predators, Gambel's quail (Callipepla gambelii) will sprint, rather than fly, into brushy vegetation.

Chapter 21: Quails, Partridges, Pheasants

The passenger pigeon (Ectopistes migratorius) sleeps with its beak tucked into its feathers mid-breast.

Chapter 39: Pigeons, Doves

At dusk there'd be no rest to the selling nor the squabbles, but it all looked pretty with the lanterns lit and hung on the bow-rungs under the white canvas bonnets of the Conestogas so they glowed like lamps monstrous big and the color of the lit moon. Plenty of men had set up for selling prospecting supplies and they were singing out: Step right up folks. We got what you need. We got picks and shovels—We got soap, sieves, knives—We got pans, piles of em. We got good boots—Hurry on over folks, we're near sold out. And the customers waving their greenbacks and muscling in. There was always a long line of prospectors waiting for the assay office to open in the morning—all rough-looking men covered with mine dust and mud but they seemed happy enough, most of them did, or drunk, and anyway always ready to talk. Talk to me. Kind to me, they were. Hello lad. Would it be worth a dime to you for keeping my place in line? What's your name son? And I told them, all of them: Billy, my name is Billy. I never said Henry like Mr. Antrim told me to say, no. Anyone who'd ask me I tell them: My name is Billy. And they knew my name. Everyone did. Hey you there Billyboy, would you hold my mule? Give you a nickel to hold my old Sally here, been with me near twenty year and wouldn't want no one taking off with her. Yes sir, I say. Happy to sir, I say. And it was fine and good to keep watch on a man's mule, though I didn't think anyone would want the old girl, but those days in Silver City you'd likely lose your britches if they weren't nailed down. You there Billy, some fella would say. Come on and mind the store a minute while I go take a piss. Or: Billyboy, go get that little señorita of yours to fix me up some of those hot corn cakes she makes.

That started it—me fetching food from señorita Jacinta's corner stand and adobe stove, or dinners from the Cave-In Café and running it back to the men at their diggings outside of town—the shafts and hillside holes and claims they staked. And they knew I wouldn't be running off with their dollar. Or their gold if they paid in flake. They knew I wouldn't get things mixed up as to who was getting what. Or which food for who. No sir, I kept it all straight. I kept me a list, so I wouldn't wind up taking taquitos out to someone who wanted tacos.

Petey Willoughby—shaft #2

5 taquitos
Arroz (a lot)
dozen churros
5 pears or apples

Mr. Bocho—red shack at the fork
4 flautas
10 green enchiladas

Fred Mokey—just upstream of Mr. Bocho
3 cemitas with jalapeños
20 corn cakes buttered
dozen tacos and tomatoes

And I wouldn't be running a batch of fried potatoes from the Cave-In Café all the way out to the mine when what someone wanted was flapjacks:

Hans Hornbeck—shaft #7
3 t bone steaks bloody
fried potatoes—double portion
2 bottles of whiskey
2 jugs cider

Johnny and Tim Quinn—shaft #9
4 apple pies
smokes & matches
Ham steak

Fatty Ray Farraagut—the undercliff diggings
3 bottles of whiskey
12 flapjacks with bacon, cook it crispy
Etc.

No one was ever complaining. No one was ever saying: Where the hell's that kid with my food? No, instead it was: Goddamn Billyboy, but ain't you the hot foot—this here tamale's still smoking. I was happy saying my name to folks who wanted to know it. I was happy them calling my name. And the ones who didn't just called me *the kid* and I was happy to hear that too: You need something, just ask the kid, that kid will do it, there's nothing that kid can't do. And in the evening when I was done running food, I was happy to hear Jacinta say my name: *Mi Billy. Mi cabro pequeño. My little Billy goat*, she called me even though she was littler than me and hardly more than a feather when I pulled her on top of me, the two of us tight together in her bed just big enough for one. I liked her long black hair, that Mexican hair of hers, the way it spilled over me, over my face and smelled like cactus flowers and her telling me *Tómame. Take me,* she said. *Mi amor, mi corazoncito* she said, but I didn't much mind her calling me her little heart, me being a shade small for nearly thirteen, but having a little darlin all my own made me no kid at all but a man, or nearly a man. And by then I didn't anymore mind that we left Irish Town and Wichita to be in Silver City. To see the kinds of birds I never did see. I was happy in Silver City. Happy to hold up my hand to myself in that pure bright light of the New Mexico sky and see what was me and always was me but I never knew it.

The broad-winged hawk (Buteo platypterus) does not immediately consume its prey, but prepares its meal by skinning its captured toads, frogs, and snake, and by first stripping the bodies of birds of their feathers.

—Birds of America and the Territories, Chapter 15: Eagles, Hawks, Kites

Chapter 30
The Family Antrim
Silver City, New Mexico
December 1873 – The Moon of Dying Fires

Thin clouds called mares' tails leave a powdering of snow.

An owl sits motionless at the entrance to its burrow behind a hillock of buffalo grass.

The burrowing owl (Athene cunic) collects the fecal matter of deer and antelope and places it just outside its burrow to attract dung beetles, which both adult and fledgling owls eat.

—Birds of America and the Territories, Chapter 42: True Owls

A dove alights on a branch of a palo verde.

The distinctive cooing call of the white-winged doves (Zenaida asiatica) resembles the spoken phrase "whooo cooks for you, hoo hoo."

Chapter 39: Pigeons, Doves

Now in this month the Apache call the Moon of Dying Fires the December transformation of the firmament begins. As the cold desert dusk descends the sky goes blue to darkest blue to black and the constellations seem brighter, closer. Orion, looming above, fastens his belt for a night of hunting. He scabbards his sword, adjusts his shield, and flings himself into the firmament.

The hardpan lays pallid by the waxing moon.

There is light enough. Billy and Joseph walk the edge of the wash shimmering with silica. They climb down the crumbly bank. There lay the rubble of wrecked and buckled timbers from mines lost and flooded. The whole of a smoke tree, branches cracked. Get that one there, says Billy. Good one, he tells Joe. But break it smaller. We've got to lug it all back. Over your knee like so. See Little Man? says Billy. Billy thirteen. Joe turned ten. Billy calling him Little Man though he's near as big as Billy is. Watch where you're stepping now, he tells Joe. You don't go putting your foot where you can't see your foot. Hands neither. Likely where snakes be sleeping. Whole nests of 'em. And mind that prickly pear behind you. You'll get an ass-full of it if you're not careful. Come here now. That's cholla stickers you got in your hair.

The wood in the dry wash is brittle and easily cracked for kindling. Branches are bundled and tied for the stove. Handfuls of flyaway leaf and straw are tied in squaw vine for tinder. Billy climbs out, up the wash-bank first, and gives Joseph a hand up. Come on Little Man, he tells Joe. Home to Mam. She'll be waiting on us then. Waiting for a fire, she will.

Orion blazes above them, the star-made hunter on the celestial equator, blind and fading now, his eyes put out during a night of bloodshed. He crawls eastward along the starpath to the rising sun where he will once again regain his sight.

Catherine Antrim coughs.

She supposed that she would mend in the clear air of New Mexico.

She supposed New Mexico would be warmer than Wichita.

William Antrim supposed that he would find silver.

He had set out before sunset set when it was still light enough to see the claim he thought he might stake, and he stood on the windy ridge taking in the lay of the land, and attempting to make sense of the scattering of rock and distribution of scrub and sage below, but there were no messages for him in the look of the terrain, no thought as to what looks lucky, what looks promising in the alluvium of a stone-and-pebble slide, in the auguries of his dirt streaked palm or the auspices of a loose flock of crows flapping overhead and laughing as they passed. The crest is unstable and weathered, strewn with pale loose rock that had weathered away. He takes a piece in his hand. In the dimming light it is almost luminous, and quite unexpectedly, recollections from a previously long-ago remove are summoned: his hand in his father's hand for a walk along Ballydonegan beach and then shaking loose to seize a cockle shell sucked seaward by the ebb of a wave—and the pieces of the bone china creamer he knocked off the cupboard shelf onto the tiles and his mother screaming—and the smooth piece of jawbone from Dukie his Kerry Blue Terrier who, they told him, had tired of being his doggie and had run off, run away—and he didn't believe it, *My Dukie would never run away no never would*, and when he found the spot under the hedge where the soil was loose and newly turned he dug the body up and there the jawbone already clean of flesh.

So when William Antrim said, *This looks promising*—said it to himself, to the sky, to the single silvery cloud he took to be the shape of a shovel blade, to the ridge, to the passing crows, to the cactus wren resting in a desert mesquite—he did not know why. *This looks promising*, he said, as so many would-be miners have said before him for their own reasons or recollections, and as so many will say in such spurious and specious circumstances, but if asked what exactly, what at all, if anything, seemed promising they could not say, and Mr. William Antrim—neither could he say, and that being said he soon enough staked a claim on that very ridge and set about digging a drift mine, sinking and timbering the semblance of a shaft as his unworked gambler's hands cracked in the desert cold and blistered over and the dusty winds scoured him sore, and he climbed in and out of the long level hole he had dug and fitted with timber and worked on a place that looked promising, that he hoped was a strike, a vein, an outcrop of ore, until one bright morning when he came limping home to the log house, gray with mine dust, his eyes rubbed red with grit, and a trickle of blood leaking down his forehead where his scalp was torn when a top beam in the makeshift shaft splintered down. After that he went back to cards and taking his chances at games of chance until things went poorly at Poker and Mexican Monte and No-Limit Faro and with his own brand of cheerful desperation, he returned to the diggings, and poked around the ridge with a pick until the day he lost his footing and slid aways down the slope clear down to the riverbank and nearly into the river. He stood himself up and smacked his trousers clear of dust, and straightaway came home to the log house, his clothes torn by the rocks and brambles and missing his hat. Dearest, he told Catherine. I'm done with it, I am. Time for traveling. Time to go and take in some cold cash.

Go where? says Catherine.

South. Otero. Maybe Texas. Easy pickins around El Paso or even somewhere else.

Dearest girl, he said, I'll be back before you'll know I'm gone.

Billy at the window watches him go. Watches him stop in the road and look back to the house and wave them goodbye with a sweep of his hat. Watches the sky as the horizon west goes red and the air goes cold and goose after goose goes over on its way to somewhere else.

The Canada goose (Branta canadensis) learns night navigation while still a very young gosling by gazing up at the stars when the skies are clear.

—Birds of America and the Territories, Chapter 13: Swans, Geese, Ducks, Mergansers

Catherine coughs and covers her mouth with her apron hem. The cloth comes away damp. She does not look to see if there are specks of blood.

Chapter 31
An Evening in the Thoroughfare
Silver City, New Mexico
April, 1874 – The Moon of Waking Bears

Torches. Shadows. Billy slipping down dim passageways between tents and wagons. Faces of tent-keepers lit by their campfires. Billy in silhouette, here and there. Quickly now. Slipping past.

Hey, you boy, you come away from there. That's not your wagon.

What you doing back there? Shoo now. No one's allowed back here.

Go on now, git.

Billy here and there.

Billy here and then not there.

Billy, our careful Billy with his hat pulled down low, loitering near the tabled display of pintail ducks and plucked quail and shuffling about, waiting until the game-seller steps away behind his tent to take a piss.

Billy, our clever Billy, pointing to the sign that lists the price of beets by the pound or the bushel—Which is the better buy, sir?—while he pockets a potato.

Billy, our quiet Billy, milling about with the crowd outside the tent of Dr. Arthur Broadwater who so far this evening has professed a cure for quinsy, consumption, dropsy, and the fantods, but in toting up tonight's sale of *Broadwater's Bodily Rejuvenator*, has discovered one bottle missing—or could it be two?

Billy, our quiet Billy, outside the tabernacle tent. The *Ransomed & Rejoicing* sign posted on a pole. *Oh Be Healed!* on banner strung above the flap. A man perched beside the entrance is on a stool the kind that dunces sit. Step on in son, take a seat before we get full up.

Billy stands with his hands in his pockets. Just having a look-see, he says.

You've got sickness about, haven't you boy. You or your Ma or Pa or someone.

Might, says Billy. Might not.

Well sure you do, the man says, or you wouldn't be standing out here looking in. We got the cure.

Which? says Billy.

Whichever, says the man. Come on in, son. Preacher here don't charge for listening.

What does he charge for? says Billy.

Old Thomas, remember him? A doubter like yourself, the man says.

Ain't no one like me, says Billy, and he steps in from the night into the lantern-bright tabernacle tent, taking a seat with the supplicants who are in the midst of singing *Washed by Blood of the Lamb.* There a crowd of both doubters and believers. Some hoping to cast off their crutches and canes and eyepatches this very night. Some praying that shaft timbers hold. Some soliciting divine intervention to punish the scallywags that sold them petered-out mines or cheated them at pot-limit poker or Omaha high-low. Some sitting with their sick children, held upright on their knees or rocked in their arms. A spatterstained face the color of wine. A right eye at odds with the left. A lip cleft and contiguous with the nose. A baby poxed and poulticed. A boy pale and propped up on a father's lap and the mother petting his hair and telling him: Soon Orville. Our Billy is in the midst of them, situating himself directly behind a miner whose last greenback slightly protrudes from a riveted pocket.

Thanks to you all and welcome, says the preacher (black suit, black shirt, white collar worn by them of the cloth.) All be seated, there's plenty of room (squeak of camp chairs unfolding. Spates of coughing. A baby cries. Shushes all around). And welcome again all who witnessed last night in this very tent the glorious healings of the lame and the poxed and the broken! (The crowd halleluiahs) of them that partook of the ancient cure known to Abraham, to Noah, and even old Moses and kept secret by the Israelites, until now friends. Until now. What our Lord and Savior himself used to cure the leper, the blind man, and yes even bring Lazarus back from the dead. Who among you are in need of it? (Hands shoot up.) You and you and you? Then yes, you shall have it. It is secret no longer, so Praise the Lord, yes you shall have it. (More hallelujahs.)

And now the flap of this canvas tabernacle opens onto the cool darkness beyond (night wind with the odor of desert primrose and penstemon, white moths flutter in) and two men come forth hauling crate between them, both a bit familiar (both participants in last night's demonstration: one repaired of his total paralysis, the other relieved of his deafness.) The brown glass bottles rattle in their slatted spaces, glint in the lantern light.

Those in the back rows stand for a better look. Billy, too. His thumb and pointing finger delicately plucking backpockets of currency as he edges forward, part of the crowd that shuffles forward. Billy appearing penitent, humble and humbly clutching the crown of his hat with the brim of it flat to his chest.

Here it is friends, the preacher says while the men uncrate the bottles and line them up. And here you shall have it. The Leviticus Elixer! Step right up.

Billy steps right up.

Yes friends. Just one single dime and your sufferings be surrendered to the Lord. Easy now folks. No need for shoving. Wait your turn now. You, young man. Yes you. You boy. I'm talking to you. Get back in line. Hey! You put that back now. That's not paid for! Grab that kid! Somebody grab that kid. Where'd he get to?

Goddamn him, where'd he go?

And where in hell's my Bible?

Billy, our thirsty Billy, at the water-seller's wagon, mouth to the barrel spigot. Hey! You there. No free samples. Off that now! Git.

Billy, our agile Billy, tripping on a leg of the fruit-seller's table, tipping the bushel of green pears and apples, overturning the tin-ware bowls of okra. So sorry sir, says Billy. Clumsy cuss, ain't I. Let me help you pick them up.

Spring again. Again the month the Apache call the Moon of Waking Bears. The foothills of Las Montañas de Sacramento take on the smell of moist and thawing earth. A she-bear pokes her head from out between the slanting slabs of shale that has been her den and sniffs the air. Her pair of cubs claw and tumble and nurse.

A mockingbird comes to perch on the ridge pole of the tabernacle tent and begins to sing in the dark as if it were nearly dawn.

Mockingbirds (Mimus polyglottos) can imitate the sounds of other birds, but also bullfrogs, crickets, squeaky doors, and pump handles.

—Birds of America and the Territories, Chapter 62: Catbirds, Mockingbirds, Thrashers

Chapter 32
In Need of Biddy Doro
Silver City, New Mexico
May, 1874 – The Moon of Come Back Birds

Mrs. Catherine Antrim bakes her cakes flavored with bits of dried persimmon. She puts out a sign at the log house door, as others have done at their tents and shacks in Silver City. *Just Baked Irish Cakes.*

She coughs to her sleeve. She spits and she sees the little red globules, the consistency of the pulpy fruit of prickly pear. I was better in New York, she says. Back there, whatever it was Miss Biddy give me, I was better.

May 10, 1874

Dear Miss Biddy Doro,

You might be remembering me and my Mister Patrick McCarty and the changeling baby we named Billy what I never got loose of.

I am remarried to Mister William Antrim who took me here to Silver City out here in the Territories, on account of my sickness, but I am coughing still. There are no cures here, none like what you give me before in New York.

If you still be in the business of bodily cures please send your licorice root and arrow weed, it helped me before.

Here is money.

Very truly yours,
Catherine McCarty Antrim
Log House on White Hog Lane
Silver City, Territory of New Mexico.

But Biddy Doro does not reply. Perhaps it is by some stroke of luck Miss Biddy actually receives a letter that travels across seven states, and she holds it in her hands and reads but has no recollection of a woman named Catherine McCarty Antrim nor her changeling baby. Perhaps she receives the letter but alas the money Catherine McCarty Antrim had so carefully placed inside wrapped in several papers has been stolen somewhere en route. Or perhaps she does not receive the letter at all, it being lost as letters sometimes or often are, spilled from the canvas mailsack that was tossed from stagecoach to stagecoach, then carried along in two trains and four carts and perhaps during one of these transfers, during any one of these loadings and unloadings, the mail sack containing her letter and other letters bound east and bearing news of everyday doings, losses, delinquencies, sufferings, apologies, promises, requests, deaths, births, and heartbreaks came undone when the rope used to fasten the sack (improperly knotted, not secured according to postal service regulations) slid through the grommets unnoticed and the very mechanism of careless flinging onto the next means of transport released the letters to the landscape, some of which were hastily retrieved and some of which fell into the muddied ruts of the road and were promptly trampled by the hoofs of a ridden horse or a mule team of twenty or were blown away into the neighboring fields or up into the trees or the sky when a rogue wind arrived forthwith and postal service onlookers assumed that the escaping correspondence would fly to the intended addressees in the manner of homing pigeons. Perhaps that. Or perhaps the letter had not gone astray in the mud or the trees or the sky, but found its way to the New York residence of Miss Biddy Doro in Dingman's Alley, but on a day that Miss Doro just happened not to be at home in her hut to receive her letter, but instead she reclined unclaimed in the city morgue, having been placed there after her removal from her hut by municipal workers alerted by neighbors to a terrible smell in the environs of her alley several weeks after the stink became more than the citizenry could ignore, the delay in investigation likely due to the curious odors that emanated from her hut on a regular basis when she brewed her tinctures and elixirs. It was these municipal workers were summoned to the scene and finding the unopened letter with a New Mexico address which had been delivered and placed by the postal service into the letter basket she kept hung on a hasp at her door, also found that basket brimming with other unopened notes and letters written by those seeking relief from their ailments and requesting her remedies. And with tightly tied rags over their municipal mouths and noses and employing a pole to poke open the unhasped door to her hut, pushed past the racks and rows of herbs hanging by their stems as the stench guided them through the gloom to the mound of oddly cloaked rot that once was Biddy Doro who had unintentionally poisoned herself some weeks prior by sampling her own elixirs for potency and efficacy—a practice she employed with regularity to minimize the possibility of inadvertently killing those who came to her seeking cures. What she had ingested—the seeds and pods and botanical buds—had already begun to sprout and leaf in the fertile slough and wet of her disintegration, thereby giving her laid-bare belly as well as her gas-ruptured gut the look of an untended garden. The cloud of flies that buzzed around her were waved away and the maggots occupying the remains of her nose and ears were doused to death in oil of camphor, and she was lifted seepage-stained sheet and all from her bed dotted with flyspeck and the fluids of decomposition, placed in a two-poled canvas carrier and carried out the unhasped door whereupon curious bystanders and interested onlookers said her name. *There goes Miss Biddy* and *Poor Miss Biddy* as well as *Good riddance* and *Roast in hell Biddy Doro you stinking old shit-witch*, and she was transported by a rattling wagon over the cobbled streets of Irish Town to the city morgue where she was placed upon the zinc tray on a squeaky-wheeled table and rolled away into the dark cavern of the waiting cabinet, pending unlikely retrieval by kin, but with none forthcoming to claim her after what is deemed a reasonable and respectable interval, she was situated inside the city-issued coffin (fragrant new boards of yellow pine) by a kindly and aged former slave turned morgue attendant who retained her sullied bedsheet as a shroud and arranged her as naturally as was humanly possible, given the degree of decay and the fragility of limbs and the lid was set and the nails were driven, and upon the lid was chiseled

Doro

d.1874

and the box then loaded on a designated short-boat that went steaming upstream through the rising mists of the East River, past the tumble-down tenements of Irish Town, past the water-swept snags where the cormorants perch in postures of charnel house guardians, and past the outcroppings of rock, while her ghost stood on the deck to gaze upon the banks of Turtle Bay she knew so well, having once gathered there all manner of medicinal flora in bud and bloom (licorice root, nightshade, arrow weed) and fauna of the smallest forms (newts, snails, stonefly nymphs) until the shore was lost in the river smoke where the water went wide and whitecapped on the western edge of the estuary and the rocky beach of Blackwell's Island came into view, and there the designated short-boat sputtered and docked at that port of the dead. And finally, it was by handcart that the coffin containing the declension of her flesh from her blighted bones was wheeled a ways to the Potter's Field and her hole was dug and she was interred by a crew of convicted felons from The House of Detention (dubbed *The Tombs* by its residents) who had been assigned to such a coveted task (a day out of shackles, a day in the open air)—and in that soil she would for eternity enjoy the companionship of fauna of the smallest forms (carrion worms, grave beetles, coffin flies) though all manner of flora in bud or bloom would be lacking, for upon that mound there were no flowers placed.

Chapter 33
Still Silver City
July, 1874 – The Moon of Long Day Heat

Catherine still cooks the purple fruit of the prickly pear and bakes on days she is able, intervals of the cough quieted and a bit steadier on her feet. Billy and Joe stand at a table in the thoroughfare, selling her cakes and pies and jars of jam. Most days, though, she is worn out with the heat of the stove and the heat of her fever and the heat of the Moon of Long Day Heat. When she coughs she holds the hem of her apron to her mouth and spits, and she no longer looks at what color comes away.

Catherine sets her rhubarb pie out to cool on the back-stoop step. A crow watches from the roof. Billy has his pencil and his list. *Crow*, he says. Already got you. Shoo now, he says.

Crows (Corvus brachyrhynchos) will surround a predator hawk perched within their territory and harass it by squawking, swooping in, or defecating on the intruder.

—Birds of America and the Territories, Chapter 54: Crows, Jays, Magpies, Ravens

A letter arrives from Mr. William Antrim:

July 20, 1874

Dearest Catherine,

Concluding business here in Casper. Did some fishing in the Platte.
Climate currently mild. Might here be our next move?
Hope to be heading on to Thermopolis, Territory of Wyoming.
Hot springs there are supposedly curative for consumption.
Will assess before sending for you and the lads.
Enclosed banknote should tide you over.
Your loving husband,
William

But there is no banknote enclosed.

There is no cold cash coming.

A band of javelina and their piglets were spotted resting in the shade of a honey mesquite.

A short-tailed hawk was seen dropping from the sky like a stone and quickly ascending again with a young rabbit in its foot.

The short-tailed hawk (Buteo brachyurus) attacks its prey by descending in a dramatic vertical swoop.

—Birds of America and the Territories, Chapter 15: Eagles, Hawks, Kites

Catherine takes to her bed. Billy sends word:

WESTERN UNION TELEGRAM CO.
SPEEDY DELIVERY GUARANTEED

DATE SENT: 6 AUG 1874
SENDING STATION: SILVER CITY
SENT BY: WM MCCARTY ANTRIM
SENT TO: WM ANTRIM
ADDRESS: HOTSPRINGS HOSTERY

THERMOPOLIS
WYOMING TERRITORY
MESSAGE: MAM WORSE STOP
COME HOME STOP
BILLY END

A letter arrives from William Antrim:

August 7, 1874

Dearest Catherine,

I have left Thermopolis behind me.

The sight of the naked and crippled soaking in the hotsprings drove me quickly away. At this writing I am in Casper Wyoming and enjoying the hospitality of the sheriff, but I will be making my way home to you as soon as possible.

My love to you Dearest and the lads,

Your loving husband,

William

August 25, 1874

Dearest Catherine,

Custer's expedition found gold in the Dakota Territory.

I am making my way to those Black Hills in hope I get there before that yellow-haired son-of-a-skunk digs it all up and carts it off.

Hope to arrive Fort Abe Lincoln likely two weeks.

Hello to the lads.

Your loving husband,

William

Chapter 34
Jacinta
Silver City, New Mexico
August 29, 1874 – The Moon of Falling Feathers

The little señorita, hastening this early Silver City morning, past the Conestogas and the buckboards, a yucca-weave basket on her arm and her indigo rebozo wrapped around her shoulders. She steps with care over the ruts, and in places where the road dust of summer is ankle deep, she takes ahold of her skirt at the hem and lifts it by the border of lace.

She hurries on now past the tables of wares cleared away and some just sheeted over until trade resumes near noon. A page of yesterday's Silver City Sentinel tumbles by. A midnight brawl in Rafferty's Barroom has left the batwing doors hanging off their hinges. Creaking. Moaning from within. Faint clink and clatter of tin-can chimes suspended somewhere, swayed by a slow wind tunneling down the deserted thoroughfare beneath a pale blue sky blanched where it meets the peaks of Los Pinos Altos but soon to deepen to lapis with more of the morning.

Here and there stirrings.

A cinnamon-coat cat appropriates a gutted quail from the bushel of bloodied birds, taking it in her mouth as gently as if it were a kitten.

A crow perched upon the bow of an uncanvassed Conestoga tilts his head to examine a watch-chain protruding from the vest pocket of a sleeper who lies drunk in the wagonbed—but thinks better of it, flies off.

A rat wriggles out from a sack of seed corn stowed on a handcart and sprints past the little señorita and across the street.

Dios mío, she whispers to herself and clutches the windings of her rebozo. She takes the turn down White Hog Lane. Two doors down to the log house. She holds the wobbly post and climbs the two shifting steps. She taps at the door.

Billy, she calls. Billy mío.

She hears the mother coughing from inside, and then the slide of the bolt, the lifting of the latch. Billy there in the doorway. Rumpled, yawning, scratching his head.

He estado buscando para usted, she says.

Well you found me, says Billy.

Ya no me amas?

Little darlin, says Billy. Claro. Of course I do. But my mother—mi madre está enferma. Muy enferma.

Si si, she says. She lifts the basket. Mira.

Que esto? says Billy.

She uncovers the cloths on each small dish. Enchiladas verdes, she says. Frijoles.

Es mi favorito, says Billy. And these here leaves. Estas hojas? What's these?

Estos? Por su mamacita, medicinas naturales.

Billy takes the basket and he sets it on the step.

Adiós mi amor, she says and she turns to go, but he pulls her back against his chest. He slips his arms under hers, his hands against her breasts to hold her fast. He puts his face into the back of her head and takes her hair into his mouth.

Ay! Ay! Eso duele! she says.

Pintail ducks, he says in her ear. Patos.

Que? She says.

Patos enamorados. Ducks in love.

Que? says the little señorita.

The courting male Pintail duck (Anas acuta) mounts the female from behind, holds her fast with an embracing maneuver of his wings, and grasps her head feathers in his mouth.

—Birds of America and the Territories, Chapter 13: Swans, Geese, Ducks, Mergansers

In this Moon of Falling Feathers, geese preen and paddle in the shallows. Antelope graze along the banks of the San Vicente Arroyo. Javelinas have been heard clacking their tusks as they roam the desert in the quiet twilight before dark.

Billy keeps a list:

Medicine for Mam from my Jacinta

1 Yerba buena last night. Working good. Less cough this morning.

2 Gum weed. Mam spits this out. Try it in soup.

3 Aloe vera. In her tea so she won't know. Still has fever.

Chapter 35
Gold

THE TERRITORY TRIBUNE

"All the News Without the Snooze"

Vol. 74 No. 8 August 30, 1874 Late Edition Price 10 cents

NEWS FROM THE BLACK HILLS: GOLD! GOLD!

Custer's Mining Company To Commence Operations

Is it not fated! Is it not writ in the stars that it would be a golden-haired warrior who delivers to us the metal of the gods! As it was in antiquity and the adventures of Jason and his Argonauts in their quest for the Golden Fleece, so it is that our glorious Lieutenant-Colonel George Armstrong Custer embarked on his expedition to the mysterious and uncharted Black Hills of the Dakota Territory, leading the 7th Cavalry into the unknown. An undertaking of monumental proportions! One thousand men in his command and as many horses, 200 wagons, 300 head of cattle to feed his courageous regiment, and artillery consisting of three Gatling guns and a canon to protect his forces from attack by the heathen Sioux. Upon his triumphant return to Fort Abraham Lincoln, the success of the undertaking was revealed, describing the Black Hills to be of "unsurpassed majesty, its equal I have never seen, with abundant game! Massive herds of elk and deer roaming the hills, flocks of comestible birdlife including woodcock, quail, and turkey filling the air, and millions of buffalo swimming the rivers, and finally—in vein upon vein glittering in the cliff-rock and in the clear rushing waters of the trout-filled streams—unfathomable quantities of pure gold." Indeed, in his letter to the President he has confided that the success of his expedition is due to "my strengths, not only as a Master of Military Strategy, but that of Indian-Fighter and Pathfinder with a vast knowledge of topography and geology unmatched in these times, and it is by both these skills and the Grace of God that I have discovered what surely will be an asset to the prosperity of this great nation." Therefore: Hark! All ye Forty-Niners who returned home empty-handed and heavy-hearted. Make ready for the next Rush! The Black Hills have California beat!

QUOTE OF THE DAY

☞ *The crucible is for silver, the furnace is for gold, but the Lord tests hearts.*

—Proverbs 17:3

Chapter 36
God-Fearing Men

The Territory Tribune
Letter to the Editor,
August 31, 1874

Regarding "News from the Black Hills" (August 30, 1874) and the expedition of our esteemed and heroic Lieutenant-Colonel George Armstrong Custer, it has become most evident that in order to reclaim what is our land and the riches rightfully ours therein, we must scour the entire Dakota Territory clean of all Indians, for they be a useless, loathsome, murderous lot, and a detriment to the growth of this nation. We must (and we will) slaughter every last one of them, the young and the old, the newborn and the unborn, and remove any survivors to the confines of designated reservations where they will wither and die off, for the good of all civilized and God-fearing men.

Col. John Milton Chivaton,
Colorado Volunteer Cavalry

Chapter 37
Letter to the President
September 2, 1874

Department of the Interior

Office of the Secretary
1849 C Street, NW
Washington D.C.

Ulysses S. Grant, President
1600 Pennsylvania Ave
Washington D.C. 2 Sept 1874

Mr. President:

I write to you regarding lands you have placed under my jurisdiction and in light of Lieutenant-General George A. Custer's recent discoveries of gold in the Black Hills of the Dakota Territory. The occupation of that region by the Indians is no longer necessary to their prosperity, their well-being, or their habits of living. It is therefore advisable that the Territory immediately be freed from Indian inhabitancy and opened to the Whites, that all prior Indians claims be extinguished as soon as practicable, and that the articles of The Treaty of Fort Laramie between the United States and tribes of the Territory including the Miniconjou, Sioux, Dakota, Yanktonai, Arapaho, and Ogalala, be declared null and void.

Respectfully,
Columbus J. Deleno
Secretary of the Interior

Chapter 38
Book Excerpt

Apache Childhood: My Years Among The People
Author: Singing-Stick, Annabelle Margaret.
Lantern Press, Albuquerque, 1890.

I was still a small girl when the Apache rode in on their spotted horses and took me from my white family. They burned my clothes and washed me in the river, and they dressed me in deerskin. From then on I learned their ways. They taught me to respect the bear because The Creator of Worlds sent magic to his heart at the moment of his birth. That is why our people never touch a bear or the hide of a bear, or its claws or teeth, or the waste from the body of a bear, and not even the place a bear has slept. It is only a healing woman who may speak with a bear. If we happen to encounter a bear in the forest, we may call him "uncle" or "father" but we will never call a bear by his name. My white family found me among The People and they ransomed me and brought me back to my old home, but they did not understand what I had been taught. They kept the hide of a bear on the floor of their house and they walked upon it. They made me walk upon it. They would not call me by my Apache name. I decided to leave my white family and go to live in the pueblo. One night I left my bed and I knelt by the hide of the bear and asked him if I could touch him. I gathered up the hide and held it to close to myself. And when I ran away from my white family, I took the hide of the bear with me.

—Annabelle Margaret Singing-Stick
Born 1804–Died 1905

Chapter 39
As *The People* So Sit
Chiricahua Apache Pueblo
September 6, 1874 – The Moon of Leaving Geese

Daybreak. The night chill persists. The campfires along the thoroughfare of Silver City have gone to embers and the air smells of smoke and sap of single-leaf pine. The cactus wren is heard along the dry arroyo and all around the pueblo past the town.

The voice of the cactus wren (Campylorhynchus brunneicapillus) can be heard well before the desert dawn as a series of sharp, staccato notes.
—Birds of America and the Territories, Chapter 61: Wrens

Here is Singing-Stick. Peering out from the hide flap of her wickiup on this bright September dawn with another autumn coming on, bearing down, told by a change of wind sliding down the Great Divide, yellowing the aspens in the foothills of Los Pinos Altos, and the cottonwoods along the Arroyo San Vicente, and sifting a light snow upon the pines that border the upper slopes. She looks there—to the mountains and to the sky above them—and then to what serves as the dusty courtyard of her habitation where all vegetation—ocotillo, rabbit bush, prickly pear—even the buffalo grass—has long since been trampled flat by those who come to sit in this space well before dawn and to wait for her to appear at the entrance of her wickiup. See, there she is. She has been spotted. The People rejoice in their hearts at the sight of her—of what they can see of her: the sooty hand that holds the flap of hide, the muss of dark hair around her face. There she is, The People whisper to each other, grateful to The Creator of Worlds that she has lived another day and night, for it is not known how long she has lived. It is not known if she is young or old. In the burnishing light of the late afternoon sun before it sets, her face is that of a woman in her prime—or at best that of a woman poised upon the brink of her decline—but a face happy and bright nevertheless, and on other days haggard, grim. On some days, in good weather, she comes forth at dawn with a firm and steady step, and on other days she is bent and decrepit. But today, yes. She is there. Singing-Stick, The People whisper to each other, but they do not call out to her in greeting. Nor would she reply nor begin her work until she sees the bear that comes to sit among this gathering, until she is certain that he has not ambled away during the night to some distant galactic abode, as she knows bears of his kind are apt to do. But she sees him this morning, sleeping on his belly in the midst of these congregants. These sufferers of every sort. Some dragged here on travois of blankets and hides. Some diminished of flesh and their skins stretched over their bones. Some with rags wound over their faces stifling coughs or hiding holes of decay. Some with shreds of cloth bound to their limbs to contain what sloughs. A man carries a limp and slavering child, its head lolling on his shoulders. A woman holds a baby bound to its cradleboard, snugly wrapped to contain what foulness seeps, and with sprigs of sage tucked into the bindings to cover the smell of decomposition. Some unable to stand on their own are helped to their feet by the others. Crutches, canes, sticks. The ones who have been sleeping are nudged awake. The boy Billy is one of this number, poked by an old man who leans on his crutch and who bears a maggoty hole in his cheek. Wake up, says the old man, his tongue alive in the hole. The old man lifts his crutch and points to Singing-Stick. There. The Healing Woman, he says. Wake up, he says.

I am, says Billy and he stands and shakes the dust from his clothes.

He is small for his age, for his thirteen, and slight of build, sloped in the shoulders.

Singing-Stick sees that the bear, too, has come awake. Rolling onto his back. Stretching his limbs. Reaching out to hold his feet in his great clawed hands as a child might do. His coat is brown as fertile earth, each hair tipped in gold, fur ruffling in the morning wind. He is a mound, a mountain. He yawns and belches. The stink of fish. Likely perch he had swatted from out the shallows of the Rio Mimbres or the rivulets of the Arroyo San Vicente where he stood midstream and slapped muskie and steelheads twisting from the water, glinting and silver in the river light. Eagles perching in the stream-bank trees ready to steal what may slip from his paws. Another belch. Teeth violently white against the deep red of his maw. He shakes his head and sneezes violently spraying an ursine slime. She sees his great clawed forepaw come up and delicately scratch his snout. The People seem not to notice. Nor does our Billy. Not even as the bear raises himself up on his great flat hind feet and stands to his full height, and sways—drifts—from side to side with his paws held limply before him as if he were a dog taught to stand and balance and beg, lifting his snout and sniffing the air to find the smell of her, for she knows he is an old bear, and his hide shows old cuts, old scars, and what appear to be old sutures on his belly, and although his sight has worsened through his misfortunes, his sense of smell has not. He snorts and grunts and Singing-Stick snorts back at him and clicks her tongue and then as if he has been told to behave himself and sit down, he is down again, foreclaws raking at the earth to clear away the dung he had passed during the night, and finally sitting himself down on his broad haunches, his great clawed hands on his knees. As The People themselves so sit. He tilts forward off his stumpy tail, briefly holds himself in that position, and releases a rumble of foul wind. Singing-Stick grimaces and waves her hand in front of her nose to fan away the stink, but again The People seem not to notice. Nor does Billy, at the edge of this assembly of the sick and the wasted and maimed. It is not possible to know who has been waiting the longest, who arrived first. The People have not considered nor encountered the concept of lines, of order, of sequence. They believe their time with Singing-Stick will come when it is meant to come, and that she will know who is meant to live and who will live and who will linger or die, and so they remain in the dusty yard outside the wickiup, wrapped in their buckskins and blankets, some with cloaks woven of palm grass and reed, and all of them shouldered against the night cold and now the morning chill.

Someone of them has made a fire in the stone circle, the place where Singing-Stick fries her bread and bakes her apples and potatoes and roasts a skinned and skewered rabbit or the butt of a javelina. Comestibles she has not come by on her own, as Singing-Stick does not hunt and she does not gather or reap. At last she steps forth from the wickiup, letting the flap fall closed behind her. She places more fuel on the fire. Pieces of white cedar and piñon. The resin sparks and pops. The air is scented piney this bright autumn morning. She sets her implements and treatments on the wide flat stone near the fire circle—pouches filled with flower petals and yucca pollen, shards of shell and splinters of bone, sprigs of desert plants she has picked and dried and tied with string. And beside these she places pieces of birds and pieces of sky—the feathers of passing eagles that spiral down at her feet in the late summer season of their molting, and in the season of the Leonides when the night sky spews stars, the pieces that lay cooling on the desert floor. These—the pinons of eagles and the parts of stars—these are for intractable cases. Swimming Cat, who carries a sharp stone in her heart. Rain Again, who hears the whir of a hummingbird in his head. Jimmy Bad Drum, born with his right foot turned the wrong-way around and the joint disintegrated, purulent. They are all here and new ones as well this autumn morning as the pine smoke rises around them, as leaves of aspen are set loose by the wind. As a strand of geese pass above on their way to winter waters. The woman bearing the baby on the cradleboard now comes forward. Singing-Stick hears the bear whine and softly growl, and she nods to him and sorts through her basket for what will be required: only this—a gourd to hold water, to be hung high on a tree limb beside the small body should its spirit thirst while it goes to bones and waits out eternity bound there in its cradleboard. The rest come along now, one by one. Billy on the sidelines, shifting his position as the congregation moves along, letting others of this assembly stagger ahead, wanting to be the last and a witness to this procession of the afflicted, as the bear is witness to Singing-Stick preparing her treatments, dispensing her remedies. Botanicals. Powders of flowers and plant parts. Dust of earth minerals and metals from heaven. Rags unwrapped. Wounds inspected, purulence expressed. Packings. Poultices. Brief chants. Notes on a reed flute. Tapping on a drum. Medicinals dispensed, wrapped in leaves that are slit and secured by the petiole run through. Little wrappings in rawhide. The sun goes low in the sky. The last of The People go tottering away or are toted away to their huts and wickiups and adobe homes. Those for whom she offers no remedy will spend another night nearby bedded only by the moon.

And now Billy.

Now you, she calls to this pinch-faced boy who has kept himself slightly apart from the rest by appearing otherwise occupied gathering sticks for the fire and pitching them in one by one. Wandering off just far enough to examine a broken wagon wheel and the nest of a cactus wren while slyly watching her. And she has been watching him. This slight, squirrely boy. Teeth somewhat rabbity. Wiry as a coatimundi. She has seen men become their spirit animals. Perhaps that is his, the coatimundi.

He steps up to the wickiup and there the flat stone. I'm here for someone else, he says. A white woman.

She sent you.

I come my own self.

Who are you?

I go by Billy.

Just Billy?

Billy Antrim. Or Billy Bonney. Whichever.

What does she go by?

Who?

The white woman.

Antrim.

Only Antrim?

Missus Antrim.

Only that?

Missus Catherine Bonney McCarty Antrim.

You are her son.

Some say so, but not likely. Since I don't favor her. She says the Wee Folk brung me.

Who?

Sprites. They bring the bad boys. What she says.

Where is she?

She's to home, he says. That log house we rent out past the dry arroyo, he says. I seen a roadrunner hunting up and down in there.

She is alone?

There's my brother Joseph.

Your big brother?

Bigger. But not older. He goes by Joe.

Bring her here, your mother. You and your brother bring her.

I'd sure like to catch me one of them birdies.

What would you do with it? says Singing-Stick.

Wouldn't do nothing with it, says Billy. I'd just have it. It'd be something to have. One time I come on feathers blowing in the road and sure enough it's one of them shot nearly to pieces, says Billy. Those boys in town they shoot at anything. It was looking right up at me when I finished him off and wrote him on my list. I took a stripy tail feather off it and carried it home, but she was too sick to give a care.

What kind of sick is she? says Singing-Stick.

The worst kind, says Billy. You ever see one of them birdies out this way? They're awful fast, he says. He gazes out past the clearing. He squints at nothing at all. Shades his eyes with his hand. Well now looky there, he says.

Singing-Stick does not look. There goes one now and damn if it ain't running backwards! You seen him? says Billy.

No, says Singing-Stick.

Too fast for you then, was he? says Billy.

Does she leave her bed?

Not no more, he says and shakes his head. Me, I'd fly if I had wings, says Billy. But them? They'd rather be running. You ever seen their tracks? Big X is all. You can't tell which way they be coming or going for looking at 'em.

Which way are you going? says Singing-Stick.

I can't be going nowhere, he says, and he tells her that he is thirteen now and in charge of this family. This boy whose mother is sick in her bed in her log house out by the dry arroyo. Spitting blood, he tells her, just like some of them sick ones I seen coming here and you curing them, says Billy.

Is she feverish?

Near burns your hand to touch her.

Where's your pa?

Don't know is where. Neither of 'em. One of 'em give me a pistol. I shot a horse once. Same way I finished off that old bird, I did.

No, he is not coatimundi, and not rabbit or squirrel, but coyote. She has seen the ones that become coyotes. The clever ones. Cautious, evasive. This boy. A trickster setting himself free of the dying, doing what he must. Killing what he must. More killing yet to come.

The day has gone cool again. More wind. Dust devils spin up and disperse. Dusk begins. The fire has gone to ash but a knot of ironwood still glows. Singing-Stick scatters strands of buffalo grass over. She leans in and breathes and a small lick of flame flares up. Now kindling twigs of tamarisk. She sees the bear trundle over, then sit himself beside the wickiup and gaze up at the darkening sky. The first lights of the Milky Way are appearing and she knows he must be remembering the glowing road he took to the stars when he was skinned and his hide was set on the floor of a house and men walked upon him.

Can you see the bear? asks Singing-Stick.

Bears don't bother me none, says Billy.

Coyote and bear, says Singing-Stick.

Coyotes neither, says Billy.

There goes a coyote now, says Singing-Stick. Too fast for you, was it?

Nothing too fast for me, Billy tells her.

She will not live, says Singing-Stick.

You don't know, says Billy.

I do, says Singing-Stick.

I see you handing out cures. So you go on then and give me the medicine like you're supposed to or you tell me where'd you get them from.

From the Old Ones, says Singing Stick. They built their cookfires in the earth before the world was made. But they are gone now. A long time gone.

Gone where? says Billy.

They climbed out and ran away.

Then it's just you. You give me the cure and you tell me what I need to do. Mix it up, eat it, smoke it, drink it, rub it on. I can read and write. I can write it down. I can make a list.

Sundown.

Evening fires are lit.

Now in this month the Apache call the Moon of Leaving Geese, the People who wait at the wikiup hear the honk and yelp of the birds beginning their migration, calling to one another as they pass overhead and under the stars.

Crackle of burning mesquite. Smell of cedar.

Leaf-nosed bats have been seen flitting above the smoke of campfires, their fanged and dark-furred faces briefly lit by the flames below and their tiny eyes glinting like pairs of rising sparks.

The X-shaped track of the roadrunner (Geococcyx californianus) does not reveal the direction that the bird is traveling, thereby confusing the predators and any malignant spirits that pursue it.

—Birds of America and the Territories, Chapter 40: Cuckoos, Roadrunners, Anis

Chapter 40
A Young Catherine McCarty (Née Bonney)
Flees the Blight in Ireland
October, 1848—Thirteen Years Before the Birth of Billy

It was late in the season when the green hills of County Cork had just begun to fade and an early frost had withered the bracken dead in Timoleague town, that Clodagh Bonney died face down in her yard with a mouthful of grass, and her husband Eamon in an unsown field, a gnarl of rot-blighted tuber in his fist. Catherine Bonney could not honor her parents' wishes—to be interred side-by-side in the church-yard—as that sacred acreage had been populated well past its intended capacity, until the vicar himself, who had presided over each internment with an unencouraging bit of Ezekiel—*Yea sayeth the Lord for ye all will fall dead in the open field and there lie as dung left unburied as food for the carrion birds of the air amen*—finally vacated the vicarage and secured less spacious subterranean accommodations himself—and Catherine Bonney being too weak for digging, piled what stones she could roll along or carry upon the corpses of Clodagh and Eamon, as the dogs of Timoleague and all of County Cork had gone unfed and feral by then but lived well enough on the carcasses of those who had pulled their threadbare blankets over and died in their beds and or those who lay down in ditches and covered themselves with handfuls of loam, and when corpses were undug and devoured, fed on particular parts of their children that mothers and fathers could not bear to boil down to a hellish soup—the heads, the tiny hands and feet, the slit or dangling nether appendages—*And look what's become of Quinn Hanlon's old spaniel Shandy, his coat gone clotted-up with thistle and what's that he's got in that baby bonnet?* Cottages had long been ransacked by those still living and cupboards held nothing but crockery, so it was Clodagh Bonney's pair of blue willow cups that Catherine Bonney wrapped in rags and tied in a bundle of the new Tricolour of Ireland along with the family's leather-bound bible and walked away to the wharf where cats by moonlight stalk the fishmongers' shut-down stalls and stevedores loiter in the shadows between bouts of labor and stranded mariners lean along the barrels and mark the empty hours between docking and departure, and in this way she fled that famished land, bound for the port of New York with great numbers of her starving countrymen, her passage paid in the sale of herself.

Chapter 41
Nary a Moon for the Mother of Billy the Kid
Silver City, New Mexico
September 7, 1874 – The Moon of Leaving Geese

Billy writes out a list:

> *These I get from the Apache woman:*
>
> *Ocotillo berries—for fever—boil into tea*
>
> *Stone crop buds—for red spit—mash up in sugar and eat*
>
> *Black cherry bark—soak in water, serve cold*
>
> *Prickly Pear paddle—for breathing—remove prickles, heat, put on chest*
>
> *Sage—light bundle, blow the fire out, wave smoke around the bed*
>
> *Reed flute—play 3 low notes at bedtime*

Billy sets out the remedies and reads again the list he has written. Yes, all there—leaf, bud, bark, berry—all that the Apache woman has given him, except the flute. No flute. Well. No matter. He gets the fire going in the stove. He puts the kettle on.

Billy steeps the ocotillo berries in the blue willow cup.

Tea for Mam, says Billy.

Don't look to be tea, she says. She sniffs. Don't smell to be tea either.

Special tea, says Billy. For fever.

She shakes her head. Keep away now. I'm knowing what you're up to.

Billy mashes the stonecrop leaves with sugar in the blue willow cup.

Here you go, Mam. Medicine, he says.

What for? she says.

You're sick.

For sure you'll be making me sicker.

Billy soaks the black cherry bark in the blue willow cup.

It's cherry, he tells her.

It's a potion, she says, eyeing him sideways. I know where you been.

Where I been? says Billy.

Up to that Apache woman, she says.

No, says Billy. Just to the doctor.

A liar, you are. I know it. Joe told.

That Joe, says Billy.

My Joe, my Joe. My only boy, she says.

Billy scrubs the prickles from a pad of prickly pear and warms it on the stove top. He wraps it in flannel, brings it bedside.

More magic, says Catherine McCarty.

It's for better breathing, he tells her.

It's Apache magic, what it is. She knows what you are, that Apache witch. You and her, says Catherine McCarty. Both friends of the devil. Birds of a feather. You'll kill me yet, or the Wee Folk will. One or the other. Get away with you now, fly away.

The doctor must be summoned. The younger son is sent. You'll go Joe, says Billy. You'll see the sign. *All Ailments*. Git.

The room has gone cold. Billy fills the kettle, feeds the stove fire. The mother moans and gasps in her sleep. He binds a bundle of sage with string—dried leaf and twig—and touches it to the flame. It quickly catches and he waves it out. Smoke wafts. Odor of the earth and the high desert at dusk.

The mother is awake now and coughing. She sees the smoking

leaves. Is it a spell? she says. Or more of the same Apache witchery? Get away with you now, she says. Fly away.

It's sage, Mam. To cure the coughing.

Or would it be the Wee Folk you're conjuring, to come in the night and do me in. She peers all around the room. Joe? she says. Where's my Joe gone? Where's my boy? You're not him. Who you are I never knew.

It's me here, Mam. It's Billy.

Out past the dry arroyo, a coyote has chased down a jackrabbit and tears into its flank. A magpie in an overhanging limb of cottonwood waits.

The black-billed magpie (Pica hudsonia) will follow a favorite coyote setting out on a hunt, observe the coyote make a kill and eat, and finally alight on the carcass to scavenge the remaining meat.

—Birds of America and the Territories, Chapter 54: Crows, Jays, Magpies, Ravens

Along the far banks of the Arroyo San Vicente, a herd of buffalo graze the sloughgrass. An old bull rests in a mud wallow. The calves nurse.

Joe now, arriving with the man he has sought—the doctor with his black and doctorly satchel-bag in hand—coming down White Hog Lane, and what would one expect a doctor in these parts to be? A learned man perhaps. A man educated in notable institutions back East, bearing certificates complete with gold seals and degrees in scrolled calligraphy attesting to years of study, or fine forgeries thereof, or forgeries even not so fine but shabbily wrought, for who in need of a physician in these the far-flung parts makes further inquiries or even takes a closer look? Or perhaps he is a doctor true, but in seeking atonement for prior professional blunders and bungles, took up doctoring in that city of immigrants—New York City—in the forlorn enclaves of the foreign born—the Irish included in that number—tending to the down-and-out and destitute, the souls scraping out a living and scorned, the consumptive, and the poxed, as well as attending to the births of living children and ones born dead and the ones he thought better off if they were—those creatures so deformed that, on more than one occasion, he surreptitiously assisted in their demise (a pinch of the tiny nose between pointing finger and thumb for the infant with a beating heart outside its chest, and for the one with an anus imperforate—*Ah Mrs. Duffy, she's with the angels now* and *So sorry Mrs. O'Hare, but it was God's will to take him*). Eventually in the course of his doctoring he became suffocated by the suffering and screams and squalor of the city, and so headed south to more seemly cities and civilized districts—Atlanta, Charleston, Charlotte, to name a few—until after a series of medical mishaps was run out of said districts on the customary rail and hightailed it in a westerly direction. Or perhaps he is a man proficient—or one not so proficient—in the doctoring of horses, hogs, and longhorns, and in the remedies for swine mange and bovine tender-teat and equine bloat but certainly not averse to expanding his services to the human breed. Or perhaps he is a man with no aptitude in medical care for man nor beast, but adept instead in taxidermy, specializing in the mounting of the heads of ungulate hunting trophies—buffalo, antelope, elk—brought down by the rich come west for shooting expeditions with their photographers in tow, and each wanting more than a gilt-framed tintype of their newly bullet-ridden kill to take home and hang on a wall. And perhaps he may even be a man moving on from furred creatures to become self-employed in the business of human taxidermy, better known as embalming, who had been kept busy at Shiloh and Chickamauga and even west to the Territories—Mesilla, Albuquerque, and Santa Fe—so many a siege and skirmish lesser named, there a witness to the carnage (once again: the suffering, screams, squalor) that created within him a heavy heart and a rage at heaven, and though he had previously lacked the knack of rejuvenating living men, discovered he had a talent in the preservation of the dead, the interruption of the rot of their bodies, the restoration of the fallen and mutilated by the minié ball by correcting the pallor of exsanguination with a slurry of flour and rouge, rebuilding shot-away sockets and noses with papier-mâché and eyes with the glass orbs he had once inserted into the heads of hunting trophies, so that the mothers and the wives and the children of the dead may one last time gaze upon what once were fathers and husbands and brothers and sons. When the killing continued with a shortage of surgeons, he volunteered his services as a doctor of medicine, and in that unquestioning chaos was readily accepted as such and when handed a bone saw, proceeded with amputations, and treated the wounded with skill and tenderness. And when that great conflict concluded, he took himself and his hardened heart forged in horror and quenched in spilled blood to territories west where disputes are negotiated with colts and carbines and frequent gunplay is a given, is nearly mythical, and opportunities for undertakers abound. And where he also might resume doctoring and take on the infirmities of those on the frontier, selling his cure-all *Broadwater's Bodily Rejuvenator* from a table set outside his tent in the thoroughfare under the signboard *All Ailments* though few would notice (nor understand) the miniscule printing that reads *Postmortem Care.*

Next house on the right sir, Billy hears Joe say.

Billy steps into the street and he sees them on their way—his brother and the doctor he has fetched along, the small boy hurrying to the long strides of the man, the two of them silhouetted in the open road by the setting sun, a bloom of clouds behind them the color of water-cut blood. The color of the stains on her pillow. The color of the glutinous fruit and clot of seeds of the prickly pear. The color of cherry bark tea untouched in the blue willow cup.

And now Billy is at the log house door. Here we are sir, says Joe. This here's Billy, my brother. Watch your step now, sir. Careful with those two steps there.

Billy hoists the lantern, and his face is suddenly illuminated—that pinched, small face of his—and the lanternlight giving his jut-out ears a translucent look. A bat, thinks Dr. Arthur Broadwater, a rabid creature flying past the moon on a night there would be a moon, and he is suddenly off-balance just enough to lose his footing on the tread that has gone to rot where it meets the riser, and he grasps for the newel post, but that too is not right, that too is wobbled, and he stumbles forward losing his grip on the handle of his satchel and bashing his nose to the post. Immediate gush of blood, brief vision of stars and bouncing black beads.

My God, says Dr. Arthur Broadwater.

Billy! cries Joe.

That damn step, says Billy, setting down the lantern and taking ahold of the doctor. Can you stand, sir? says Billy.

The doctor tries to stand. His knees buckle under and he sinks again. The beefsteak and beer he recently swallowed at the Hotspot Hotel comes up sour in his mouth and spills onto his shirt. He looks down at the mess, brushes at the cloth with the back of his hand. I'll just sit a minute, he says. Stars fade. Black balls recede. Yes, yes. I'm alright. He touches his nose, blood there on his fingers. That step, he says.

It's a killer for sure, says Billy, our small but strong Billy hoisting the doctor who staggers and leans against him. Do you need a doctor? says Billy.

Billy hangs the lantern, turns up the wick. There the one room and all within it discernable at a glance. Table, big chair, stove, small chair, bed, and blankets over the mound of the mother more diminished by the day. Here sir, says Joe. They sit the doctor in the big chair by the bed, where Mrs. Catherine Antrim faintly coughs in her sleep, faced away to the wall. Billy has brought him a clean rag to hold against his smashed nose. Broken most like, says Billy.

Dr. Arthur Broadwater chomps his teeth together and wiggles an incisor with his finger.

Your teeth too then? says Billy.

Loose, he says, but likely won't lose it. He looks up at Billy. He sees that this boy is not so much a bat—those ears, yes—but that overbite and malocclusion reminiscent more of a muskrat. Or rabbit. Yes, rabbit, such as the rabbit-looking baby he now recalls from his doctoring days in New York a decade ago, oh a decade at least—called to an Irish family such as this one and the baby being born with a deformity such as this one, if you could even call it that. Newborn and toothless, of course, but a narrow and forward held mandible and, as he also recalls—a difficult delivery. The nuchal cord. The gasps, the release. And the family's name? What was their name? Not Antrim, no. It was Mc something. Or Mac something. Something like that and in Irish Town. Irish Town most definitely. McDonnel or McOwen. Or was it just Owen.

We have the kettle on, says Joe. We have tea, sir.

I thank you, but let's see what we can do for your mother here.

Billy leans in and whispers in her ear. Mam, wake up.

What now? she says. The Wee Folk to fret a poor sick woman?

What's that she's saying, says Dr. Arthur Broadwater.

Just an Irish thing, says Billy. Pay no mind.

Mam, says Joe. We have the doctor. I fetched him myself. Come, roll over and see.

It's doctor Broadwater, says Billy. There's a good Mam, he says.

Broadwater? says Catherine. She rolls away from the wall and turns to face them, and Dr. Arthur Broadwater sees her eyes deep in their dusky craters. The hollows at her temples. Her lips drawn back over her teeth, gums gone pale as lifeblood seeps into the cavities where there once were lungs. But he has seen the look of the slowly dying and nearly dead before, the good doctor has. He has attended the consumptives of the cities—chests caved, barely breathing—and the skeleton-men let loose from Andersonville at the close of the war—beyond help but shipped back north. But this woman—her face bears a familiarity beyond that of the wasted he has known.

Dr. Arthur Broadwater moves his chair closer in. Good evening to you, Mrs. Antrim.

And yourself sir, she says.

Your boy Joe here. He tells me you've been poorly.

Joseph, yes. My Joe. My youngest, she says. Where you be, lad?

Right here Mam, says Joe and he steps closer.

And your oldest? he says and nods toward Billy.

That one goes by Billy. Thirteen year that one, says Mrs. Catherine Antrim. But you'd hardly know it. He's born small, she says. Nearly strangled in me. He just barely lived.

Dr. Arthur Broadwater looks Billy over, as if to make a well-considered assessment. He notes that yes, the boy is small. He notes the protrusion of his incisors—likely malocclusion, likely congenital. He notes the sloping shoulders—undoubtedly a weakness of the trapezius musculature. And lastly: that fullness of his shirt across the upper back, the excess fold of cloth, the way the garment has been loosely tucked into the boy's belt—oh yes, most probably due some deformity, likely a winging of the scapula pressed against the cloth. All in all, mild bodily malformations. And yet, there be a brightness to the boy. A strength. A quickness that compensates for any disproportions.

Well now Billy, says Dr. Arthur Broadwater. Not to worry. You've got plenty time for growing still ahead of you, son.

Hasn't yet, says Mrs. Catherine Antrim. She feels around in the bed, under the blanket, under the pillow.

What you looking for Mam? says Joe.

My spit rag, she says. Where'd it get to?

Dr. Arthur Broadwater soon concludes the examination of his patient, the reason he was summoned. He has looked into her mouth and asked her to lift her tongue. He has placed his fingers at the angle of her mandible and felt there the tender swellings of scrofula. He has sounded her chest with a thump of his finger and heard not resonance of air-filled spaces but as expected, the dullness of suppuration. He has unfastened the upper buttons on her camisole in the disinterested manner befitting a physician opening a patient's clothing and has produced a stethoscope from his satchel-bag. He has taken a moment to adjust the earpieces, to warm the bell in his hand, to sound the diaphragm with a tap of his finger. He has deliberately yawned to banish any perception of personal interest before he pressed the bell of it to her in the spaces above and under her meager breasts—alternating left-right, left-right—and he has listened there with an expression of benign interest and not of disgust as he smelled the rose-water she had sprinkled on herself to mask the odor of necrosis. He has tilted her forward to rest against her forehead against his shoulder, assisted in that positioning by youngest son (Joe come help me here), and he has again listened within spaces between and below her shoulder blades. He has stayed some minutes in this position, hearing the bubbling of pus and blood and in some places nothing at all, but frowning slightly so that his assessment does not appear perfunctory, but instead an attempt to sort things out, make a decision, come up with—with something, while only dreading the pronouncements he will be expected to make. He has—with a bit of fumbling—refastened the buttons of her camisole. (There you go, Mrs. Antrim. Do I have that right?) Fluffed and re-adjusted her pillow. Eased her back onto it. (How is that, fairly comfortable? Or a little bit higher?) He has asked to see what medicines she is taking. He has inquired, as is expected of him, as to which may be providing a degree of relief and which are decidedly not. He has been shown the bottles of assorted concoctions, teas, elixirs. He has examined the leaves and stems and the little bundles of sage.

What about these? Billy says. These ones Apache. These ones Mexican.

You can keep on trying with these, says Dr. Arthur Broadwater, if she'll take them.

I won't, says Catherine Antrim, still facing the wall.

This one's from the preacher, says Joe. *Leviticus Elixir.*

No, not that one. Don't bother with that one.

Or this? says Billy. *Broadwater's Bodily Rejuvenator.*

Well now, says Dr. Arthur Broadwater. Just when did you buy that?

I didn't, says Billy.

I see, says Dr. Arthur Broadwater.

Should we keep on giving it? She'll take it time to time.

No. Don't bother her with that one either. It's just soda-water and cayenne.

He puts on his hat. He takes up his doctorly satchel. He steps to the bed. Goodbye Mrs. Antrim, he says. I am sorry we have met under these . . . but she has put her face to the wall again.

Doctor Broadwater's leaving Mam, says Joe.

Broadwater? she says.

Dr. Arthur Broadwater and Billy at the log-house door, on the log-house step. The doctor puts his hand on the newel post, then thinks better of it. Well now, he says to Billy.

She asked for a doctor, so we brung you, says Billy.

I'm sorry, son. But there's nothing I can do. There's nothing to be done.

One thing, says Billy.

Certainly, says Dr. Arthur Broadwater.

Don't be calling me son. I ain't. Not nobody's, Billy says. He lifts the lantern. Now mind that step, he says. And turns away once the doctor has descended.

Dr. Arthur Broadwater stands in the road for a moment. Still night. No cover of clouds. No moon. Still September, but the year soon will be ending. A pulmonary vessel will break and blood will rise in her throat and fill her mouth and she too will soon be ending. He has attended more deaths than births of late. Bloody events—both coming and going. As it was when he was summoned in New York's Irish Town. *Doctor—it's my missus—something's gone wrong—please come.* The mother past scream and shrieks, now only moaning. The child already emerging. A blue-faced bit of a baby. Dusky blue, the color of twilight. One gasp, then nothing. Its eyes open but dimming. The limbs coming next gone limp. Its neck noosed in the birth cordage. He recalls the slime and the blood, and he shudders—he had never gotten used to the horrid quagmire of being born, never gotten used to having his hands in the slickness of it. And this one was worse, even worse: sliding his fingers through the mucous and blood and slipping them under this slackless and twisting cincture, this snare. Finally digging under the child's chin and finding purchase there on an unslimed fold of its mottling skin, freeing him, unraveling this runt who now breathes, screams. Lives. Its tweaked little face gone from twilight to daybreak, bright with its howling. So small, and its mouth a bit odd, the maxilla a bit pronounced, likely to be bucked of tooth, but no matter: alive, oh alive. *Oh Doctor. Oh let me see him. Oh the poor little lad.* And then the stink of a strange first shit foul as fresh pig dung, smooth as a black slug sliding out from its anus. McBean? McKenna? What was that name? Perhaps McCarty? Yes, McCarty. That was it. That was the name. He wonders what has become of them, that family of McCartys of Irish Town. He remembers the howls and whimpers of that odd little fellow. He hears the yip and talk of coyotes somewhere near.

And he hears the nighttime tumult coming from the thoroughfare of Silver City—the shouts of the sellers, the clamor of commerce. He hears the farrier still at work in the livery—the clang of the anvil and hammer. He hears the preacher still at work in his tent, leading the ransomed and the rejoicing in the singing of *I'll Fly Away.*

Once more comes the chorus of coyotes, nearly a song itself. Melancholy what most might say. Dr. Arthur Broadwater looks skyward: there the stars everywhere stars, some bright, some dim, some seen only with a wayward glance, of looking but looking away. And that one there, steady and unshimmering. Unlike the rest of the lights in the sky. That one he knew, had learned as a boy. Jupiter, in the paw of the lion. And a comfort to see every night before it fades with the dawn. And a moon, any bit of a moon, would be a kind of a comfort. But nary a moon tonight, not even a sliver to sing to. And yet, the coyotes make their joyful noise. Dr. Arthur Broadwater says it aloud: A joyful noise.

And from just past the town comes the syncopated thump and drive of the silver dredgers and the rumblings of detonation in the mine-works.

And finally from most far off comes the lowing of the last of the bison fording the cold waters of the Arroyo San Vicente. So the same, he thinks, as the moan of a woman giving birth or summoning death.

Billy back at her bedside. Will you take some tea, mam? We have crackers, too. And cake. Your cake.

She looks past him. At nothing. At the walls. The air.

Mam, says Billy, do you know who I am?

Joe. You're my Joe, she says.

No, says Billy. I'm the other one. I'm Billy.

You, she says. I say it now and always. I never knew who you were.

I never knew who I was neither, says Billy.

Magpies roost in the chokecherry on White Hog Lane. They softly clack and chatter to each other before they sleep. Quiet now, says Billy. He swivels open his boot-heel. He adds to his list: *magpie.*

The woodstove door creaks open.

Catherine awakens and finds a gathering of Wee Folk there, dressed in their little coats and mouse-skin capes and their miniscule knitted caps, tossing bits of straw and creosote twigs into the fire and clapping their tiny mittened hands when the straws glow and curl and the twigs spark.

She raises herself up. She sees the firelight flicker across their small faces. What do you want? she says. Have you come back for the boy?

The one of them in green britches speaks. Do you mean your Billy?

No, Catherine. We come for you. We've been wanting to hear you sing an Irish tune. We've been waiting to hear.

I don't do no singing. Not no more, says Catherine.

Come now Catherine, says the one cloaked in mouse-skin. You must try while you still have your breath.

Billy's the one you want, she says. You brung him to me and you'll take him back.

Not Billy not now, says the one in green. But go on then, he says. Sing it for us, that's a good Mam.

Catherine falls back against her pillow. He wasn't mine, she says. I always known it. But I raised him best I could.

Out past the dry arroyo, the coyote has eaten its fill. The magpie flies down from its perch.

The vocalizations of the black-billed magpie (Pica hudsonia) include a melodious call to a mate, an anguished cry when seized by a predator, and a grieving song that summons other birds to what is known as a magpie funeral—a gathering around a dead or dying member of their flock.

—Birds of America and the Territories, Chapter 54: Crows, Jays, Magpies, Ravens

Chapter 42
Death Notices

SILVER CITY SENTINEL

"TRUTH UNTARNISHED"

Vol. 74, No. 9 September 21, 1874 Price 12 cents

DEATH NOTICES THIS WEEK

Antrim, Catherine age 45 years died September 16 with sons William age 13 and Joseph age 9 at her bedside. Catherine's husband could not be reached for notification of her demise. A noon Sunday service is planned on White Hog Lane.

Pearson, Issac and Pee Wee, both dead September 15. Pee Wee was put down by Mr. Pearson himself by order of the sheriff when the dog exhibited signs of rabies. Mr. Pearson died by a self-inflicted gunshot wound. Services for Isaac and Pee Wee will be held in their home on Friday noon. All welcome.

Ingleby, Malachy. Arlo Ingleby announced the death of his son Malachy, age 2 years, due to a dog bite. Malachy's mother, Martha Ingleby, died during the boy's birth. Malachy will be interred beside his her in the Blessed Lamb churchyard in Pinos Altos.

IN MEMORIAM

For our *Johnny Rand* 6/4/1855–10/6/1867, now 7 years in heaven, but forever in our hearts. We all miss you. George, Brutus, and Pincus

Help us be patient while we wait to meet you at the open gate.

LOCAL MAN REPORTS HORSE THEFT

Jacey Joe Owens over on Pepper Creek asks that we be on the lookout for a horse taken from his barn Tuesday noon. The stolen animal is a brown-and-white paint with a white muzzle. "He's my little girl's horse," said Jacey Joe.

"Deaths" and "In Memoriam" announcements should be brought to the Sentinel office before noon for the next day's edition. Written notices are preferable but May Alice in the obituary department will gladly write it out for you if you can't.

Chapter 43
We Leave the Log House
by Billy Henry Antrim
Silver City, New Mexico
September 26, 1874

She kept right on singing the Timoleague tune she liked to sing sometimes, but it was different every time, and the last time or near the last time it went

> *Feathered angels for my death,*
> *One to take away my breath.*
> *And when the final bell does toll,*
> *One to bear away my soul*

and I tell her: Mam quit it—quit the singing and the dying both but I was sorry I said it. Not then was I sorry but later or someday sorry maybe. I still heard it inside my head in the morning while we waited out front of the Hot Spot for the stage and Mr. Antrim, and it comes and him in it. Lads, he says.

The three of us we walk up the thoroughfare past the tents and the shacks out to where the road splits—straight goes on to Pinos Altos, left goes to the grave hill. Me and Joe showed him where they put her. There was no stone, just a stick the diggers had set. He stood looking down at the dirt. Catherine—that's all he said. He picked up some of the pile of earth and he held it a while. And then let it fly away from his fingers. I saw some crows go over. Like they do most mornings.

Would he just turn us loose now was what I was wondering. But he takes me one-handed by the shoulder and Joe other-handed and tell us: Sorry lads, but me taking the two of you is too too much. And I say: What about one of us? Just take Joe. Joe wouldn't be too much, I say. Him being the better brother.

Joe is holding my leg and snuffing. Mr. Antrim looks Joe over. Someone might take Joe, he says. Him being the younger. Maybe the Crowleys, he says. Been a year now since they lost their boy, so maybe those folks will take Joe. But a lad of thirteen? he tells me. Not likely we'd have much luck.

We wait while he is gone off and asking around. The log house is locked to us now, so we sit on the step with what we have, what little there is of it. Joe and his little bundle. Me and my old flintlock Collier. We had a kettle and some cups and cutlery, but that's gone, gone somewhere when we cleared out of the log house and my bird book gone with it, but it was torn up and spine-broke, and anyways I knew what all it said. So we sit on the broken porch step. It's a long time. I look at the sky and see the same crows I saw this early morning going over and now flying back where they come from come sundown. We kept on sitting. Joe said, Maybe we should be going.

And where is it we should we be going? I ask Joe.

So we keep to where we was, both of us going so cold with nothing for covers but sometimes sleeping anyway. I rouse myself up when a wagon comes rattling and it turns down White Hog Lane with a lantern swinging on the side bow. It's the Crowleys—the mister and the missus I seen selling trousers in the thoroughfare. Crowley's Trousers. I once picked me up a pair of course not paying and am wearing those very ones, so I hope they wouldn't notice. And once I seen them singing in the tent of *Ransomed and Rejoicing* with their pale little boy Orville propped up between them and waiting on his healing. They were saying the amens and the halleluiahs like they were supposed to but their boy died all the same.

Whoa now Tucker, Mister Crowley tells the horse he's driving and he pulls up right in front. Missus and Mister Crowley look both of us over and he tells her something into her bonnet and she says something back with her hand hiding her mouth and he says: I'll ask them. He turns back to us and says: Which of you be the younger brother?

Mister Crowley makes room for Joe among the bundles—piles of trousers and bales of canvas—and he tells me: Mr. Antrim says to say he be back for you right shortly.

Yes sir, I say.

I pet the horse. He's a bay, the same as old Finn was but no stripe, just snip of white on his nose. He nickers low and leans into me a little.

Been around horses, have you? says Mister Crowley.

But I don't say about that.

Well lad you're good with 'em, he says. It takes a certain kind to know the beasts.

What kind is that? is what I want to say but I don't say it.

Then we shake hands, me and Joe—like men do—and I tell him: Alright now Little Man—what I still call him though he's big as me—We'll be seeing you then.

Go on Tucker, Mr. Crowley tells his horse. Time to get on now.

And then they pull away.

Joe turns around in the wagon so he's facing back my way and I wave but he doesn't wave me back not then or when the wagon rolls down White Hog Lane and turns and turns once more and gone. Then there I am. Being still and quiet the way Mam was after the last of her blood came up and we were pulling the covers over. The way my Da used to be telling me: Keep quiet is what he told me. Keep your gob shut when it needs shutting and pay attention to what is coming so you'll hear just what you're supposed to hear.

And soon enough it comes—a whippoorwill out there in the dark, calling its name and my name over and over the way they do: poor-will, poor-will. But we're not poor wills. Not neither of us is. Even with everyone going off and leaving us be, we're not poor wills. I'm still here and he's out there, close by likely. Folks who'll be hunting him can hunt all they want, they won't be finding him. And when the sun comes up they'll be thinking: Now I'll get him, now I'll catch him but no they won't, not even if he's right there in front of them sitting at their feet. Likely they'll wear themselves out with looking. And if it comes down to it, I'll do what my Da told me: Get them off guard, then clobber them. That's the way of it, it is. Will be from here on. When we went to Wichita I thought I found a way to live. But it wasn't so. And neither was it so here in Silver City.

The whippoorwill (Antrostomus arizonae) derives its name from its call, a repetitive "poor-will" uttered throughout the night. It is seldom seen due to its cryptically colored plumage. If approached by humans, it will remain where it rests unless almost stepped on, and only then take flight.

—Birds of America and the Territories, Chapter 43: Goatsuckers, Nightjars

Chapter 44
The First Cold Winds Coming
Silver City, New Mexico
October 1, 1874 – The Moon of Yellow Trees

He was asleep, back in the empty log house, having nowhere else to go when the first wind of winter swept down from the mountains of Los Pinos Altos and rode above the waters of Arroyo San Vicente in that space the river makes. The sliver of new moon quaked and dished in the eddies along the banks where the cottonwoods turned their catkins loose and acorns rattled down from the chinquapins. The wind was scarcely a sigh in the last of the leaves, a hush in the needles of the ponderosa pine and upland piñon, although for some—those on the brink of things—it came as a whistling, as the low and somber notes from an ancestral puebloan's bird-bone flute to summon up Brother Coyote or Big Owl, or a shaman's composition to carry a soul to the Land of Ever Summer, even now in this cold season and a greater cold coming, in this month the Apache call the Moon of Yellow Trees.

He heard it in his sleep, hollow and resonant, coming as it had for as long as the rivers were and the mountains were and long before The People were, and loud enough—this harbinger of winter's misery—loud enough for a lone coyote to hear and answer with the first gust-ruffling of its fur and then to stop mid-trot along the hunt-worn path he followed through the bigleaf sage, past the dens where the ground squirrel and the Apache pocket mouse will winter until the coyotes dig them out and take them in their sleep. But now with day breaking, the hunt has ended and the new moon is descending. He turns off the hardpan path and takes to the road at the edge of the end of the town. He pauses with forepaw raised, poised, his ears aswivel, his snout testing the air. And yes, there it is—the scent of the kind of cold that will split rock and stop a river and snap a sinew. Yes, it's come. Winter and the new moon, both—just a bit of a moon, a scant rib of a moon in moonset as he utters a low whine of lament.

Billy hears the song in the stovepipe. He had not shut the damper and the flue shook as freezing air poured down into the room through the open woodstove door. He had not built a fire. There should be no smoke rising from the chimneystack of a house where the tenants had moved on. He lay on the bare slatted bed he had shared with his brother and he listened. Daybreak birdsong. The rumble of a wagon coming on. Louder now. Passing by. Rumbling away. Then nothing. Then the bark, then the whine. Billy crept to the window and raised himself up to eye level at the sill and looked out. Now in the dim light of dawning, cowbirds crouch and peck in the roadside dust. But a larger shape beyond. At first he was not sure what it was, that shape a ways down the road. Small deer or big rabbit or dog. But none of these, no. He had never seen a coyote standing still. And this one seemed to be gazing at him, seeing the little bit of Billy that showed above the sill. But he knew this could not be so—it was too far away. And he knew it could not be so when it seemed to Billy that he might become a coyote, clever coyote, stopping in the road and seeing himself peeking from a window in an empty house, cold but too cautious to lay a fire in the stove and wondering what sort of life would his new life be but knowing what was left of it would be without restraint and lived in joyful desolation.

The cowbird (Molothrus ater) *does not raise her own young, but instead lays her eggs in the nest of another bird species (the host) when the owner of the nest is momentarily absent. The cowbird egg hatches first, and the cowbird hatchling pushes the other eggs out of the nest and is raised by the host bird.*

Occasionally, if the host species recognizes the cowbird nestling as an intruder, she will refuse it food, fling it to the ground, or peck it to death.

—Birds of America and the Territories, Chapter 74: Blackbirds, Cowbirds, Grackles, Orioles

Chapter 45
Astray in Silver City
1874 to 1875—A Year of Apache Moons

Cold mornings. Crows warm themselves on chimney rims.

The colors of dawn light the rifted hills facing east.

Now the days of Billy astray in Silver City.

He was seen in the thoroughfare, and along the dry arroyo, and walking the pueblo road. He was seen in the restaurants, wiping tables, pouring coffee. He washed plates and pots and platters in the kitchen of the Cave-In Café and peeled potatoes in the Tiltin Timbers. He swept the floor at the assay office and mucked out the stalls in the livery. He hauled water for the water-seller, nails for the farrier. He ran hot meals from the Timbers and the Cave-In to the guests in the Dance Hall and to devotees and those desperately seeking cures at the tent meetings and to the miners at their diggings.

Dr. Arthur Broadwater caught sight of him hurrying along with a canvas delivery bag on his back and rows of lunch buckets and baskets slung shoulder to shoulder on a pole. He noted the boy was thinner, not dressed for winter. He watched him take orders from the men lined up at the assay office and vendors at their wagons and people in the street. Yes, sir. That's four orders of beefsteak and fried potatoes. Whiskey, beer, or water? Thank you, much appreciated. They've got some nice pie over at the Timbers. Could fetch you a few, save you the trouble. Apple or pear?

The doctor had been sitting out front of his medical tent where his new banners had been erected (*Rejuvenating Treatments on Premises—Free Antitubercular Tincture Included*). He sat with his chair slightly atilt to the rear, his feet upon his display table (a few bottles of his *Bodily Rejuvenator* at the ready for purchase by passersby) and reading the morning edition of the *Silver City Sentinel* when he spied Billy on the other side of the thoroughfare, gazing at the sky. He lowered his newspaper, and, as folks will do, looked up. A hawk was flying over, a small varmint of some kind—mouse or ground squirrel or rat—in its talons. And he watched it fly high and then out of sight.

When he looked over at Billy again, the boy had taken a pencil from his hatband and a scrap from his boot-heel, and was writing on the paper pressed to his knee.

Dr. Arthur put down his newspaper and crossed the street.

What was that? says Dr. Arthur Broadwater.

What was what? says Billy, and he slide his list back into his trouser pocket.

That what just flew over. Some kind of buzzard was it?

Hawk, says Billy. Red-tailed.

Well now, says Dr. Arthur Broadwater. How do you know? They all look pretty much the same to me.

It has a red tail. That's how.

You don't say, says Dr. Arthur Broadwater.

Billy reaches up and tucks his pencil stub back under the hatband.

I attended to your mother, says Dr. Arthur Broadwater. It's nearly a year now she's gone, isn't it?

I've got to git, says Billy.

Where is it you're staying these days? says Dr. Arthur Broadwater.

Here and there.

I see. And where might that be? said Dr. Arthur Broadwater.

Here, mostly. Depends.

My place is right over there, says Dr. Arthur Broadwater. Fourth tent down. See it?

I know where, says Billy. Been there.

There's a spare cot for folks coming in for doctoring, but most times they send someone over to fetch me out.

Well, says Billy.

Folks pay me in pies and potatoes, if they pay me at all. I've got plenty, if you're hungry. Are you?

Ain't everybody? Says Billy.

Listen. Even if I'm not there, just go on in, says Dr. Arthur Broadwater. Anytime.

Just might, says Billy.

You come by then, says Dr. Arthur Broadwater. Come say hey.

Now I've got to git, says Billy.

The red-tailed hawk (Buteo jamaicensis) takes small rodents and snakes in its talons and swallow them whole. But when it captures other birds, they are first beheaded and plucked.

—Birds of America and the Territories, Chapter 15: Eagles, Hawks, Kites

Jacinta, the little señorita, went looking for Billy at the log house on White Hog Lane one Sunday early. She climbed the shifting steps, took hold of the wobbly newel post. Lightly knocked. Listened. Billy, she said. Billy? She leaned over the step-rail and put her face to the window and her shadowed shape filled the square of light on the floor boards. She could see the stove but there were no signs of a fire glowing between the seams. A dog barked from somewhere, and she took it as a warning and hurried away from the log house and down White Hog Lane and back to a busier part of town.

Midwinter, she returned to the log house when she saw smoke rising from the chimney stack. The broken post had been hammered fast.

And the rotted stair had been replaced with a new unpainted board that squeaked under her step. Before she could knock or call out for Billy, she heard the bolt, the latch, the hinges. The door was opened. An old man stood at the top of the step, bearded and bent, wearing long-underwear sagged out at the knees, stained on the crotch and the chest, his eyes all gone to a milky gray and wandering deep in their sockets. Who's there? he said. He reached his arms out into the darkness before him as a sleepwalker might, but she had already stepped back into the street. I know someone's there, he said.

Lo siento señor, she said.

What do you want?

Nada, she said. Perdóname. And went on.

In early spring she caught sight of Billy across the thoroughfare, sitting out front of the medical tent with Dr. Arthur Broadwater, both of them smoking cheroots. Billy's hair had grown long, to his shoulders, and he wore a frayed length of burlap sacking around his neck against the cold. She called to him and she crossed the roadway and she came to him.

Poor little one, she said. Mi pobrecito.

Gently he took her by the shoulders. He turned her around and away from him, and sent her walking toward the street.

It was on some late winter sunrise that Singing-Stick too caught sight of Billy when she peered out from the flap of her wickiup—Billy there, beside the stone circle where she made her fire, setting down a bundle of fuelwood. She saw him again at the rubbish heap, shaking a dusting of snow from his throw-away clothes. She did not see him at all the next spring, and she did not see him that summer. She never left the pueblo and he did not come to her. It was not until the autumn one day at dusk when the cottonwoods had already gone yellow and her crowd of the failing and infirm were dispersing that she saw him. Jimmy Bad Drum with the festering foot spotted Billy on the ridge above the Chiricauhua pueblo and called to her and pointed.

There. Billy in silhouette, sighting the birds crossing the continent ahead of the coming cold, some from as far north as the Yukon and boreal forests, and as far east as Labrador and Thunder Bay. Some coming from as near as the Pecos Plains and La Luna Blanca and summer habitats in the Sangre de Cristos and the Sonora and the basins of the Chihuahua. He knows them by their songs and by the ways they make their way through the air: the rapid wing-strokes of bufflehead ducks through the cold autumn air, the undulating flight of finches as they drop and rise and drop and rise as if they might be mechanical birds in a potshot arcade.

Bufflehead ducks (Bucephala albeola) will escort their newly hatched ducklings to the water from the nest, but that is the only time in their lives that they walk on dry land.

—Birds of America and the Territories, Chapter 13: Swans, Geese, Ducks, Mergansers

The crimson plumage of the male house finch (Haemorhous mexicanus) is due to the assortment of red berries in its diet.

Chapter 76: Grosbeaks, Finches

They passed above him on the updrafts off the ridge as a scattering of birds in loose flocks, and geese in skeins of hundreds, and passenger pigeons in clusters so dense they seemed to be billows of smoke or swarms of bees or locusts on the move, shifting position in unison—a thousand birds—no ten thousands, and together flashing gray to white to gone with a wing-tilt and turn.

Some birds in pairs. Some solitary fliers, alone amid the multitudes of their kind, but all summoned away from what had been home for a spring and a summer by the new slant of the sun and the early frost on the grass. High and lonesome came their calls over lakes and plains, over rivers and ranges, against headwinds and through the high thin air, their causeways created by the pull of the poles on the magnetized bits of the planet deep within their brains and the motions of the stars. He heard the bleating of geese, plaintive and piercing his heart as it would—it must—the heart of anyone who understands that the journey's end will be sepulcher or earth or urn. That laceration of the heart might be cleanly made as if by flint flaked to a deadly point, or the kind of cut that festers with regret, suppurates former despicable deeds, and thereby kills slowly with the seep of decay and despair spreading through the body—and why would it matter which?

Singing-Stick looked to the ridge. There the leaves loosed of the cottonwoods and spinning in their disorderly courses, but the birds unswerving. A solitary thrush. A flock of ducks. A skein of geese borne on a flyway wind. A harrier hawk rising, beat-beat-glide.

But it was not Billy that she saw there in silhouette, not Billy in the shape of Billy, no—but instead the boy in his coyote shape, sitting on his haunches, unfolding his list.

Mice and voles are the preferred prey of the northern harrier hawk (Circus hudsonius) but it will also take geese and rabbits, killing these larger animals by carrying them to water and plunging them under.

—Birds of America and the Territories, Chapter 15: Eagles, Hawks, Kites

A pair of javelinas and four piglets snuffle in a patch of prickly pear.

Townsend's solitaire (Myadestes townsendi) often goes unnoticed. When this thrush is observed, it is alone, as its name implies. Its call-note has been likened to the tolling of a distant bell. It frequently sings during flight.

Chapter 63: Thrushes, Solitaires, Bluebirds

Chapter 46
No Danger to the Public

SILVER CITY SENTINEL

"TRUTH UNTARNISHED"

Vol. 74, No. 11 November 1, 1874 Price 12 cents

LOCAL DOCTOR SOUGHT IN CHILD'S DEATH

Dr. Arthur W. Broadwater, age 38, is currently wanted by Grant County authorities for failure to appear at the deposition regarding the September death of Silver City resident Malachy Ingelby, age 2 years. The boy's father, Arlo Ingleby, has publicly accused Dr. Broadwater of negligence, specifically his failure to recognize that his son's symptoms were that of rabies, which ultimately led to the boy's death.

Attempts to locate Broadwater have been unsuccessful. He attended Malachy's funeral service at the *Church of the Blessed Lamb*, but left abruptly after the boy's father produced a pistol and fired at Broadwater, missing him but shooting off the foot off a plaster saint and causing funeral attendees to scatter. Broadwater abandoned his tent, leaving behind several crates of *Broadwater's Bodily Rejuvinator.*

Dr. Broadwater's medical credentials are under investigation. Reports from Philadelphia indicate that he may have not completed medical training. However, many residents have come to his defense, stating he treated them even when they could not afford to pay. In addition, he allowed an orphaned youth to share his lodging and victuals. Jacob Cornelisse recalled "the doc saved my leg" after a mineshaft mishap. George

Hirschberger, whom Broadwater treated for dropsy remarked, “He was a good dresser.”

Broadwater has not as been officially charged with a crime, but an individual fitting his description was seen entering the livery and leaving on a sorrel mare belonging to a hotel patron. The horse has not been recovered and the culprit has eluded capture. Broadwater is 6 ft tall, approximately 180 lbs. and sports a mustache which he may have shaved to alter his appearance. Sheriff Whitehill asks that citizens contact local authorities if Broadwater is spotted, but adds there is no reason to believe that he is a danger to the public.

QUOTE OF THE DAY

☞ *A merry heart doeth good as medicine, but a broken spirit drieth the bones.*
—Proverbs 17:22

Chapter 47
Last Days and Dreams in Silver City
November 10, 1874 – The Moon of Moving Waters

Now again night. Billy is bedded down in the somewheres of Silver City but remembering his nights back in Wichita in the shuttered house, perched on the bedrail and waiting for the warm midwestern wind to swing the shutters wide, and then taking to the air, taking flight away from the shuttered house, over the barn where the horse Finn slept, the fields where the mice traveled the corridors of Kansas corn, the forests of oak and ash where the deer settle in, the part of the river where the buzzards waited for the pieces of cows to tumble from the slaughterhouse pipe, and past the upriver riffles where the water is pure and swift. But the winged dreams of Wichita are long gone. Billy now sleeps in the hidey-holes of Silver City, in empty sheds and abandoned wagons, and in sleep he is winged once more, and once more taking flight, this time over the tents and shacks of the ramshackle parts of Silver City, through the rising smoke of the log house on White Hog Lane that was once his home, over the graveyard where the tidy rows of oblong holes await their tenants, and at last leaving the town behind and skimming the tops of the piñon pines and paolo verde, then following the pale sands of the sandy wash-bottom that meanders through the hardpan. Now gaining altitude above the ridge. Now updraft. Now headwind. Stronger now against it. Wingbeat. Wingbeat. Higher now. Goodbye. Get on. Got to get on.

Scaup ducks are seen in a quiet inlet of the Gila River, brought down by the storms during their journey from Saskatchewan to the Gulf of Mexico.

Blue-winged teal begin flocking in a marsh pond, gathering for the fall migration as they do every year in the Moon of Moving Waters.

Large flocks of scaup ducks (Aythya marila) gather on rivers where they ride facing upstream and into the current. After being carried backward for a length of several hundred yards, a scaup will fly back to the head of the flock to maintain position.

—Birds of America and the Territories, Chapter 13: Swans, Geese, Ducks, Mergansers

Four elk were shot dead at dusk while bedding down in a grove of junipers. Skinned, gutted. Two unborn calves were left behind, dusted with the early snow.

Blue-winged teal (Spatula discors) are the first ducks to migrate south in autumn and the last ones to return north in springtime.

Chapter 13: Swans, Geese, Ducks, Mergansers

Chapter 48
My First Arrest and Swift Departure
by Billy Bonney McCarty Antrim
September 23, 1875

What I took wasn't much, but enough to get me sent to the Silver City lockup. A room off the courthouse kitchen was all they have for a cell in this town, since citizens hereabouts take care of thieving and murdering mainly by their own selves and not needing help from the law. Shootouts and lynchings and such being preferable to folks been wronged and no patience for some desperado just waiting on the circuit judge, which could be a stretch if his honor has met with mishap, is how they put it. In this territory, it would more likely he's met with a waylay along the way and left for the buzzard birds. Who we waiting on? I ask Sheriff Whitehill.

Judge Oliver, says the sheriff. Been sent for. Old Hard-On Ollie. Been twice shot by stick-up men, twice ambushed by Apache, and once rode into town with an arrow in his ass, but you can't kill off old Ollie no how. He'll be here. Likely leaving Santa Fe sometime soon, the sheriff says, but don't count on him being too happy sent all this way for a delinquent such as you.

And I am thinking: No he won't be too happy about that, me being just small potatoes. Those little red ones you dig in the spring ha ha. I was surprised the sheriff even bothered to run me in. Sheriff Whitehill. But he had to. That sneaky Ira Rand from over at the Cave-In Café. He's the one made a federal case out of a missing T-bone and a buckwheat biscuit. Red-handed, he said. And telling the sheriff I done it once before. Which wasn't true at all, no sir. I been robbing his dinners all winter.

Taking you in, the sheriff had said, and I didn't make a fuss when he showed me the room off the kitchen. You're here till the hearing, he says. So go on then, make yourself to home.

There's a little bed. A boy-size bed. A table for sitting at and taking dinner. A cane-bottom chair with the cane part busted. A window to look out of between the bars and some old lacey curtains strung across there on a stick. There's a fireplace full of ash and cold stones in the grate. There's the sheriff saying he'll go easy on me. Behave yourself Billy and I'll go easy, he says when he sees my trousers gone to threads at the knees and my boots scraped-up and shoddy and me looking long at the boots he is sporting. Black bullhide buckaroos with yellow stitching and sewn-in yellow stars, like I never saw the likes of.

If there's some test for sheriff, I said, then sign me up if its paying for boots of such a degree. Unless I'm disqualified getting arrested.

These, he says. The wifey sent for them special order from Abilene. Or Laredo maybe. For our anniversary, he said.

Which one? I ask him.

Our twenty year, me and my Sally. These boots, I first get 'em I never wore 'em. Saving 'em God know what for. Now I wear 'em or they be outlasting me. My Sally. Gone a year she is, he says and he's tearing up some. Then he's fussing with the window curtains, old and faded lace things, tucking them behind the bars. Then he's poking in the fireplace with the fire iron though there's nothing needing poking, only ash. Then he says, But you—young feller like yourself. I seen that little señorita scouting you.

Which one? I say, and it got him to laughing a little. Then he gave me a wool blanket for the bed—brown with green and blue stripes wove in—and he gives me a pillow. He sets an old tin-punch lantern down on the table, and a stone pitcher and a stone cup same color as the pitcher. Then he works the door latch up and down. This here door, he says. I've got deputy Bedloe sitting right outside, he says. Isn't you Izzy? he calls.

The deputy pokes his head in. You call me, Sheriff?

Just letting the kid here know he's got no call for rascality.

He ain't no kid.

He's thirteen. You thirteen, Billy?

Fourteen, I tell him. I already turned fourteen.

He's just a small man is what he is, says Deputy Izzy. Them Irish, they got dwarf people. Most of them is over in Irishland. Ain't that so Billyboy? says the deputy.

Sure is, I tell the deputy. Back in Irishland there's us dwarf people all over.

They come smaller than you, don't they? Some real teensy.

Alright Izz, says the sheriff.

You ever seen them real teensy ones? the deputy says.

Not too many, I tell him. They mostly hide out in tree-holes and stones.

Alright Izz, the sheriff says. You go have your dinner and then get yourself back here straightaway. You Billy, you'll just have to sit tight a while. Meantime you're locked in and I've got Izzy right outside the door.

Right outside, says the deputy and he looks at me. Got me a Colt here, he says and he pats his right hip. Got me a Schoefield here, and he pats the left. Been keeping both of them nice and handy, he says. Try anything and out it comes to pop you.

Which one? I ask him.

I wait out the day.

Sheriff Whitehill brings me dinner. Buttered cornbread and a bowl of Brunswick stew. Two gingersnap cookies. And milk. You're not too grown up for milk now, are you Billy? he says. He sits with me while I eat. We're talking. I'm thinking. I'm making a list in my mind, what I need when I leave this town, so as not to forget:

new hat
jacket
pants
canteen
pistol
matches
another pistol
pencil
sour balls
ammo
biscuits
horse

but mainly it's him talking. Telling me about how there's cattle rustlers camped along the Pecos, and how about that new Mercantile store supposedly coming to Lincoln, and how about the doctor skipping town so what in hell is sick folks around here supposed to do for doctoring, and wasn't that a hell of a wind last night? Tore loose a tent or two out along the thoroughfare and flies one away like a big balloon. Hereabouts, he says, the wind gets to blowing so bad that when it stops the chickens fall over. Did I ever hear that one, he says, and I tell him no never did. Though I did. I guess everyone did.

It was getting near to sunset then. Outside the birds start their chittering the way they do before dark, some with their little chips and tweets coming down the chimney, and some would be somewhere else hopping branch to branch in the cottonwoods and the sage along the dry arroyo, flitting and jittery the way I seen them do, finding their places to bed down safe and I'm getting a little of the jitters myself waiting for the sheriff to get on. Well then, he says, let's get you settled, and he slaps his knees and gets up. He lights the tin-punch lantern and it spatters a pattern of stars along the walls. He dims down the wick. He pours a cup of water from the stone pitcher into the stone cup. Fixes the pillow square on the bed. Spreads the wool blanket out. Was my boy's bed, the sheriff says.

He pulls the shabby old curtains shut.

And these, he says. Was my Sally sewed these curtains, he says. Used to be hanging in our boy's room.

He's grown now, I say. Your boy.

No. He never got the chance to get grown, says the sheriff. He'd be near about your age, if he had.

And the sheriff doesn't tell anything more about that and I'm not asking. He takes up my plate and spoon. He takes ahold of the door latch and gives it a jiggle. Izz? You awake? You out here? he calls.

Been out here. Just waiting on you Sheriff, calls the Deputy.

Billy, you need something, you just knock. Izzy's right outside. Hear that, Izz?

At your every beck and call Billyboy, calls Izzy.

Unlock me out then, the sheriff tells him and then he's gone.

They came soon enough, the swifts did, squeaking soft and sending bits of soot and bird shit to the hearth as they come zipping a ways down the chimney and clinging to the brick walls like bats. I've seen them before. Before I got myself into this fix. Back in Wichita Kansas they'd be flying above the river hunting mayflies and catching wind-spiders spinning out their spidery threads, and come sundown one by one diving down the chimney of our shuttered house. And here in Silver City I seen them, going over the town, flitting over the courthouse, here where they have me captured.

I set my ear to the door and lean myself into it and keep it there a good long while until Deputy Izzy comes knocking right where I planted by ear. Whoa. It nearly set me off, but I stay put. I stay still. Hey, you up Billyboy? he says. Hey, he says. But I keep my gob shut like I'm supposed to, like my Da, my old Da used to tell me: Billy, you keep your gob shut when it needs shutting and pay attention to what is coming so you'll hear just what you're supposed to hear.

And it comes. Sure it does. Right what I'm supposed to hear. The sound of a chair getting shifted around on the boards. Likely the deputy making himself comfortable and paying no mind to a desperado such as me cooped up in a cozy little room off the courthouse kitchen with a dead boy's curtains hanging in the window and me supposed to be asleep by now in a dead boy's bed. Likely not considering that I could might set the whole damn place afire with the lit lantern they left me, and likely not concerned, no not one bit about leaving a criminal in a lockup with a hearth as cold as little duck's ass.

Not considering none of it.

In another minute more comes of what I'm supposed to hear, which is nothing but calm and quiet on the other side of the locked latched door. I wait some more and now here comes a wheezy sort of whistle, a snore, a whistle, a snore, a longer drawn-out snort snort snort and you get the idea.

I get myself down in the ash and see up the chimney. There's the clump of darkness along one wall. That being the birds. I know the kind. Already on my list. *Chimney swift*. And way up top there's the chimney rim lit by the moon and a nice square of starry sky. That being where I'm going.

Worst part is getting started, but I plant my feet on one wall and get my back and hands hard against the other and push up, push up. A slow go, I tell you. The slowest go, with each push against the bricks hardly an inch higher and all the while I'm listening for the door latch and the deputy. And listening to the birds making little peeps—the whole huddled pack of them holding fast to the wall with their bellies to the bricks and their eyes shining like little black seeds by what bit of moonlight there is. Likely they're surprised seeing someone sidling past them on the way up their chimney. And likely they're thinking: Well hell Billy, now ain't you the clever one sneaking on out the same way we come in.

Chimney swifts (Chaetura pelagica) bathe by gliding above lakes and ponds, striking the water with their breasts, and without the slightest lapse in speed, continue their path of flight.

—Birds of America and the Territories, Chapter 44: Swifts

Chapter 49
First Light and Last Look
Silver City, New Mexico
September 24, 1875 – The Moon of Leaving Geese

He stood on the roof, bent and breathing hard, his back abraded clean through his shirt by the press and scrape of his ascent, his hands bloodied by the roughened chimney bricks, and he licked at the wounds on his palms like a dog. It had been a slow climb. The moon had moved closer to the horizon illuminating the slopes of Los Pinos Altos where the first snow of the season lay brilliant white against the outcroppings of rock and where a family of ravens had hunched and roosted for the night, now stirring with the coming sun. To the south spread the desert, the span of hardpan flat and pale and broken only by wash, boulder, dry arroyo. Beyond that was the Apache pueblo, and beyond the pueblo the ridge with its scattering of piñon, and beyond the ridge just stars and sky. He stood and he looked all about and below him. There the cemetery just outside of town, where the gravestones and the mounds beside the waiting holes are shadowed long by the slant of the descending moon. There the shapes of shacks and cabins out past the thoroughfare. There the thoroughfare, the sleeping thoroughfare, with a few lanterns still lit and illuminating from within the tents and the canvas-covered wagons. There a light in the corner food stand where the little señorita has already fired up her adobe stove and a thin sting of smoke is rising. There the last campfires and cooking fires gone to embers. The torches left to burn themselves out but still glowing. A dog going midroad—or what seemed to be a dog and then closer—but no. A lone coyote. Billy considered calling to it. A soft yip yip would do: I'm here, brother coyote, up here and it is only the two of us awake now in the world, only the two of us knowing what might be dreams and what are not while the world sleeps. But there was no need to call. No need. Brother coyote on its way down the thoroughfare was watching our Billy on the courthouse roof, and as it passed, lifted its snout to the scent of Billy's blood on the air. And where the thoroughfare ended without torch or campfire or lantern, it turned for one last look back at Billy before trotting away into the night.

There was some wind. Billy had left behind his raggedy coat—it would have been too tight for his trip up the chimney—and early on, partway up he had tossed his hat down to the hearth, and he was cold. The wind carried the smell of the drying September sage and the smell of white cedar smoke from the fire that the Apache woman Singing-Stick set near her wickiup before every dawn. Now he knew he must get on. Now the moon was nearly set. Now the morning stars were shining. Mercury. Venus. Names he did not know, and did not know what these celestial lights might be, but considered they could be whatever kind of cover the sky was, or perhaps perforations in a great tin-punch lantern and night being its dimming when the great wick of the sun is turned down by the concealed hand of the creator of all things that walk the earth or burrow under or swim in the rivers or ride above ridges on updrafts by day and by night travel on tailwinds that bear them along or the wuthering headwinds that bring them down.

He thought that he might see the geese, might hear their hooting overhead in the cold morning air. Another fall migration, the closing of another year. Another passing of the Moon of Leaving Geese.

He stood a moment more, waiting for their hooting calls but none came.

The voice of the raven (Corvus corax) is similar to that of a croaking toad, but it is able to mimic any sound. If a member of the flock is missing or lost, another raven will reproduce the calls of the lost bird to hasten its return.

—*Birds of America and the Territories, Chapter 54: Crows, Jays, Magpies, Ravens*

Chapter 50
Up the Chimney

SILVER CITY SENTINEL

"TRUTH UNTARNISHED"

Vol. 75, No. 9 September 25, 1875 Price 12 cents

SUSPECT ESCAPES, DEPUTY ON DUTY

A local youth detained in the courthouse lockup broke out sometime last night. William Antrim, who also goes by Billy and William Bonney McCarty, had been accused of stealing food from the Cave-In Café where he was employed. After his escape he returned to the Café and absconded with two six-shooters that had been hidden in the cutlery cabinet and a jar of sourball candies. In addition, the City Laundry is missing a bundle of clothes and the livery is short a horse. The boy's disappearance was discovered when Sheriff Whitehill arrived with Billy's breakfast. The window bars were intact and the door remained locked, so it is presumed that he escaped up the chimney. Deputy Isadore "Izzy" Bedloe was on duty at the time and when questioned by Sheriff Whitehill stated, "I ain't been drinking, I swear it." Billy was familiar to Silver City residents and known for his speedy dinner deliveries, courteous service, and pleasant manner. However, in light of the missing pistols, he may be armed and dangerous. He is fourteen years old, 5' 6" with a slim build and slightly protruding ears and teeth. Sheriff Whitehill accepted responsibility for the boy's departure up the chimney. "I should have figured it," said the sheriff. "He was just a little feller."

THIS WEEK IN SILVER CITY

Sept 20. Julia Elmers reported a large white dog tearing up her petunias.

Sept 21. Sheriff Whitehill responded to an altercation at the Timbers restaurant. Customer Bob Bobenhouser refused to pay for his chicken dinner and was shot dead by proprietor Jack Goodnough who claims self-defense.

Sept 23. Welcome to Miss Susan Bobenhouser arriving from Carson City but too late for her brother Bob's funeral service held earlier this week.

QUOTE OF THE DAY

☞ *Behold! The man was gone and all the birds had fled.*
—Jeremiah 4:25

Chapter 51
"The Livery is Short a Horse"
—*Silver City Sentinel*, Sept 25, 1875

The horse was a Choctaw piebald, its great-granddam a brindle mare called *Ofunlo*—the Owl. She was named for her owlish eyes and her wise ways by the family Shakcuckla in the clan of the Beloved Crayfish People.

In the fall of 1831, the brindle mare wore tiny bells that the family Shakcuckla tied to her mane so they would hear music as they trudged the thousand miles in silence, and the bells tinkled as she walked with the other Choctaw horses—the pintos and the buckskins and the yellow duns—and the other families of Choctaws—the clans of the Reed People and the Divided People as they passed through the groves of cherrybark oak and palmetto and touched the trees and told the sweet gum and tupelo goodbye, there at the beginning of the long Trail of Tears on the flat-topped Mississippi ridge between the Petickfa Creek and the Creek of Black Water.

For a while, they went along a barely trampled path, but by the final trek of the Choctaw thousands—the tens of thousands—it was worn away to shoulder deep and deeper still, so that settlers of the countryside sitting on their porches or tilling the fields or hunting in the wildwoods would hear the faint tinkling of bells and the footfall of the multitudes, but would see only the heads of horses passing by on that nearly a tunnel of a trail.

For a while, the brindle mare had carried what little the family Shakcuckla had been permitted to bring: parched corn and dried pumpkin and smoked strips of flatfish and chub, and they shared the corn with her, and they drank as she did from the streams and springs. And when all they had carried was gone, the brindle mare showed the family Shakcuckla the sprigs of peppergrass and the hogweed trailside and the family clans of the Beloved Crayfish people and the Reed People and the Divided People went into the meadows as far as the soldiers allowed them to go. And they fell to all fours and pulled at the peppergrass and the hogweed with their mouths like horses.

For a while, the brindle mare carried the lame grandmother called Pokes With Her Little Finger until they reached the border of the Arkansas Territory. There the old woman climbed down and sat herself in the dust and decided to die.

For a while, the brindle mare carried the young boy called Plays Where Tadpoles Live, and as the boy rode he remembered the pools along the Creek of Black Water where the tadpoles wriggled through his fingers, and he saw them in his mind before he died in a fever. The mother of the boy was called Sits In Pretty Places and she put a bit of peppergrass and a pumpkin seed in his slack mouth and she wound his body in strips of blanket. The father of the boy was called Drinks The Juice Of Stones, and he asked the soldiers if he might stop and build the *illi a shol*—the high bier—for the body of the boy so it would return to the power of the sun. But the soldiers put their hands on their rifles and said there was no time, no time, you must go on, and the father of the boy tied the body as high as he was able to a limb of a loblolly pine. And with the brindle mare *Ofunlo* beside them and the tiny bells in her mane tinkling, the mother and the father of the boy they left tied to the loblolly pine walked on.

For a while, the woman called Sits In Pretty Places walked beside the brindle mare and beside the man called Drinks The Juice Of Stones until she could walk no more.

For a while more, the woman rode on the back of the brindle mare until they neared the end of the Trail of Tears, and there the snow began, and her pains came on. The brindle mare stamped and pawed the earth at the woman's cries and at the smell of birth waters that seeped out of her. The soldiers lowered their rifles, and the woman climbed down from the brindle mare leaving a circle of blood where she had sat, and the last of the family Shakcuckla in the clan of the Beloved Crayfish People were permitted to stop, to build a fire, to take shelter under the brindle mare. The snow blew hard around them and the water in the hollow hoofprints of the horse became cups of ice, and in the night the baby they named Brought To The World In A Blizzard was born. The woman called Sits In Pretty Places held the child to her body but come morning they both were the color of the snow. The man called Drinks The Juice Of Stones tied them together. He threw the rope that bound them over the limb of a honey locust and the snow on the limb filtered down in a small separate storm as he hoisted the two of them hand over hand as high as he could to the power of the morning sun. The sky had cleared. The wind had stilled. Small stars, little flames in the bright fallen snow. A nuthatch circled down the trunk of the honey locust. A tree creeper crept. A crow and his consorts alighted beside the bodies. Somewhere beyond lay the land of Indian Resettlement. The brindle mare nickered and stamped and the snow that had settled in her mane flew around her. And with the brindle mare beside him and the last of her tiny bells tinkling, the man called Drinks The Juice Of Stones went on.

He did not look back to see the crows in the honey locust. He knew the crows would come as that is what crows do. He knew they would take the meat of the woman and the child into their mouths and their stomachs and fly away higher than the highest limbs of the honey locust that he could ever reach.

And he walked on.

The man called Drinks The Juice Of Stones of the clan of the Beloved Crayfish People, and the families of the Reed People and the

Divided People walked on. Come dusk, each took their turnip and spoonful of parched corn from the soldiers and they ate sheltered under their horses and looked out into the night where the small cold lights of fireflies flashed and the glowing heart of *Hashok Okwa Huiga* rose from the swamp smoke and floated on the forest mist. Come dawn, they lifted the dead into the trees, and they walked on.

They walked on. The brindle mare called *Ofula* and the piebalds and the buckskins and the yellow duns all walked on to the confluence of the Red and Kiamichi Rivers where whooping cranes foraged in the shallows, but at the arrival of those thousands of the displaced and dying, the cranes rose together in a great wave of white on their black-fringed wings with the tangles of wet river-reed dripping from their strange back-jointed legs. The brindle mare and the other Choctaw horses trembled and shied at the sight of it and the cranes circled above the river in the shape of a bright cloud for as long as their wings would hold them in the air and finally the birds turned and rode the north wind away from the river, away from the dying and the nearly dead, there at the new Territory of Indian Resettlement at the end of the Trail of Tears

The man called Drinks The Juice Of Stones—of the Family Shakcuckla in the clan of the Beloved Crayfish People—lived. The mare called *Ofunlo* lived. She had never been saddled. She had never worn a bridle or harness. She had never pulled a plow. He fitted her with a breast collar and withers strap. He backed her into the traces, then hitched her to the whipple and the whipple to the plough. He stood behind her at the edge of the field he had cleared and he talked to the mare and told her what must be done, what they must do. What she must do. Then he walked behind her and placed his hands on the handles of the plow. *Ofunlo*, he called, and she turned to look at him. He called again and flapped the reins onto her rump. *Ai! Ofunlo*, he said, *Ai!* But she stood waiting for him to climb on her back or lead her forward as he had always done. Drinks The Juice Of Stones dropped the reins.

He went to the row of wet ditches along the length of the field and cut a wand of willow switch. He took up the handles of the plough and called *Ai Ofunlo* and snapped the switch to her rump. She had never been struck. She lunged forward at the pain of it and turned around in her traces to look at him. *Ai!* he called. She pulled against the breast collar and the withers strap, and the plough blade made its furrow-cut as she went on. She went on.

In 1845, at the age of fifteen, the brindle mare *Ofunlo* was bred and bore a filly. The man's new wife named her *Fichik*—Star—for the mark on her forehead.

In 1860, *Fichik* was bred, and she too bore a filly. The man's daughter named her *Shapo*—Hat—for the white patch between her ears.

In 1870, *Shapo* bore a colt. The man's son named him *Bakoa*—Piebald—for his color, and in 1875 sold him to a cavalry officer who was passing though the Land of Indian Resettlement near the Kiamichi River, on his way to the Territory of New Mexico. And who, upon his arrival in Silver City, boarded his Choctaw piebald in the City Livery while he had a bath at the Bedrock Bath & Spirits, a hot meal at the Cave-In Café, and a woman at the Half Moon Dance Hall. That evening, a local youth by the name of Billy Antrim—also known as William Henry McCarty and Billy Bonney—who had been arrested for thievery and held in the courthouse lockup, escaped by ascending the chimney, scrambling down from roof to ledge, entering the livery and finding there among the stalls of boarded horses a fine Choctaw pony, a piebald. The air was sweet and rich with the smell of hay and their droppings. Billy stood listening. No sound but the flit and flutter of barn swallows in the roofbeams. The soft nickering of the horses at his presence. The grinding of grain in their mouths. The piebald Indian pony stopped chewing and looked at the squirrely boy standing in his stall.

Hurry up there and finish your dinner, said Billy. We ain't got much time.

Barn swallows (Hirundo rustica) never alight to drink, but skim the surface of streams and ponds, taking water on the wing.

—Birds of America and the Territories, Chapter 53: Swallows, Martins, Saw-Wings

Chapter 52
With Two Rivers Behind Me
by Billy Bonney
November, 1875

Likely they'd be hunting me south to Hidalgo and more south on into Mexico where most desperados go. So I went north—we went north—following along the foothills for a time, then crossing the Gila, then turning east to the banks of the Rio Grande, me and the piebald Indian pony I found with his nose in the feed bucket in the livery of Silver City. I took him to be a Choctaw—I'd seen the breed before. And this one—the one I took to be my own—he had the little ears the Choctaw horses have and a nose dished in just a bit and a double mane: one black as crows and over that another one pure white and hanging long nearly to his withers and all straggly wild between his ears. And one thing he had I never did see in a horse. A little bit of blue there in the brown of his eye. Just on the right. Just there. Small enough you'd have to get in nearly eye to eye to see it, but I seen it and right then I give him his name. Cielo. Sky. His name kept just in my mind but never will say it. Cielo then, for however long we'd be keeping on. And we were keeping on. Five days and nights went by, following the river through some rough country with boulders tumbled down clear to the banks and hardly a place for the Choctaw to set his foot. But we kept on until the bluffs bottomed out and we crossed ourselves over where the river ran a muddy red and easy. With two rivers behind me I figured us clear enough of Silver City and likely safe enough away to be hunting work in the ranches, but none would have me. Not a one. It was always the same—someone telling me I'm too puny to take on as a hand, too small, just a kid, and then someone would get to talking about the Choctaw. What a fine face he had, and you don't come by so many piebalds nowadays except if you're an Indian, and so forth. Wherever we went was someone asking if I might be selling that horse. I swear that pony he didn't like that talk and set to stamping and twisting around. Once bent his neck clear around and took a nip of my foot where it set in the stirrup. He was smart a fellow as I ever did see, those ears of his turning at the littlest sound—a ground squirrel scratching in the mesquite, a jaybird calling in a piñon. And unspookable too, standing still as a stone when I was in the saddle taking aim and shooting at some dinner. Stayed put the same when I bed myself down and nearly froze those nights on a sandy bar or tucked myself under some overhang, and soon I'd be asleep to the talk a river makes when its open and sliding over stones and the sound of him pulling at the winter grass on the bank. Or stepping in the shallows where the thin icy places are crackling and tinkling under his foot. Giving a little snort if the wind came up or tree limb creaked. Good as any hound you might keep to keep watch. Come morning, he was close by me, us both drinking from the river where a flock of merganser ducks out in the cold midcurrent were swimming and dipping under, then popping up and shaking the wet off their shaggy head-feathers. Gulping down the little fishes still wriggling in their mouths and diving again the way they do, disappearing, escaping along the river bottom. And me cold and hungry on the bank with nothing better to do than be betting myself where one of them will come up. Maybe there, by that big gray rock? Or will it be that shady spot there where a willow branch sweeps clear down to the water? Or might he been swimming upstream making his way against the current just to fool my fool ass while I'm standing here watching ducks and should be getting on, or did he already come up somewheres downstream when I wasn't looking or so far off I missed him. And while I'm guessing and wondering, why up he pops, and wouldn't you know it, he's never where you'd think he be, no never. I watch a while until they're done diving and dipping this stretch of river and the whole flock starts to skitter and run, yes sir I said run with those paddly feet right along the surface, never sinking, never going under as long as they kept on running, flapping and slapping with the sunlit water sparking off their wings and then up, up, they go and gone. I knew then how it would be for me from now on. How I'd be running as long as I have left in this life to be running, escaping across this dry and dusty desert earth as fast as I can before I sink into it, because I'll never get off the ground. Mam said my splayed-out shoulder blades were wings stuck in me, folded up wrong-ways inside of me but never to be doing me no good the way they are. And never will I be knowing how to set them loose to lift me up and get me gone. So I saddle up again and go.

The common merganser (Mergus merganser) will rise from the water by flapping as it runs along the surface to gain momentum to ascend. Once in the air, the merganser's flight is rapid and strong.

—Birds of America and the Territories, Chapter 13: Swans, Geese, Ducks, Mergansers

Chapter 53
Billy Comes Upon the Rustlers
Las Cruces, New Mexico
May 5, 1876 – The Moon of Come Back Birds

He came upon them and their branding fire in a box canyon a half-day's ride outside Las Cruces and long after the sun had set. He had first seen the wavering glow along a flange of ledge while still nearly a mile away and following a faint trail atop the tableland, a territory of upheaved slabs and plates of sea-bottom stone marked with the ripples of a primordial tide, and firelight again as he passed through a district of lightning strikes told by a scattering of black and splintered bristlecone conifers that had long ago taken up residence in the smooth channels of sandstone worn so by millennia of infrequent rain, and these had been turned to torches and to char.

He had not eaten for days, except for a handful of rushpeas and a woodrat's cache of pine nuts—but had found water in a dished rock protected by a wedge of boulders, and there he bashed and ate the spadefoot toad he found sleeping with its tiny bulbed foretoes tucked to its chest in the cool sand of this shaded seep, and he and the Choctaw horse drank the pool dry, and rested, and with nightfall went on. Long tracts of stone lay ahead of him and he could not see the mouth of the canyon nor the canyon floor where the men had corralled their stolen stock and had assembled their fire of deadwood spruce. The limbs were dry and streaked with pitch that flared and popped, and the flames illuminated the surrounding rock faces and sent sparks spiraling out of the canyon on a wind of the fire's own making up to the rock rim where they winked out against the night sky like dying stars while true stars beyond shimmered on the heat. The light on the canyon's far scarp seemed to come from some subterranean conflagration, and he recalled the Apache woman's telling of the ones she called The Old Ones who long ago lived in the earth waiting for the world to be made and tending their cookfires that blazed up through smokeholes until they finally doused the flames and leaving their underground homes behind they climbed out through the holes to live in the world—though he wondered if some had decided to return after a stint in it. They went on, Billy vigilant in that vast and open country, listening to the Choctaw's steady hoofstrike. Seeing its ears flick at every sound. Squeak of the saddle. Ring of a pebble kicked loose. The trill of a lone nighthawk zigzagging over. He halts the Choctaw and listens. Nighthawk, he says. He's on my list. And then the sound of something else, something like the murmur of far-off thunder, though the night sky is clear and pierced with stars and there is no sign of storm. The Choctaw steps sideways, uneasy and unused to this barren upland. It's alright, Billy whispers to the horse but it is more a comfort to himself, and he begins to hum the Timoleague tune his mother used to sing and it takes him back to Irish Town where is a small boy again and his mother is tucking his shirt into his trousers then pulling it free and loose to hide his poked-out shoulder bones—*Billy stop your fidgeting.* And once more he is back at her bedside—*It's me, Ma. It's your Billy*—while her breathing becomes a rattle in her throat as she tells him *Get away with you Billy, fly away* and the silence between each breath grows longer and he is wondering *Is that the last of it? Let that be the last of it, let her now be done with it* until the final surge of liquified lung fills her mouth, overflowing to pillow, neck, breast. *Mam?* A gurgling. *Mam.* And again, now in this clean night air, he can smell the rot of his mother on the rag he uses to wipe what clings to her lips, face, settles between her breasts. The awful looseness of the newly dead in turning her over, of her limbs lifted and spread. The filth between her legs. *No Joe. I'll do this little brother. Little Man. You, you get the fire going.* Billy bundles up her nightdress, spit rag, pillow cover. Joseph kneels at the ironcast stove with paper, straw, twigs, sticks. The fuel catches. Spark. Smoke. Breath. Flame. *Out of the way Joe*, says Billy. He shoves the stinking bundle of bedclothes into the flame and kicks the stove door shut but they are damp and slow to catch and they smolder and smoke. The smell of what had leaked out her now seeps through the cookplates. *Get the window Joe*, says Billy and in comes the cold of a New Mexico morning and the scent of snow blowing in from the mountains that rise beyond Los Pinos Altos.

The Choctaw horse snorts. The trance of the Timoleague tune broken.

The air smells slightly of singed hair and roasting meat.

And what seemed be a far-off thunder now seems to be the low wail of a yawning wind, the heave of swaying trees. But there are no trees left standing atop the tableland. No wind. It comes on louder and lifting from within the box canyon. The lowing of the captured longhorns that a believer might take to be the pleading calls and lamentations of condemned souls, and the chasm to be an aperture from which the heat of hell escapes. Sprout wings, said the preacher back in Silver City. Sprout 'em and head on up to heaven or be cast into the scorching pit. Heaven or hellfire, you pick.

The flamelight wavers on the rise of ridgeline. I guess that's where we're headed, says Billy. Let's git.

The lesser nighthawk (Chordeiles acutipennis) lays its eggs on gravel or bare rock.

—Birds of America and the Territories, Chapter 43:Goatsuckers, Nightjars

He nudged the Choctaw on until it balked and would go no further. Alright then, said Billy. If you say so. He slid off frontwise leg-over-leg and let the reins fall to the rock. He began to walk, but before the canyon rim he went down on his belly and in this way crept ahead on his elbows, and with pistol in hand he reached the edge and peered over. Had the men watched the flight of the rising sparks to the top of the canyon they would have seen the small face of a boy bright in their firelight and the gun glinting in his hand. Billy looked down and took stock. There were four of them. Two were dragging deadwood into piles around the longhorns huddled against the canyon wall, a herd—Billy figured—of near twenty. One man knelt feeding the cookfire. One skinning the hide from a slab of meat and the last man skewering chunks of it on a branding iron rock-propped over the flames. An unbound calf lay on its side nearby, moaning and mewing. It thrashed and twisted to get its legs under, and finally pushed its face into the dirt and with great effort leveraged itself upright, and momentarily stood so that Billy could see that its flank had been opened and the flesh cut away before it tottered, folded its forelegs, and tumbled down into the dust where it did not move or mew again.

Billy slides away from the canyon rim on his belly.

The Choctaw pony waits. He stamps and blows for Billy but does not nicker.

A scorpion out hunting carries her clutch of pale soft young on her back. She senses the horse's footfall too late. All are crushed by the hoof.

A coyote rests on an overlook above the box canyon, the slickrock under her haunches still warm with the heat of the day. She looks down upon the activities of cows and men. Her pups nearby and partly grown scrap and growl at the smell of the bloody calf and the fired-braised meat and their faces come and go in the veils of the rising smoke like ghost dogs or visions of dogs or dogs destined for dreams.

Soon will come the Moon of Coyotes Singing. Soon the pups will be foraging on their own. The bigleaf sage will be blooming.

Chapter 54
I Take Up with The Boys
May 5, 1876
by Billy Henry Bonney

Warn't no hellfire. Nothing but a box canyon with cows and men. And me just looking down at them, it seemed to be a grim sort of gathering and none too friendly—the cow and cow thieves both—so not to spook them into shooting I pitched down a pebble but no one takes no notice. Twenty or so pebbles later and they're pulling pieces of hot steaks off the spit. I wait a while more till they're all hunched fireside and busy with eating and I set a nice-size rock on the edge and give it a little push, and damn but doesn't it go wild bouncing off boulders and going higher and wilder with each bounce on the way down and nearly beans one of them. He looks up. And there I am, most of me flat to the rock but peeking over. Hello boys, I holler. They drop their steaks in a hurry and draw their pistols and dive for cover behind the cows and the crooks in the rocks. One of them I can't see starts shooting up at nothing, and I can't tell which one where, but there's sparks flying off the stone.

Who's it up there, Jake? Can you see?

Don't have to see. It's the goddamn sheriff is who, come hunting us.

I ain't no sheriff, I call.

Like hell you ain't.

Damn, Elroy. It sounds like some kid.

I ain't no kid.

It ain't the sheriff, Petey Ray.

It's some kid, I tell ya.

What you doing up there kid?

I'm just waiting on you to look up, I say.

You hear this kid?

I hear 'em.

Can I come on down?

Take the trail just back from the drop off.

Can you see him, John? Got a bead on him?

I'm telling you Elroy, it's the sheriff.

And I'm telling you Jake, it's just some damn kid. Yeah you come on down kid. Watch out for the quick switchback. You can miss it in the dark.

Chapter 55
The Box Canyon Before Daybreak
Las Cruces, New Mexico
May 6, 1876 – The Moon of Come Back Birds

They called themselves The Boys, and they were waiting for him. Their horses stood slumped, an old red Appaloosa, a liver chestnut, a bay mare, a dapple gray, all with their heads held low and line-tied to a rope woven through the debris of deadwood stumps and roots and branches. A sad and wasted lot these broken beasts—rheumy of eye, ulcerated withers, foundered and footsore. Their hides slung in hollows hipcrest to hipcrest. Rib slats sharp against their heaving sides. The dapple gray attempted to lie itself down but the tether was too short and it half stood, head suspended, neck upstretched, and foreleg lame-bent at the knee and bearing no weight. Each in mute misery, these creatures that can overtake the wind with footfalls the very sound of thunder, here broken of everything except their confederacy, and for this they lifted their heads as best they could toward Billy's Choctaw and they softly nickered their greeting. The Choctaw nickered back.

Billy halted his horse. There appeared to be no one about. The fire appeared to be recently stoked. Crackled. A log thudded out. Sparked. Billy heard the ratcheting of a hammer cocked. A twig snapped. A short two-note tweet came from behind a behind a boulder. An answer came from beyond a clump of burrow-brush.

Hello boys, said Billy.

One man stepped out from behind a cow. How'd you know? he said.

Ain't no birdy tweets that way, said Billy. Least not none I ever heard.

No, you dumb-ass. How'd you know we're The Boys?

There were four of them, having stepped one by one into the firelight, grim faces and shaggy heads all with an assortment of beards and mustaches except for the one named Petey Ray Maxwell, who sported a smile and big cactus spine between his teeth. The one named Jake Perlmutter was somewhat pustular around the mouth, but likely bearing similar suppurations on his overused lower regions given the exudative stains crotchwise. The man beady of eye and leg-bowed and somewhat the leader was named Elroy Ellison and known by the rest to be always the first of them going for his gun. The fourth one was named John James Glasser but on account of the fissure through his philtrum ridge from nostril to lip and so long in his life been called Rabbit or Hare or Harry he took it for his name. All of them formerly drovers, drifters, ranch hands, felons, fallen in together by frayed threads of acquaintance. Having worked the same ranches in the Hidalgo or part-time in Piedra Negra three winters ago. Or being half-brothers perhaps, or other relations founded upon unfounded rumors of mutual fathers. Or cell-mates once in El Paso or Tucson or Yuma. Or colleagues in crimes of one sort or another down Santa Fe way. All of them now in the habit of spending away in a single night a month's wages on grain spirits and blackstrap bourbon, on the company of companionable women, and on craps and cards, and most recently on outfitting themselves in whatever fancy goods their rustling money would buy though none of it suitable to their way of living: shirts that once may have been white complete with wrist frills partially attached, gone at the shoulder seams; sporting odd scarves and bright neckerchiefs and one wearing a cravat threaded through a buttonhole and retied in a bow; silk vests gone buttonless, blackened with spots of grease and soot; trousers of worsted and herringbone and tweed clotted with mud and shot through with little scorch holes. They wore peewee boots and imported pull-ons of ostrich-leg leather and gator-back and caiman-belly. Cuban Heels. Spurs. Small city hats. Narrow brimmed. They carried silver flasks holding water—though not nearly enough and nearly useless after the last bit of whiskey went, and brass stickpins set with cut-glass heads purchased from an open-coat vendor who claimed they were gemstone and gold, though no matter—these they used to pick their teeth. They owned watch fobs and pocket watches as well, though none of them knew the art of telling the time of day more than it be morning or night. New saddles too, with Mexican tooling and tapaderos, though nary a thought did they have as to the care of the horses on which those fancy saddles sat. No, the four fading specimens they owned were not alive to their way of thinking but ornery machines fueled infrequently and only if necessary to make them go. Nor considered alive were the unfortunate cows they stole and drove with hardly a thought to their comfort or sustenance. Or to their calves downed and trampled or carved or killed for a portion of meat. They stepped forth, this unseemly quartet, pistols drawn.

See Jake? Just some dumb-ass kid, said Elroy Ellison

Ain't neither, said Billy.

Where you from, kid?

Up there is where.

That's some fine-looking horse you got there, said Jake. Ain't that some fine-looking horse, Elroy?

How'd you come by that horsey, kid?

How'd you come by that dead calf yonder? said Billy

Mouthy little son of a bitch, says Petey Ray.

What might be your name be?

It might be William, but my friends call me Billy.

Your friends. You thinking we be friends?

No, says Billy. I'm not thinking that. That's the one thing I'm not thinking.

Before daybreak, the mother coyote had returned to the pups and there disgorged her kills. Two rabbits, one kangaroo rat, four fledgling burrowing owls. A pup tried to nurse but the coyote nipped him on the snout.

Before daybreak, Billy had moved the cows to the seep pool at the mouth of the box canyon. He watered and fed his Choctaw. He watered and fed their horses.

Before daybreak, he had split the dead calf's skull with a rock and fried its brains in its fat for their breakfasts and concocted a semblance of coffee from sow thistle and acorns of gamble oak.

Before daybreak, he had seen the coyote

Before daybreak, Billy had become the newest member of The Boys, skinning and butchering the calf, slicing it into strips for smoking, and thrusting his hands into the blood.

The burrowing owls (Athene cunicularia) nests in a vacant prairie dog den and will place coyote dung around the entrance to attract dung beetles, which both the adult bird and its fledglings will eat.

—Birds of America and the Territories, Chapter 42: True Owls

It was just daybreak when they decided on a foray for fresh horses.

Elroy Ellison came forward carrying a new tooled saddle set with silver star conchas and roughly hoisted it onto the back of the lame dapple gray. The animal spread its legs and swayed but stayed upright until Ellison tightened the girth and it collapsed upon its knees. Goddamn get up, he said. Kicking it in the head. Its eyes rolled to white and it let out a shudder. Billy slid down off his horse and came up behind Ellison. Leave it, Billy told him. It's dead. No it ain't, said Ellison as he kicked it again. Billy knelt beside the animal and put his palm to its muzzle. A faint bit of breath, a nearly inaudible wheeze. My mistake, said Billy and he pulled his pistol from his waistband and put it to the horse's eye and fired. Now it is, said Billy. He was still kneeling and off balance when Ellison fell upon him and with his pistol between them, Billy pushed the barrel into Ellison's neck and let loose a shot. Ellison sputtered some sort of speech as he felt for the hole with his fingers and his blood sprayed Billy in the face. Then stopped spraying. Get him off me, Billy said. Petey Ray Maxwell rolled the body over. He looked down at Elroy Ellison, then took off his hat and held it to his chest. Elroy was my half-brother, said Petey Ray. Or half-cousin. I forget which. My ma never liked him though, said Petey Ray.

Me neither, said Hare Glasser.

Billy wiped the blood from his face with his sleeve and climbed back on the Choctaw. Let's git, he said.

Well now, said Jake Permutter. You don't seem much aggrieved.

I've killed me one the same way before, said Billy.

Self-defense was it?

Billy looked up at him. I was talking about the horse.

Sunup had come and gone when they left the box canyon behind and turned southwest to the town of Tortuga, a two-day's ride. The surface terrain was rust-tinted by the weathering of the surrounding escarpments that in millennia past had been mountain-high dunes tamped into sandstone by time and the trickle of alkali, and sealed in that strata of rose-red and yellow and brick lay the petrified bodies of beasts that once roamed these regions, the first sedimentary deposition bearing the bones of upright reptiles the size of the very hills that quaked at their lumbering, and above these lay rodents bigger than boulders, and higher still the three-toed horses as small as dogs, and soon the dapple gray that died that morning would take its place above those ancestral remains, as would the liver chestnut and the red Appaloosa and the bay, soon to be stripped of muscle and hide by the creatures that consume carrion in these districts of hardpan and heat, that being the birds that thrust their featherless faces into decay, the dung beetles that burrow through the innards, and the flesh-flies that swarm and hatch and swarm again—until the desert does its work entombing their bones under silt and sand becoming bands of stone the color of sundown and watered blood.

The land was mainly level, scored with dry washes and barren draws. The Choctaw pony kept on, going sure and steady, but the others stumbled among the stands of chaparral sage and chamisa where fly-catchers rose from their perches in the brush at their approach. It was near midday when they turned their horses away from Las Cruces—too big a town for unauthorized horse trading, they agreed—and headed south on the Jornada del Muerto. It was just sundown when the bay mare and the liver chestnut went lame and the red Appaloosa began blowing pink foam from its nostrils.

And it was just past dusk when Petey Ray Maxwell and Hare Glass-er and Jake Perlmutter and Billy Antrim Bonney rode into the oxbow town of Tortuga. And when Billy opened his boot-heel, unfolded the paper he kept secreted there, and added *flycatcher* to his list.

The willow flycatcher (Empidonax traillii) perches atop willow thickets near water and stands of salt cedar where flies out, captures insects in flight, and return to the same perch.

—Birds of America and the Territories, Chapter 51: Tyrant Flycatchers

Chapter 56
The Turtles of Tortuga
Tortuga, New Mexico
May 7, 1876 – The Moon of Come Back Birds

Five horses stood side by side in the small corral with the cold night air misting around their muzzles. At the arrival of the riders they pricked their ears and trotted to the rail. Billy raised his hand for quiet and the men sat in silence waiting for a dog to bark, for a door to swing open, for a lantern to be lifted. Waiting for a shout or the sound of gunshot. None came.

A trough had been set just inside the gate, and the liver chestnut and the Choctaw dipped their heads under the rail and drank but the red Appaloosa and the bay mare stood apart from the others and too near to dying to drink. The horses in the corral began to snort and nicker and circle nervously, but still the town was quiet when they hitched their animals to the posts and started down the deserted thoroughfare on foot, past the shacks and adobes where nary a candle or lamp was lit, through a small flagstoned square where the stalls and trundle carts stood empty, past a straggly grove of cottonwoods in which a cuckoo was calling, and on to the tin-roofed cantina bearing a sign above the lintel beam—Comida y Bebida. A small dog lay motionless in the doorway in the long light the lamp within cast out onto the street where two old men sat in old cane chairs tending a cookfire under a piglet skewered through mouth to tail on a stove-poker. Buenas noches, said Billy. Both fire-tenders nodded. One stood. Por favor, he said, waving them in.

The old man comes tableside, a clean white waiter's cloth folded on his forearm. Señores? he says.

Whiskey all around, says Petey Ray Maxwell.

Billy sits adding to his list: *yellow-billed cuckoo*. He does not look up. None for me, says Billy.

Lo siento señor. No lo tenemos. Solamente cervezas, says the old man.

What's he saying? askes Petey Ray.

He says only beer, says Billy.

Beer then, says Petey Ray. Cervezas. But the kid here will take a sasperilly.

Un que? says the old man.

Tiene refresco? says Billy.

Ah, soda. Sí, says the old man. Refresco de limón.

We eat, Perlmutter tells the old man while gesturing with an invisible fork. Go on Billy, says Perlmutter. You ask him what's to eat.

Billy inquires as to the bill of fare. The old man speaks rapidly at length. Mañana tenemos cochinillo asado—rio—seco—agua—tortuga—sopa—ha ha ha.

Goddamn, says Glasser.

He says roast pig, but not till tomorrow.

What else?

They used to serve tortuga.

Tortuga. Ain't we in Tortuga?

Sí. Sí. Tortuga, says the old man making swimming motions with cupped hands.

Turtles, says Billy. The river used to be full up with turtles.

What they do, make soup? says Perlmutter.

Used to, says Billy. But they're all gone now.

No mas, says the old man. He holds up his empty hands, palms up, as if to show he has not been concealing a turtle.

Where'd they go? says Petey Ray.

Ate 'em, says Billy.

The old man leans slightly into the table. No mas tortugas, he says with a conspiratorial wink. He taps his upper lip with his finger and jerks his head in the direction of Hare Glasser. Pero, he says, qué tal conejo?

Now what's he got? says Glasser.

He's calling you a conejo.

Is that so, says Glasser. Well now. So I'm a conejo, Glasser says and he takes his hands from the table and slides them under.

The old man steps back, his palms held up before him. Una broma, he says. Solo una broma.

Sí, señor. Una broma, says Billy. Just a joke.

The old man delivers to the table a two-handled stoneware pitcher of beer and a bottle of yellow-tinged soda and four glasses. Billy invites him to come sit, please and por favor sit with us and relájate por un momento, says Billy. Relax for a moment. Yes, sí the men tell him. Sit and have a drink with us. But the old man declines and declines twice more until there comes a pistol click from somewhere under, and he says gracias, gracias. He sits and he immediately begins to talk, mainly to our Billy, but turning to the others when he employs the few English words he knows: horses, cowboys, wife, sickness, fever, dog. He speaks about the process of roasting a pig and how such a thing must not be rushed and that he is sorry it was not ready for their dinners. He speaks about how expensive it is to serve good beer here in his cantina, but oh no and make no mistake—please understand! There will be no charge this evening, none at all señores. Never a charge for my American friends. Vaqueros. Cowboy amigos. It is his pleasure to be of service and he wishes he had tequila to offer but the agave are small this year and there is very little to be had in these parts and he talks of the sickness of his wife who lies so many days now—no, actually weeks—how he does lose track of time—confined to her bed in the room at the back of the cantina, suffering with a problemas intestinales and with his sons both grown and gone, how he—the old man—must wash his wife because she cannot, she is too weak to clean herself, and it is so many times every day he must wash her as she soils herself both ways and how it difficult it is—muy dificil!—to run the cantina but he must so he can feed the poor woman though sometimes she is unable to eat because there is much vomitando, but he must keep working to pay for her medicine, and the four of them, the three men and Billy all nod and finish their beer and soda, and when at last they leave the cantina, the old man is sitting in a corner spitting teeth though an upper lip split and his nose off center and dripping blood, while the dog still lies in the doorway and a nudge from Perlmutter's boot raises a whiff of putrefaction and disturbs a cluster of small white worms that crawl out from under it. In the street the cookfire has gone to smoke and char and the men who had been tending the cookfire and roasting the piglet are gone. As well as the piglet itself.

It was barely daybreak when they unhitched their horses—the red Appaloosa and the liver chestnut and the bay mare from the post and turned them loose into the corral. And in exchange, they led out three horses of other horses and saddled them up, and in that early light they saw they were black-stocking bays, all three.

We sure traded up, says Hare Glasser.

It's something for our trouble, says Petey Ray.

Near killed that waiter, says Jake Perlmutter.

Near was enough, says Billy.

Billy, says Hare Glasser.

What now? says Billy.

Tell me what the hell's a conejo?

And they rode the three black-stocking bays from out the oxbow town of Tortuga where turtles once lived in the river—Hare Glasser and

Petey Ray Maxwell and Jake Perlmutter. And in the lead rides Billy the Kid on his piebald Choctaw, bound for the longhorns where they had left them lowing in the box canyon outside of Las Cruces.

Most birds are unable to digest hairy caterpillars, but the yellow-billed cuckoo (Coccyzus amerianus) will take these creatures in its beak and beat them against a branch to remove the bristly tufts before consumption.

—Birds of America and the Territories, Chapter 40: Cuckoos, Roadrunners, Anis

Chapter 57
Coulees, Canyons
New Mexico and Moving On
October 1, 1876 – The Moon of Yellow Trees

They headed east across the Territory where the trees had turned with the season and the herds would be wintering. Cold days and nights, thievery along the Pecos and the high plains of Llano Estacado. Cutting fences and taking ten or so head at a time. Too easy, Billy told them and from then on it was ten times ten. They kept to the edges of the herds where cows will wander away into the gullies and go unnoticed by the lookouts the ranchers paid and posted. Billy on his Choctaw horse outrunning and outriding the sentinels, dodging their guns, becoming a rough-and-ready rustler. The rest of The Boys take note while Billy takes chances and takes charge, changing their hideouts in coulees and canyons, a different one with every raid. Hard riding, their hands cracked by the dry desert cold, skinned by the slide of a runaway rope, or burnt by mishaps with a running iron. Then the days of waiting on agents ready to pay for cows to be driven farther on to markets in Kansas or south to Mexico. When it came time to split the loot four ways it was Billy elected to those calculations, and no complaints were lodged when he wrote out a list and put a portion aside for provisions:

rope
gloves
cartridges
matches

bacon
flour
lard
oats
cornmeal
beans
tea
salt
wire cutter
coffee
sugar
soap
pencils
hat.

When it came time to spend it, it was the four of them together in any town with facilities serving spirits and sarsaparilla or refresco de limón and playing poker and faro, and after a day or two of general carrying on, too soon they'd be wondering where it all went.

Grimly they went on. The next raid. The next agent. Tracts of ironweed, brittle bush pale with a sifting of last night's snow.

At times they drove their stolen herd a hundred miles through buffalo grass and gamma, but all of it flattened by frost and their cows and horses gone footsore and thinner and they arrived at the points of delivery with the steers diminished, payment reduced, and the money running through their fingers like quicksilver. Like the last of the sugar. Like the ice-crystalled sand in the cold dry bed of a wash. Then back out on the range again. Out of salt. Out of coffee. Out of coulees and hideaway canyons. They kept on. Lawmen and ranchers supposed the gang to be more than four men, so frequent the raids, so heavy the losses.

Wanted posters began appearing in all parts of the Territory:

!WANTED!

OCTOBER 1876

THE ENTIRE GANG OF MURDERERS AND CATTLE RUSTLERS CALLING THEMSELVES "THE BOYS"

William H. Bonney, Henry Will McCarty,
Billy Antrim, Jake Perlmutter, P. Maxwell,
Kid Bonney, Hare Glasser, John J. Glasser,
Willy Kidd, Petey Ray, and Bill McBonney
for the killing of an unarmed Tortuga man
and the theft of a thousand Longhorn cattle

$$$ 100.00 REWARD offered $$$

For the apprehension of all of them,
already strung up dead or still living.
Contact Cattlemen's Association, Santa Fe
Or any Sheriff of the Territory.

They began lying low again, waiting out trouble. Now the idle days of blame and accusation, apathy and blood sport. Potshots at creatures that eke out their winter living in the high desert cold and happen to creep or trot or fly into killing range. Ringtails and foxes. Woodrats. Explosions of fur and bone. A slaughter of jackrabbits, but only one collected and skinned for the stew. Ground squirrel. Rock squirrel. Weasel. A sparrow alights in the sage. Burst of feathers, winter winds, no trace. Flocks.

Bet I can pick 'em all off at once, says Jake Perlmutter. He fires upward at nothing and cloud of birds rise from the brush then shot after shot they drop one by one. See that boys? Brought 'em all down.

You'll be bringing the goddamn law down on us is what, says Petey Ray Maxwell. You goddamn fool.

See that buzzard? says Hare Glasser, pointing to a large bird gliding in a thermal high in the pale winter blue. He fires. It seems to break apart, tilts on one wing as if to gain altitude or change direction, then spirals down to the desert floor, to somewhere beyond the next rise.

Got 'em, says Glasser. Like to kill them. All them buzzards.

Ain't no buzzard, says Billy. It's a hawk.

It's dead, what it is, says Glasser.

It's not even that, says Billy walking away while loading his pistol.

It had walked a ways—a hawk walking—one wing extended and dragging beside it until finally it stopped in the shadow of a boulder out of the way of the sun. It did not crouch or cower when it heard a stirring in the brush—Billy coming through the dry winter sage and over the rise.

That's right, said Billy, hunching down and rocking back on his boot-heels. There's no reason to run and you know it.

The hawk stood fast, facing him. Talons curved against the pebbly ground. Clear yellow eye. Wing torn away at the shoulder and held on by a bit of bone.

There's no fixing it, Billy told it. None that I know.

Billy stood. That time's arrived, he said. It come to us all, that time when you know it's better to be dead than be taken.

He takes his pistol from the holster. Easy now, he says. It'll be alright. I know what you are. I'll be writing your name.

The broad-winged hawk (Buteo platypterus) rarely drinks from ponds or streams but survives on the water content in the blood of the prey.

—Birds of America and the Territories, Chapter 15: Eagles, Hawks, Kites

Now in this month the Apache call the Moon of Dying Fires the desert holly shines silvery in the high winter light, the bigleaf sage withered.

Then the winter months.

The Moon of Hungry Crows.

The Moon of Sleeping Bears.

The Moon of Dying Snow brings the thaw along the Pecos Valley and the high plains of the Llano Estacado.

Then the months of spring.

The Moon of Waking Bears.

The Moon of Come Back Birds brings the longleaf sage a tinge of green again.

New grass. Longhorn calves born to longhorn cows.

Fulltime rustling again all the spring and summer long.

Hideouts. Hiding. Hard riding. Hunted. Hard riding.

Winter.

Spring.

The Moon of Waking Bears.

Chapter 58
He Goes by Billy
Fort Stanton, Territory of New Mexico
October 20, 1876 – The Moon of Yellow Trees

The Major did not look up from his desk when the Sergeant set his face to the window of the officer's annex and cupped his hands in a hollow around his eyes against the glare of the sun at his back and the moving reflections of the wind-tossed boughs of the ponderosa pines that lined the yard. He peered in. There the Major seated in his swivel chair, leaning over a large oaken desk covered by an accumulation of papers, some stacked, most scattered, and although the Sergeant's shadow was cast upon the page currently under the Major's scrutiny and had darkened the room therein, the Major did not cease in his endeavors nor did he look to the window to ascertain who or what was blocking the light. A document bearing a circular seal at the bottom of the page was positioned under his pen. The remaining mass of papers were secured with a variety of weighty objects: a horseshoe, a humidor, a fine crystal paperweight bearing on its base an engraving of a neoclassical edifice magnified nicely by the convexity of the dome and identified as Cadet Chapel West Point, and a fist-sized chunk of milky quartz bearing a vein of pure gold, this a memento of his 1874 trek with General George Armstrong Custer on Old Yellow Hair's expedition into the Black Hills of the Dakota Territory. Several packets of correspondence had been spread out and held down with a particularly heavy saber laid across them, a specimen known by cavalrymen as The Wrist Breaker. Amid the mess, a damp cigar stub rested on the rim of an empty sardine can filled with ash, and beside it sat a tin army-issue cup of tea. At least it appeared to be tea. Slightly apart from the clutter stood a miniature easel displaying a small gold-framed tintype of young woman in black crepe holding an infant in a white gown that cascaded across her lap, the child so dressed as if for a baptism though its pale hands were crossed at the wrists and held in place with a bit of ribbon, its lidded eyes were sunk in shadow, and its image had been hand-colored so that its cheeks were delicately pink. As was the bit of ribbon.

Two ladder-backed chairs had been set side-by-side against the far wall. One held a standard-issue McClellan saddle. The other, a very old Chiricahua Apache who bore a stump where once had been his left knee, lately wrapped in soiled rags and bound with strips of rawhide. The old man's hands were in irons, though not secured to the chair. The Sergeant tapped at the window. The Major seemed not to hear.

The Sergeant left the window and moved to the door. Rapped lightly. The Major did not respond. The Sergeant knocked again, this time with greater enthusiasm. When this did not produce a response, he opened the door just wide enough to put his head in, and as he did so the papers on the Major's desk lifted and fluttered under their anchors. Without looking up, the Major reached out to still them from escape and then bent back to his work. The Sergeant quickly entered and shut the door behind him. He stood before the Major at his desk, a sheaf of papers of his own in hand. The Major did not look up. The old Apache did not look over. The Sergeant coughed. Sir, he said. The tick of the clock on a shelf behind the desk. The scratching of the Major's pen. The muted chatter of a bird somewhere beyond the window. The Sergeant sniffed loudly. I see you, said the Major. Go away.

Sir, said the Sergeant once again. This shouldn't wait.

The Major looked at him. What shouldn't.

Another raid on cavalry horses.

I've been previously informed, Sergeant. Thank you. Dismissed

Sir.

Something else Sergeant?

Whoever he was he rode them out of here just last night.

Post a guard. Post two.

Been posted, Sir. But they cleaned us out anyhow.

The Major set his pen on the edge of the sardine tin. He put the cigar stub in his mouth briefly and he took it out. He drained the tin cup. He tilted back in his oak swivel chair. You are aware Sergeant, that matters more pressing than horse thieving comes across this desk. As you are also aware that I and I alone am responsible for the every misdeed of every savage in this territory? And that the Apaches under my jurisdiction will not stay put on the land we have allotted them, having convinced ourselves such was a generous act. And that it was just two days ago when a band of Papago slaughtered forty Coyotero Apaches on the west bank of the Mimbres and a contingency of Chiricahua Apaches no less than fifty miles south ritually mutilated a wagonful of Mexicans, of which the surviving child now rests in our infirmary with suppurating wounds, attended to by none other than the camp cook until a doctor—and the only one for 800 miles, who, I am told, may actually be a wanted man in possession of fraudulent professional credentials—arrives here from Silver City. You are also aware—and I know you are because you yourself run them in—that we have six starving Mescalero Apache families in the yard awaiting placement God knows where, and we are expected to round up several hundred more. And finally, you must be aware that the loss of horses from our corral is ongoing. Is not urgent. Is not new. Is expected. Losses are expected. This is the age of unexpected losses. A territory of losses. Perhaps a nation of losses, if one cares to view the big picture which you apparently do not or cannot. And the losses of which you speak are largely due to our lack of scrutiny. So. You have already been aware or have just been made aware of the fact that I have bigger fish to fry. He glances to the Apache. Or hang.

Sir. If I may. That scrutiny part. We got scrutiny. Plenty of scrutiny.

How so, Sergeant? And are you referring to the nation in general or this here shithole we call a cavalry fort in particular.

Here. This here shithole. Sir.

Enlighten me, Sergeant.

We got two men at the corral round the clock. Overlap at shift change. Everyone requiring a horse gets logged in and out. Officers and enlisted both now. Civilians are required to show documents of identity. So, plenty of scrutiny. Losses at ninety percent. At present we have eleven horses in the coral, four of which are not ours.

Not ours. Whose are they?

Damned if I know. Likely whosever taking ours out. Damned if I know that either.

Any ideas.

Fort Grant, night raid, same thing. The corporal assigned corral detail goes off for a friendly smoke with some young fella—a civilian—while his accomplices ride off with a dozen new ponies just come in. They got him though. Stuck him right quick in their stockade.

Have we a name for this friendly civilian?

We think it's William Bonney. Or William Antrim. But he goes by Billy. Just Billy. Young fella. He's done his share of rustling before, but now all these is federal crimes.

Well Sergeant, let's get this young fella down here.

Not possible Sir.

Tell me he escaped.

Yes Sir.

Yes you're going to tell me or yes he escaped.

Escaped. Sir.

Enlighten me once more, Sergeant, as to the means of escape from a cavalry fort stockade.

That wasn't clear. But he was a little fella. Hardly bigger than a kid. Wrangled his way out somehow. Not quite clear, as I said.

So. We have eleven serviceable horses for 177 men, is that correct?

No Sir. We have seven serviceable horses. The four not ours are lame.

The Major turned slightly in his swivel chair and reached down. Opened a drawer in his desk. Produced a bottle of whiskey. Squeak of the cork. He raised the bottle and an eyebrow ever so slightly to the Sergeant.

No thank you, Sir.

The Major poured a few glugs into the tin cup, recorked, and scored the label with his thumbnail at the level of what was left. He smacked the cork in with his palm and replaced the bottle and closed the drawer but he did not take a drink.

Now tell me this, Sergeant. How we are to operate a cavalry post with seven horses?

We got forty or so fresh ponies coming in tomorrow morning. Just broke I'm told but ridable.

Forty.

Yes Sir. Though I expect that number to be down some by tomorrow night.

On account of this young and friendly little fella on the loose.

That's about the size of it. Sir.

What do you suggest, Sergeant.

Well that's the thing, Sir. I was hoping you'd tell me.

Alright. Close the fort to civilians till we get this sorted out.

Yes Sir.

Dismissed, said the Major. And Sergeant, get a few guards in here to take this old man out to the stockade. Might have to carry him.

The Sergeant looked at the old Apache who now sat slumped forward in his chair and appeared to have fallen asleep. The rawhide strip had become unwound some and the ragged wrapping dangled from the stump.

And Sergeant, said the Major.

Sir?
Try not to let him escape.

Chapter 59
Reward!

REWARD!

NOVEMBER 1876

GANG LEADER OF THE BOYS

WILLIAM BONNEY, alias
Billy Antrim, Billy the Kid
Outlaw and Federal Fugitive

WANTED FOR FEDERAL OFFENSES

Including horse theft & acts detrimental to
the Peace & Safety of these United States.
$200.00 in gold coin will be paid by the

US GOVERNMENT

for his capture and delivery dead or alive.
He is Friendly but Cagey & Dangerous.
Telegraph the US Cavalry Commander
Fort Stanton, Territory of New Mexico.

Chapter 60
Abilene
by Billy Bonney
New Mexico, Kansas, Texas—November 1876

Was me got The Boys off cows. Had to, with every rancher and drover in the territory on the lookout and ready to blow all our heads off and mine in particular, no questions asked. We just about cleaned out every longhorn herd in ten counties and the ones up and down the Pecos Valley and when there wasn't nary a cow left for us to rustle, we ran raids through west Texas where the Stockman's Association hired a posse to track me down, noose me up, and whack my Choctaw rumpwise to set me swinging from the nearest cottonwood limb. So we took it up with horses instead, mustangs first since they was free for the taking, running loose and fierce from as long as some say since forever and breeding out in every kind and color, like the little herd of broncs we caught up with crossing Carrizo Creek:

3 paints
1 red dun
3 bays
1 buckskin dun
2 sorrel grays
2 appaloosa
2 roans

and a few of them with coats I couldn't name or there wasn't names invented. And we roped saddle horses right out of the remudas when the wranglers weren't looking and sometimes even when they were, and hell, didn't we even steal ponies where they stood tied to the rail outside saloons where the cowhands what owned them were inside drinking and whoring and carrying on. We ran horses off ranches and we ran them off the cavalry forts, some being riding ponies and some just recent tame and some being wild-tailed mustangs right off the plains. Most we drove them clear across the Territory to Tucumcari into Texas and we crossed the Prairie Dog Town Fork where flocks of little bluebills rose up in dark clouds of them when we splashed on through and then straight south and across the Rio Grande into Mexico and the big cattle spreads that bought from us as many horses we could fetch them. When the law got too close in Texas, we did our rustling in Arizona along the dry Santa Cruz, got them ponies shoed up by the smith at Fort Grant, and took them into Mexico by way of Nogales. Some we sold off across the Texas border in Kansas where they would go on by rail from Abilene. But one time I went all the way to Abilene. One time. We drove those ponies out of the traps and up the ramps. Some of them was mares with their little foals trying to hold close to their mamas, but all of them, all of them, getting whupped into the boxcars and packed in every which way so they couldn't stand but with their heads hung on the backs of each other and when the big doors slid shut they were on their way to cities in the East to be spending the rest of their lives not even being rode but dragging coal carts and wagons over the stone streets where they would never more see a blade of buffalo grass or drink from rivers or feel wind not full of smoke and soot. No more life like that, no. Now it would be blinders on their eyes and getting whipped and beat until they dropped. I seen it myself back in Irish Town, the horses. And that one time when I drove them all the way through Kansas, I seen them loaded up at Abilene. That one time. Some wouldn't go, and that's would be just the start of more whipping to come. When those boxcar doors slid closed, one of them he gets his big horse eye up against an opening in the slats. I knew that eye. I knew that color. It was the buckskin dun. I remember when I roped him up around Carrizo Creek. Gave me a hell of a chase that one, the buckskin dun. And now there he is looking at me through the slats and at my Choctaw pony where I'm sitting. The train starts to go and that's when I hear them wild things in the boxcar start to stomping as if they was running, as if they got themselves loose and free and gone. The train going on then. Pulling away. And me, I'm not knowing if what I'm hearing is the steam whistle of the big smoking locomotive leaving out the station yard or is it them ponies that's screaming inside that boxcar dark. I heard it in my head a good while after it was way gone, I did. That one time I drove those ponies clear through to Abilene.

The little bluebill or lesser scaup (Aythya affinis), is a small fresh-water diving duck that forages by sifting bottom-mud for small crustaceans and vegetation.

—Birds of America and the Territories, Chapter 13: Swans, Geese, Ducks, Mergansers

Chapter 61
Killing Mister Cahill
January 18, 1877
by Billy Bonney

I knew there'd be some killing coming, this shoe-smith out on Aravaipa Creek being the sort he was. And being as big as he was but did you ever know some smith that wasn't? And me, well. Me being on the sort of small side and being the sort I am, I figured him dead first and then his friends finishing me off. His friends being everyone in that sorry little town, all of them calling him Windy Cahill behind his back on account he's a bigmouth and always running it while everyone is taking his orders, running his errands. Running scared it seemed to me and calling him Mister to his face whenever we came in to get all them ponies we'd be catching shoed. Yes Mister Cahill. No Mister Cahill. Right away Mister Cahill. Laughing at whatever he wanted them to be laughing at. Ha ha Mister Cahill. He had them laughing first time we come in. He's poking in the forge fire, stoking the coals. Good afternoon sir. That's all I say. He turns around to see who's doing the talking. I see his big face full of sweat and soot and grit and his eyebrows and eyelashes singed from the forge. He has his poker still handy and he comes closer to look me over. Well now, he says, but ain't you the polite pipsqueak! Ain't he now, lads? Sure is, Mister Cahill, his friends are saying. Bobbin their heads and laughing. Ha ha Mr. Cahill. And The Boys, my boys—Petey Ray Maxwell and Jake Perlmutter and John James Glasser—all of my boys laughing right along with these so-called friends of his and forgetting we have buyers wanting their stolen ponies shoed and I'm the one they elected to do the talking. But I go on. I just go on. I tell him, We got fourteen horses need shoeing, ones that will stand still for it.

Well now, he says. What do you know. Tell us lads, he says, who is it went and put the runt of the litter in charge?

I seen his sort before. All my life so far I seen it. So what I do, I woof. Like a pup. Like the runt I am.

Well damn, he says. Ain't you just the smart little doggie? Fourteen is it? You're counting that high then. Me, I once seen a smart little doggie count to fourteen with his feet. Fourteen. Well now, he says. Where you got 'em stowed?

And so we get on with it. But it's the same then every time from then on. Peewee this or pipsqueak that or mouse or kitten-pie or peanut. Look out now lads, he says. He's back again, he is. It's the pipsqueak himself, he says. And by jaysus, he says, is he not the very measure of the Wee Folk we got frolicking the green hills back home?

But I go right on. I tell him how many. We've got seven more horses this time Mister Cahill.

He says, Do you now, little doggie? Well, you just keep them coming.

We keep them coming. He keeps on getting them shoed. And he keeps right on funning with me. Jabbing at me with his poker. Grabbing me with the hoof nippers. Snatching off my hat and dunking it in the quench bucket. Ha ha Mister Cahill. He'd be pitching cinders at the sparrows that fly partways in the barn for bits of straw and sometimes he'd be calling his old black dog here boy come on over here and when the old boy comes slinking like it don't want to come on over Mister Cahill gets it sitting up begging and tosses it a cinder. Ha ha Mister Cahill. One time he takes ahold of my coat with his hot tongs. Scorching it good, that's what. And scorching me too, right through it. And that last time, walking up on me flapping his big leather apron, shoo, shoo, shoo little mouse and pushing his big belly out and me into a corner.

When they pulled him off me he's groaning some and holding his big belly with both his hands and between his fingers the bullet hole I made is leaking blood and then they tell me: He had it coming Billy, you had no choice Billy. That's what his friends said, so I guess they wasn't. They sure didn't do much tending to him, but still he didn't die right then. Next day he did, is how I heard it long after I'm long gone. Stick around Billy, is what they were saying, and don't you worry none. They'd tell the sheriff how they'd seen how it was, how he set his own self up for a killing. How surprised they were I let him come at me so damn many times before.

But me, I wasn't surprised. No, Mister Cahill, no I wasn't. Like I said, I figured on it. Straightaway, I did. I come to know right off when trouble is standing in front of me. It takes me no time at all.

The field sparrow (Spizella pusilla) weaves its nest in a low thicket or cluster of grass. To lure predators away from its young, the adult bird will fling itself from its nest and feign a broken wing. The predator chases the apparently injured bird as it struggles to drag itself away. At a safe distance from its nest the sparrow then flies off, leaving the predator dumfounded.

—Birds of America and the Territories, Chapter 77: New World Sparrows, Juncos

Chapter 62
Wanted!

WANTED!

JANUARY 19, 1877

BILLY BONNEY

Alias W. Antrim & W. McCarty
Better Known As Billy the Kid
Age 18, Height Approx. 5 feet 5 inches,
Do not be misled by his Diminutive
Stature or his Pleasant Demeanor!

HE IS SHREWD & DANGEROUS

Wanted for Criminal Activities and
Multiple Murders in Three Counties
Including the Cold-Blooded Killing
of an Unarmed Blacksmith outside
US Fort Grant, Territory of Arizona
Reward offered: $300 Upon Capture
Or Convincing Proof of his Death

Chapter 63
The Ranch on Rio Feliz
Lincoln County, New Mexico
February 1, 1877
by Billy Bonney

I was done with The Boys. Done with rustling, for all it got me. I was long gone from The Boys and going on my own by the time a posse strung up Jake Perlmutter and John James Glasser. Knowing Petey Maxwell, I figured he got out of Lincoln right quick headed for the house he kept at as hideout up around Fort Sumner. And me? If the law didn't yet catch up with me and kill me for the killing I'd done, I knew it would for all the thieving, no matter and never mind how much I keep on running. I run off from the pokey in Silver City going up a chimney. I been on the run in Texas and Arizona both and finding neither of them places none friendlier, I figured get back to New Mexico. The territory was big enough. If I stayed east of the river. If I went wide around cavalry forts. And if I steered clear of Silver City and all the ranches we'd hit.

So I went south again, through Stinking Springs and then through the desert where the hills are every color you could name and some you couldn't, and the rocks along the cliffs are set every which way and looking like they're just about to tumble down but you can tell they've been sitting there that way for nearly forever or as long as there's been rocks. And except for rabbits and pack rats and peccaries there's not a soul that I'm seeing, not for days, and no Indian war parties neither, but plenty of cactus in those parts with spines as big as fish hooks. But some with small stickers too, smaller than splinters and too small to see but I damn sure could feel them in my fingers at night when I start feeling every pebble under my butt poking at me and every burr in my blanket. The cold weather come on fast, and the nights went fast to freezing so even a fire burning right in front of me was keeping only the front half of me warm while I'm looking up at the stars and wondering the way I always do what keeps them lit. I wish I knew. I wish I knew the names of all the stars the way I hear some folks do. Or say they do. I wish I knew the names of all the birds there is. That would be something to know. Something I could say and folks would see there are things I know. Something I could have. But see, right then I have the Choctaw pony for company and a gun for hunting and seep-water for drinking. It's everything I need to be riding north again into New Mexico, staying east of the Rio Grande. Light-hearted. So I've heard it called. Which to my way of thinking is just the same as being empty-hearted, going on, seeing no one, hearing nothing but the wind sweeping up dust devils and the birds that were staying put for winter singing somewhere in the sage the way I am sometimes singing to myself what I remember of my Mam's Timoleague tune on those days birdsong might not be enough, and overhead the buzzards are spinning up so high in that big bright blue that I lose sight of them just by blinking, but they're still up there, for sure they are, turning and tilting in their slow circles, looking down on me and maybe mistaking me for a dead man. But not yet.

So I went on. Wondering what was next out in front of me. And it was a ways further on outside Lincoln we come upon a pretty spread set near the banks of the Rio Feliz.

It was a big ranch house framed in round timbers of peeled pine, red-stone steps to the pine-plank porch, glass and curtains in all the windows. And brass lanterns, the biggest I ever did see and with mirrors set of three ways inside of them, are mounted up on either side of the door.

Big bunkhouse too. Fire going in the corral. Cowhands, all of them Mexicans, smacking calves through the chute one little whiteface at a time, then one of them sitting on its head and one wrapping its hindlegs in rope and one holding the iron to the branding fire. And what I took to be the foreman resting his boot on the rail. They burn the last one and turn it loose and it runs off bawling for its mother. But there is no mother. Not there. Alright muchachos, the foreman tells the Mexicans. Enough for today. Sufficiente. He watches them kick sand on the fire and he doesn't even turn to look my way when he says, Looking for me?

Looking for work, I tell him.

He calls to one of the muchachos. Miguel! That fire ain't out boy, he calls. Sí, el fuego. Ever done any ranching?

Been doing it, I say.

Where you done it?

On ranches. All over.

All over. See them boys? he says and now he's looking in my direction. Thems all Mexicans.

I talk Mexican, I tell him.

He rubs his chin. How old did you say you be? says the foreman

Didn't say, but I'm fifteen.

Small for fifteen, ain't you.

I've seen smaller, I tell him.

You're a light one for wrangling, he says.

I done it plenty, I say.

I don't think so, son. I don't think so.

And then he calls to the Mexicans, Buenas noches, boys. Hasta mañana.

And he tells me, We're done here for today. I've got my own ranch to run.

I don't suppose you need a hand out there, I tell him. Wherever that is.

You don't quit boy, do you? he says.

Haven't yet, I say.

He takes his hat off and looks inside it and sets it back on same way he had it before. Dick Brewer, he says and he puts out his hand.

Will Antrim, I say and I put out mine.

Well now Will, you go get yourself some supper before you go. Get on in there with the boys and you can all talk Mexican together. Go on then, he says.

He calls to one of the men to take my horse. Carlito! Su caballo. And Carlito comes over. He lets my Choctaw drink slow and long from the deep wood-trough in the yard and takes him to the barn, talking to him low and soft. Buen chico, he tells it. Venga.

I take it your horse talks Mexican too, the foreman says. Segundo, find this man a place at the table. Sí sí una comida, he says and me and Segundo and the rest of the muchachos head in for supper.

The old cook they call Encendio is standing at the cookstove, and he's got a string of dried poblanos strung round his neck and a giant spoon in his hand to swat the muchachos off when they start in lifting lids and sniffing and pulling on his apron ties above his big behind. Then it's platters passed around, frijoles charros and tortillas with habichuelas and chorizo and all of it hottern hell, the way my little señorita Jacinta used to fix them, and the men dishing it up in a pile on my plate saying más, más, take some more. Two of them are called Jose and two are Diego and one is Segundo and one is Miguel and there's a Paulito, a Matteo, and a Davito who is the son of Encendio the cook. And me? Me they start right in calling me Billy El Nino. What's a kid doing up this way all by your lonesome, Billy El Nino? Donde esta su mama y su papa? And I tell them, Muertos. Both dead, I tell them. Segundo puts his hand on my shoulder, whispers, Qué pasó? I don't answer right away. I just sit. I wait a bit more. Las maté, I say. I killed them. The two Diegos slap their hands to their mouths. Dios mió, says Davito. And it only takes a minute more when they see me smiling that they all bust out laughing and hooting and smacking me pretty good. Carlito starts clapping and one of the Joses starts on a guitar and someone starts singing and Matteo pulls me out from my chair and swings me around dancing, and we are dancing like crazy people until I need to set myself down. Loco! says Davito. And the cook Encendio starts hollering for us to stop stop stop and he sets down a dish piled up with little sweet cakes and cups of coffee with milk and sugar and we eat all that. All of it. Davito hands around a pack of cheroots, and we smoke and cuss and someone untucks out my shirt and flaps it around back and someone steals off my hat and puts it on his head brimmed up and backways and someone tips back my chair and I fall over and this is as good a place as I've ever been. As good a place.

And then we're done.

We go out the yard. It's near sunset now, but the yard is bright by the mirrors on the brass lanterns and the lanterns lit. Encendio comes out too, calling after me, Billeee! Tu comida! with a little package of some of those frijoles of his wrapped up in paper. Carlito fetches my horse out the barn. He's got bits of oats stuck to his nose, and I can see he's been wet down and curried over. And he's got a new saddle blanket, Mexican style, orange and green weaves. And there's a braid wove in the white and black hairs of his mane with a tiny bell tied in. The way the old Indians used to do.

Everyone comes down off the porch to see us off. To see my Choctaw and asking Dónde lo encontraste? So I tell them I stole him off a Choctaw chief when he wasn't looking, that's where. And that starts them laughing and shoving me around all over again. The two Diegos and Segundo are running their hands over him and feeling his knees and petting his head, but he stands still and blowing big blows hard out his nose and he's looking straight ahead of him, but turning his eyes to the whites to see me, making sure all this poking and patting is something I'm allowing, and that's when I knew he is mine for sure. And muy guapo, they say, pero pequeno. Sí, I say. Pequeño pero fuerte. He is small but strong. The same as me. Cuanto es el caballo? they are asking. But I say oh no, I won't sell him. Not for no money. Well would I trade him for a different horse, another horse, a bigger horse, or even two horses? One for riding and one for packing? But I say no, and gracias, I'm just looking for work, I just got to get on.

I'm ready to get on but the foreman comes over. Dick Brewer. Hold up there son, he says. Mr. Tunstall wants a word with you.

Mr. Tunstall. Coming down the porch steps. Older than me but not by much. Twenty-two or so I'd say and looking like he never gets nowhere near a longhorn cow. Blue shirt peeking out from a black-and-white checkered coat. A stickpin made from a chunk of turquoise set in silver and stuck in the pocket. Pants the color of sand and blue rattler-skin boots peeking out the cuffs and a cattleman's hat that matches. I can't tell if he's toting a gun from the cut of the coat, but I doubt it since he's not out riding down rustlers at the moment.

Spiffing beast, he says. Splendid conformation, though a tad small for my tastes. But quite spiffing, he says and I guess he's talking about my horse.

Allow me to introduce myself, and he puts out his hand and I shake it. John Tunstall, he says.

They call me Will.

Will. Do tell, he says. What might else they call you?

They might else call me William or Willy. Wills. Wilson. Wiley. Or Henry. Or Bill. Or Mr. Bonney. Or they just might call me to dinner. Like they did.

I see. The cheeky sort. Have I seen you somewhere before?

You'd know that better'n I would.

Possibly a picture. A crude drawing on the post office wall.

I don't look like my pictures.

Perhaps you've heard there's been a dodgy character at large, thieving through three counties with his gang of rustlers. Described as a pleasant chap, diminutive but bloody dangerous.

I ain't neither though I don't know about the dim part, I tell him.

Quite the desperado, as you Americans romantically refer to such individuals.

Dodgy, I say.

He's cost us considerable losses. Prime stock.

Do tell, I say.

Given the circumstances, says John Tunstall, such an individual might bloody well consider alternative employment, he says and it's just about now I'm thinking what my Da told me: Keep your gob shut when it needs shutting and pay attention. So I start keeping it shut and the Choctaw keeps on pawing and tossing, telling me let's get going, let's get on out of here and I should be listening to him when this John Tunstall slides the flap of his black and white checkered coat back from his hip and there's the holster I didn't see before and the grip of the pistol inlaid with silver I didn't see before neither.

As it happens we've had a spate of rather annoying incidents of late, says John Tunstall. Occasional gunplay. A business rival seems to be quite resentful of some friendly competition.

Ranchers? I ask him.

Hardly, he says. A Mr. Murphy and a Mr. Dolan, the men who own what they call the Mercantile. A sizable enterprise. Dry goods, sundries, an assortment of staples. Quite the pair and nothing but trouble.

I'm good with trouble, I tell him and I'm wanting to say I'm good with occasional gunplay but I don't.

I'd consider hiring someone who knows his way around the county.

Or even three counties, I tell him.

Considerable losses, says John Tunstall and he still has his hand on his silver-stock pistol. Longhorns primarily, he says.

It's a fine night. No wind where we are in the yard. The trough is near to brimming but the surface stays still as glass and the moon is laid down on it with nary a ripple until a hushing starts in the tops of the trees. It's about that time now, just after sundown when the first chill sets in that the owls are waking up to start their hunting.

Perchance you were the leader of such a gang? he says.

And it's a quiet night. No crickets now. None so late in the year. It's the cold that quiets them. Or kills them. There's only the mournful bawl of a calf looking for its mam out there in the dark. And the tinkle of that tiny bell tied to my Choctaw, so faint you'd hardly hear it if you didn't know it was there. And then comes the whistle of a screechy owl from somewhere. I can see the tops of the pines out past the bunkhouse and I figure that's his hiding place. They like pine trees better'n most, most owls do. It doesn't matter summer or winter, pine trees always have dark places for hiding even when other trees won't and they grow high enough to catch the cold wind where other birds won't go. Beyond the treetops the clouds are moving fast now and steady, lit by that moon. It's not a regular round moon. Just half of a moon. But there's more moon up there by the shape of it along the edge where it goes from bright to dark. I wonder what's in the dark parts. I wonder what the moon is. Once my mam told me if you keep on looking you can see the man in the moon. After that I always looked and looked, but all I saw were just the white and empty places on the moon, white as the old bones you come across in the desert, and gray patches the color of ash where the fire was when it's gone cold come morning. But no man up there, no. None I never did see. Once when I looked long enough I thought I saw a bird. A bird in the moon. One wing up and one wing down, or maybe that one wing wasn't there at all but tore clear off.

I was never the leader of a gang, I tell him. I was never the leader of anybody. I was always just for me, Billy.

The call of the western screech owl (Megascops kennicottii) is a descending whistle with occasional barks and screeches. Its diet consists of rats, mice, and birds, but it will take small trout from streams during the night.

—Birds of America and the Territories, Chapter 42: True Owls

Chapter 64

Journal Entry of John H. Tunstall, February 3, 1877

Statements of the Mexicans in My Employ
Regarding Newly Hired Hand, Wm. Bonney:

Él trabaja duro. Es un buen amigo. Me gusta mucho.
—José Septimo Munõz, ranch hand

Billy he good boy. No trouble, no kill nobody.
—José Gabrielle Jorge Lopez, ranch hand and drover

After he eat, he come la cocina, he say gracias Encendio.
—Encendio Julio Tomás Contreras, cook

Es más listo que la jefa.
—Davito Leo Contreras, drover and son of the cook

His horse eat before he eat.
—Carlito Cruz de Juárez, stable hand

Él era un muchacho ordinario.
—Paulito Alejandro Chávez, ranch hand and wrangler

Le gusta ver pájaros. Always he looks at birds.
—Matteo del Mundo, ranch hand

Uno pequeño. A small one.
—Diego Arroyo, drover

He will leave us. Muy pronto.
—Diego Ismael Leandro, ranch hand

He bad inside him. Muy malo.
—Miguel Mercuerio, drover

He say he likes las señoritas, but he has none.
—Segundo Arbolito, drover

Chapter 65
Bloody Hell

The Lincoln County Ledger

"Listen Up"

Vol. 77, No. 2 | February 15, 1877 | Price 12 cents

NEWCOMER TO LINCOLN COUNTY

Ranchers and residents hereabouts are no longer obliged to trade at what has been the only store in all of Lincoln County, that being the Murphy & Dolan Mercantile. John Tunstall, a 23-year-old entrepreneur and newcomer to The Territory by way of London, has announced that his Emporium offers "fair deals and quality goods at reasonable prices." The Emporium has a full inventory of ranch and homestead necessities, "Everything from carpet to corsets," says Tunstall, including his own brand of canvas clothing favored by miners and ranchers alike. In addition, Tunstall has launched a banking enterprise, promising "secure loans at better rates than the Dolan Savings & Loan". Mercantile proprietors Lawrence Murphy and James Dolan have expressed their consternation, as many of their former customers who complained of the high prices set by Murphy & Dolan have already taken their trade to Tunstall's. Skirmishes and bouts of gunplay have occurred between the Irish owners of the Mercantile and British-born Tunstall, and acts of vandalism have been reported. When asked if he means to take trade away from the Mercantile and from Dolan's Savings & Loan, he stated, "Bloody hell yes" and characterized the business dealings of Murphy & Dolan as "dodgy". Tunstall has already established a 3200-acre ranch on Rio Feliz and has accumulated 4,000 head. He is currently hiring armed ranch hands and wranglers, as well as stockboys and clerks for his new Emporium. *The Ledger* bids a heartfelt "Howdy Do" to the Brit in our midst!

LOCAL WOMAN WINS COMPETITION

Hattie "Huck-Towel" McLendon has again garnered 1st prize in the county-wide baking competition for her hummingbird cake. She credits the win to her "secret" filling. When asked for the recipe, Hattie replied, "It's a secret."

QUOTE OF THE DAY

☞ *The Passenger Pigeon is doomed to disappear from our skies, and ornithologists will find them no more, except those specimens of taxidermy in museums of natural history.*

—Bénédict Henry Révoil

Chapter 66
John Tunstall's Emporium
Lincoln, New Mexico
February 28, 1877 – The Moon of Sleeping Bears

Now in this month the Apache call the Moon of Sleeping Bears, the last of the rotting leaves hang black and ragged in the cottonwoods and the manzanita is rimmed with frost. Stones open at their seams, fissures sprout crystals. Beds of shale heave along primordial planes. A coyote goes cold and alone amid the withered sage, its muzzle beaded with ice, its paw-pad imprint dark on the snowdust. Above him a goshawk hunts in the clear winter blue. A jackrabbit shirks. The goshawk soars, dives. A brief chase ensues through a tangle of salt cedar and the rabbit tumbles headfirst in mad abandon, its haunches awry over the slope of a draw as the goshawk is wingspread upon it. The rabbit is gently enfolded, the talons sunk in. The sun ascends. South of the town of Lincoln, the pure light of morning goes pale gold on the peaks. To the north spreads an open terrain spotted with new snow and a scattering of blue juniper and piñon extending upland to Las Montañas Capitan. Cloud shadows climb the foothills, break and bend to the rifts and faults. Great sweeps of snow rise from the crests of pitchstone and feldspar where the wind that scours the hardpan is born and descends though the stands of spruce and ponderosa pine crowding the slopes below the timberline. It folds the browning buffalo grass along the banks of Rio Feliz where two thousand head of John Tunstall's longhorns graze and turn their hindquarters into it, and it spins through the rutted thoroughfare of Lincoln, the county's sole outpost of commerce, rattling the doors and windows of the meager assortment of storefronts and establishments of trade.

Livery Horses Boarded & For Hire

J. H. Holliday, Dentist

J. Riley Restaurant & Rooms

Cards & Kinship, Fine Liquor & Ladies

Lawrence Murphy Assay & Ore Recovery

Traveling Tintypist—Expert Images

James Dolan Savings & Loan

The Mercantile Store—Assorted Provisions—Murphy & Dolan, Prop.

wherein its Irishmen proprietors Murphy and Dolan seethe and scheme, their monopoly broken. Bankruptcy looms. They have been undersold by J. Tunstall Enterprises, in both the cattle market and the Mercantile. Lucrative beef contracts dissolved, foot traffic at the Mercantile diminished. Cashflow has slowed to a trickle. Moth worms are hatching in their bales of woolens. Flour turning rancid in the sacks. In the storage bins of the Mercantile cellar, pumpkins kept in beds of straw leak their liquefied innards, strung-up onions sprout limp stalks, and pink protuberances resembling infants' toes poke crookedly from the potatoes. Greenmold slimes the sides of beef and bacon hooked and hanging in the meat shed. There are cottony patches on the slabs of elk. There are weevils in the cracker barrel.

There are gunmen on the porch.

They call themselves a posse, having been appointed by the sheriff of Lincoln County, one W. B. Brady, another Irishman, who happens to be deep in cahoots with his countrymen Murphy and Dolan as well as deep in their pockets. They spend their days in shifts on the Mercantile porch, wrapped in their thick canvas coats, warming themselves with smokes and pulls from a bottle they pass one to another, their chairs tipped back on the floorboards and their boots propped along the rail. Come nightfall, they untilt their chairs and unprop their boots. They stand and stamp away the stiffness and cold. And they saddle up and they ride out. Sometimes somewhat drunk. Sometimes with the sheriff himself, who has essentially given up on keeping the peace.

And when they are done with their evening's doings—those being riding through the open range and John Tunstall's vast acreage, cutting his fences, tossing torches into his grazing lands, stealing his horses and longhorns—they return and sit suchwise on the porch of the Mercantile as they have so sat since spring and the months the Apache call the Moon of Waking Bears and the Moon of Come Back Birds. As they have so sat through the midsummer months the Apache call the Moon of Long Day Heat and the Moon of Falling Feathers, and on into the autumn of the year with the passing of the Moon of Leaving Geese—sat with their breech-loading carbines and Winchester repeaters laid across their laps or lifted with gunsights set on former customers from far and wide within the county as well as familiar townsfolk and past patrons of the Mercantile who now turn up their collars and hurry past as fast as is possible without breaking into a run and proceed instead on to Tunstall's Emporium as the posse shoots off their hats and sometimes wings a few of them while calling them out with an assortment of hoots and threats.

That you Davey? Yeah you bet it's you, we see you taking your trade to that damn Limey.

Hey, Calvin. Where you think you're going? The bank's thataway and your loan's past due.

Howdy there, Leahy. You too, Mam. A bit risky toting your wife to town these days, don't you think?

Well now, if it ain't Ed Newcomb. Walking on by like he never knowed us. Fucking turncoat.

Hey mister. Yeah you. You're looking for trouble doing business with that Brit. We'd hardly recommend it.

Looky there, boys. It be Red-Feather Ed, the Emporium injun. You goddamn heathen. Wasn't that your boy I seen out hunting on the East Branch Creek? Likely to wind up shooting his own self he's not careful.

Why Tom-Bob Conroy! What you looking so riled about? Was that a new hat? Go on then, report it to Sheriff Brady. Go get me arrested.

And one door down from this posse of louts on the Mercantile porch is the printing office of

The Lincoln County Ledger: "Listen Up"

and one more past that,

The Emporium—J. Tunstall, prop.
Staples & Fancy Goods—Cash or Credit

where Tim Miles oversees the ground floor (boots and clothing, notions, dry goods, canned goods, produce, pantry staples, feed) and the long marble counter that holds the gleaming brass-keyed register and the lidded glass jars of jaw busters and candy sticks and the mahogany box that holds the loose tobacco and cheroots.

Billy Bonney runs the second floor (tack, hardware, farm and household) where he keeps accounts and keeps watch on activities in the street. He has informed John Tunstall that he can read, write, count, shoot, ride, wrangle, rope, brand, rustle, rotate stock, correspond, deal with complaints, and cipher. He has been given a workplace beside the window. Small desk and chair. Ledger, pen, inkpot. He records transactions. Tabulates customer debt and credit. Tracks inventory. He stocks and restocks. He makes note of supplies and sundries, surplus and shortages. And he makes lists:

Shelves #1 to 5:
Hats, 1 doz Stetson Mallory, half doz Range Rider, half doz straw
Trousers, assorted sizes, 2 bales denim, 2 bales checkered

Shelves #6 to 11:
Sack coats & frock coats, 6, each, one size (reorder first of month)
Slickers & dusters (fresh out, delivery expected)
Fabric in full bolts, 15 yards each—calico, stripe, gingham, flannel
Assorted notions (full stock)—needles, spools, buttons, rickrack

Bin # 1 to 4:
Cracked corn, 40-lb sacks, 34
Whole corn, 40-lb sacks, 80
Chicken scratch, 50-lb sacks, 210
Salt licks, 3 now. Delivery 12 days
Winter wren (new one)
Crows (all around town)
White-crowned sparrow (new one)
White-winged dove (already got him)

Tack—2nd floor:
Bosal hackamores, 11
Bridles, snaffle and bitless, 22 each
McClellan saddle, US Army issue, 40
Saddle pads and blankets, 7 & 11

He sweeps, mops. Chops wood, the axe sparking where it strikes the seams of ice. He stokes the stove. The days are short. The nights arrive early and go long. At dusk the celestial hunter and his star dog rise above the southwest horizon and wait for the bear that roams the sky.

He is hungry. But he is an old bear. His eyes are weak and his claws are dull and there is little in the winter heavens to eat. The hunter puts cornmeal in the bowl of the big dipper and waits for the bear. The old bear with his old eyes does not see the hunter. The sky dog leaps ahead. The cornmeal spills from the bowl. The bear bounds away, but he is slow and his tracks are made of stars and he is easy to follow. The hunter takes an arrow from the quiver. He nocks the arrow to the bowstring. He draws the bow and lets the arrow fly and it finds the heart of the bear. Blood runs from the wound. The scattered cornmeal becomes the Milky Way. The blood that pours from the heart of the bear becomes the color of the daybreak sky in the east. Morning winds. Empty seedpods of devil's claw rattle on the desert flats. Stalks of saltbush tremble in the gravelly ruts. Some birds have come down from the tundra. Some are stragglers and some turned off-course by storms. Some have come by way of the Milky Way and in flight have fed on the cornmeal spilled from the dipper. Some are winter visitors. The dove on the livery roof. White-crowned sparrow in the creosote brush behind the bank. Billy can see the thoroughfare and the porch of the Mercantile. The posse. The potshots. In the roadway now goes a dog no one lays claim to but sleeps among the horses in the livery hay. Now a ball of thistle weed tumbles adrift. And now comes John Tunstall in his shahtoosh coat and cashmere muffler, astride his horse, a stockinged chestnut thoroughbred. Its oiled hoofs, its braided mane. Past the weathered boards of the storefronts and shops. Livery. The Lincoln County Ledger. Now past Murphy & Dolan Mercantile. Coming straight along now, unwavering. Not so much as a glance to the men and their guns on the porch. Touching his hat brim to the very few townsfolk out and about on the rough-cut sidewalk boards. Tying the thoroughbred to the Emporium rail. Now coming through the Emporium door. The jamb bells jingle.

John Tunstall huffs on his hands and stamps as if there is snow or mud on his boots. Abysmal weather, Timothy old bean! he says. Utterly abysmal.

Beans? says Tim Miles. Kidney and pinto most likely, just ask Billy. Billy keeps the list, he says but John Tunstall has already strolled away, inspecting his store as he is fond of doing. A bit of a strut. A nod to a line of boots, a display of crockery, a row of Stetsons set on pegs. Attempting to engage the customers in conversation, a sullen crowd of late, given the coldness of the day and the gunplay in the street.

Ah Mr. Tolliver, finding what you need?

Good day, Mr. Conroy. I believe I spied your newly apertured hat in the thoroughfare.

Calico, Mrs. Leahy? We have calico in stock. And gingham, if you need it. And I believe we just received a new bolt of flannel.

He peers up the staircase. Billyboy! he calls. Are you there?

Billy pokes his head over the upstairs rail. Billy looking down. That curious face. Those ears, that bucky mouth.

Yessir Mr. Tunstall? says Billy. I'm here.

Hello Billy, says John Tunstall. Come down here just half a tick, would you? Show this good lady our fabric selection. And perhaps our display of notions.

John Tunstall peers out the window at the Mercantile porch. There sit the Mercantile sentries. Have a look Billyboy, he says. See the one with the limp? He's Buckshot Roberts, maimed in your Civil War. And that one with the cigar, that would be the sheriff, one W. B. Brady. A proper collection of drunkards. Miscreants. A rather ghastly lot. They've even enlisted new arrivals from Ireland.

Yessir, Mr. Tunstall.

Just John, says John Tunstall.

John. Yessir, says Billy.

Listen here Billyboy, he says, leaning close in. I hereby give you the nod. Feel free to shoot them all on sight.

Yessir, says Billy. I'll go load up.

Ha ha, dear Billyboy. Absolutely marvelous, John Tunstall says. But of course I jest. My feeble attempt at drollery.

Though they are a rather ghastly lot, says Billy.

I say Billyboy! says John Tunstall. You'll be speaking the king's English in no time.

He takes his pocket watch on its chain from his pocket. I'd better be off then, he says and heads for the door. We've got two hundred cows headed to Fort Stanton today, two hundred more to Camp Grant tomorrow.

He adjusts his hat in the mirror at the Stetson display. He adjusts his muffler. He goes to Tim Miles stationed at the counter. Tallyho then, Timothy, he says.

Close up at seven Billyboy, he tells Billy. Then come up the ranch for spot of supper, eh. I'll tell Guadalupe. Tonight's likely cat's arse and cabbage, says John Tunstall.

How does she fix it? says Billy.

The jamb bells jingle.

Tim Miles is toting up Mr. Tom-Bob Conroy's purchases. One hackamore. One claw hammer. Tom-Bob, says Tim Miles, go fetch yourself another one of these, this handle is cracked. Molasses one half gallon. White flour ten pounds. Would the missus be doing some baking? One Stetson. Well now Tom-Bob, ain't this pretty. I expect you'll be wearing it home.

Billy on his way back upstairs, calls to Tim Miles. Tallyho Timothy, he says. Timothy old bean.

Pinto and kidney, says Tim Miles. We got both.

Billy upstairs. Desk and chair at the second-floor window. Three men are sitting on the Mercantile porch. He points at one of the men with his pointing finger. Bang, he says. Then bang to the other. A third man sits on the Mercantile steps.

Bang, says Billy. A jest, says Billy. That's what you'd call it.

Bin #5–9:
Sugar, 10-lb sacks, 44
White flour, 10-lb sacks, 22
Molasses, half gal jugs, 7
Kidney beans, 20-lb sacks, 16
Pinto beans, 20-lb sacks, 9

Hardware—2nd floor:
Saws—carcass, ripcut, crosscut, keyhole, 2 man—3 doz each
Axes—long handled, 5 (5 more expected next week)
Hammers—ball peen, claw, dead-blow –not counted
Rope—10 spools each—jute, sisal, hemp, 150-ft lengths
Misc—spirit level 2, yardstick 3, trowel 4, spade 1
Goshhawk (new one)
Turkey vulture (are they following me? Ha ha)
Lesser goldfinch (new one)

Counter:
Jaw busters (delivery Tuesday)
Sassafras candy sticks (full jar)
Tobacco pouches, papers, matches, cheroots—3 doz each

The Moon of Dying Snow is coming. Though the buffalo grass is not yet greening. Berry buds still closed tight on the white cedar. Jackrabbits have already been seen sunning themselves when the sun is highest. Antelope have been spotted on the lower slopes.

The next moon will be the Moon of Waking Bears. They will stretch their great limbs, restless in their sleep. They will hold their new cubs to their bodies. The new cubs will coo and grunt and suckle while their mothers sleep.

The Moon of Come Back Birds will follow. But until then the birds are scarce, except for those that know the ways of overwintering or the ones who were too old or weak for going when the going was good, when summer was ending and the winds of migration would have carried them away. Dusky flycatcher on a spear of Spanish bayonet. A goldfinch falling from its perch.

And always, there are the raptors. They have no need to leave. They watch and wait for whatever is skittering for cover or trembling in the brush, whatever tries to make itself small and unnoticed in this open country where by day all is illuminated: every pebble, seed, footprint, track, and twig; every slender blade of buffalo grass or creosote leaf; every barb of barrel cactus or cliff-rose thorn; every cast-off feather or left-behind bone or wind-scoured carcass or clump of fur blown by the wind and snagged in the spines of a prickly pear. They watch from the air where they tilt their wings to the updrafts and glide and hover, and from treetops and upland overhangs. They take the creatures who run from them until their hearts split as frozen stones will do, and they take the creatures who do not run at all, the ones slowed with the cold who sense that their days are done and so rest themselves, warm themselves in plain view and the sunny places. And always, there are the buzzards to feed on what is left of the fallen.

The white-crowned sparrow (Zonotrichia leucophrys) does not fly to its nest directly when returning with food for its nestlings. Instead, it lands nearby and cautiously creeps the remaining distance as would a fugitive on foot to conceal the nest location from predators.

—Birds of America and the Territories, Chapter 77: New World Sparrows, Juncos

The goshawk (Accipiter gentilis) is a fearless hunter, capable of chasing ground prey through woodlands and dense vegetation with its seemingly reckless acrobatics on the wing.

Chapter 15: Eagles, Hawks, Kites

The undulating flight of lesser goldfinch (Spinus psaltria) confuses predator hawks that hunt it in the air.

Chapter 76: Grosbeaks, Finches

During the nesting season, the tiny winter wren (Troglodytes hiemalis) will destroy the eggs of other birds by puncturing them with its beak or ruin their nests by filling them up with debris.

Chapter 61: Wrens

Chapter 67
The Night She Goes
The Ranch on Rio Feliz
March 1, 1877 – The Moon of Dying Snow

Hollow hoof-clop. The Choctaw pony on the hardpacked courtyard earth. Billy riding in. No moon, the waxing crescent already descended. The morning stars persist without a trace of daybreak in the East. Carlito waiting at the barn door and holding a lantern aloft by its wire bale. Señor Billy, he says in the quiet voice befitting the early hour and the windless night and the final yip-yip-hoos from a distant company of coyotes discussing the disappearance of the moon and the winter dearth of rabbits and the heliacle rising of the dog star after its season behind the sun.

Billy swings his legs right over left and slides from the saddle, both feet to the ground. Buenas noches, says Billy.

The night she goes, says Carlito. He takes the reins. He pats the horse on its neck, the dark sepia patch of hide under the fringe of double-colored mane. Mi chico, he tells it. Mi buen chico.

Who's a good boy? says Billy. Me or my horsey?

Carlito smiles and shakes his head. You good boy Billy, he says.

Me good boy, says Billy.

The big lanterns on either side of the ranch house door have long been put out, but the long windows along the porch wall are lit from within, the light wavering from the fire in the hearth. Above the roof, chimney smoke rises straight up. No drift. So calm the wind. So close and clear the sounds of the Choctaw's nickering from inside the barn. The rapid pattering of grain sliding into a pail like birdshot spilling. A single hollow note from up in the pines past the bunkhouse where they stand peaked in silhouette blacker than the star-dusted sky behind. Not quite a whistle. Not quite a coo. Billy looks. Out there somewheres. Or up there somewheres. Not the wind because there is no wind to creak a limb or pipe on through a tree hollow or a woodpecker hideout. Been fooled before. He waits but the sound does not come again. He cups his hands to his mouth and calls a string of hoots. Waits again. Come on, you *owl*. I know it's you. And then there it is, coming back to him from the tops of the pines—whistling hoots so the same as the ones he sent.

I knew it was you, says Billy. Right off, I knew.

Now on the porch. The brass door knocker in the shape of a longhorn's head with a nose ring to grasp for the knocking. Billy does not knock. He goes quietly. Measured steps. The boards too new and well-placed to squeak. Edging to the long windows, closed against the winter air. Almost a sidle. Curtains held away with tassel tiebacks. The pattern ivy and vine. The gauzy cotton sort Billy's mother had hung in the log house on White Hog Lane that turned gray with stove soot and red-flecked from the spew of her cough. But an odd sort of curtain for a man's house, for a ranch house window, but selected by Tunstall himself, remembering the same pattern in his grandmother's house when he was a boy, where every spring Grandma Tunstall stood on a chair and slid the curtains from the rod and stepped down from the chair, and washed them by hand and rehung them fresh and white again, until that spring she became fearful of falling, of standing on a chair, of reaching up and sliding them off the rod, and that was the spring she left them yellowing in the window of the room where she sat, where she kept a sky-blue parakeet named FiFi in a cage by the window. So it could hear the birds outside, young Tunstall was told. Until it escaped the cage one day, claws caught in the curtain threads but too high and out of reach for his grandmother to retrieve and there it hung and died of the struggle and there it stayed until both were found. Oh both were found. Oh yes he remembered. Grandmother Tunstall in her chair, mottled and cold. The parakeet an empty husk of itself and its sky-blue feathers faded by the sun coming through the curtains. How well he remembered. How strange and hollow the remorse he had felt. But here he has them, here they are hanging in John Turnstall's ranch house, in John Tunstall's windows, though impractical in these parts and already tinged with desert dust.

Beyond the curtains, the room is richly lit by hearthfire, logs racked on andirons topped with snail-coil finials and by standing a pair of candelabra shoulder-high and in the Spanish style of curlicues and scrollwork wrought in iron. Their twenty candles lit and dripping. The waxcatchers clotted. On the ledgestone mantlepiece sits a mahogany clock and a display of little ambrotypes in frames of gutta-percha and gilt. Mother. Father. A tiny lad astride a horse. A sidetable veneered in golden oak, and partly covered with a chevroned runner of a rough Apache weave, and placed upon it two crystal-cut glasses, thick-bottomed for weight, and a crystal decanter of amber spirits topped by a crystal stopper. The settee is upholstered in red-brown cowhide and studded in brass and there John Tunstall presently sits, his feet arranged foot over foot on the matching tussock. His fine slim boots. Feather stitching. Soles barely scuffed. An assortment of books lay scattered about on settee and sidetable and floor. Some leather-bound with gold-embossed spines but mostly dime novels thoroughly thumbed, an assortment of titles and frayed covers with illustrations. *Apache Massacre* (tomahawk beside a blood-spattered prairie bonnet). *I Joined the Jesse James Gang* (squinty eyes above a bandana). *Dead Man's Hand—The Killing of Bill Hickock* (aces and eights). And *Badlands Vigilante*. And *Santa Fe Sharpshooter*. And *Heroes of the Alamo*. To name a few. *Young Gunslinger* is open and face down in his lap. And the one John Tunstall sits reading, currently become his favorite: *Boy Desperado* (both six-shooters blazing).

Billy takes his pistol from his holster and taps the business end to the windowglass. John Tunstall throws down his books, scrambles to his feet. Billy there at the window doffing his hat.

Marvelous, says John Tunstall, at the door. Absolutely brilliant. Well come on then, my young desperado. Come in and show me that gun.

Hawks kill by puncturing vital organs with their talons, but owls squeeze their prey to death with their large robust feet and wide toe-span. The long-eared owl (Asio otus) will conceal itself deep within an evergreen, leaving to hunt and returning throughout the night and in the hours before dawn.

—Birds of America and the Territories, Chapter 42: True Owls

Chapter 68
The Friendship on the Rio Feliz
April 9, 1877 – The Moon of Waking Bears

Winter went away with green stems sprouting from the straw-beds of old buffalo grass. Berry buds opened on the twigs of white cedar. The Moon of Waking Bears was full. Antelope had been spotted browsing where the snow fields shrank away from the lower slopes. Billy rode out with John Tunstall to hunt. Deer, antelope, and elk. Grouse and rabbit. John Tunstall declared rabbit was most delicious when prepared as lapin au vin, but of course shallots were impossible to come by in these parts, and the last time he gathered his own champignons he nearly poisoned himself, and anyway his Mexican cook Guadalupe had ignored his instructions entirely and made a fiery hot conejo stew with corn and chili sauce instead. Billy brought down an antelope nearly two miles off. John Tunstall was a poor shot. Though a fine horseman. Quite the figure astride his thoroughbred chestnut by the name of Sutton Star. It had traveled transatlantic with him on the Cunard Line, he said. Just ten days to cross the Atlantic! Liverpool to New York aboard the fabulous Scythia on her maiden voyage. A horse on the sea in a stateroom converted to stable! said John Tunstall. I dare say the cost was astronomical. Quite. But the service? Impeccable. Proper chuffed, I was. The cuisine first rate, although the wine list was lacking a decent selection of cabernets. And the aperitifs?—limited, unfortunately, to amontillado, sherry, and pernod anise. But the chateaubriand that was served on the last night of the voyage—captain's table and all that rot—quite good, quite good, although the sauce béarnaise could have used a tad more salt, at which point Billy inquired if that sauce was any good on bear. Oh marvelous, said John Tunstall, and he put his hand on Billy's shoulder. I so enjoy these hunts with you, old chap. Comparable, he said, to fox hunting with the Quorn, riding the hounds in the rolling grasslands of Leicestershire and the fox thickets of Burley-on-the-Hill.

Good eating, them foxes? asked Billy.

Ha! said John Tunstall. Just brilliant.

Unlike other birds, dusky grouse (Dendragapus obscurus) move to higher elevations in winter and consume the green needles of the Douglas fir, hemlock, and pine.

—Birds of America and the Territories, Chapter 20: Grouses, Ptarmigans

Chapter 69
Guns and Ghost Horses
The Ranch on Rio Feliz,
Spring and Summer – 1877

Now the Moon of Come Back Birds. The cows bear their calves. Olive warblers nest in the ponderosa pines. Spring nights are cool and the night skies so clear. The constellation of the kite rises and flies. Arcturus at its tail. The calves tremble and tuck close to their mothers. The spring grass is tender but they do not eat. Kinglets in the conifers. Dick Brenner stays on as foreman. The muchachos are up with the sun and stoking their fires but there are many calves and more hands are needed for branding. John Tunstall turns Billy loose from the Emporium and sends him back to the ranch. Back to the muchachos. Encendio is cooking up a great earthenware pot of habichuelas and chiles and chorizo when he sees Billy in the courtyard and he comes running. Billeee! he calls, Ven aqui! Billy weaves and dodges away. Then the muchachos. Sequndo releases a calf and Miguel throws down his iron and they climb the corral fence. Now here comes Paulito, Matteo, Davito, Carlito, the two Joses, the two Diegos. Our Billy, they call. Our Billy he returns. They hug him hello. Push him to the ground. Carlito throws him over his shoulder and marches around. Ayuda ayuda! says Billy smacking Carlito in the head. Dick Brenner comes over and puts his boot to the rail. Boys, he says, them cows don't be branding themselves.

Brenner hires two new ranch hands. Neither are Mexican. Both are handy with guns.

One is Charles Bowdre, son of a cotton farmer and when at forty years old he decides he is done with the family plantation and the privilege of riches, done with the pretentions of southern gentility, goddamn it, and with civility and civilization in general, he leaves Georgia behind him and heads west to New Mexico. In Bernalillo he marries the seamstress señorita Manuela Herrera and he treats her with tenderness, but he is mostly gone, putting loot in pocket. He joins a posse or two and is paid to catch rustlers, though he is known to lynch a few on his own while they're still in his custody. He is considered good company by the men he meets and even the men who fear him, and known to be steadfast in all his endeavors but quick to avenge a double cross. A man who weighs his options with consideration, generally a quiet man, self-contained you might say, though recently shoot-em-up drunk in the thoroughfare of Lincoln where he killed a bystander who didn't run for cover quite fast enough and another one who did.

The other gun is Tom O'Folliard, just turned twenty-one, orphaned in childhood and left to his own devices. Drifting through Texas in early spring, the month the Apache call the Moon of Waking Bears. A skirmish here, a tussle or two there. Goaded into a gunfight just outside Galveston. One dead and one wounded. And in Corpus Christi, killed a man he caught stealing the bloodbay he named Bo. Then arrested. Released. Ranch work. Running. Taking a northwest turn for the Territory of New Mexico by way of the Panhandle through Palo Duro Canyon. There riding a narrow trail through the sand-scoured bones of Kiowa ponies slaughtered by the Cavalry. Piebalds, duns, palominos, Appaloosas, all. His horse goes wary with eyes rolling to white and ears pricked at old echoes of gunshot ricochet and the ghost horses' screams as they try to climb the canyon walls, the slide and crash of loose rock. The sounds that only a horse could hear. Though Tom himself is somewhat spooked by the silence. No birdsong. No wind. No insect rasp or drum. Only hoofbeats. Tom keeping the horse to a trot. Steady now Bo, he whispers. Easy now, he says. He is cold without knowing why as he rides the terrain that keeps the corpses of Chief Lone Wolf and Chief Woman's Heart. And others unnamed, become skullbones peeping up from the hardpan and desert dust. Eye sockets growing sage and buffalo grass. Teeth tiles of polished stone. Nothing here is newly dead or decaying and yet there are buzzards winding clockwise high above him and knowing only what buzzards could know. Up ahead, the escarpments part. The mouth of the gorge. Then on he goes. Lubbock. Briscoe. Amarillo in April. Through the Llano Estacado and the high plateau in the Moon of Come Back Birds. And finally turning his horse toward the Territory of New Mexico. Birdsong in the sage and the hardpan burning and sometimes the buzzards still spinning above him.

The two men arrive at the ranch on Rio Feliz in summer. Charlie Bowdre in August, the month the Apache call the Moon of Falling Feathers. And Tom O'Folliard in July, the Moon of Long Day Heat, but still feeling the Palo Duro cold.

The olive warbler (Peucedramus olivaceous) nests high atop the Ponderosa Pines where it is believed to creep along the branches foraging for insects in the tree's needles. It is never seen at eye level and very little is known about its life.

—Birds of America and the Territories, Chapter 72: Wood Warblers

The weight of the tiny golden-crowned kinglet (Regulus satrapa) is approximately that of a copper penny.

Chapter 64: Gnatcatchers, Kinglets

Chapter 70
The Peacemaker

THE ROYAL ARMORIES MUSEUM OF LONDON

Hall of American Weaponry

Exhibit 22: Colt Single Action Revolver

On loan from the Tunstall Estate, The Royal Armouries Museum presents this Colt six-shooter belonging to John H. Tunstall, friend to that desperado of the American West, "Billy the Kid." The revolver, also called "The Peacemaker," is mentioned in a letter (Exhibit 23) penned by Tunstall in 1877 while at his ranch in the American Territory of New Mexico and sent to his father living in London. It was in February of the following year that the young outlaw set out to avenge John Tunstall's murder.

Chapter 71
John Tunstall's Letter

THE ROYAL ARMORIES MUSEUM OF LONDON
Hall of Archived Correspondence
Exhibit 23: Letter of John Turnstall to His Father

September 18, 1877. Lincoln New Mexico
Dear Father,

I again take pen in hand to inform you that I remain in the land of the living, and beg your forgiveness for the delay in correspondence. Having voiced your concerns upon my departure from London, and your doubts regarding my ability to establish either a retail venture or a ranching enterprise, especially in light of my lack of experience at both, let me now reassure you: Your investment is secure and all is well! I have staked my claim, as is said hereabouts, and as is also said, business is booming at both ends, despite what most entrepreneurs and lesser men might count as insurmountable obstacles. Most encumbering has been the absence of a structured law system in these largely unsettled territories of which New Mexico is no exception. As a result, local citizens hire the most violent individuals to maintain a semblance of order. Many of these so-called peacekeepers are simply killers looking for steady work, or as in the case in this district, cowards employed to do the bidding of political and economic forces. And while the rules of government and society as we know them do not exist here, there are unwritten codes of conduct that I find quite amusing. Allow me to present two examples: "Remove your guns before sitting at the dining table," and "Never try on another man's hat." This, Father, is what passes here for law.

I have, however, managed to overcome the prejudices and presumptions that inhabitants of this county previously harbored about doing business with a foreigner such as myself. They have abandoned their long-standing trade relations with my sole competitor, the Murphy & Dolan Mercantile, and its banking, ranching, and retail operations, having been persuaded by the fine and fairly priced selection of goods at my Emporium. Rifles, for example, as well as ranching necessities and homesteading staples, are, if you would indulge me in another purely American colloquialism, selling like hotcakes. In addition, Father, I have garnered the US Cavalry contracts for beef by undercutting those prices set by Messrs. Murphy and Dolan to their great consternation and embarrassment. And due to my determined efforts to become the richest man in the Territory of New Mexico and thereby restoring the Tunstall family name to the upper echelons of British society, I shall soon drive this Irish duo into bankruptcy by my economic acumen, business intuition, and refusal to yield to intimidation. Oh, yes, Father. Intimidation! Allow me to elucidate. They have collected an assortment of thugs to harass me, have paid the so-called county sheriff—a sniveling pawn in their game—for his partisanship, and have gone on to call this ridiculous assemblage a "posse." How quaint a notion! On several occasions they have attempted to set my barn and grazing lands afire, stolen a number of my cattle breeding stock, as well as several horses on their raids. You inquired in your last letter about reporting these felonies to the authorities. Such action on my part would be fruitless, given that the Territorial Governor turns a blind eye and that the local sheriff, a pawn in their game by the name of W. B. Garrett, aligns himself with these criminals and openly participates in these nefarious activities. You would be enthralled, as I am, by their recklessness, their pathetic displays of bravado, and their attempts at coercion. Rather than succumb, however, I have acquired a fine center-fire six-shooter and have hired several competent individuals, skilled marksmen all, to protect my property. One young man in particular, though accused of an assortment of crimes throughout the Territory, has proven to be a hard worker, amiable companion, and trustworthy friend. My foreman, Mr. Brenner, who is usually quite the level-headed sort, has urged that we retaliate against the Mercantile proprietors, but I have restrained him from such deeds which these bullies would find provocative. In the end, I believe that Mr. Murphy and Mr. Dolan will acknowledge defeat and that gunplay can be avoided. It is my hope that they will withdraw as gentlemen should, when I appeal in earnest to their sense of decency and fair play and simply inquire, "Might we be civil?"

And now I must conclude. Give my love to Mother. I trust you both attended the Christmas Concert Spectacular at Albert Hall. Such things are unknown in this country. It is currently are quite cold here, but dry, and I think often of your enduring the meteorological inevitability of a drizzly London winter. And lastly, in your most recent letter you did not mention the health of our spaniel or whether the leg has healed. Dear old Prince. Please advise me of his condition in your very next correspondence.

In the meantime, I shall keep on here, but you need not worry for my happiness. I have grown fond of this land, the mountains that surround me, and its broad and barren vistas. It is wild with adventure.

And I do not trouble yourself with fears for my safety. I have the situation well in hand.

With most sincere regards, I remain your devoted son.
John Henry Tunstall

Author's Note: Daybreak

Daybreak. A cool morning along the Rio Feliz. The month the Apache call the Moon of Leaving Geese. John Tunstall has decided to ride today, perhaps to shoot duck on the Rio Feliz, though he hasn't had much luck with hunting. Or perhaps, instead, take a ride into town. Head out along the river and at the fork take the trail to Lincoln. Yes, that's the ticket. An unscheduled visit to the Emporium. Always wise to observe the doings of that Mercantile establishment nearly next door and prepare, if need be, for some new sort of trouble on the part of Messrs. Murphy and Dolan, its pesky proprietors. Always wise, is it not, to keep a finger on the pulse of one's enterprise? Carlito has readied the thoroughbred chestnut. Curried, brushed, saddled. John Tunstall presses his palm to the window glass. Ah, cooler than expected, even for September. A jacket will be required. No, not the shahtoosh coat this time. The reliable herringbone tweed instead. A better choice. A more rugged look, that. He slips it on before the full-length mirror fixed to the back of the bedroom door. He fastens only the waist-level button. He adjusts the collar. He adjusts the knot in his silk cravat. He sets his Stetson on his head and checks the placement in the mirror, then readjusts it with the front brim tilted back. There now, a slightly jaunty look. Bordering on rakish, but a bit. He straightens his stance and nods to his image. He smiles and he touches his hat. Pardon me? he says. Are you addressing me, sir? His expression now faintly incredulous, quizzical. Then fading to concern, possibly annoyance. So sorry to hear that, he says. Now a bit of frown. Furrowed. No need to raise your voice, sir. No need to take that tone, sir. He takes a step back. Gentlemen, he says, might we be civil? and his smile returns, though nearly imperceptible. Well then, he says. So be it. He one-handedly unbuttons the black and white checked jacket. It falls open. Revealing the holster. Hand tooled with a thick-stitched border, center concho, silver rivets. Revealing the pistol. Walnut grip, with JHT in silver inlay. His hand now beside the holster. Now closer to the grip. A dramatic twitch of the fingers. Now the swift arc of the hand to pistol, cocked and pointed and clicked.

Does he blow imaginary smoke from the muzzle before he places the pistol back in the hand-tooled holster? Yes, he does. Of course he does.

Does he wonder how many more times he will be allowed to decide between the shahtooh coat and the herringbone tweed? Or how many more mornings he will have a chance to ride his thoroughbred along the river?

Fee-Fie-Foe-Fum.
I smell the blood of an Englishman.
—Historical rhyming couplet, origin obscure

Chapter 72
Final Fall on the Rio Feliz
September 1877 – The Moon of Leaving Geese

The towhee nests stand empty in the tangled brush of the chaparral. The days are cool, the nights cold.

The men set out for open range. Foreman Dick Brenner. Tom O'Folliard. Charles Bowdre. Billy Antrim. Days now of riding and roundup of the Tunstall herd, collecting the strays. Billy keeps count and makes the list:

bull steer 417
calf 1375
cow 1960
heifer 868
breeding stock 91

and some cut from the herd to remain on the rangelands for wintering. Some to be sold to the US Cavalry at Fort Stanton to feed the captive Apaches. And the rest are sent off with the wranglers and the drovers on the long drive west into Texas and north along the Chisolm Trail to the depot town of Abilene and its vast stockyards of the damned, there to wait with the others of their kind, the herds of a thousand and the herds of tens of thousands in this metropolis of pens and chutes and mazes of gates. The bellowing unending. Now the train. The boxcars readied. The ramps are set. Now driven in. Whips and sticks. The unyielding are roped and dragged. The ones that stumble on the ramps trampled, bone broke, left. The heavy doors are slid closed and bolted and with the great lurching of the locomotive and its coupling rods in motion and the smokebox hot and the billows of steam up the chimney stack, the journey to oblivion begins. Now rumbling on, clickity clack and clickity clack on the jointed rails. They are joggled. Rocked. Shifted by the turn and the pitch of the tracks. Heads straining high to rest on the backs of each other on account of the closeness, on account of their horns. Leg-sore and scuffed as they stand and thirst. Days in the dark. Tongues dry and swollen. Their bellowing ceased. Strips of light between the slats. Stripes of the final sunlight over their faces, over their eyes. Squinting. Peering. Days of high desert and open country. Then passing pastures. Green hills. Fields and fences where their own kind stand grazing. There a horse running, foal by her side. Oh little one, with your new legs so long and still unsteady. Following. Frolicsome. This world, this world in the glint of a river. Clickity clack, as they stagger and quake and lose their footing, slipping in the slime of their urine and dung but there are so many, so pressed to each other, there is no place to fall so they stand and sway until the slaughterhouses of Chicago. Behold now the great moaning heard before the doors are unbolted and thrown open to another ramp. Tremulous of leg they go, sightless in the sudden light and stumbling forward on the rungs. The living are unloaded. The still-standing dead and dying fall. Shoved along and shoveled out. All sent on to the cavernous dark. The chute narrows. Ten cows abreast. Then eight. Then four. Then two by two under the men with the death hammers. The momentum of the swing. The weight of the head. The skull split. Then the blade. The blood. Their bodies disassembled.

Grebes take flight from the eddy pools along the Rio Felix and embark for the Salton Sea.

Newly-hatched chicks of eared grebes (Podiceps nigricollis) ride on the backs of their parents for several weeks even though they are fully able to dive and swim.
—Birds of America and the Territories, Chapter 3: Grebes

The preferred habitat of the canyon towhee (Melozone fusca) is the chaparral.
Chapter 77: New World Sparrows, Juncos

Chapter 73
Final Winter on the Rio Feliz
December 1877 – The Moon of Dying Fires

Snow falls on Las Montañas de Sacramento but there is grass enough for John Tunstall's longhorns on the rangelands and along the Rio Felix. Wintering geese feed in the open waters. Jays forage on the slopes in the ponderosa pine and piñon. The Mercantile posse rides nightly, cutting cattle from Tunstall's herd, stampeding horses from Tunstall's corral. Cloud shadows sweep the cold desert hardpan, ascend the foothills and darken the stands of conifers, then disappear above the timberline and the treeless peaks. Snow funnels spin along the thoroughfare in Lincoln.

The Mercantile posse waits for a moonless night to ransack The Emporium, loot, smash. The big windows of Tunstall's store are shattered. The front door demolished.

Billy lists the damage, itemizes the destruction:

7 grain barrels spilled out
12 flour sacks split.
1 bolt gingham unraveled and shit on
1 bolt flannel set fire
3 cases of notions: missing
3 nail barrels broken
9 pairs boots missing, 5 pair filled with molasses

countertop tobacco missing
countertop candy jars upside down empty

The men of the posse have filled their mouths with cinnamon jawbreakers and their arms with stolen goods. They sit biding their time on the porch of the Mercantile, sporting Stetsons and slickers, brand new boots, checkered trousers and smirks while John Tunstall oversees repairs to the Emporium, Dick Brenner seethes and urges retaliation, and crates of replacement goods arrive daily.

February, The Moon of Sleeping Bears. Quail scratch and peck under the pine-oak and juniper. Tunstall takes on more protection. Grouse hide along the borders of the conifer forests. Billy and Tunstall head out together on milder winter days, riding for miles, following along the Rio Feliz for hours. Finding their way back well after dark. They ride into the foothills of Las Montañas Capitan. Game is scarce, but there are birds. Tunstall's shooting has not improved. Oh dear, he says when the birds take flight at his rifle fire. I so would have liked a nice breast of quail with pearl onions and a green pea puree. They rest the horses on the sandy riverbank. Billy builds a fire. John Tunstall opens the saddlebags. Or grouse, he says, a fine bird for baking in pastry with buttered truffles the way my mum would fix it for Christmas.

Billy boils the coffee. He heats the biscuits. He asks John Tunstall about his mother. Did she ever fry up them little birdies like picnic chicken? Oh clever Billyboy, says John Tunstall. He speaks of England. His father's debts. His mother's garden. Her jam roly-polies. His spaniel Prince. Likely dead by now, he says. I have written and asked, he says, but neither Mum nor Father will say. And he talks of the library near Charing Cross and the stables at Belsize Park. The wind comes up. They move closer to the fire. The stars loom. Ancient lights. Whole shoals unclustered. The sky teeming.

The horses pull at the dry grass and drink at the river. Billy's piebald Choctaw. Tunstall's chestnut thoroughbred. The eastern sky is not yet lit, but yellow warblers have begun to twitter.

Their fire is out. We should get on, says Billy.

You take my Sutton Star, says John Tunstall. Let me have a go at your Indian pony.

Best not, says Billy. He won't let you.

Of course he would, says John Tunstall, patting the Choctaw on its neck. It stands trembling, ears pinned back. Then a show of teeth.

Ah. Perhaps not, says John Tunstall, backing away. But a fine animal nonetheless, he says. I have always thought so. Did you ever name him?

No, says Billy. Never been sure how long he's mine for.

Billy kicks sand on the embers. They mount their horses. The river sings. Billy points at the moon, nearly set now and ringed with nimbus. See there? says Billy. That's bad weather coming. It's not just me who says it. A moon like that, anyone would know.

The Steller's Jay (Cyanocitta stelleri) can imitate the calls of predator hawks, warning other birds to flee.

—Birds of America and the Territories, Chapter 54: Crows, Jays, Magpies, Ravens

The yellow warbler (Setophaga petechia) favors a riparian habitat.

Chapter 72: Wood Warblers

Chapter 74
Muy Bello: Andrew Roberts Arrives at the Ranch
January 1878

Andrew L. Roberts was well out of Lincoln and riding the road along the Rio Feliz when a high wind came up shifting the night clouds covering and uncovering the moon, so that shadows among the boulders and slopes of rubble stone seemed at times to overtake him, and then retreat, and supposing that John Tunstall might have posted gunmen on that route, he came along warily. His horse, too. A dappled gray with black points. Ears, mane, tail, and legs. The very color of General Lee's Traveller, as it had been pointed out to him throughout the war. It had been his mount since Shiloh in the spring of sixty-two and was with him when he was wounded at Chickamauga Creek in the fall of sixty-three. Struck with buckshot from a confederate musket. Smooth-ball, thirty-one caliber. Right shoulder socket. Left hip. He had limped into the medical tent where a young doctor stood in the lantern light, stripped bare to the waist, slick with blood, and a pile of limbs beside him. He would have limped out again, but the doctor held out a bottle and offered him a swig of whiskey. Another swig. Several more. He remembered being led to a cot and being suddenly oh so tired and deciding to sit. Yes, better to sit. A brief rest, just a minute or so, that's all I need, he thought, and I'll be on my way, I'll be sneaking away before someone picks up a bone-saw and begins to cut.

He remembered the doctor easing him down. A countenance benevolent and shining there above him, asking his name, asking his regiment.

Roberts, he said. Andrew Roberts, sir. First Texas Cavalry, he told the doctor.

Basin, the doctor said to someone else. Retractor. Tenaculum.

He remembered the cold of the chloroform-soaked cloth laid upon his nose and his mouth while the face of the doctor grew smaller and smaller as a closing circle of darkness took it away and away and then after some strange compression of memory and time and a sleep without dreams he remembered awakening on a litter loaded into an ambulance wagon and wondering if parts of himself now lay in the pile. He felt for his limbs and finding them intact called out to know the name of the doctor. That would be Doctor Arthur, someone said. Arthur Broadcreek or Broadwater or something like that, though he could hardly hear amid the shouts of the battlefield and the fusillade of fire. The wagon's dropboard is lifted. The hinges creak. Then slammed shut and the keeper bolts thrown. Molly old girl, the driver calls to the mule, for he knows she'd been standing asleep in the traces all during that din, and she swivels her big mule ears back to the driver to hear. Come on sleepy head, he says and she answers with a sort of a bray, a sort of a whimper. Get on Molly girl, the driver calls and they start off. A heave forward. Rattling along. A hill. A ridge. Explosions. He sees the canvas roof and walls around him lit bright and briefly glowing red and dark again. He smells blood and flesh, gunpowder and piss, and the piney new-cut wagon boards and he is overtaken by a sudden longing, by wistful recollection of the big longstraw pine that grew beside the barn, that farm Pa worked just outside of San Antone. Ma kept hollering. But I kept climbing. Andrew you come down from there this minute. The crack of a branch, the smell of pine wood, a tumble through the needles. Scrapes and bruises, nothing more. The whooping Pa gave me was so much worse, he remembers, and he sleeps again. Awakened once more by the moaning beside him, a legless man there, begging to be dead and another man cries water please, please some water. Just over the next rise the canvas walls go blinding bright as the mule and the driver burst into pieces. The wagon tilts. Teeters. Rolls over once, twice, and rocks to an unsteady stop in at the edge of a swamp. The man who had cried for water lands face-down in the shallows, his head and neck in misalignment. The legless man was already dead when the wagon rolled and the body is thrown on top of him. He creeps from under the corpse and out of the wreckage to the front to look to the driver. To look to the mule. I always liked mules, I'm partial to mules, he says out loud as he crawls through the mud and the brackish water. A leg in a boot is still set to the toeboard. Pieces of the mule hang in the traces. In half a day he finds his way back to his regiment where he lies pained and fevered and when that is over he asks after his horse—Have you seen him, a big dappled gray with black points?—and he fights again. Kennesaw Mountain. Chattahoochee River. Missionary Ridge. Right shoulder tendons have been snapped and tangled, but he learns to handle a gun with his left. His hip still holds a spray of buckshot, so that he walks with a hitch and winces with every step.

The night sky had cleared of clouds and his shadow goes long in the moon-silvered courtyard of the ranch on the River Feliz. Singing comes from the bunkhouse accompanied by a tender Spanish guitar. Palomita negra, adónde vas? Where are you going, little black dove. Several of the muchachos stand smoking their Te Amo cigars on the bunkhouse step and nod buenas noches as he descends from the saddle and throws the reins over the rail. He nods back. Carlito inquires does the horse need attending to and he thanks him yes. They note his holster and cavalry revolver, hipped for a left-handed draw. They watch him undo the rawhide tie-string encircling his thigh and unbuckle his gunbelt from around his waist and they watch him buckle it back again for hanging from the pommel. He nods to them once again and unison they nod back. Thank you, he says. De nada, says Carlito. They note that his walk is off-kilter. As if he might fall, but that he doesn't. A limb that lags. A foot twisted off center. They note that his right arm hangs stiffly from the shoulder. Somewhat drooped. No swing. They watch him turn and look back to his horse. A dappled gray with black points. Ears, mane, tail, and legs. Though grizzled around the muzzle. Carlito there, walking it to the trough. Muy bello, Carlito says. He very beautiful, señor.

He is old, he tells Carlito as he takes ahold of the ranch house rail. An old horse, he says.

They watch him take the ranch house steps one by one. Onto the porch. He removes his hat. John Tunstall is there, opening the door before Andrew Buckshot Roberts lets the brass knocker drop.

I see you have arrived without your employers this evening, says John Tunstall. Unless a Murphy and Dolan contingency is not far behind.

They ain't, says Andrew Roberts.

Then I shall assume that you are no longer in their employ, Mr. Roberts.

I ain't.

And that you have no intent to do me harm.

Unarmed, says Andrew Roberts.

Unless you have concealed a derringer somewhere about your person. Or perhaps some other sort of clever American weaponry.

There's a Spanish folding knife in my left boot, says Andrew Roberts. And a Brit vest-pocket pistol in the right. As I don't wear a vest.

Then do come in, sir.

Ain't here for socializing, Mr. Tunstall. I'm here to say I'm done with the Mercantile. I'm selling my place outside Ruidoso and leaving New Mexico. Yourself might consider doing suchwise.

Your admonition is appreciated, Mr. Roberts. But abandoning my enterprise is not an option.

Well killing you is, Mr. Tunstall. But this ain't my fight no more. So kindly keep your boys off me. I had my share of shooting and shot at.

Ah yes, says John Tunstall. They call you Buckshot, do they not?

Them that do, says Andrew Roberts, it's only once.

The dappled gray stands ready at the rail and gives a soft nicker at his approach. Carlito has been waiting. He pats the horse on the neck. He hands the reins to Andrew Roberts. Vaya con Dios, Carlito tells him.

He leans into his horse. His left boot in the stirrup. His left hand on the pommel. His right hand hangs down as pulls himself up. A hop and a step and he swings his leg over.

He looks out at the dark hills that lay beyond the house. A nighthawk dives and swerves above him. The lights in the bunkhouse window have gone out. And now there is no singing, no guitar.

The common nighthawk (Chordeiles minor) forages in the air, and more frequently on moonlit nights.

—Birds of America and the Territories, Chapter 43: Goatsuckers, Nightjars

Chapter 75
The Source of the Limp
Near the Ranch on Rio Feliz
February 18, 1878 – The Moon of Sleeping Bears

They came upon him while he knelt. The stockinged chestnut had been favoring a foreleg. It had come on suddenly over rough ground. So fine a horseman, he could feel it from the saddle. A change in its gait. The cant and bob of its head somewhat off and rising just slightly with the right hoof strike. Perhaps a small break in the coffin bone. Or more likely a ligamentous strain—he had seen it before, a similar injury with a bay mare he once stabled at Belsize Park. Examined there by a farrier of that London borough. But then, this is not London. This is a wild country where horses are had for the taking, whole herds thundering over the plains until they are corralled howling and bucking, ridden by wrangler and drovers. No, this is not London. But this change in gait, this unstable hoof strike—he'd seen it back home. That bay mare. Likely the same sort of trouble now with Sutton Star. Requiring compression with a wrap of bandages, carefully applied counterclockwise. Was that correct? Yes, that was it. Clockwise left leg, counterclock right. And of course, requiring rest. Yes, likely just that. But possibly just a bruise on the underside of the hoof. He recollected a ride through a dry arroyo, the stony slope, the stones in the bed. So perhaps just a bruise. Common enough. Come old boy, he told the horse. Let's have a look. He leaned into the horse's shoulder and it shifted its weight to the opposite leg. He picked up its foot. No stone there, no bruise or crack.

And now he knelt. He ran his hand down its foreleg, knee to hoof and back up again. He carefully examined the cannon bone for swelling. He placed his palms to the pastern and the fetlock and felt for heat. The horse snorted. Nostrils wide. Ears perked. John Tunstall stood up. Dust was rising a quarter mile off. Is it two of them? Three? A blur of dust. Billy had warned him. Don't ride out alone. Don't get so ahead of me when I'm riding behind. The terrain's too open. No place to take cover. And now there is only the buffalo grass around him, a sparse scattering of sagebrush, and the bright winter sky above. They must have been somewhere close by, following, waiting, and ready to ambush. And he remembered passing a shallow side-canyon. Just minutes ago. Yes, that's where they were. Where they must have been, hidden amidst the boulders and the brush while he rode on by without so much as a glance. He had been incautious, unwary. He had been occupied with the gait of the stockinged chestnut. That right foreleg. It seemed off. Hoof strike. Head bob. Coffin bone. Compression. Come on old boy, let's have a look.

He thought to ride off, but there wasn't time. Remount, turn, push the horse on. And the horse would go. This he knew. It had always done whatever he had asked it to. But that leg would suffer. And they would likely outrun him anyway.

Or stay home, Billy had told him. For a time at least. Set yourself on that cozy settee by the fire and read one of your books about desperados. Such as me. Or such as them.

They were coming on still, faster is seemed, closer now. Bearing down on him with their shroud of dust.

Stay out of the open, Billy had said. Stay at the store. Putter around. Clean up the mess. Check the accounts. Go do whatever it is you do. Just stay off the range.

They charged on. Three men. It seemed almost as if they might run him down. But they rear in their horses not ten feet from him. Pulling in the reins. Their horses lathered and stepping nervously in their places.

John Tunstall looks up at them. He touches his hat brim. Gentlemen, he says.

All three men carry firearms. Of course they do. One sits with his rifle propped in front of him, stock set down, barrel skyward. Finger on the trigger. One keeping his rifle strap-slung over the shoulder. The third unholsters his pistol and rests it on the pommel.

The stockinged chestnut stamps. A bird calls from the buffalo grass. A chirp, a trill. John Tunstall raises his hands shoulder height, palms facing the three men on their horses. Please, he says. Might we be civil?

He takes a step back, away from his horse. His checkered coat has fallen open. There the holster. There the grip of his gun inlaid with silver.

Ain't that pretty, says the man with the upright rifle.

Which, says the second man with his rifle still shouldered. The horse or the gun?

All three of them is which, the third man says and he raises his pistol.

The stockinged chestnut screams and shies at the sound. John Tunstall now with his hands to his chest. *Oh Mum, is that you? Taking your Yorkshire pudding hot from the oven. And Father, too. Carving the roast. Not so thick dear. John mind your manners. Eat your vegetables. Perfectly delicious turnips. Pass the butter. Prince is there under the table. Sneaking him the turnips. Summer sky. Sunup on the Thames. Tide out. Mudlarks. A misty day at Belsize Park. My bay mare waiting at the gate. Looking for me, Polly old girl? Here I am. It's me . . .*

The second shot, this one to the head.

A sagebrush sparrow rises from the buffalo grass. A second follows. The hardpan takes up the blood but the blood-smell rises. A buzzard pair glides past, tilt and turn and circle back. So quickly detecting the scent.

Chapter 76
Riding the Drag
by Billy Bonney
February 18, 1878
Morning

It was just six horses. One of them a little bay mare he took a liking to, being it the same color as a horse he left back home in London, or maybe that was a mare he used to have but died a long while ago or maybe I'm mixing that up with a dog of his that died. Prince it was or Rex or some doggie name. Or Polly. But Polly might have been the London mare. I don't know. But this bay mare, the one from the remuda was the one he wanted. Sure he had that chestnut thoroughbred, the one he was always riding, the one he was riding that day. Sutton Star. Big horse. White stockings up to its knees, little white star just between its eyes. Brung it here on a boat, he did. You heard me right. A horse going over the ocean in a boat. Once I asked him if he was thinking we didn't have horses here in the territories. Brilliant, Billyboy, is what he said, but Billyboy not a one would have been a Sutton Star. So he had a horse. A fine one too, that thoroughbred. But the little bay mare in our remuda was the one he wanted kept safe, and with the posse stealing every horse but these last six, we were running all six of them back to the ranch. Dick Brenner on the point. Charlie Bowdre on the flank. Tom O'Folliard at the swing. And me, I was riding the drag. And John's keeping himself a ways more back, staying out of the sand and hardpan we're stirring up. I look back and yep there he is, but he's getting behinder all the time. Slowing down. What in good god damn, I'm wondering. What in good god damn do you think you're doing John and I holler for him to git on, stay with us. John, John. Let's go boy, that's what I'm hollering over the thundering hoof sound of six range horses running and the sound of Tom and Charlie and Dick whooping them on. And the last I see of a living John Tunstall is when I look back and he's getting off his horse. He's kneeling down and by the time I hear the shot, there's nothing to see but dust. That's how it is when you're riding the drag. Everyone's dust thrown up in your face and your eyes and blowing all around you. So there he was, then. Kneeling alongside that thoroughbred, and that was the end of it. All around me it was nothing but dust.

His horse was spooked some but hadn't run off. Sutton Star still standing but stamping and scared near witless. That bit of white star between the eyes, like I said. Did I tell you he brought that horse here on a boat? Could be I did. I got the horse steady. I picked up his pistol. I picked up his hat. There was so much sun. It was me who slung him over his horse and tightened the rope. Didn't want him sliding off. I fixed his hat so it'd stay put. Draw string and bead. Sparrows were fliting around in the brush. I couldn't tell which. Too hard to tell. Just too damn hard. I got the reins from the thoroughbred. John Tunstall there, head down, belly down, slung over. It was me who went back and checked the rope. It was me on my Choctaw to be leading his horse with him on it, taking him home.

The sparrows fly up from the sage. I couldn't tell how many.

There was no one I could kill, not right then. But I knew I would.

I surely would.

The sagebrush sparrow (Artemisiospiza nevadensis) is an inconspicuous bird, often missed until flushed from the grass or the desert scrub.

—Birds of America and the Territories, Chapter 77: New World Sparrows, Juncos

Chapter 77
We Load Up
by Billy Antrim Bonney
February 18, 1878
Afternoon

We carried him in. Tom O'Folliard and me. I'm telling Tom to watch it now, be careful and Tom is telling me, Billy get ahold of his head. We lay him on the settee. Two wounds. Face and chest. Little holes that make you dead. Don't ask me how, I seen it plenty before but I can't figure it out.

Guadalupe brings the basin and the cloth. I set to washing off the blood what's leaked from his mouth down around his neck and wiping away the white pieces of whatever it is coming out his ear and Tom starts fiddling with the shirt buttons but it's all slippery bloody and anyway he's sniffing and wiping at his eyes so I tell him go on then Tommy, you go with Guadalupe and get all what we need and I write him a list of what all to fetch:

blue shirt, pearl buttons
tan canvas pants
tan coat with tiny checkers
blue rattler boots
comb
brown hat

and I tell him while they're at it go find that fancy turquoise stickpin of his and that's what they go and do.

We are getting John sitting up on the settee to get the bloody shirt off him and his new one put on but he's not gone stiff as yet and still flopping all around when Charlie Bowdre comes in and sees what we're up to. He stands there with his teeth clenched and fists tight at his side and saying nothing. Not a word. Tom tells him, Give us a hand here Charlie. But he doesn't give us a hand, no. He goes to the fireplace and shoves over the big iron curlicue candlesticks and then he sweeps his hand across the mantlepiece and there goes the little gold frames with John's pictures of people in England and dogs and one with a little lad on a horse and such and next it's good-bye to the mahogany clock that chimes once when it hits the floor, and one by one he throws John's gunslinger shoot-em-up books hard into the hearthfire. Guadalupe sits down with the grave clothes folded on her lap and starts in rocking and calling Dios mío, Dios mío and damn if she won't hardly shut up.

We get his pants off him. Tom and me. Wet where he pissed. No shit though, I'm glad for that. Next it's the boots, putting them off and on. Ever take boots off a dead man? As bad as putting them on. The fancy blue rattlers he liked. The ones he was wearing the first time I met him, the only time, that I saw. I make sure right's on the right and left's on the left so not having to do it over. I get done and they look like they are supposed to look but Tom says you forgot socks, and I say goddamn to hell and didn't I now, but to hell with it. Tom buttons the blue shirt. I get his arms up straight over his head and that way get the tan checkered coat on him and stick the stickpin on the pocket. Then button the pants. Then his hair. The comb sticky with blood. Water on his head and that takes it off pretty good and I comb his hair it over the hole. Next his hands. Laid across each other the way they always do it. Get the eyes shut right. I did that first thing finding him but they opened on their own. Maybe from all that joggling on the ride in, tied to his horse the way I done him. Or maybe moving around on the settee with the shirt, getting it on. His mouth just hung open. Tom says it won't stay shut no how. I tell Tom, well that figures since he hardly never did shut up, now did he? And feeling not so good about me saying that so I tell him, Right John? You always be talking. And we finally get it fixed with me holding his jaw up for a bit and letting it go real slow and then it stays put. I know it's me doing all these things I have to do but seems not me too. I've seen the dead before. I've been the one done it. With my Mam I knew her dying was coming by the smell of her, and by the owl hoots from somewhere outside. I fixed my Mam some when she was done spitting up the last of her blood and she had gone still as a stone, but that was Mam. She wasn't old, my Mam. But years of sick sure turned her old and with Mam I knew what was coming. Not the same with John Tunstall, no. Him being hardly older than me, so you could say I didn't know what was coming. But maybe I did. The way he was doing things, the goddamn fool, maybe I did. And if I'd been thinking that most dying comes from being older, well that makes me a goddamn fool myself. But that's what I'm thinking when we stand back and look how we fixed him. And we remember the brown hat and do that. He's better with the hat. Maybe everyone is. Anyway, he's looking the best as we can get him. Best you can get a dead person to look. Under them fancy clothes, he's not John Tunstall no more. He's only what a buzzard might smell and start picking over or what spooks you in the dark some lonely night and you hear a screech owl calling.

Tom says let's put him on the table and tote him out to the porch. For the muchachos to see. I say leave him be, they can see him good enough right there on the settee where we got him. Tom says it's too warm in here with the fire going. In here he'll start stinking. We should put him on the porch where it's cold, he says. But I say no, the coyotes. Then we'll keep watch, says Tom, and right then Charlie who's been quiet since he smashed things up stomps on over and throws the basin of bloody wash-water on the fire. It steams up and smells bad. There damn it, he says. Now it's cold.

Dick Brewer comes in. He says the muchachos are all outside and want to come in. Charlie goes to the window to look out but there's those fancy white curtains strung across and he snatches them down with his hand, tiebacks and all, and he says, Well bring them the fuck in then. And he smashes something else. Dick opens the door. Venga venga he calls to the muchachos. Here they come, shuffling and stumbling. The two Joses and two Diegos, and Encendio the cook his son Davito, and Carlito the stable hand, and Paulito, Matteo, Segundo, and Miguel. The ones with hats take them off and hold them in both hands or set them pressed to their chests. Nuestro señor, they say. Nuestro jefe. Mateo leans over and tells John in his ear, No worry Señor Juan. We kill them. Paulito catches me aside and he tells me, We come with you Billy. Los mataremos. We kill them. Todos.

Segundo twists the corners of his neckerchief and dabs at his eyes. Davito has a jug of sotol and passes it around. The last man taking a swig is Diego, the second Diego, and he puts the mouth of the jug to John's dead mouth but wasn't it hard enough us getting it to stay closed so I tell Diego to quit it. Gimme that, says Charlie and he takes a big glug. Dick Brenner gets ahold of John's fancy glass bottle of whiskey and pours all of it out in that set of John's fancy glass glasses and holds his up. To John Tunstall, says Dick. That man could ride, says Tom. Couldn't shoot worth a shit though, says Charlie Bowdre. After a while Dick opens the door. It's time, he tells muchachos. Es el momento. Gracias muchachos. Gracias and Adios. And they go.

Encendio and his son Matteo stay on the porch. Charlie goes to the window where the curtain is torn and halfway hanging. They ain't going, he says. Dick, he says, go on out and see. Dick goes out to see. Qué es? he says. Matteo tells him, Por favor Señor Brenner. Qué debemos hacer? What do we do? The men, they want to know. Dónde debemos? Where do we go?

Dick Brenner goes to the long glass case that keeps the guns. He starts pulling on the latch but it's locked, and while he's yanking on it Tom starts looking for the key, opening the drawers and throwing papers all around. But Charlie, he goes ahead and kicks it in. Just the way I'd expect him to. Wood and glass smashing. Pieces of glass are still sticking up in the frame and he kicks at them too but they stay in the frame and he reaches in through the glass and he says goddamn get them guns. All them guns. I already got mine and John's silver-grip pistol I took off him when I found him dead. Get them rifles, Dick says. Charlie Bowdre is opening cabinet doors, pulling everything out, slamming them back. Packing our kits. Stuffing our saddlebags. Ammo. Knives. Tinderbox. Matches. I tell Charlie, Hold on there.

Charlie. I'll make a list of what we're taking, but he goes right on and Dick looks at me funny and says, A list Billy? What in hell for, Billy? You tell me that, what in hell for, you and your goddamn lists.

Tom O'Folliard hands the rifles out and he says he expects he'll be the next one of us dying. Dick tells him, We'll all be dying next Tom. Ain't that so Charlie? he says.

Well now, says Charlie Bowdre, anything's possible since there's no telling ever what might be coming your way or when. Never was and never will be.

I look at John Tunstall. He's there on the settee. Sitting up, no less. Tom's got him sitting up, settee cushions holding him, and one leg crossed over the other, just like he'd do, that sissy way of sitting like he'd do. But not quite. Not quite. He's sitting there, but he's not. Both. Where did some part of him go, I'm thinking. Where my Mam went? And my Da? Folks say they are gone to some other world up there in the stars and anybody can get there just by believing it. But hell no, there's nothing you can get from just believing it. Some nights when I look at stars I am wondering where they go when the night is over. Seems to me that the stars you see at night are still there in the morning but the sun won't let you see them. So it must be that if you find yourself shot dead some morning you'd have wait until dark so there will be stars you can see to get yourself going. If stars is where you want to go.

Dick Brenner sees me standing there quiet and thinking things over and he puts his hand on my shoulder and he tells me, Come on there Billy. Let's git son. It'll all be alright.

Sure it will, says Charlie Bowdre just as he's got a rifle raised up and aimed out the window with his eye to the sights.

He hands Dick Brenner a rifle. Here you go Dick, he says. And this one's for you Tom.

And he has one for me, too. The Winchester. Go on and take it Billy, says Charlie. If he could he'd be giving it to you hisself.

Load up boys, he says.

And we do.

The call of the whiskered screech owl (Megascops trichopsis) is a haunting sequence of eight hoots beginning with low notes, rising in the middle, fading to lower notes at the end, and according to Apache legend, producing the ghostly song of the wandering dead.

—Birds of America and the Territories, Chapter 42: True Owls

Chapter 78
Adios to the Ranch on the Rio Feliz
February 19, 1878 – The Moon of Sleeping Bears
Before Dawn

They rode out in that early hour before dawn when the air is already filled with birdsong and in that final starlight the desert glows ghostly blue. They had readied their horses with care that morning. Curry and brush. Saddle and bridle. Charlie Bowdre on a slate grullo from out of the remuda. Billy on his Choctaw. Dick Brewer on his buckskin. Tom O'Fallion on his bloodbay Bo. They bid adios to Carlito who came solemnly from the stable and spoke to each horse softly in Spanish and stroked their long noses and offered each a small yellow apple on the flat of his palm. And they bid adios to Encendio who had filled their canteens with water flavored with lemon rind and pressed upon each of them parcels of dried figs and soft corn taquitos filled with cheese and wrapped in paper and tied in twine. As if their absences would be long. As if their journey would be far. Or as if they might not return at all. They turned their horses away from the ranchyard and set off one by one as a flock of birds leaving their perches from a single tree might do, and though they had no need to speak each to each, they soon found themselves riding abreast with their horses going the same easy lope and falling into the same rocking rhythm while the four of them—three men and the boy Billy—felt the cadence of the gait of the horses under them lifting into their loins, lulling away the clamor of anger within them and turning it into tranquility borne of an acceptance of their approaching ruination, and a sense of rapture in which the desert that stretched out before them became boundless and strangely resplendent in the morning starlight, and although they had often traveled that singular tract of country, on this morning, in this fleeting twilight before daylight, that terrain so familiar now presents itself anew as if in the precincts of dreams where the spines of the cholla are gossamer and translucent, the hardpan silvered, and the silhouettes of Las Montañas de Sacramento backlit by moonset, and where their horses' hoofsounds fade into silence as they no longer touch the ground but ascend above the desert in this new day dawning, below them the river braided and burnished by the first light of the sun, a coyote in mid-trot now stopping to look up at them and they rise over the ranches and fences on the road to Lincoln, over the thoroughfare of the town and the tin roof of the livery, the cedar shingles of Riley's restaurant, the patchboard of the dentist's shack, the tarpaper topping of the assay office, and over the smoke and flames engulfing the roof of John Tunstall's Emporium set afire by the very men they have sought who sit and watch it burn from their places on the porch of the Murphy & Dolan Mercantile.

And if they would not be roused from their collective reverie, the four of them—the three men and the boy Billy—would never descend to the streets of Lincoln to slay this posse of arsonists and assassins, but instead would leave those ordained to die far behind them, to be dispatched by someone else's justice. It is only in this waking dream that the four of them ride on escaping their own destruction, and ride on and ride on joyously relinquishing their revenge and all the grief they had known and all hope they had ever held and all that they had desired.

What was it that returned them to their purpose, their ride on to Lincoln and retribution? Perhaps the recollection of the Englishman's body now gone stiff and mottled on the ranch house settee. Or the history of killing that Charlie Bowdre and Tom O'Folliard and Billy Antrim carried with them. Or the smoldering sense of revenge Dick Brewer had long suppressed in accord with John Tunstall's preference for what he called decency and fair play, that desire for retaliation now unleased with John Tunstall dead. Or perhaps their reverie was interrupted by a glimpse of the ash-pale moon about to set or the faintest glint of daybreak on the snowy crests of Las Montañas de Sacramento. Perhaps it was the sight of the coyote now hurrying home with a broken magpie wing-fanned in its mouth or the smell of rot from a pronghorn where sat a tribe of black buzzards that levitated above the carcass at their approach and alighted once again, resettling among the slats of bone as they passed and rode on. But it matters little what reminded them of their mission. Only that they rode on.

The Apache believe a Magpie (Pica hudsonia) will become the sky guardian of the human that approaches it with reverence.

—Birds of America and the Territories, Chapter 54: Crows, Jays, Magpies, Ravens

The black buzzard (Coragyps atratus) or black vulture regurgitates its meal when approached by predators, thereby decreasing its weight for takeoff and flight.

Chapter 14: New World Vultures, Condors

Chapter 79
Heading to Lincoln: Morning
February 19, 1878

Lincoln lay twenty miles to the west, and for a time they rode the river trail until it was lost in a wind-sheltered marsh where wigeon ducks slept among the sedges and sloughgrass. When the terrain went bare and dry they turned into the stretch of scrub desert sparse with homesteads shacks and ranch houses and they watched lights move in the disembodying dark as ranchers and their sons and hired hands carried lanterns to their early-morning chores and kitchen windows went bright as wives and daughters laid breakfast fires in cookstoves and hearths to set the coffee boiling in graniteware pots and soft white biscuit dough baking in cast-iron pans and setting trails of smoke rising from the chimneys of stone and adobe. As the four of them—the three men and the boy Billy—rode up, the occupants halted their chores and held up their lanterns, having heard them coming or seeing their approaching dust ghostly in the predawn dark. Few words were then spoken. Or no words were spoken. Some shook their heads and wished them luck and some said they would meet them in Lincoln, would catch up with the four of them in Lincoln, where they might find the streets empty of law-abiding citizens and where the first of the killings would commence.

American wigeons (Mareca americana) are referred to as a robber ducks. They float innocently beside species of diving ducks feeding on submerged vegetation, then snatch their food away when they resurface.

—Birds of America and the Territories, Chapter 13: Swans, Geese, Ducks, Mergansers

Chapter 80
Our Tom Dead and Gone in Lincoln
February 19, 1878
By Billy Bonney

It was Tom they took down early on, Tom O'Folliard that first gunfight in Lincoln. Tom being the first of us to fall. We didn't see where they was shooting from when they started shooting. Or maybe we were the ones it was started shooting. But there was nothing and no one to see. Not a Murphy & Dolan man in sight. No one sitting on the Mercantile porch or poking a rifle out a Mercantile window. No one on the roof of the newspaper office or the assay office or the livery. And no one on the roof of John Tunstall's Emporium, seeing how there was no roof left anyway, just a burned crisscross pile of caved-in timbers. And not a regular citizen in sight neither except a few I spied cowering behind their curtains or a face at a window before a shade rolled down. Elsewise nothing moved until a cold wind sprung up catching a strayed-off page of *The Lincoln County Ledger*, whiffing it through the thoroughfare right on past us and our horses already skitterish and my Choctaw pony riled up all the more as a gust took it up and up, scaring a rain dove whistling off the restaurant roof and that's when I look up and bam bam bam the shooting starts. It's coming at us from where we can't see until someone on the roof raises up a little bit and what flashes bright in that morning sun is the tin star pinned to the sheriff. Charlie he starts shooting aiming at the roof while is running hunched across the thoroughfare to behind the trough for hiding himself while more shooting keeps coming at us from someone else in the livery corral and bullets raising up little poofs of street dust, bam bam bam. Tom jolts back in the saddle and throws up his hands and pitches backwards off his horse Bo and bam bam bam comes again and now Bo stumbles and goes down on its knees and then rolls on its side screaming. I see Tom down in the dirt leaking a bloody trail as he goes crawling to his horse and me thinking I better go get him or he'll go tear the hearts out of them who killed his Bo and they'll kill him right back, so I give my Choctaw a go-boy-go! while I'm way atilt over in the saddle and ready to give Tom my hand to take. Tom, Tom, take it, take it, take it, look here Tommy, my hand, take my hand. Oh come on Tommy, and he's supposed to take it. Supposed to pull himself up behind me and we'll get away since Charlie's the real gunslinger of us and the best one to be killing them off, them we can't see or where they're all shooting from, but Dick he's right there keeping Charlie covered, and I'm shooting at everything and nothing as I ride off and Tom is supposed to be up in the saddle with me and holding on and Charlie and Dick is supposed to be riding up the rear behind me but that wasn't the way it was, no. Tom's horse Bo is lying beside him rocking and pushing its head into the dirt trying to get up until it lets go with a long cry from inside and goes still. See you Bo, Tommy tells it. Oh hell Tommy, come on, you have to go now, I say. I take ahold of his hand, try to, but he hits my hand away. He says, You too Billy. And it's bam bam bam some more coming at us, and the last thing he says is: Billy you'd better. So I do.

The wings of the mourning dove or rain dove (Zenaida macroura) produce a distinctive whistling sound as it rises, which warns other members of the flock of approaching danger and the need for flight.

—Birds of America and the Territories, Chapter 39: Pigeons, Doves

Chapter 81
Hard Times and Hiding Out But We Keep On
by William H. Bonney
March 19, 1878

We done a load of shooting that last day in Lincoln. Them and us. Tom gone, and I mourned it, much as I could. Knowing what I knowed. Knowing they took him in. After. Half dead he was, but they kicked him around some anyway. So I'm told. But Tom wouldn't tell nothing, first off since I know he wouldn't, and second he was barely breathing breath enough to be talking at all, and third they kept on hunting us high and low but just guessing where might get to. Me and Dick and Charlie, we hid out as long as we could. I knew all the places from my rustling days and then some, and there was ranchers enough around the county that the Murphy and Dolan boys done dirt to. Ranchers who wouldn't have another go at a gunfight, but they would take us in for a time when we showed up between hideouts and running. That shootout in Lincoln got everything turned around. That was the start of it. Sure, it's John Tunstall lying dead but then it's us they're hunting since it was one of us—or all of us and me included—looking up to see who's shooting at us from the roof of the restaurant, seeing that tin star up there flashing in the sunrise sun, and didn't me and Tom and Charlie and Dick know it was pinned on the shirt of the sheriff himself? Sure we did. So it was one of us or all of us what put a bullet in Sheriff W. B. Brady when he raised himself up. And it was one of us or all of us put one in Deputy Hindman hiding in the corral and doing his own shooting.

So. It's not one but two lawmen dead in Lincoln. Charlie says he likely done it both, being the best shot and the real gunslinger of our bunch, the one the law would find most worth catching up to, the one most worth hanging, but I knew that wasn't exactly the way it was. It could have been anyone of us who did it. The law would be happy to be hanging any one of us. Or all three of us. Or any one of the ranchers who partly took up with us. Them who put down their morning doings and caught up with us into Lincoln. But damn didn't they ride out quick enough when the sheriff and the deputy went down. Quick as some roadrunner going off and chasing its dinner. Or getting chased. That quick.

The roadrunner (Geococcyx californianus)is able to fly, but it prefers to run.

They frequently consume desert lizards, often killing these creatures by battering them against the ground.

—Birds of America and the Territories, Chapter 40: Cuckoos, Roadrunners, Anis

I hoped my rustling days were behind me when John Tunstall took me on. And him hiring Tom O'Folliard, that had me near believing it could come to be, Tom and me partners someday. I knew he was hoping it the same. Tom being from Galveston Texas, when he left home he rode north to New Mexico by way of the panhandle, through some real fine ranching country. So we talked about the two of us taking up legit cattle doings there one day, saving up our wages and buying a decent spread on the Red River or the Prairie Dog Town Fork but somehow our pay kept running through our fingers. We mighta gone on with fooling ourselves forever if Tom didn't die. It pained me to think on it but Texas was still pretty much on my mind. Dick Brewer knew about running a ranch, not only his own but being foreman for John Tunstall there on the River Feliz, and having a pal somewhere on the panhandle with a big parcel. So there was still that sort of thinking, that sort of talking while the three of us—Charlie Bowdre, Dick Brewer, and me—were on the run. But Charlie said count him out since he had a wife in Bernalillo to get back to and anyways he'd likely be dying any time now with his luck gone slim after slipping through more scrapes than a man of his sins had a right to. So. That's how we figured it. The three of us planning on killing off every one of them who killed John Tunstall and our Tom—the whole damn Murphy Dolan gang included, when they catch up with us or we catch up with them. Charlie planning on dying. Dick planning on running a ranch. Me planning on putting this way of living away again, behind me again, and heading for the panhandle.

Chapter 82
Our Very Own Billy

THE NEW YORK IRISH NEWS

"Ni neart go cur le cheile."

Vol. 79 No. 11 | November 8, 1879 | Price 15 Cents

OUR DASHING IRISH LAD

News of the escapades of one of our city's native sons has traveled from the wild and wooly Western Territories to us here in New York. Billy Bonney Antrim, born William Henry McCarty, and known throughout the land as Billy the Kid, is the fair-haired Irish lad with a bent for adventure who is living the Irish tradition of rebellion against tyranny. His exploits have become legendary, and he is known to be charming, clever, and devilishly handsome, as well as a marksman and horseman of the first order. In the lawless desolation of New Mexico, he and his band of daring lads have taken to the countryside, living by their wits, evading capture, and bringing to justice the murderers, thieves, and corrupt officials who prey upon the poor. Indeed, as it is for so many of our doughty countrymen, young Billy carries a bounty on his head, but it is certain he will outwit his oppressors with his cunning and courage. Even now, as brave young men back in Ireland continue the hundred-year fight for freedom from British oppression, our very own Billy the Kid is taking a stand against injustice and iniquity in the West.

MORE ON THE MIRACLE OF KNOCK

The Ecclesiastical Commission has concluded its investigation into the appearance of The Holy Mother and The Lamb of God on a church wall in the village of Knock, County Mayo. Reliable witnesses have stated that the apparition was bathed in light and surrounded by flying angels. Although the church wall has since been chipped apart by townspeople seeking souvenirs, a miraculous cure has already occurred. A local woman visiting the site with her deaf daughter placed a tiny piece of the concrete wall in the child's ear, resulting in a complete healing. The New York Irish News will organize a pilgrimage to Knock later this year, details to be announced.

The Quote for Today:
Drochubh, drochéan. (A bad egg, a bad bird.)

Chapter 83
Blazer's Mill
by Billy Antrim Bonney
December 20, 1880

So we left Lincoln behind us and started south for Texas, riding through the Mescalero Reservation and stopping at a shabby little settlement name of Blazer's Mill not far from Ruidoso. Not much to the town. Post office. Sawmill. Office of Indian Affairs. A general store with tins of food and feed and such. A tiny cantina. Three seats. One table. An Apache girl comes over. She's thirteen maybe fourteen, and black-black hair down her shoulders and turquoise in her ears. I ask her what's on the menu, even though there isn't any menu. Eggs and tomatoes, she says. And corn. So soft I can hardly hear her. Alright, I tell her. The same for everybody. And coffee. So we wait. Dick sits fiddling with his pistol. Charlie gets to writing his wife Manuela back in Bernalillo. The Apache girl comes back and as she's leaning in and setting down the cutlery she touches my shoulder so light you'd hardly notice but I sure do, and then we wait. I figure there's a week's worth of riding ahead of us and the store's got supplies so I write a list:

coffee
potatoes
cornmeal
sugar
lard

beans
bacon
and salt

at least. Dick sets down his pistol. He turns his chair around and sits looking out the window. But it seems to me there's not much out there to see. An old woman with a parcel coming from out from of the post office. A man with a lame leg hobbling on in. A magpie squawking on the roof. A boy leading a goat. A dog trotting by with a chicken in its mouth. Someone looking out the Indian Office window. The Apache girl comes back with our plates of tomatoes and eggs and fry bread and corn and she sets it all down. She's trying hard not to look at me, but I see her doing it with the smallest kind of smile you can have and still not be smiling. Charlie looks at me and looks at her and says, Don't go bothering with no Apaches, Billy.

She puts extra butter on my corn.

Ain't you something, says Dick Brewer and he punches me in the shoulder.

The rest of us, we don't rate no extra butter, says Charlie Bowdre.

So we eat. She fills our coffee cups from a big silver pot. Mine first. Charlie rolls himself a smoke. So does Dick. Me, I don't. Maybe a cheroot once or twice a while back but never took it up. We drink our coffee. The Apache girl passes by. She puts down a dish. Three little squares of piñon nut cake. Charlie Bowdre rolls his eyes. Go ahead there Billy, I do believe them all three is for you, he says. And Dick Brewer, he says, Dang me Billy.

We eat the cake. We finish our coffee. We watch out the window.

The magpie has flown off. The dog with the chicken has git. So's the boy with the goat. The shade goes down in the Indian Affairs office. The man with the lame leg comes hobbling out from the post office and heads to his horse. He's collecting the reins and getting ready to ride and now I see he's got a gimpy arm to boot.

We get up from the table. We put down our dollar. This is where the Apache girl comes back with the coffee pot. I tell her no thank you little darlin. She's smiling more now, a little bit more, and I see she's got a front tooth missing. But that's alright with me. That would have been alright.

I look to see if Dick's looking. But he's already gone straight out the door ahead of me and he's calling out to the man untying his horse. It's an old boy, this horse. A dappled gray with dark points. Buckshot, Dick calls. You. Buckshot Roberts.

Hello Dick, says Buckshot Roberts.

Hold on right there, says Dick.

You hold on, says Buckshot Roberts. I'm done with Murphy and Dolan and that godamned Mercantile. Been done.

I don't think you are, says Dick and already he's got his hand at his holster.

My ranch outside Ruidoso's been sold, says Roberts. I'm here just getting the last of my mail and I'll be getting on.

This is where Dick has his hand on his pistol.

It wasn't me what killed John Tunstall, says Roberts. And this is where he puts his good hand on his gun.

Charlie's right there coming up behind. He's never been one for much talking. He's never been one for waiting things out neither.

This is where Roberts draws his gun. And where Charlie Bowdre shoots him in the gut.

But Roberts is pretty damn good with a gun for a gimp. And one with a bullet in his belly. He gets two shots off before he goes down dying. His first shot is wide, but he manages to graze me pretty good just over my ear. I shoot back and if I hit him or missed him, I couldn't tell. And that's when he's got enough life left in him for his second shot which blows Dick Brenner's eye clean through his head and drops Dick in the dirt with his brains spit out behind him.

So. Dick, then. Not Charlie. Charlie expected himself being the next one dead. I hated to think it, but sure. Why not. Him being quicker at killing than most. So it didn't turn out the way I figured it. But then you tell me what does.

The Apache girl comes running out. She's still holding the silver coffee pot. Her hair is flying behind and shining in the sunlight. The turquoise in her ears. I liked her putting butter on my corn without me asking. It was good cake. I might have worked in that kitchen. Cooking or chopping or cleaning up. I done it before. Or in that general store, keeping accounts and toting up the price of coffee and potatoes. Done that too. But that could never happen. Shoot-out or no it never could. And now she's screaming something in Apache, or just screaming. I don't know which.

Get inside. That's what I tell her. Get now. Just get away.

According to Apache custom, it is advisable to say Da'anzho Ya'ateh ("Hello") when encountering a magpie (Pica hudsonia), and Egogahan ("Until we meet again") when leaving its presence.

—Birds of America and the Territories, Chapter 54: Crows, Jays, Magpies, Ravens

Chapter 84
Wanted For Murder!

Wanted for Murder!

DECEMBER 2, 1880

THE BOY DESPERADO

Known as Billy Bonney, Wm. Antrim,
Wm. Henry McCarty, & Billy the Kid
for the murders of multiple persons including
our two Courageous Lincoln County Lawmen
Sheriff W. B. Brady & Deputy George Hindman
and the unarmed blacksmith Frank "Windy" Cahill,
and the crook-armed lame gimp Civil War Veteran
Sgt. Andrew "Buckshot" Roberts at Blazer's Mill.
Caution: The Kid is likely wounded & desperate.
Do not be fooled by his age, size, or his clever talk!

$400.00 REWARD

Guaranteed paid for his capture and delivery be it
Living or Dead to Governor Lew Wallace, Santa Fe
or
Patrick F. Garrett, the Sheriff of Lincoln County,
Territory of New Mexico

Chapter 85
Sojourn to Stinking Springs
December 21, 1880 – The Moon of Dying Fires

Billy Bonney and Charlie Bowdre headed north through long stretches of sagebrush and needlegrass. The terrain they traveled was not level but slow rise hill after slow rise hill, and it seemed as if those first bits of stinging white that blew into their faces were ash unleased from an unseen fire just over the next crest. It had been a dry winter but now the snow was falling. They both looked up. To wonder, as one does, what is coming. There the firmament pale, opaque. The glow of a waxing moon lighting the thin cover of cloudwork. Charlie retied his blue neckerchief bandit style. Billy pulled his hat down tight to his head. The wound above his left ear leaked, and although his scalp was split open to the bone, he felt only a trickle of wet on his neck. They both adjusted their collars and went on.

They went on through an expanse of sloughgrass blown flat and slick and soon there was no grass to be seen and the horses blinked into the wind with heads dropped low and pushed through snow now drifting to their knees. And if a moon had persisted behind the clouds there now was no trace of it, and in darkness they went on. Presently the Choctaw stopped. Come on, said Billy. The Choctaw tossed and twisted his head around to a stirrup and baring its teeth sunk them into Billy's boot toe and began to back up as a group of wolves appeared, an apparition of gray shifting within the tattered and trailing curtains of white. They stood, snouts lifted and sniffing with mist streaming from their muzzles and briefly suspended in the air until taken forthwith by the wind. The snow rose and spun around them and they were hidden for an instant and when the wind died again they were gone.

Billy urged the Choctaw forward. Charlie Bowdre followed on his slate grullo a horse-length behind. They climbed a slope set with shortleaf pine that had long ago found sapling rootholds among the multitudes of close-set stones. The horses stepped uneasily. Charlie and Billy slacked their reins and spoke to them kindly and softly and slowly they went on, but soon enough they were passing through a wide slide of snow-laden boulders with hardly a space between to set a hoof. Once more the Indian pony stopped. Billy just sat. The trickle of wet from the wound above his ear had turned yellow and foul and froze along his neck. Billy? Charlie called. You awake? The Choctaw snorted and swung his head around and looked back. Billy dropped the reins and slumped forward onto the Indian pony's neck, his face in its mane crusted with rime.

By daybreak the storm had begun to lift. A dim but silvery stripe of sky in the east. Billy woke to find his head resting upon Charlie Bowdre's leg, his mouth full of snow, and a junco chittering in the boughs of the juniper above them. Charlie pushed him upright and propped him back against the trunk. Billy wondered if a piece of himself was missing as half of his head had gone numb. He raised his hand and felt for his ear. The wound had been scrubbed with snow and covered with Charlie's neckerchief wadded up. You owe me a neckerchief, Charlie said. Blue, preferably.

Billy tried to speak but he could not. He choked and coughed and started to spit snow. Better swallow that, Charlie told him. You was hot.

The Apache believe that the yellow-eyed junco (Junco phaeonotus) absorbs sunlight in the daytime and releases it at night though its bright golden eyes.

—Birds of America and the Territories, Chapter 77: New World Sparrows, Juncos

They sat wrapped in their rough saddle blankets, immobile and feeble with cold. They had no provisions, having hightailed it out of Blazer's Mill leaving behind the bodies of Dick Brewer and Buckshot Roberts, but Charlie Bowdre found a dusty fig and a few coffee beans at the bottom of his kit. He chomped off half the fig in the manner of taking a chaw from a plug of tobacco and he placed the other half into Billy's mouth. Chew, he told Billy. I ain't be doing it for you. He counted out the beans and divided them up between them and these they sucked with bits of snow for hours while the day began to brighten. A fire was considered, briefly discussed regarding the cover of snow, the continuing wind, the dearth of kindling dry enough to ignite. Charlie thought to peel strips of shagbark from the juniper trunk and he managed to strike a match to his fingernail and cup the flame as he touched it to those shredded bits, but the wind stole the first sparks from that paltry tinder time after time. By midmorning the snowfall had ceased. The horses that had been standing with their heads down and rumps to the wind now stamped at the snow and pawed through to the strands of brown grass and began to eat. A pair of hunting hawks cried from somewhere above while they sat in their blankets and looked up through the crosshatch of boughs so they might see the hawk pair passing but what they saw was only blue. Billy tried to stand. Where you going? Charlie said. Billy knelt and clutched the trunk and took hold of a lower branch to pull himself upwards but he lost his grip and again went to his knees shaking down a little blizzard of snow on both of them. Charlie calmly brushed himself off. Try that again and I'll shoot you, he said.

By afternoon the wind had stilled. The air gone colder or seeming so. Before dusk the hawk pair passed overhead again. Billy stood up. Unsteady still but standing. He shaded his eyes against the slant of final light in the west. Red-tails, he said as the ruddering of their tails flashed rust in the last of the sun and they few on to some citadel in this district of treetops and ledge-rock, arriving at that promontory with feathered legs outstretched and talons reaching to take hold of a perch. And there they hunched and plumped their dense underdown in preparation for the freezing night ahead.

The cry of the red-tailed hawk (Buteo jamaicensis) has been likened to the shrill note of an Apache ceremonial whistle.

—Birds of America and the Territories, Chapter 15: Eagles, Hawks, Kites

Dawn on a bright winter's day. The canyon lies sunlit below them. The limbs of pine along the slopes sag with snow that sparks in the cold winter light of perigee as the earth's circuit brings it closest to its nearest star. Their upland climb through the storm had taken them to the top of a mesa and now from that overlook they beheld the miles of chaparral ahead, the dry sage and olive-green chamisa on a field of white, and beyond that vermillion cliffs crossbedded by limestone and an ancient lava flow. The mesa was banked by an escarpment of rockslide and rubble revealing no path for descent until they spied a party of deer making their way down a distant incline, disappearing and appearing in and out the pines, seen and not seen, some already descended to the lower slopes and stopping to forage amid the scrub oak for acorns fallen a season ago and unsprouted under the snow. We'll go that way, Billy said, saddling up.

Taking charge again, are ya? said Charlie.

They came upon the doe partway down the slope. A straggler. The rest had thrown up their tails at the scent of men and the smell of horses or the sound of hoofs cracking the snowcover, and bounded away with weightless grace over downed trees and drifts, but the doe made only a faltering start, spotting the snow with bits of red around her as she scrambled off the trodden path and crashed through the scrub oak and they saw the ragged tear in the hide of her hindquarters and the open strip of blood-clotted sinew, and Billy raised his Winchester and took her down in one shot.

They traveled on through the chaparral, passing the pale green spikes of Spanish bayonet arranged in giant rosettes and scatterings of olive-green sage and the horses grazed the patches of last summer's galleta grass showing through the scant snowfall of the desert floor.

At dusk they followed a dry wash that wandered into a canyon, and there they took shelter in an alcove of rock carved into the canyon wall by a river that had run this way millennia ago until the earth buckled and folded it over. The space was wide and deep enough for themselves and the horses with an overhang of stone from which blades of ice hung at the lip of it and dripped. The floor of the alcove was hard-packed sand marked with the tracks of animals and strewn with dry drifted cottonwood, some of it blackened by other burnings. They built a fire. They skinned and butchered the doe. They set sticks into the sand and hung them with strip of the flesh bent into the flames and smoke. It had begun to snow again. Specks of white flew past the alcove opening from the vast blackness beyond. The sky briefly flashed white and they wondered if the rumblings they heard were distant gunshots or thunder. They sat in the rock hollow and gazed upon the cavern walls decorated with curious images, the shapes of ancient hands outlined in sprays of sepia pigment, and whole processions of pronghorn antelope and deer and sheep with huge coiled horns and the renderings of turtles with shells of concentric circles and big-eyed spiders seated in geometric webs, and lightning bolts, arrows, spears, spirals, stars, suns, moons in a series of waning phases, and stick-figures playing reed pipes, and fantastic limbless beings bearing antlers and antennae and wings, and they studied all of it in the flickering of the firelight as they took the hot meat in their fingers and their mouths and tore it apart with their teeth, much the same as those ancient artists had done long ago in the very places they now sat.

What do you make of it? said Billy.

Needs salt, Charlie said.

A coyote pup appeared at the mouth of the alcove. It sat facing them with its head resting on its forelegs in the way dogs have done since the first cookfires of the world were set, its eyes dark tarns of firelight. Billy clicked his tongue and held up a piece of meat but it would not come and he pitched it just beyond its reach. It crept forward watching them all the while, even as it extended a paw to pull the meat closer and as it crept in reverse the same. Next it'll be bringing the whole pack of its pals in here, said Charlie as he laid his rifle beside him and pulled his saddle blanket over and stuffed his hat under his head for sleep.

Billy woke during the night. The fire had burned low. The pup was still there curled on itself against the cold with tail draped over its snout and its limbs folded and tucked. It opened its eyes and lifted its ears at Billy's stirring but it did not raise its head to look. Come morning when they awoke it was gone. They wrapped the smoked meat in pieces of the newly skinned hide and they packed these parcels into their saddlebags.

They rode out along the dry wash and onto the treeless plain. The sun commencing its shallow arc of solstice. The wash-bed lightly sifted with snow. A goshawk passed high above them but seen only as a shadow-shape silently climbing the canyon wall, bending in accommodation to the stoneface slants and outcroppings in its ascent to the top, and then disappearing into the cerulean blue.

When goshawk pairs (Accipiter gentili) hunt other birds in flight, one goshawk distracts the prey by flying in plain view, while the other swoops in from behind and ambushes the victim.

—Birds of America and the Territories, Chapter 15: Eagles, Hawks, Kites

Chapter 86
List of Pictures in the Rock Hollow
by Billy Bonney
December 21, 1880

5 handprints
12 pronghorns
7 deer
2 big horns
2 turtles
1 tarantula spider or some other kind
zig zags I think is lightning
arrow, spears
stars too many
suns
shapes of the moon just like you see it come and go
squiggles, likely snakes
circles
bird people with deer heads
other things but too far in for me to be going.
a coyote pup (real one)

Chapter 87
The Stone House at Stinking Springs
December 24, 1880 – The Moon of Dying Fires

Early dusk. The sky bear written in strung stars crouches in sleep below the northwest horizon. In the east the moon rides above the heads of Gemini. This winter sky. Some stars glittering and some dim motes so far flung from any knowing that they fade from the eye when pondered.

They camped in the ruins of a small stone house, a solitary structure in that expanse of sagebrush steppe, treeless except for a dead mesquite beside it and hung with old pods. The walls were the same rough gray rocks as those strewn over the surrounding terrain, and these had been stacked and fitted one to another without benefit of mortar or masonry, and grown over with circular crusts of lichen, red and yellow and peridot green. The roof was old wattle and daub and in places open to the stars, and the widow was silled in stone and open to the wind. The lintel beam had collapsed into the doorless doorway where a large paddle leaf cactus stood with its shriveled globes of fruit.

The hearth held the fallen chimney stones. They built a small mesquite fire that did little to warm them, but they melted snow in their tin cups enough to steep a bitter mesquite tea. A thin braid of smoke lit by the moon coiled from the broken chimney. They lay on the frozen earthen floor as close to the fire as that small space afforded, legs folded to their chests, their bodies bent and braced against the cold.

They talked awhile about getting to Texas. It better be warmer, said Billy. Some parts, said Charlie. And he said that his wife might like Texas. My Manuela, he said. She'd like me staying put for once and homesteading on the panhandle. Good grazing country, Charlie said. Long on grass and short on fences.

What'll we do for cows? said Billy.

Cows? said Charlie. Hell, cows is nothing. You and me, we just rustle us some stock and stake a settler's claim somewhere along the Pecos. And damn, in three years we all be sitting pretty.

Three years, Charlie? I guess you've gone off thinking you're dying any time soon.

No I ain't, he said. Not never gone off dying.

It is sometime before dawn when the horses snort and steam the air around their faces. Billy crawls to the window on his elbows, his six-shooter cocked. I'll take the door, Charlie whispers. They look out upon the unforested plain to the edge of the world where the far away mesas stand black against the backdrop of stars, and the clumps of sagebrush shine silvery gray, and every boulder and stone in that level desolation sits apart from every other and within its singular shadow shortened by the overhead moon. The sky bear wakes and shows himself just above the western horizon before lost again in the sunrise. No wind. No sound. And then again the horses' skitterish snorts and nickers.

Hear that? says Billy.

Could be they're smelling something. Likely some wolves out hunting, says Charlie.

Could be somebody hunting us, says Billy.

Garrett if it's anybody, says Charlie.

He's been gunning for us, says Billy.

You name someone who ain't, says Charlie.

They keep watch until the sameness of the terrain takes over. You seeing anything? says Billy. Charlie rubs his fists into his eyes. I don't know what in hell I'm seeing, he says, but damn if all them rocks out there ain't turning into turtles.

It comes soon after dawn.

The sun sits low in Sagittarius and the rock shadows are drawn long. The underfolds of the clouds shot through with copper and gold and rust. Billy kneels at the broken hearth. He fans the last embers alive with his hat. We could do with more tinder, he says. Charlie stands at the stone house window for a look-see out at the lay of the land in daylight. A jackrabbit sits hunched in a patch of sage. *That's hardly hiding. You're an easy shot if I happened to be out hunting. There goes a crow. Here comes another. Could be ravens. I could ask Billy. Billy would know, always writing down birdy names. Keeping his damn list.* New sunlight now on the patches of snow. Charlie squints. Beyond stand the faraway mesas that through the night stood in black silhouette against the spangled sky, now becoming sandstone and sienna in this light and green-topped with the forests of shortleaf pine they had passed through. The cloud colors beginning to fade from gilt to gray. The slate grullo screams. Gunfire comes from somewhere. Billy's Choctaw pony crashes through the cactus paddle-tails and stands trembling in the doorway. Billy reels him in. Charlie slumps down with a wound to his shoulder. Bullets spark and sing off the rocks. Charlie on his knees and hands now, creeping to the window. There the Grullo is on its side. Blood pouring from the hole in its belly. Blood pumping from the hole in its neck. Charlie raises up, a gun in each hand, fires, and he is hit again. This time mid-chest. Billy sidles to the door. There's four of them Charlie, Billy says of the men coming on, closing in, hunched as they come and cowering stone to stone on that treeless plain. Maybe five. Billy takes aim. Fires. The Choctaw shies and presses to the far wall. Got one, he calls to Charlie. Charlie is down again, blood in his mouth. Texas, he says.

The slate grullo still thrashes, its legs moving as if it were running.

When ravens (Corvus cora) come upon a dead animal, they invite wolves to the carcass by calling them in. Wolves recognize the ravens' call, and arrive to tear through the dead animal's hide and expose the flesh, which is then easily be consumed by the birds.

—Birds of America and the Territories, Chapter 54: Crows, Jays, Magpies, Ravens

Chapter 88
Leaving Stinking Springs
December 25, 1880
by Billy Bonney

His name was Stockton. The deputy I shot. Doyle Stockton. Young fella. Twenty-two, they told me. Just recent deputized, the sheriff said.

It was the sheriff who let me ride my Choctaw back to Lincoln. Sheriff Patrick Garrett. He had to, seeing that Indian pony pitched him right off on his first try and the same with the deputies, both of them.

They slung Charlie Bowdre belly down on the packhorse they brung along when they come hunting us. They sacked his head the way they would do for a hanging and they roped him tight behind the bedrolls and saddlebags.

The one of them I shot, the deputy, they wrapped in a blanket and laid him on his own horse the same way belly down and him they covered over.

So. There's two dead men riding. Three if you're counting me.

We left the grullo there to rot. Or get ate. Buzzards, crows, coyotes, polecats. There's plenty of varmints in that open stretch of nothing but stones and sage.

It's a hungry country.

We had a long ways to go.

The bright red head of the turkey vulture (Catharses aura) or buzzard is featherless, thereby preventing rotting bits of carrion from sticking to its face when thrust into a decomposing carcass.

—Birds of America and the Territories, Chapter 14: New World Vultures, Condors

Chapter 89
Mrs. Emma Bea Stockton
Jemez Springs, New Mexico
January 7, 1881 – The Moon of Hungry Crows

They were on the move now. These two deputies, two dead men, one sheriff, one Billy.

They rode south along the San Juan River, a region of buttes and badlands, and turning east at the Chaco tributary, followed its sandy-bottomed course into the flatland of the great caldera. Before sunset they camped along pools kept simmering by the ancient heat of a deep and sleeping volcano, itself fed by the molten core of earth's creation, and all around them fumaroles fizzed and smoked and the groundwater steamed up into the air. Soon after moonrise flurries began to fall and pair of elk stepped out of the cold and stood veiled in the warm mists and the falling flakes, and these they shot and skinned and flung away the innards, and they cut huge steaks for themselves and poached them in the bubbling shallows.

Come morning, a trio of vultures had taken their posts in the trees above the cast-off viscera, and these watched the sheriff and his two deputies as they butchered what remained of the elk and packed the meat in skins and snow, and it was already turning twilight when they entered the settlement of Jemez Springs to deliver the body of deputy Doyle Stockton to his mother. She had been sweeping a dusting of snow from the porch of her clapboard house and at the sight of the men riding up to the gate with bodies bound to their horses she set the broom against the post and fell to her knees, crying into her frail and wrinkled hands. One of the deputies came down from his horse and strode up the steps. He gathered her shawl around her and lifted her up and carried her inside. He sat her in her kitchen. He waited until she dabbed at her eyes with a handkerchief she produced from her sleeve. She asked if he would care for a cup of tea. She asked if he'd help her search for her brass candlesticks and candles. Yes ma'am, he said. You just tell me where. Oh dear, she said. I last used them when the mister died, oh when was that, oh dear.

He went about opening and closing cabinets and drawers and loudly rummaging around but none were found. He asked her where, please tell me where would you like your boy. That was how he put it. She sat silently for a moment tapping her fingertips to her chin. Well, she said. Back in his bed I suppose. And he'll be needing an extra blanket tonight, she said, that nice wool one folded at the foot and the extra pillow so he's comfy.

Well Ma'am, he said. I expect some folks will be coming by, he said, paying their respects and such. Oh yes, she said. I do expect they will. He let her sit and ponder this a moment and she said, The parlor would be better. The parlor would certainly do.

Let me, he told her, and he left her where she sat in the kitchen. She could hear him in another part of the house moving things about. The thump and clunk of furniture. The sound of something falling. The sound of window sash lifted. As cold air found its way to the kitchen the curtains briefly billowed and she pulled her shawl closer. He came back to the kitchen. She watched him put away the things on the table. Teacups. Spoons. Creamer. Sugar pot. Bluebird salt, redbird pepper. He tilted the table up on its side and with great effort lifted it pressed it to his chest and in that way lumbered along through kitchen and corridor, his steps heavy and hard on the wide plank floor as he carried it away to the space he had cleared in the parlor.

The turkey vulture (Cathartes aura) has no song or call, but it is able to softly grunt and hiss.

—Birds of America and the Territories, Chapter 14: New World Vultures, Condors

Chapter 90
Mrs. Manuela Herrera Bowdre
Socorro, New Mexico
January 14, 1881 – The Moon of Hungry Crows

They rode south along the Rio Grande following the rift valley formed in that remote millennium when liquid rock from the earth's innards spumed up fracturing its crust and hardening into great swales of basalt. They rode past distant cinder cones and through tracts of scrub strewn with oddly pocked boulders and black flows of stone and wondered how these rivers of dark rock so unlike the surrounding sunset-colored hills and mesas came to be.

The body of Charlie Bowdre was carried by packhorse at the rear of the party. Billy rode out front on the Choctaw with a deputy's gun fixed in his direction, his arms tied behind. The iron cuffs had they carried for their purpose were found to be too large to contain him, and they wrapped strips of rawhide around his wrists and over these they clamped the cuffs which were then made snug enough. These wore against his tendons but mostly his hands were too numb for him to notice. Come sunset they made their camps leeward of canyon walls or tucked under outcroppings. They unsaddled their horses and relieved the packhorse of the burden of Charlie Bowdre, and hobbled them all except the Choctaw. On their first night out, it had been standing patiently while one of the men knelt to rope its forelegs when it took the man's hair in his teeth and flung him away, inciting hoots all around and deeming the animal henceforth unlikely to run off and leave their prisoner behind.

Billy was kept wrist-cuffed and rawhide-tied from behind when he sat with them at their nightly fires. When he asked for food, scraps were placed on the bare ground a distance before him and on his knees he shuffled toward it and he put his face into meat and dirt and on his belly he ate. When he asked for water, it was poured into a pan and he lapped it up. When he asked that his hands be released to unbutton his trousers, he was told go right ahead there Billyboy, go piss and shit yourself. And this he did and his parts were rubbed bleeding raw by the waste and the wet and the rhythm of the riding. He was not asked how he fared, or if he was poorly or well, or if one blanket was enough, or if he felt something akin to sorrow or remorse or regret nor did he attempt to tell. And so it went. On the morning of their third day of travel they woke and found the tracks of coyotes and the body of Charlie Bowdre dragged into the brush just beyond their camp.

The sack that had covered his head lay beside him. His face had been torn away from his mouth up to his empty eye sockets and his neck had been stripped of all flesh and vessels and laid open to the bone-stack of his spine.

They fitted the sack over his head once more, and loaded him to the packhorse. And they traveled on.

They traveled on through broad alkaline flats of hedgehog agave and up through the grassland foothills of the Montañas Magdalena where their horses grazed upon burro-grass and galleta. Scatterings of spruce and juniper. Bear sign was seen on the trunks where small birds crept. Icy springs trickled through the rocks. As the terrain rose the air grew colder. That night they made a fire of scrub oak. A gray fox circled them unseen while they slept, sniffing as it went and moving on. Come sunrise they broke camp and by late afternoon they reached the old pueblo town of Socorro.

They rode along the only thoroughfare. Shacks of juniper shakes. Adobes much the same as the homes of the old puebloans, built with bricks cut from canyon sandstone, mortared with the clay of a dry desert basin, and raftered with enormous rounds of ponderosa pine. These with small yards fenced by chunks of lava rock. A pair of winter wrens hopped in a garden of dry weedstalks and hollow cornstalks, their leaves gone pale as paper.

The last house in town was made from child-sized boulders of scoria that had been spewed miles from some primordial vent-hole, and the porch was roofed in a weave of Spanish bayonet. A terra-cotta flowerpot held a withered perennial. A hook held windchimes of green bottleglass shards. A plaster Saint Veronica, patron of the seamstress, had been set beside the door. From inside came the tick tick tick of a sewing machine and the metered squeak of a treadle.

They had wrapped what was left of the body in an old hairless hide. A swath of burlap was bunched over the head and secured there with a rope to keep the fleshless face from view. The two deputies came down from their horses and took their tin five-point stars from their pockets and pinned them prominently to their coats. Billy started to slide down from the Choctaw. Sheriff Pat Garrett pointed his pistol. Clicked the hammer. Finger on the trigger. You Billyboy, he said. You stay put.

They hauled their consignment down from the packhorse and carried it along the crushed cinderstone path to the porch. One man smacked his head on the windchimes. The other knocked over the flowerpot. The plaster Veronica teetered. The sewing machine sounds from within the house ceased.

Manuela Herrera Bowdre had been sitting at her sewing. A special order for her niece's fiesta de quinceañera. A skirt of sky-blue satin with a petticoat of white organza and a trim of sky-blue tulle. At the noise on the porch she took her foot from the treadle. She stood and coiled her long hair to the back of her head and tucked the ends under. She brushed bits of blue thread from her skirt. She took her shears in her hand and she went to the door.

Señora Bowdre?

Sí, Sí. Soy la señora Bowdre.

Sorry mam, said the deputy. Mucho siento.

Qué pasó? she said.

The second deputy nudged the package with his foot. Señor Bowdre, he said.

Mi esposo? she said. Dónde?

Here. This.

She frowned. Que? she said. Que? They did not answer. She looked down at the bundle wrapped in hide. Esta? she said. This? She waited. She looked into their faces. One then the other as she turned her shears in her hand. Palm to the handle. Daggerwise. And then she went at them, throwing herself upon them, the blades aligned and going down like a knife.

Señora! called Billy.

The men on the porch held her. She struggled to be free of them. She kicked. They pulled the shears out of her hand and tossed it into the garden. She wrenched her arms free and lunged and scratched at their faces. Two men could hardly contain her. She screamed and screamed until she spit blood and until no sound came.

Señora! called Billy from out past the yard. Aquí! he called, raising himself up in the saddle. Mira aquí señora! Look here!

They had her down now, beside the gunnysack. Her hair had come undone and hung in her face as she lifted her head and looked toward the horses in the street and to the one who was shouting, but she could not hear.

Yo era su amigo, Billy cried. I was his friend.

No, said the sheriff. You wasn't.

Chapter 91

The Town Turned Out

The Lincoln County Ledger

"Listen Up"

Vol. 81, No. 2 February 2, 1881 Price 12 cents

THE KID IN CUSTODY!

News of the capture of Billy the Kid has been trickling south from Jemez Springs and Socorro for weeks now, and today with the announcement that the Kid and his captors were approaching town, excitement here in Lincoln reached a fever pitch! The entire town turned out, as well as folks as far from Capitan and Ruidoso, all for a look at the young desperado.

The cold morning air did not keep crowds from gathering along the thoroughfare for a glimpse of Sheriff Patrick "Pat" Garrett, his two deputies, and their murderous captive. All were expected to arrive last month, but bad weather to the north made the trek more arduous and lengthy than expected. Garrett and his deputies appeared triumphant upon their arrival, but Billy Bonney Antrim, age nineteen, looked trail-worn and weary. However, as he was herded into the courthouse, several children called out, "Billy! Billy!" at which point he responded with a smile, and though his wrists were in irons, he pointed a finger at them, uttered "Bang", and blew away a puff of imaginary smoke, much to their delight.

Billy is quite the prize for the 32-year-old Garrett in light of his recent election as Sheriff. When asked for details of Billy's capture at Stinking Springs, he declined to elucidate or to discuss the $500 reward.

The Kid will remain in the courthouse lockup until his trial, likely to commence in the coming months. He is accused of killing Sheriff W. B. Brady and his Deputy George Hindman, as well as blacksmith Windy Cahill, and most recently Deputy Doyle Stockton at Stinking Springs, and of cattle rustling throughout the county. A guilty verdict and execution are expected.

TWO-HEADED CALF AT THE DOUBLE-D

Dan Degan reports the birth of a two-headed calf on his Double-D ranch. Anyone wanting a look at the creature, go on by before it's dead.

QUOTE OF THE DAY

☞ *Thus sayeth the Lord, your Redeemer, who formed you from the womb: "I am the Lord, who made all things."*

—Isaiah 44:24

Chapter 92
I Hope There's a Window Where They Put Me
by Billy H. Bonney
Lincoln Courthouse
February 2, 1881

The town turned out.

All along the thoroughfare was folks wanting a look at us as we rode in, Garrett and his deputies and me on the Choctaw and then we whoa up at the rail out front of the lockup. They had me cuffed frontwise by then, me being too weak for riding without holding on, and I sat my horse while Garrett made his little speech about how Lincoln County, no—how the entire Territory would be better off with Billy Bonney put away or maybe what he said was put down. Put down. That was it. I just sat.

I looked into the faces of the folks that come from around the county to see me. They'd heard the stories. Some what's been writ. Some just told, one man to the next. None of them not looking too happy, not by my lights. Not Garrett neither. It seemed to me he took no joy in it. How could he. He'd been where I was sitting once or twice himself or in some similar fix and him same as me had to be hoping to wriggle out of it, since he'd done his share of killing on his own long before he got made sheriff and the county started paying him to. I'm thinking he is ready to haul me off my horse but he says, Hold up there Billyboy, since now there's the reporter from the *Lincoln Ledger* come running with a pencil in his hand and he's writing right while he's running, and next comes the silver agent from the assay office, and out from the hotel restaurant a mother and a father with two little boys in tow and them both still wearing their napkins under their chins, and now the liveryman from out the livery and now the people from the bank. Men in white shirts and eyeshades and regular folks who been banking. A few looked at me kindly but mostly they just looked. Garrett tells them, Nothing to be feared of folks. He was sure right about that. Nothing to be feared in getting a look at a killer up close when he's just about done in anyway which I was from that hell of a trip down from Stinking Springs and when he's good and tied and cuffed-up to boot which I also was. So they all inch in a little closer.

I see one man in a porkpie swigging from a bottle. He stops swigging and starts yelling, String 'em up now, why don't we? he says and next he whips out his pistol and fires straight up and there's screams from the ladies in the crowd and the men are laughing when he yells Whoopie we're overdue for a hanging ain't we? That'll be enough of that Horace, says Sheriff Patrick Garrett. Get on home now Horace, he tells him and this Horace mutters something and the crowd makes way. There's all kinds in the crowd. Men dressed fancied up and some plain and rough looking, and drovers, and ranchers, and wives and children, and few little lads waving at me. Way back some there's a lady wearing a cotton bonnet the same color my Mam used to wear, bow-tied to the side of her chin the way Mam tied it, and set on her head just the same and for a quick minute I was thinking—well you know what I was thinking. But Mam was long gone and likely rot away where we put her in the soil of Silver City. So I paid no mind to that what I was seeing. She never cared much for me, my Mam. But she was my Mam all the same, and when I saw that bow-tied bonnet, I felt something of what some might call happy, so maybe I wasn't so bad if she was coming to mind right then. But fast as that thinking came on me, I let it go. A foolish notion was all it was. Two foolish notions, those being a bonnet fetching my Mam to my mind and me being happy, both. So I just sat, looking at all them folks who come to look me over and one lady dabbing her eye with her handkerchief and I thought maybe it was that I'd killed some kin of hers but she says, Oh my he's just a boy, a smidgen of a lad!—the way my Da told me he said it when he sees me newly born. But it wasn't so. I wasn't no boy right then. I wasn't no lad neither. Not no more. I was nineteen years old and fully growed but even before growing I never was one. I never knew what I was. My Mam, she told me I wasn't no boy of hers but most likely kin to the Wee Folk and Sprites who just flew in and left me for her to be raising, but didn't she wish I'd grow wings from my crooked back wingbones so I'd just go on back to whatever dark place I come from. Well, them wings never did grow and they never would, though there were plenty times I wish they did. I'd just lift up and flap off and keep on going, I would. Like those little brown sparrows there hopping and pecking in the dust at my Choctaw's feet, not a bit scared of all the people in the street since any time at all they can fly away safe from trouble coming, but I can't. And now I wouldn't no how, not with this Choctaw pony I'm sat on wondering why I'd left him and where I'd got to. He turns his head way around and does what he does when it's time to be getting on, and what that is he gives my boot-toe a nip. Alright Cielo, I tell him. I'm as ready as you are to be getting on. Cielo. That's the name I give him, since he's got one blue eye, sky blue, but I swore I'd never say that name on account of the way my life's always been going, since there was no telling how long he'd be mine for. And this situation right here, this may be when him being mine is just about over. So I let him bite. Why not. I got it coming. It's a real fool I've been and a real fool doesn't know any other way to live than foolish. Bite me then, boy. Clear through my boot and to the bone if you want. Was me got us into every trouble there is. This here included. And now they had me for sure but hell, I'll find a way to get away. Always did. In the meantime they'd take me. And the Choctaw? A full-blood Indian pony strong and sound? They'd take him too for sure. They might not tell me where he's got to, but I'd figure a way to find him. So I just sat. I wanted that Choctaw horse knowing

I wasn't going off and leaving him on no will of my own. So I sat. Not saying nothing, the way my Da would always be telling me Billy, you keep your gob shut when it needs shutting and your eyes open and pay attention to what is coming. I know what's coming, I do. It comes right soon the speechmaking's done with and the lockup's waiting. Alright Billyboy, Garrett says. Let's go. Get on down, he says. But I sit. And keep on sitting. The sheriff and the two deputies come over and put their hands on me, and I tell him, You go on then. Pull me off my horse, boys. Pull me down if you have to, but don't expect I'm coming easy, so pull me down and damn they did.

House sparrows (Passer domesticus) often nest near human habitation where both parents participate in feeding their nestlings. However, a single parent will take over their care if the other dies. If both parents are killed or die, the begging cries of the orphaned young will attract other adults who will feed them until they are able to fend for themselves outside of the nest.

—Birds of America and the Territories, Chapter 78: Old World Sparrows

Chapter 93
Governor Lew Wallace Writes to Wm. H. Antrim
February, 1881

Office of the Governor

Territory of New Mexico

February 14, 1881
Wm. H. Antrim:

After careful review, I find no evidence implicating Messrs. Murphy and Dolan in the death of J. Tunstall in February of 1879. What remains under investigation are the misguided attempts at retaliation by you and your gang, resulting in the murders of lawmen and private citizens of Lincoln County.

As Governor, I have been entrusted to uphold the highest standards of public service. My official duties include a multitude of complex issues, and there are personal literary obligations to which I must attend. In order to fulfill my many commitments, I must bring this time-consuming affair to its conclusion. Members of your gang have since met their demise, but testimony from a participant such as yourself would give credence to final judgments and settle this matter in the eyes of the law. I have authority to exempt you from prosecution if you will testify and state for the record what you know. Inform Sheriff Garrett, in whose custody you remain, of your intentions.

Lew Wallace,
Territorial Governor

Chapter 94
Wm. H. Bonney Writes to Governor Lew Wallace
February, March, and April, 1881

To His Excellency, Governor Lew Wallace
February 16, 1881
Dear Sir,

I will testify in exchange for a Pardon.

Your faithful servant,

Wm. H. Bonney. Antrim was my stepfather's name.

To His Excellency, Governor Lew Wallace
March 18, 1881
Dear Sir,

thank you for allowing me to testify about John Tunstall's murder.

I await your reply with news of my Pardon. As ever,

Wm. H. Bonney

To Lew Wallace, Esteemed Governor
April 10, 1881
Dear Sir,

I am writing you again from the Lincoln lockup but you know where I am. I ask Sheriff Garrett if you received my letters and he says you are busy selling your book about Mr. Ben Hur and the Romans. As you see I can read and write and will read it myself if someone gets it to me. In the meantime I expect you forgot you offered me a Pardon if I would testify to circumstances of the shooting of the Englishman John Tunstall in 1879 to provide Final Judgements and square things with the law, as you said. I stood up in court and done everything you asked, but here I still sit convicted of murder and sentenced to hang while Sheriff Garrett lets in Every Stranger that comes to see me from Curiosity but never the person took custody of my Horse, and never my attorney who done all he can for me up to now. For the last time I ask, Will you keep your promise? Excuse my bad writing, which is because of handcuffs.

Respectfully waiting for your reply.
Wm. H. Bonney

Chapter 95
We Return to the Young Desperado in Shackles
Lincoln County Courthouse and Lockup,
April 28, 1881 – The Moon of Waking Bears

Noon. Or nearly so. Mourning doves cry Oooo-wee-oo from their perch in the cottonwood.

Billy swivels open his boot-heel, works the folded paper from the hollow, and adds to his list: *mourning dove*. He pivots it back in place and secures the nail with a stamp of his foot.

Now comes Deputy James Lee Bell to fetch the crockery—the posole bowl looking licked clean but having been dumped unbeknownst into the piss bucket.

Well, says James Lee Bell. You done real good for someone ain't eating. Slide it this away under.

He slides it under.

Deputy, says Billy. Nature calls.

Use your bucket, says James Lee Bell.

Bucket's full, says Billy. I better hit the privy.

No can do, says deputy Bell. Strict orders from Sheriff Garrett.

Go fetch the other deputy.

No can do not that neither. Ollie's at lunch.

Suit yourself, Mr. Bell. I'll be pissing and shitting on the floor then. And you'll be swamping it up.

And so it began, as this sort of thing does, with a scuffle. The captive, though small of build and just past his boyhood and said by some to be downright puny, is nonetheless agile, and as his father liked to say: You're too small to be landing a punch, Billy, but you'll win in a fight by dancing around and making the other feller dizzy.

Deputy James Lee Bell, however, is a large and lumber-footed man, too talkative at times but liked by all, and the disadvantage of his size worsened by the off-kilter stance required to sort through a jangle of keys on a ring, fit the key in the lock, slide a bolt, slide another bolt, lift the hasp-hold, swing the cell door and sidestep allowing the prisoner egress while manipulating and pointing a pistol, his new Colt Peacemaker, and maintaining aim. Billy stands. They have not taken his boots, as has been noted. Hat, yes. As has been said. As well as his Choctaw, his piebald pony. Ooooh wee oooh, says Billy. Croons Billy.

What say? says Deputy Bell, nervous now at that sound from Billy. He takes a step back.

Dove-call, says Billy. I heard you shooting. Sing out a dove-call next time just before you take your shot.

Oooh oooh? says Deputy Bell.

Ooooh WEE ooh, says Billy. Distracts 'em good, says Billy.

Ooooh wee oooh, says Deputy Bell.

Yep, says Billy. You got it now.

Well thanky, says Deputy Bell.

Sure, says Billy who has managed to wrangle one hand free from the cuff irons, due to a deformity of the wrist and a laxity of ligaments enabling the thumb joint to fold unnaturally palmwise, the result of an untreated childhood mishap, namely falling from a tree. *You tell me how it is a little squirt like thisn gets himself down the stair without breaking his feckin' neck and out the door and through the alley and up a persimmon tree,* his father said. *You look at that wrist of his swell up and tell me how to be paying for doctoring that, you go ahead and tell me that and while you're at it, you tell me why it is you're not watching him, Catherine, why is that?*

Say, where'd my hat get to? says Billy.

Had one when you come in, did you? says Deputy Bell.

Sure did, says Billy bending for a look-see under the cot.

None of that now, says Deputy Bell, suspecting a trick. You straighten up now, says Bell and Billy straightens up to standing and swings and the dangling wrist-iron connects with the mandible of James Lee Bell. Teeth spewed, bloody spit. Bell flung backward, still with his pistol. Manages a shot. Then a second. Nearly wings him, but Billy is dancing. Dodging. Bell winds up. Throws a wide right hook, over-extended. The hazards of a haymaker. Billy takes a side-step. Bell throws another. Billy dodges. Bell off balance. Billy goes for his neck. Chain held taut. An artery occluded. James Lee Bell sees the contents of the room go by slowly counterclockwise, then speed up, now spinning, now reversing, spinning and reversing, spinning and his vision goes hazy and transiently fades. Gasps and wheezes emanate from both parties. Gurgles, in fact. Bell still grips his pistol. Won't unclutch it. Won't or can't. Billy has Bell's hand bent backwards beyond the range of normal extension, a popping in the sockets at the point of dislocation. Howls emanate from both parties. Struggling for the gun continues (to be reported in tomorrow's early edition of *The Lincoln County Ledger* as *grappling for the gun* and *accounts vary*, though no witnesses remained, one being dead and the other *fled the scene*). Is the weapon pressed in between the chests of both men, or the bellies of both men, or is it held overhead and discharged with bits of the ceiling debris falling on their heads (the resulting gap and crack in the plaster later enhanced and promoted as a local attraction) or is said pistol finally seized by the abrupt twisting of the wrist and the rearrangement of the small bones therein? And is the Colt Peacemaker deliberately thrown down, or inadvertently dropped, or possibly deliberately or inadvertently kicked away and slid just out of reach of both parties, or perhaps either party, or just one party, and then recovered, while both parties remain engaged in the maneuver already termed grappling? No matter though, as the final engagement spills out onto the landing, the weight of them thrown against the creaking banister with the crack of polewood, until at last the fatal shot is fired—oh yes, it is our Billy just past his boyhood that fires (also reported in *The Lincoln County Ledger* and in most accounts of gunplay as the usual *shots rang out*), the passage of leadshot entering the back just shy of the shoulder blade of Deputy James Lee Bell (*dedicated public servant, cold blooded murder, shot in the line of duty*, etc.) and continuing in a slightly downward trajectory though parenchyma of lung, though a chamber of the heart, and lodging in the breastbone, effectively finishing off the recipient of said leadshot, and in turn completing the collapse of the balustrade as his body crashes through it. Toppling. Head first. An ear snagged on a rogue post-nail, torn from its cartilaginous attachments to hang there skewered. Blood in the stair-step cracks and piney knot-holes. The final thudding of Deputy James Lee Bell, a talkative man, too much at times but liked by all—upon the hard-trodden earth of the courtyard, sending the pair of doves newly perched in the cottonwood away in a burst of flight and a bustling of wings.

As fate would have it and certainly always or often has it, Sheriff Patrick Garrett happened to be out collecting county taxes, and four other prisoners who were regular guests of the Lincoln lockup and charged with crimes more minor than Billy's (bad checks, public nuisance, foreclosure hold-outs) had been detained in first floor of the jail annex and permitted to take their meals off premises. It happened to be lunch time, and deputy Bob "Ollie" Olinger with his Winchester at the ready was designated to escort this shuffling procession of line-shackled jailbirds to the Lincoln Chow Down just across the street. The sound of gunshot coming from the lockup was heard between the special (green chili stew) and the peach hand-pies. Spoonfuls of stew held midair between mouth and bowl. Deputy Olinger out of his seat. You men stay put, says Olinger on his way out of the Chow Down door and sprinting across the street. There the body in the piazza. Beside it broken timber. Up here deputy, calls Billy, our Billy still standing on the splintered remains of the second-floor landing. Taking aim with Deputy Bell's brand-new Peacemaker pistol. Up here Olinger, says Billy, drawing a bead on Bob "Ollie" Olinger who lifts his Winchester too late.

The four men at the Lincoln Lunch do not finish their green chili stew. They pocket the peach hand-pies. They stand in unison. Shackled together. They do not stay put.

Billy is seen by the upstairs ladies of the Cards & Kinship who peer through the shabby curtain-lace as he makes his hobbled run to the livery. There tools aplenty. He selects a pick-axe. He selects a hammer. Smash and smash. The horses go skitterish and snorting and knocking about in their stalls: bay, roan, and a black Appaloosa. Untethered at the haycrib stands an old mule, his eyes closed and set deep in their orbits. Which? The black Appaloosa—a mare—rump spotted white—the prettiest. There are saddles on the rack, bridles on a hook. He clutches a fistful of the Appaloosa's mane and swings himself up. Go giddy-up there girly, says Billy. Saddleless. Sans bridle. The mule opens his gray-lashed eyes, brays wheezily and low. The Appaloosa nickering. Tell him adios, he says and she does. He leans forward on her pretty neck, reining her out though the slide-bar doors, whacking her rumpwise with his hat. Or someone's hat. The Appaloosa is plucky, young. Hoofbeats of a hard gallop athunder through the thoroughfare, the usual getaway display: kicked-up dust and a woman nearly run over, shrieking and clutching her child (who drops his pinwheel sucker on a stick) to her skirt. The dun-coat dog dives under the sidewalk boards. A lone leghorn—coop fugitive—hotfoots it to cover. The mourning doves scatter.

Now the men are mounting up and shouting to each other even as they take up the reins and swing astride.

He got James Lee, shouts someone.

And Ollie, shouts someone else. He got Ollie.

He's armed boys. Done took their guns.

Who the hell was watching this guy?

Where is Garrett? Where's that damn sheriff at?

Forget the sheriff.

Let's go boys.

Where's my horse? Where'd she'd get to.

Which is your horse?

My mare Ed. The black Appaloosa.

That's the one he done took.

And now the men setting their spurs to the flanks of the horses rearing and turning, and now all of them, all of the horses, turning.

Wherein the early hour it had brightly hung beyond the limbs of cottonwood, the morning moon has begun to fade—blanched now, the color of campfire ash and fragile as weathered desert bones but riding high a length or two behind him. Oh he would see it if he had looked back as he rode on, had glanced over his shoulder, but he does not and he does not see it racing with him, but never catching up.

The mourning dove (Zenaida macroura) is sometimes called a rain dove as the Apache and the Choctaw believe its cooing causes rainfall.

—Birds of America and the Territories, Chapter 39: Pigeons, Doves

Chapter 96
Wanted Dead or Alive

Wanted Dead or Alive

APRIL 28, 1881

MULTIPLE MURDERS!

William Henry McCarty, Alias Billy Bonney
and better known to all as Billy the Kid,
for the Cold-Blooded Killing of Lincoln County
Deputies James Lee Bell & Bob "Ollie" Ollinger,
during his daring jail-break from the Lincoln
Lockup where he awaited his death by hanging,
as well as the ruthless murders of other lawmen
shot down in the line of duty & several innocent,
law-abiding citizens of the Territory!
He is armed and has killed without provocation.

$500 REWARD FOR HIS APPREHENSION

And delivery dead or alive and in any condition
to Sheriff Pat Garrett, Lincoln County

Chapter 97
Where You Be?
Las Montañas Capitan
April 29, 1881 – The Moon of Waking Bears

He took the trail south out of Lincoln but soon turned north against the flow of the Rio Bonito and into the cold shadows of Las Montañas Capitan. That first night he came upon a rubble of rockslide that had taken down with it a slope of pine and juniper. There he took cover behind the tangle of branch and brush and pitched-over stones and boulders, and with the reins wound around his hand he reeled the black Appaloosa mare partway in. He lay face down upon a shelf of bare stone and put his parched mouth to the slow trickle of snowmelt seeping along the fractured slabs of shale. From time to time he lifted his head from the rock to see the Appaloosa pulling sprigs of the new grass that had sprung from the wet between the rocks, and then he slept. He did not feel the reins slip from his hands and when he woke in the night he had lost sight of the Appaloosa, and he tried to stand but tottered and fell back to the stone. The moon was just new. What light it gave was lost behind a bank of clouds and it was very dark. Where you be girl? he called softly and cursed himself for his foolishness, for his hunger and thirst, and for letting the reins slide away and for losing her, but by and by she drifted back into view not as a whole horse but as the disembodied spots of her white-dotted rump faintly glowing in the gloom and then drifting away once again, and he slept. Come dawn he woke to the calls of foraging piñon jays and there she was beside him. He stood now on his trembling legs and leaned a while against her for warmth with his hands on her flank and finally heaved himself upon her. And then he went back the way he had come, skirting the city limits of Lincoln, and then turning east with the Rio Ruidoso and into Las Montañas de Sacramento.

A foraging piñon jay (Gymnorhinus cyanocephalus) will determine if a piñon seed is empty or contains a nut by tapping the seed with its beak and listening for a solid or a hollow sound.

—Birds of America and the Territories, Chapter 54: Crows, Jays, Magpies, Ravens

Chapter 98
East Now and Running with the Rivers
Rio Ruidoso
May 1, 1881 – The Moon of Come Back Birds

He made his way east through Las Montañas de Sacramento with the Rio Ruidoso running clear and snowmelt cold amidst the early springtime blooms of yellow chamisa and Apache plume. The returning birds chittering. The bellows of elk. The river singing in its cobbled bed. He speaks to the purloined Appaloosa as they go, and she turns her ears to hear, and they keep on, winding up and down the foothills of the Las Montañas and into the forest cover of spruce. He rides with his pistol holstered and his rifle carried crosswise and ready. Rabbit. Mule deer. Nesting quail in the lee of a boulder. Easy kills. He returns riverside before nightfall and nightly makes his camps and cookfires in places where the Ruidoso bends and eddies. Bankside groves of gamble oak to hide them. A sprinkling of stars emerge at dusk. Betelgeuse arrives as a glowing speck of blood-spatter to the west. Clear nights. His smokey fires cure the cuts of butchered elk for keeping. Game roasts on a greenstick spit. River cress. Wild honey. Chicory tea. Balmy days. Shaded pools. The brown trout hold steady in the current, their noses point upriver. A hummingbird buzzes at a fireweed flower. A blue heron stands on stilted legs in the shallows, its long beak pointed fishward and ready to strike. The curve of its long neck extends so imperceptibly that it seems not to move at all.

He rode out from the mountains with a westerly wind at his back. He went on, still following the Rio Ruidoso as it joined the Rio Hondo, stopping at the trading post in Villa Nueva where he sold off his parcel of rabbit hides and read his list to the proprietor:

soap
pepper
salt
oats
knife
spoon
sugar
tinderbox
matches
gloves
coat
cartridges

and went on to the settlement of Picacho where an itinerant tintypist took his picture, and then turned northeast, heading for the Rio Pecos with the dry and windswept districts of New Mexico still ahead of him.

The Apache consider it a sign of good fortune for anyone who sees the feather of a blue heron (Ardea herodias) fall from the sky and land in his vicinity.
—Birds of America and the Territories, Chapter 22: Herons, Bitterns

Many birds die during migration, brought down by storms or starvation, and many more die of exhaustion at the end of their journey. The tiny calliope hummingbird (Selasphoras calliope) lessens these dangers by riding on the backs of geese during its 2000-mile flight from the Western Territories to Central America.
Chapter 45: Hummingbirds

Chapter 99
The Tintypist Starts His Circuit
Lincoln County
May 2, 1881 – The Moon of Come Back Birds

Ezra Dodson had wrapped and bound the bodies of his wife and daughter during a snowstorm in February, the month the Apache call the Moon of Sleeping Bears, and had sunk them beneath the ice of the Rio Hondo. He watched the hole he had hacked close over as clear as any lens, and with the coming of spring, he awaited the arrival of the itinerant tintypist while the river ran cold enough to keep them.

The itinerant tintypist could not recall when he had acquired the mule or how old it was, but it seemed to him it had lived longer than any horse he had ever owned and was wiser than most of them as well. In its younger years it had been surefooted, stoic and reliable, pulling an old Conestoga over both mountain roads and desert hardpan, cautious and discerning about where it was best to cross a creek or set up camp or what new trail to take when the usual route was washed out or slid over with rock rubble. When in doubt I let my mule decide, the tintypist liked to say. But now the mule had gone gray in the muzzle and cloudy in its vision. And although it was willing to keep on, it had become unsteady on even a coating of snow, and the tintypist had taken to spending his winters in Lincoln. Come the thaw he loaded the wagon with staples for the trail and the equipment of tintyping. Stacks of engraving plates, foldable tripod, carboys of chemicals, and the mahogany box-camera carefully crated. With the mule newly shod, he set out on his circuit of settlements where year after year there were ranchers and townsfolk and homesteaders expecting his visit. *Yep, he comes through here every spring. Pretty regular too, I'd say, unless he breaks an axle oversteering that old wagon like he did a few years back or that old mule of his goes laid up lame.*

It was in early May, the month the Apache call the Moon of Come Back Birds, that the tintypist started his yearly trek, heading west out of Lincoln.

Stopping for a spell at Fort Stanton and pulling his wagon into the space designated for sutlers and their tables and tents where they kept up a steady trade selling spirits and tobacco and wool socks and such to the cavalry soldiers, and there he set up his camera-works and took their pictures in military poses for sending home. Pistols drawn. Fierce looks. Cavalry kepis. Salutes and sabers. Dinnertime at the enlisted men's mess. A corporal takes up his pen. *Dearest Mother, got my picture took today so you can see that I am eating alright and taking to army life well enough.*

On then through Nogal. A bride and groom married the prior autumn now hauling the gown and suit out from the cedar chest and dressing again as if for a second wedding. The bride pinches her cheeks but the rosiness quickly fades. *Take her hand there, sir. Get in a little closer to that man of yours, ma'am. Alright, don't move. Breathing is permissible.*

On to Capitan. New babies. Twins. Wriggling in the mother's arms. *Try keeping those little fellers still or they'll be a blur.*

Turning south then to Oscura. An old hunter sits on the steps of his falling-down house and holds something furred in his lap. *This here? He's my old Bobby Blue. Tick hound. Right natural don't you think? Stuffed him myself, corn shucks and mattress cotton. I could do that old mule of yours when you're through with him, standing up if that's the way you want him.*

On to Three Rivers and the one-room school. Five children in the yard, the schoolmarm severe. *Excuse me Ma'am but might we leave the switch out of the picture?*

Pocito, Perrito, Berryville, Laughton. A family of ten gathered under the trees. Kitchen chairs. The daughters dressed from the same bolt of forget-me-not flowered calico. *Back row there Davey, you're the tallest. Girls be still now, enough of them fidgets. We want those pretty faces coming out perfect in the picture.*

On then, to Tularosa. Patrons at the trading post stepping out into the sunlight. Proprietor on the porch still merchandising up to the last minute. *How about a brandy-new pulling bridle for that mule? I may be fresh out next time you're passing through.*

From there, east through Coyote Hills, stopping a while in Mescalero. Cattle ranch. Hired hands, mostly Mexicans, lining up. Inside the ranch house a grandfather sits on the horsehair sofa. His old wife beside him, her hand on his shoulder. *Come on now, Baxter. Keep them eyes open.*

Then north again into Ruidoso. The farrier's shop. The farrier out front in his leather apron, arms folded. *Hold on there, let me fetch my hammer.* Then on to the livery. A new foal, skittish. The mare watchful, nickering. *Somebody get a grip of that sweet little critter.* A hand in the picture holding the halter. Its legs a cloud of motion.

On to Alto. A cemetery behind the house. Fenced in white picket. Old headstones, some askew. A grave newly dug and waiting. *Our dear Auntie Jean, I do believe she held on these last weeks for when you was coming.* The darkened parlor. Here and there candles. The odor of candlewax. Lifting the lid. The old aunt displayed in her clothes long unused, long packed away. Now a waft of camphor. Woolen fichu tied at her chest and kept with a cameo brooch. Blue gingham dress. The parlor too dark for a proper tintype. The curtains are thrown open. The candles are brought closer. A grandfather clock stands near the door. A chalk dog on the mantle. Chipped at the foot. Eyes of glass amber. A bird cage of brass-wire with a brass birdy finial and a domed roof sloping into the curlicued eaves. There the dead canary, the empty seedcup. *A pair it was. One dead when she forgot to feed it. The other we turned loose, barely living.* The old aunt is positioned. Partially propped. *Horace, fetch your Auntie another pillow please, that would help some.* The tintypist lifts his shroud-cloth and ducks his head under. Adjusts the focus. Slides in the plate. Takes a final look. A sister of the corpse pipes up *Don't move, Auntie Jean.* The tintypist opens the shutter. A long stillness seeps through the room. An unseen cricket calls from a corner. Tick and tock. The minute hand moves a half-click back, then lurches forward and clicks into place. Back a half-click, lurch, click. Back a half-click, lurch, click. Tick and tock. *All right then folks.* The curtains are drawn again. The lid lowered. *Ease it down, Horace, that's right, watch your fingers.* The candles are snuffed.

Ditchville, Pararito, Cold Canyon, La Quinta. A new barn. New outhouse. Little Jimmy peeking out. *Boy you get out from there and come sit for your picture now, well ain't he just the dickens.*

Now through the settlement at Low Water Hollow. *Come on Martha, he's here. He's got that same old mule, too. Bring the boy on out.* The mother hurries, fastens her hair with a comb. She carries out the son, a spindly and wasted bit of a boy. *This here's our Martin. We were hoping you'd be coming through soon.* The mother positions the boy on her knee, supports his wobbly head against her chest. *Say hello Martin. This man's taking our picture.*

Late May now, and on to the towns along the Rio Hondo: Tinne, Los Gatos, Poco, and Picacho. Picacho of course. This trip he'd be stopping at Picacho for certain, where some folks had put up their cabin right there on the river. As the tintypist remembered it. Dodson, that was the name. Ezra Dodson. Just him and his missus, Alma Dodson. A year ago, last June it was, when Ezra asked the tintypist to please come back next spring or so. The baby is due next winter, Ezra had said. Next February, said Alma, that's by my reckoning. A girl, she had said. A daughter, you'll see. Come next May, she will be four months old, she told the tintypist. The perfect age for a picture.

Canaries (Crithagra flaviventril) seen in the wild are those turned loose or escaped from their cages. These will not survive the winter or even a cold spell and are doomed to die well before the first frost.

—Birds of America and the Territories, Chapter 79: Escaped Species

Chapter 100
The Tintype of Billy the Kid
Along the Rio Hondo
May 16, 1881 – The Moon of Comeback Birds

They had died during a February snowfall, the month the Apache call the Moon of Sleeping Bears, when animals lie still and dreaming in their dens and would not stir to take them.

It was fortunate, the husband would tell the tintypist, that they lived near the river and that they had known he would be returning in the coming spring.

And fortunate, the husband would tell Billy, that they had died—his wife and his daughter both—when the Rio Hondo was frozen in its shallows but flowing midstream at its coldest.

The husband had done what he could to clean away the blood before he wrapped them in gunnysacking and brought them to the river. There had been so much of it. More, it seemed, than such a small and fragile woman could contain. So much that he had stuffed a rag into the wound he had made in her belly to sop up the pool of it that remained, forgetting that the river would wash her, wash all of it away. She had screamed his name so many days. Ezra. Ezra. And then just screaming. Bled for so many days. When the screaming stopped she lay still but still bleeding. A spreading stain on the ticking under her and the sheet he had put between her legs. He bent to her chest. Heart sounds. He heard them. Or was it the wind thudding the shutters. Or was it the dull hammering in his head. Or the dog thumping his tail against the bedstead as it sat smelling the blood. And then, so quickly, she became the color of weathered bone. The color of buttermilk. The color of the clouds. The color of the sheet when it was still clean before all that coming of the blood when it was still early in her screaming. He lifted the sheet. He dared to look. The hole, the cleft. There the protrusion of a tiny foot. Pink, wrinkled. Covered in slime. The smell of dung. The knife was ready. Hunting, skinning, honed with care, back and forth, with attention to the point. He placed it on the square of flannel she had saved. A pattern of tendrils and tiny roses. Alma dear, he said. My Alma, he said as he pushed in the point and he felt the skin and muscle give way as if the blade had entered an empty space and he turned the knife and made a slit hip to hip in the place he thought a slit should be made. There the child. Bloody but uncut. He took it by the shoulders. The arms limp. The head lolling, flopping back. As she said it would. Months before she had sewn a doll from scraps of cloth. Stuffed with gramma grass. You'll hold her like so, she had said. Her? he said. I can tell, she said. A daughter, he said. What will we name her? Mary Delia, he suggested, after my mother. Not now, she said. Bad luck to be naming or be talking of names. And she took up the doll and held it out to him. Your hand goes here, she said, on the back of her head until she can hold it up herself. Yes, he remembered how it should be done, how he had to do it. He reached into the wound he had made. He slid his hand behind its head. *Until she can hold it up herself.* The eyes were closed. The mouth full of dung. The body was stuck with patches of white. He began to lift it, to pull it out of her. But it would not give. It would not give. He adjusted his grasp. It would not give. The foot caught under the ramus of bone. He ran his fingers along the limb. Its knee. Its ankle. A tug, a thrust. A release. A kind of a pop. A cork from a bottle. The cluck of the tongue that tells a horse to go.

He cleaned out its mouth with a sweep of his fingers. He wiped the patches of white from its face with his shirt, careful in the creases along the nose, the hollows of the eyes. There now, he told it. He pushed the lids open with his thumbs. The pupils wide. Boreholes of blackness. He looked to his wife. Her mouth had gone slack. Her lips dry and fissured. Her eyes were open. There the same void, the same vacancy. The same black apertures filling the spaces. He wrapped the small body in the square of flannel. The pattern of tendrils and tiny roses. A fold, a tuck. See Alma? he said and held it to her. It's our Mary Delia, he said. He set it beside her. He turned her head to face it. And see, she has your eyes. My ears, I'd say. But Alma, your eyes for certain.

The snow was still falling when they went into the river. Ezra Dodson had wrapped them together with lengths of sacking in that singular shape of a body that has been bound for the shelf of a crypt or for burial in the earth and had circled this bundle with a crisscross of rope, leaving a good length of it loose at the foot and by this he slid it along behind him through a stand of evergreens and over a little rise on his way to the river. Winding through the grove of old trees, bark clotted with pitch. Piney scent of sap. Pushing past the low-slung branches. Sprays of snow dusting this shrouded bale of the dead. The dog following behind on the snow-tamped path the parcel made. Tiny cones and needles strewn in its wake.

At the river he set it on the bank. When he had hacked a hole in a frozen eddy he lowered in the gunnied bundle and tethered it to the trunk of a large cottonwood growing streamside. The flow in the eddy was slower than the rest of the river, and new ice soon closed the hole over and he was glad of that at dusk when he heard the coyotes afoot and singing their incantations of the hunt.

From time to time he went to the river to clear away new snow that had fallen on the ice so that he might gaze down and watch that long dark shape waver with the current as if it were some giant bottom-feeder that had swum upstream to spawn, and sometimes he went just to tug on the rope and feel the weight of them.

And there they stayed through the month the Apache call the Moon of Dying Snow, and on through the thaw and ice going thin in the Moon of Waking Bears, and on through the new buds on the cottonwood when the river still ran cold with mountain snowmelt. And it was in May, the month the Apache call the Moon of Come Back Birds, when a goldfinch nested in the cottonwood and Ezra Dodson finished sanding the pinewood box and the tintypist with his mule and wagon rode in. Been expecting you right about now, said Ezra Dodson.

The tintypist climbed down from the wagon and patted his mule. This old boy, I thought he'd have some trouble with the trail up Cold Canyon or that ford at Ditchtown, but we took it easy, didn't we old boy? Sure we did, he said, and he turned the mule loose from its traces. If I rightly recollect, he said, your wife was predicting a daughter.

Yes, said Ezra Dodson. A daughter. It was a daughter.

Well now, said the tintypist. Are they about ready for a picture?

Yes, said Ezra Dodson. I'll go fetch them.

When predators approach the nest of the American goldfinch (Spinus tristis), the adult bird calls to its nestlings as a warning to crouch lower in the nest and to stop their peeping, thereby becoming less noticeable.

—Birds of America and the Territories, Chapter 76: Grosbeaks, Finches

Near as pretty as she ever was, the tintypist said when Ezra Dodson hauled them from the river, untied the ropes, and unwrapped them, and he gazed upon what was Eza Dodson's wife. There was, of course, the damage that death will do. The sharper margins of the nose, the general blanching of the skin. But the gunnysacking had saved her from all but the slightest bit of sloughing at the jaw line and the chin, and the waxy deposit that forms on the faces of the submerged dead had given hers a translucent look. The wound was bloodless, fringed in white shreds of flesh. The gown washed clean. Her eyes settled into their craters. Her hair a tangle of moist tendrils. Yes, said Ezra Dodson, and he smoothed away the tangle. I do believe she is, he said.

The child, however, had shrunk somewhat. Puckered at the mouth. Pursed. The tiny fingers shriveled and fisted. The brow creased, the countenance glowering. As if she was aggrieved, said Ezra Dodson.

No, said the tintypist, as he set his camera on the tripod. That's just when she was leaving. By now she's become an angel for certain.

A rocking chair was placed beside the cabin steps. The mother and child were lifted in. The mother's arm arranged with a bend at the elbow, her head inclined toward the swaddled child in the crook. And the child? Positioned as in sleep. Should we open their eyes? asked Ezra Dodson.

No, said the tintypist who in his years of travelling for his trade had done this all before. Better to not, he said.

The dog had been crouched under the cabin steps and now crawled out along its belly and lay at their feet. Let me back us up a bit, said the tintypist as he lifted the tripod. That way we get your dog in the picture.

The tintypist dipped his head under the camera cloth once more and adjusted the focus for the change in distance. A small shadow briefly passes over the posed tableau. As a cloud on the wind might do. Or a buzzard soaring above the evergreens. And then another. Their slow convolutions. Their easy circles. Damn, said Ezra Dodson, peering up.

The tintypist threw off the cloth and looked. They won't be bothering her none, he said. Nor the little one. We're just about ready, he said. Just about.

Ezra took his place behind her, his hands on her shoulders. At the last moment he had brought forth her summer bonnet and this was set on her head to hide her hollowed eyes in the shadow of its brim.

The tintypist knew just the right tilt.

I hope it is to your liking, the tintypist said when he handed Ezra Dodson the finished plate.

Ezra Dodson took it in his hands and looked a while and wept.

The wife and daughter looked natural enough. With just a dappling of sunlight coming through the trees, but the image clear and sharp. As was the dog. Though its tail was just a blur.

Ezra Dodson was digging the grave and the tintypist was harnessing his mule when a black Appaloosa and its rider came through the grove of evergreens and started down the rise to the cabin. The mule gave a soft bray and tossed its head. The tintypist looked where the mule was looking. Is it your wife's kin you're expecting? asked the tintypist.

No kin, said Ezra Dodson.

Well here comes someone yonder, said the tintypist. Hello young fella.

Ezra Dodson stopped his digging and climbed from the hole. He leaned his shovel beside the pinewood box.

Billy climbed down from the Appaloosa. He touched his hat. He nodded toward the hole and turned to Ezra Dodson. Need a hand with that mister?

There was not much more to be done. A few more shovelfuls to be flung out. Hammering the lid. The box roped and lowered in. Billy in the hole. Easy now. Hold on, he said. Take that up again, sir. Right there's good. Ain't quite level. Send me down that shovel. Oh see, there it is. It's a damn root that's catching, that's what. Likely that big old tree. There's no telling when it comes to roots. Fetch down an axe. All right then. Let's see how it sits. Send it on down again. Easy now. Yep, that's right level. That's fine. Is that to your liking, Mr. Dodson?

Billy climbed out. The tintypist took up the shovel. The soil was pitched in. Tamped. Hats held. Words spoken.

I'm beholden, said Ezra Dodson.

It's all right, said the tintypist.

Weren't nothing, said Billy.

What might be your name son, asked Ezra Dodson.

William Henry.

The tintypist shook his head. Aw now, he said. His name is Billy. Billy Bonney.

Ezra Dodson scratched his head. You two been prior acquainted?

This here's Billy the Kid, says the tintypist. You ain't heard of him?

We never got much news, says Ezra Dodson.

Well now Billy, said the tintypist. I seen you in Lincoln, he tells Billy, the day you rode in with the sheriff. You give him the slip, I see.

So it appears, said Billy.

That face they drawed on them wanted posters don't come close, says the tintypist.

Not all of it's true, said Billy.

All of what? said Ezra Dodson.

All of what them wanted posters say he's wanted for, said the tintypist.

I'd better be getting on, said Billy, heading for his horse.

Listen here Mister Billy the Kid Bonney, said the tintypist. I don't take a whit of it as true, you being on the run but still taking the time for a man what's lost his family.

I'm getting pretty worn down on my running, said Billy.

Well then, said the tintypist. It's likely you'd hold still long enough for a picture.

The afternoon sun had lent a coppery slant to the cabin steps where Billy sat. He watched the tintypist setting up his box-camera. Sliding open the accordion bellows. Patting the bright mahogany wood and asking the camera, Ready for another one?

What say? asked Billy.

Didn't say, said the tintypist. Soon though.

Billy sat. The tintypist leveled the tripod, adjusted the legs. He opened a little latched slot on the top of the box. Dropped in the plate. Reset the latch. Almost there, he said.

How does this work? said Billy.

An underexposed negative image on a colloidal emulsion mounted to a black metal plate appears positive, he said.

Well sure, said Billy.

The tintypist covered his head with the black camera cloth and set his eye to the lens. He slid the bellows forward and back adjusting the focus. An upside-down and antipodal Billy came into view. There you are, the tintypist told it. He peeked out from the cloth, leaned sideways. Frowning. Hmm, he said. Let's get you standing. Give you some height.

Billy stood. He took off his hat.

Hat back on, said the tintypist. He flung the cloth from his head and stepped slightly away from the camera, rubbing his jaw. He looked at Billy. It's crook to the left, he said.

My own Da give me this here hat, said Billy. This is just how I always been wearing it.

The tintypist squinted. You've got yourself standing near stiff as a dead man. Let's see what you look like toting that Winchester.

Billy took up his rifle and set it beside him stock down to the boards.

Better, said the tintypist. And smiling is permissible.

My teeth ain't right, said Billy. Rabbity, what my Mam always said.

You got reason to be smiling, Mister Billy the Kid Bonney. They ain't strung you up just yet.

The tintypist took a last look at Billy. The right-side-up Billy. We're all set then, he said. Now just pick out something to look at.

Billy looked. Past the brim of his hat. Beyond the shrouded tintypist and his camera. There the clouds changing shape as they streamed along. The afternoon sun gliding the edges. The light through the needles of the spruce grove. Small cones suspended. Ezra Dodson setting stones along the border or the grave mound, their shadows long in the raking light. The dark soil drying. The Appaloosa just beyond, head down, pulling grass with its teeth as it went along. The scattering of the spots on its rump forming a pattern, as if they could be connected to make a picture or the parts of a picture with some parts missing. The mule's ears turning toward the trees. A kinglet peeping in the spruce, pecking along a branch.

You need to stay still, the tintypist told Billy. But breathing is permissible.

He lifted the camera cloth and bowed his head under. Staring now, he said.

He opened the shutter and exposed the plate.

The diminutive (3-inch-long) golden-crowned kinglet (Regulus satrapa) uses spiderwebs to suspend its nest from twigs along a branch of spruce.

—Birds of America and the Territories, Chapter 64: Gnatcatchers, Kinglets

The sun was nearly set and the afternoon had grown colder when the tintypist held aside the canvas curtain he had hung to the back of his wagon and climbed down. He had wrapped the tintype in a scrap of muslin. Here you go son, he told Billy. Take a looksee.

Billy carefully folded back the cloth.

Go on. You can't hurt it none, said the tintypist. It's ready for looking at.

Billy turned his back to the low-lying sun and held the tintype in front of him. Well now, he said. That's my Winchester alright, he said. So that must be me.

Spittin' image, said the tintypist.

I can't recall when last I seen myself, said Billy.

Give it here, said Ezra Dodson. He took the tintype, cloth and all. Yep, he said nodding his head and passing it back to Billy. Yep, he told Billy. He got you good.

No sir, Billy told Mr. Dodson. He got me better than I am.

Well I do thank you, said the tintypist. But it ain't my doing. This here camera, it don't lie. That's what I tell folks. Go get yourself gussied up or don't gussy, or whatever which way you want it. It don't matter none. This here camera, he said patting the rich mahogany wood. It sees. More than you be seeing. This here camera.

Billy put his hand to his vest pocket.

The tintypist stepped back and put up his hands. I ain't taking nothing for it, Mister Billy the Kid Bonney. Might be worth something to you someday. Mayhaps it brings you luck.

You keep it for me, said Billy. I'm beholden to you if you did.

Me keep it? Oh no, son. I never did it that way. That ain't how it's done, he said.

Billy took a last look at himself and folded the cloth back over. The way things are, said Billy, this is the best way to be doing it.

He took up the reins of the Appaloosa. He stirruped his foot and threw his leg over. He turned the horse out through the evergreen grove, heading for Fort Sumner and an old acquaintance there, by way of the plains west of the Pecos.

The sun sets. The kinglet forages on until dark.

The night are cool these parts in May, the Moon of Come Back Birds.

Ezra Dodson lights a fire in the hearth.

The dog sits at the cabin door and whines to be let out.

The Rio Hondo had been muddied where Ezra Dodson had waded in to haul his parcel onto the bank, and there the river fronds are flattened and tangled. But the current made its repairs. By nightfall the pebbles on the riverbed had rolled back into their places and bottom silt had settled. And the river ran clear again, as if no disturbance had occurred. As if it had never been sullied.

The golden-crowned kinglet (Regulus satrapa) is forever on the move as it forages along the limbs of spruce trees. However, it remains a mystery how this tiny songbird survives, as it appears to constantly peck at seemingly invisible prey.

—Birds of America and the Territories, Chapter 64: Gnatcatchers, Kinglets

Chapter 101
The Apache Ponies Do Not Answer
The Plains West of the Pecos
Late May, 1881 – The Moon of Come Back Birds

The terrain turned flat and treeless, beset with outcroppings of jagged rock angled aslant to the earth and great plates fractured along fault lines where they had been folded over on themselves again and again into scarps and scars of granite and tuft. The pleats of rock stood sharp and clean in shades of red and rust, but free of signs of weathering and the passage of time as if newly thrust by some unseen force deep below the surface and by this he thought they must be moving even now, slipping and buckling upward, the ridges rising even as he looked, even as they seemed not to move at all but must be in motion by some trick of time too slow to see, some clock apart from the one that ticks and tocks the region of the world where blue herons stalk along the river bank. The clock that unwinds the heron's neck before the strike.

He met no other riders except a troupe of Apaches. Ten or so men, a hunting party homeward on their wild range ponies. Palominos, duns, pintos coming on at an easy lope, fitted with old cavalry saddles covered in hide, the pommel-horns hung with quail strung in bunches. The riders were dressed in deerskin shirts and deerskin breeches, some with their dark hair loose along their shoulders and some with it evenly cropped at the neck, and all with wide deerskin bands wrapped across their foreheads and tied from behind. They came toward him, upright and astride in postures natural and rocking with the gait of their animals. Billy halted his Appaloosa. He took off his hat. They came on, steady and unswerving. Billy held up his hand, but they did not stop and when they rode so closely by on either side of him he saw that their faces were rigid and cast in the very colors of the rocks, and that they looked past him and ahead to the far horizon. The Appaloosa nickered as horses greeting horses will do, but the Apache ponies did not answer and went on.

He turned to look at their leaving, at the swinging bundles of quail hanging head down and wingspread, the gutted pronghorns trussed and slung across the rumps of their horses, the hoof-strike dust rising around them.

Billy put on his hat. He looked at the hand he had raised. Yes, it was his hand. He put his hand on the neck of the Appaloosa. Yes, she was there. Her hide stiff and smooth. He tugged at her mane. She turned to look at him, her eye clear and gleaming. You see me, he said.

When a predator is in the vicinity, the bobwhite quail (Coinus viginianus) will crouch amid ground vegetation to avoid detection. When closely stalked, it will startle the predator by bursting into flight.
—Birds of America and the Territories, Chapter 21: Quails, Partridges, Pheasants

Chapter 102
Renegades

The Lincoln County Ledger

"Listen Up"

Vol. 81, No. 5 — May 30, 1881 — Price 12 cents

SKIRMISH WEST OF THE PECOS

Congratulations to Company B of the Sixth Cavalry upon the apprehension of a band of hostile Apache renegades recently escaped from the confines of their reservation and illegally taking game in their former hunting grounds in that arid stretch of terrain between Lincoln and the Pecos. Lieutenant Luther Smithson and his company confronted the Apaches, who were led by the notorious instigator known as *I Saw Six Birds*. All of the Apache hostiles were summarily dispatched as they attempted to flee, except for an elderly man named *Hides His Foot*, who surrendered but died in transit back to the reservation near Lincoln. The Apache ponies were taken into custody, and will be sold at slaughter.

RUSTLER AND MURDERER STILL SOUGHT

The hunt continues for William Bonney Antrim, known throughout The Territory as Billy the Kid. An individual fitting his description was spotted in several settlements along the Rio Hondo and its environs. In addition to his extensive career as horse thief and cattle rustler, Bonney has murdered nineteen men, one for every year of his life. His victims include both innocent civilians and peace-keeping lawmen, among them two deputies killed during his escape from the Lincoln County Courthouse. Sheriff Patrick F. Garrett requests information as to the Kid's whereabouts and cautions the public against confronting this killer themselves.

QUOTE OF THE DAY

☞ *Do you give the horse his might? With fierceness and rage he swallows the ground; he cannot stand still at the sound of a trumpet.*
—Job 39:19

Chapter 103
Company
by Billy Bonney
June 15, 1881—Still West of the Pecos

He came out of the sage running the way them roadrunners do, and next thing I know he's running along beside us—me and the Appaloosa going at an easy trot since the midday heat's coming on. He could outrace us easy if he wanted to but he didn't. At first I thought he was chasing down something to eat, the way I seen them do. Catching lizards and snakes and such and just about any little thing that hops or crawls. But he wasn't hunting. He was just running. And he kept on, staying right with us. He didn't mind us none. Not looking right or left, just watching ahead. Striding out the way they do. Legs going so fast you don't know what they're doing. Neck stretched out ahead and that long tail streaming. He stayed with us for a few miles before he took off, not flying mind you. Just still running. Faster than we wanted to go. I got to wondering: What did he want with me? And then I figured that he just wanted some company, is all. I was happy seeing him for as long as I did. I took it as a bit of luck.

Many tribes of the Territories believe that the roadrunner has magical powers, and that its song—a long and descending "Cooooo"—will cause the listener to feel tired and look for a place to lie down and sleep.

—Birds of America, Chapter 40: Cuckoos, Roadrunners, Anis

Chapter 104
One More River
Eastern New Mexico
Mid-June, 1881 – The Moon of Coyotes Singing

He reached the banks of the Rio Pecos at a bend where it had long left behind its wilderness headwaters on the slopes of the Sangre de Cristos, had traveled through both granite canyons and high mountain meadows. Here the river ran through an arid and treeless country scattered with isolated mesas and rocky peaks rising from a vast and level landscape, barren but for blue sage and cholla cactus in bloom. And although he could have crossed it at any gravelly bar jutting into the current, or any narrow and shallow strand of it, he turned his horse north and rode riverside against its southward flow through sparse groves of cottonwood and salt cedar, and broad green sweeps of new cheat grass and woad, and though the horse found the going easy, it went on, ever as watchful, as vigilant, as the rider upon it.

Toward evening, he made a fire. Dry strands of Spanish bayonet for tinder and sage twigs for kindling, and when a small flame rose he cracked lengths of long-dead cholla over his knee and set them in. A soft wind blew in from the river and fed the fire. Small brown trout began to rise to a stonefly hatch in the shallows, and these he took with his hands and set them belly-slit and headless to cook on a slab of river stone. Elf owls in the salt cedar were calling yip yip yip much the way a coyote pup would do, and as the fire grew brighter they flittered outside the circle of heat and sparks, catching the moths that spiraled into the light.

He sat and watched the embered chunks of cholla break and fall in on each other. He crossed leg over leg and took ahold of his boot-heel. There the nail loose in its hammer hole. He took it by a fingernail and pulled it out and swiveled his boot-heel and removed the tightly folded square of paper there. He regarded the list by the firelight. First bird. Last bird. He found his pencil nub in his pocket and leaned to a rock and wrote some more. He refolded the paper and pushed it back tight into its boot-heel hollow and swiveled it back into place. He stood and stamped his foot to send in the nail. He steeped a handful of desert amaranth for tea.

At the approach of a predator, the elf owl (Micrathene whitneyi) will draw a wing across the front of its body, covering its light-colored chest, pale feathered abdomen, and most of its face, but leaving its eyes uncovered. This maneuver provides camouflage but allows the bird to peer out over the top of its wing, the way a bandit with a kerchief would do.

—Birds of America and the Territories, Chapter 42: True Owls

He woke during the night to rumblings that might have been drums or hoofs or thunder. He sat listening a good long while, and when it did not come again, he slept. He woke again in the cold that comes before every dawn and he stirred the dead fire for a spark. A flame sprang up. Once again he took the nail from his boot-heel and the folded paper from the hollow and he wrote until the sound came again. He walked to the river bank and it was louder still, but nothing more than the sound of water riding the stones. He saddled the Appaloosa. And he went on. North.

If not for the river, he would have drifted, succumbing to the mystery of time and distance in these stretches of desolation. The faraway peak rising from the desert floor some distance from the river's east bank imperceptibly crossed over and rode along with him on the west. The mesa that he judged to be a day's ride away at dawn seemed only to retreat as he rode on and was no closer at dusk. At times when he wondered if he was moving at all, he turned in the saddle to see the tracks his horse had left behind him, and these he took as proof that he was being carried onward, no matter what the trickery of the terrain might tell him, no matter that the wind would take the dust and cover every trace.

When an elf owl is captured and held in the mouth of a coyote or bobcat, it does not struggle to escape. Instead, it becomes limp, quiet, and seemingly lifeless. This adaptation prompts the predator to loosen its hold, allowing the owl to fly away.

Chapter 42: True Owls

Chapter 105
List
by Me, Billy
June 30, 1881

Finn in Wichita
Elroy Ellison
Maybe the Tortuga waiter, maybe not
The blacksmith Windy Cahill
Sheriff W. B. Brady
Deputy George Hindman
Buckshot Roberts
Deputy Doyle Stockton
Deputy James Lee Bell
Deputy Ollie Ollinger

Chapter 106
I Remember Some of It
by Billy Bonney
July 2, 1881

I've been riding north, but what does that matter. Any direction could be away from whatever I'm running from. Or maybe closer to. This Appaloosa mare, she's a good horse, she is. Smart. Like the Choctaw I had before, but Appaloosa smart. She knows same as me that something's closing in behind me. Or coming up ahead. One or the other. Or both. It might could be the law, and likely is, since it was the law what got most of The Boys, except for the one of them I got myself. Same as some other killings I done by just me, Billy. So sure, it's the law I'm watching out for. But it's more than that. It's what's been coming my way every sunup, every sundown. It's over the next hill or on the other side of every mountain pass. And I'm always wondering what's next or who's there and when if it turns out to be nothing, well that's almost worse. I ride on but what I wish is to be done out-running trouble. My Mam, poor Mam. She knew I was trouble. She knew about me and what I was, seeing my stuck-out shoulder wings and knowing I was not some natural child—not born to her, oh no—but likely kin to Wee Folk. And some parts of me believing it. She saw what I was right off.

She tried her damnedest to set me loose or just get free of me. Sometimes I remember some of it. Sometimes when I'm camped along this river and hid in a grove of trees and the afternoon sun is slanting in and there's a little wind, the light coming through the leaves goes bright and dark and bright and dark, and that's when it seems to me I've been somewhere just the same as this but a long time ago. Me up some tree and seeing those sparks of sunlight. And hearing my Mam calling for the Wee Folk to snatch me away but I don't go, I stay in the lights and the leaves until they start fetching me down, and I am going down and going down to my Da. Down to my Da. He's gone now, my Da is. And my Mam too. She died still waiting for my shoulder-blade bones to sprout feathers and for me to take off. I can feel those shoulder bones that never did grow. I feel them aching to come out when I'm lying on my thin bedroll spread along this hard ground and the heat of the day is leaving this earth and the cold is seeping in. It's just about the time that the sky goes dark enough for stars and stars and stars. One of them's what they call the pole star. It's pointing north, which is where I'm going. I've always been going against something. This this time it's against the way the river's running.

According to Apache myth, the first magpie in the world flew up to the lodestar to steal it from the sky, sending its enemies off course. Forever after, the black-billed magpie (Pica hudsonia) has been fond of collecting shiny trinkets.

—Birds of America and the Territories, Chapter 54: Crows, Jays, Magpies, Ravens

Author's Note: First Light

First light. A clear desert morning in summer. The month the Apache call the Moon of Long Day Heat. Early birdsong always wakes him. Cactus wren. Dove. The far-flung mesas and the slides of red scree along their walls still stand in darkness as the sun gilds the rims of caprock. Within the stratified sandstone and shale reside the fossil bodies of creatures that once lived in this district of ancient oceans, many more of them than ever swam this river. This Rio Pecos. Flowing south, bearing red silt and the slightest tang of the salt it sweeps from a seabed emptied in millennia long past. Billy the Kid, awake now, considering a thread of smoke-rise from the blackened cholla of last night's fire. Considering its rekindling. Considering his contingencies. The Appaloosa stops her grazing. She lifts her head and looks down river. Ears pricked forward. A snort. Billy stands. He no longer asks his horse: What is it? The long view of the river lies before him, flowing south, banded by thick stands of salt cedar and scattered cottonwoods. Oh the muddy stream. He judges the flow and the gentle slope to the water, considering a crossing here. Considering his options and how they have diminished. As we might well consider how our own diminish day by day, hour by hour. He looks beyond the opposite bank and considers a landscape that seems to unfold into infinity might reveal the path that provides safe passage there. As we choose our direction by what we deem a pole star among the infinite spread of stars and reckon the time required to so travel. Or by the notion that the hands of a clock more rightly measure the irreversible succession of events than would a twig turning in the foam of an eddy. Here is Billy the Kid, still numbering his days. Why do we not begin our counting but instead dismiss the stalking shadow until it is upon us and we utter, Who is it? Billy's shadow appears long in the early light, much the same as the shadows of the men who had walked forth from the Lincoln courthouse carrying the rope tied with a tallowed noose. This time the shadow is his alone and growing shorter as the sun rises. The slant of it. He looks again and now the mesa walls are lit. From dim to bright too soon. The sun too hurried. But how lovely are the colors. Chalk white, bone white, cloud white, ash gray, smoke gray, horn yellow, umber and rust, coral, carnelian, cinnabar. How strange and new are the pale flowers of the mariposa lily and the bright yellow blooms of the blue agave, and the feathered mite that hovers there. How curious are the whorled spikes of Spanish bayonet.

The lucifer hummingbird (Calothorax lucifer) feeds on agave nectar.
—Birds of America and the Territories, Chapter 45: Hummingbirds

Chapter 107
Another List
by Me, Billy
Still South of Fort Sumner
Might Be July, 1881

Da
Mam
Joe
Miss Biddy
Jacinta
Singing Stick
Dr. Arthur Broadwater
John Tunstall
Tom O'Folliard
Charlie Bowdre
Dick Brewer
José Munõz
José Lopez
Encendio Contreras
Davito Contreras
Carlito Cruz de Juárez
Paulito Chávez
Matteo del Mundo
Diego Arroyo
Diego Ismael Leandro
Miguel Mercuerio

Segundo Arbolito
Cielo my Choctaw
Finn in Wichita
This here Appaloosa

Chapter 108
The Sheepherder's House
The Settlement at Fort Sumner
Before Sunset, July 13, 1881 – The Moon of Long Day Heat

Soon after Sheriff Garrett caught up with John James Glasser and Jake Perlmutter, he hanged them both for rustling. Petey Ray Maxwell took the hint and high-tailed it out of Lincoln County. He hired on here and there as a ranch hand for a while, but soon enough went back to small time cow-thieving, cutting longhorns from herds along the upper Pecos and selling them off around Fort Sumner. He had taken up residence in a sheepherder's house in the settlement not far from the old fort, and it was just as he was in the midst of fixing shingles to the ramshackle roof when a lone rider on a black Appaloosa came into view. Petey Ray stood for a moment and gazed out over the darkening plain shot with clumps of sage and the Rio Pecos running coppery and wrinkled in the light of the late day sun. And then he knelt again and went back to his hammering. The rider came on. He reined his horse to a walk as he rode through the half-hinged gate and into the dry and weedy yard and he sat in the saddle looking up at Petey Ray, who eventually spoke, head down and between hammer strikes. Thought you was good and dead by now, he said. Shot or hanged, but either way collected on.

I could say the same for you, said Billy.

Not likely, said Petey Ray.

Too damn bad about John James and Jake, said Billy.

They had it coming.

Didn't we all, said Billy.

Not them that gets away they don't, said Petey Ray. He had stopped hammering and looked down at Billy. He hitched the hammer to his belt and started down the ladder.

Anyone see you ride in? said Petey Ray.

Some Mexicans.

What did they say? said Petey Ray.

Quién es usted? said Billy. Who are you.

It was just Mexicans then, or some other folks?

Some other folks. They shook my hand and said hello. And some said they seen me on the wanted posters.

Hell. What did you say?

I said hello back.

Sure you did, said Petey Ray, you not being the sort for lying low. He sat himself on the edge of the trough and wiped his face with a palmful of water. He looked up at Billy, who sat slumped in the saddle. Haggard. His shoulders shrugged against the coming night's cold and the sun low in the sky.

You seen them buzzards? said Petey Ray,

I seen 'em, said Billy. I'm always seeing 'em.

That's a doe hung up in the shed what they're smelling, said Petey Ray. She's already skinned and part-way butchered. Go cut yourself a steak if you want it. The stove's still hot and a greased pan's sitting on the grate.

I've been missing a meal or two, said Billy.

You help yourself Billyboy, said Petey Ray. I'll ride out and fetch us some whisky.

That's alright, said Billy.

Take the room off the kitchen, if you're planning on staying put, said Petey Ray.

Staying put keeps getting harder, said Billy. The same for planning.

Just passing though then?

Might go either way, said Billy. Depends on who might want to know.

The sheriff for one. Pat Garrett. He been up this way, said Petey Ray. Just passing though hisself he said.

What did you tell him?

What did you think I tell him.

Hard to know, said Billy.

I tell him I ain't seen you. And I ain't.

Alright, said Billy.

But now I have, said Petey Ray.

The turkey vulture or buzzard (Cathartes aura) does not kill the creature it intends to eat, but patiently waits nearby for its death.

—Birds of America and the Territories, Chapter 14: New World Vultures, Condors

Author's Note: Noon
July 14, 1881

Midday in the month the Apache call the Moon of Long Day Heat. A windy day in the town of Fort Sumner, so named as it grew around the old military post. A small settlement. A single treeless thoroughfare. General store, feed store, mail office, sawmill, church. A blacksmith and a livery. McKee's Café has rooms to let. Wood-frame homes, most well-kept, and the usual assortment of outhouses and shacks scoured of paint by years of desert wind. Little Ralphie Smoot catches a cinder in his eye while he is running with his kite. A gust sends George Tuttle chasing his hat. Running, reaching. Damn it all, I almost had it, there it goes again.

Two sawhorses have been placed on the shady porch of Otis Feed and General Sundries. Otis Raffel, sole proprietor. On these the narrow box is set. The lid rests against the porch rail beside a hammer and nails in a carpenter's carry-all. The townspeople begin to arrive in a slow and somewhat solemn procession along the dusty street, except for a band of small boys who are always running everywhere. One with a slingshot in hand. One with a little rat terrier trotting beside him. One with a rabbit's foot protruding from his pocket. Now the farrier, the seamstress, the shopkeeper, the postmaster, the preacher. Others. Some from homesteads and trails beyond. Fathers and sons from outlying ranches. Drovers passing through. Hey Johnny Bill, did you hear? They got the Kid. Yep. It's him. Let's ride into town and take a look.

The coroner had decided that the coffin lid would not be nailed in place. Not yet. After all, they have come to see a dead desperado and that is what they shall see. The slope of his shoulders. The rent in his shirt. The holes in his woolen socks. The raggedy cloth wrapped around his left hand. His slightly protruding teeth and squirrely face, already changed. A pale and waxen hue. A sharper angle to the jaw. Billy but not Billy.

The coroner is wearing a suit. Starched collar. Bowler hat. Showing the death certificate around and pointing out his signature to anyone interested, presiding over the viewing, as these things are sometimes called. Too bad that tintype feller ain't coming round, he says.

Lamont Coombs has come in from his ranch on the Pecos, five miles south. He leans into the coffin for a better look. What happened to his hand? he asks the coroner. Where's his boots got to?

George Tuttle is dusting off his hat after chasing it down in the wind. Never mind the boots, he says. Where the hell's his gun I wonder. Likely worth something, don't you think?

Here comes little Cora May Bowstock, calico and pigtails, walking with her father, holding his hand. They stop at the porch steps. She presses her face into his trouser leg, then peeks out. Don't be afeared none, Cora May. Daddy's here. Daddy's here. In the blue above, a trio of buzzards begin their widening ellipsis, detecting the first notes of rising rot.

Here's old Logan Carter who can't recall when he last strapped on a firearm but hearing the name of the dead on display, he decided he'd better. He steps up onto the porch. Surprised now, peering into the box. So it's come to this has it? he says. The law's got nothin' better to do than be shooting down boys?

Now a couple, arm in arm. Alejandro Palacios who raises milkgoats on a small ranch north of Clovis, and his wife Marisol. Aye, Dios, says Alejandro Palacios. Pobre niño pequeño, says Marisol.

Otis Raffel, whose store it is, whose porch it is, has set out a table of odds and ends. A half bolt of blue flannel. A selection of mismatched cutlery. A box of assorted nails. Jars of jam, jars of honey. He is wearing his apron. He stands beside the table. He adjusts the sign: All Items Half-Price. That's right folks, he announces. Today only.

Colin McKee has come down from the café. Business has been brisk today. He sidles in among the lookers for a look. Jaysus, he says. A fair-haired lad he was.

Mr. Smoot is here with Ralphie, still red-eyed from the cinder. He lifts Ralphie up. See there? says Mr. Smoot. Bad man, he says. Ain't that so Reverend?

Reverend Fletcher, Sumner Church of Holy Light. Yes indeed, he says, and the inevitable end for them that lives by the sword.

Where's his sword Papa? says Ralphie.

Now here's Mrs. Hannah Jane Gilligan. She has grown gray and frail these past years and steadies herself at the rim of the box. Oh my goodness, she says. He's just about the age my boy Wesley Cole was when I saw him last. She sees that his eyes are open, just the tiniest of slits, and while she can't see that they are blue, she knows that they are, that they must be. Blue as her boy's ever was. And that his hair is the same light brown as Wesley Cole's, though that she might be misremembering. It has been so long now, so many years gone now since he was killed in a minor skirmish by a confederate minié ball, boxed and shipped back home with a note pinned to his jacket, positioned over the hole and the dark stain:

Wesley Cole Gilligan, Private.
1st New Mexico Volunteer Infantry.
Fallen in battle, Courageous in the Cause.
I shared in your grief while preparing his body.
"May he meet you again in that pleasant land."
With deepest sympathy,
Arthur L. Broadwater, Physician & Embalmer.

And now, here she is, standing again beside another box. She reaches in. Her hand wrinkled and spotted. She smooths back a wisp of the light-brown hair that has fallen on his brow. Reverend Fletcher steps in. Alright Hanna Jane, he says. That's enough.

Now lastly the sheriff. No one walks beside him. He tips his hat to the women as he passes. Good day Ma'am. Good day. A bit windy though. But they all hurry along without so much as a nod. The coroner comes down from the porch. He is carrying a sheaf of papers, striding up beside the sheriff and catching him by his sleeve. The sheriff stops and presses the paper to his knee. He signs where the coroner is pointing. Patrick F. Garrett. His horse at the porch rail untethered. A bay with a blaze and foreleg stockings. He mounts his horse and a few men walk over and some reach up to shake his hand. He looks back at the porch. He turns his horse and heads out of town. The small boys run after him. One tells the rat terrier, Go get him Rexie. One fires his slingshot. One throws stones.

We're through here, the coroner announces. But the townspeople do not yet disperse. They stay for a while, some in the yard, some on the porch. They speak quietly, one to another, before returning to their horses and wagons, before returning to their ranches and desert camps and wood-frame homes where they will feed the chickens and mend the downed fences and brand calves and haul feed and sweep the floor and chop the wood and stoke the cookstove and roll out the biscuit dough and peel the potatoes and sit down to dinner. They will talk about today. They will tell it to their children and grandchildren and perhaps more children after that, but soon there will be no one left to tell it. No one left to recall the events of today or the talk of the townspeople here in the settlement at Fort Sumner, Territory of New Mexico. Myths and stories will abound for a time. Recollections will fade. Deeds will be misremembered. As it is with every death. As it will be when we are lifted from our deathbeds and the final obligatory remarks are made and we are covered with earth or reduced to ash and flung into the wind or strewn upon the water.

Turkey vultures (Cathartes aura) are scorned for feeding on carrion. However, they would kindly devour anyone of us who has succumbed and been left unattended, thereby sparing the rest of us the sight of that final maggoty banquet and the unpleasant slough of our flesh.

—Birds of America and the Territories, Chapter 14: New World Vultures, Condors

Chapter 109
Auction
1960

Upcoming Auction - September 8, 1960
Art and Artifacts of the American West
Hosted by *Americana Auctions & Appraisals, Inc.*
Lot 3 - Item #1: *Glass Jar Containing Trigger Finger of Billy the Kid*

We are pleased to present a must-have item for the serious collector of curios of the Old West. This unique artifact was taken from the hand of William Henry McCarty, better known as Billy the Kid, apprehended and killed by Sheriff Patrick Garrett in 1881. It is believed that Garrett's deputy John W. Poe bribed the coroner to amputate the digit before the corpse was displayed for public viewing. Poe's career was advanced by his participation in Billy's killing, and the following year he was elected sheriff. Upon his retirement from law enforcement, Poe opened a bank in Roswell, New Mexico, where he kept the jar with Billy's finger prominently displayed. The amputation was made just above the knuckle, which helped to determine that the severed appendage is the left 2nd finger. The myth that Billy was left-handed was based upon a tintype taken by an itinerant photographer and showing Billy's revolver holstered on his left hip. However, what had not been taken into account was the fact that tintypes reverse the image, so his pistol was actually on his right hip, confirming that he was right-handed after all. That his corpse was mutilated based upon the left-handed misconception makes this artifact an even more valuable find. The digit has been preserved in a clear liquid and shows a bit of ragged flesh at the amputated end. The canning jar containing the specimen bears the molded embossing *Mason's Patented Jar* and a hand-written label that remains legible: *Triger (sic) of Wm. Billy Bonney Antrim, d. 1881.* The metal lid is intact and sealed with pitch.

This one-of-a-kind item is a true museum piece, and will be accompanied by a certificate of authenticity issued by The Authentication Committee of the Academy of the American West. Lots are available for in-person viewing by appointment only. All transactions are fully bonded and insured. Absentee bids welcome.

—*Auction News Monthly, September 1960*

Chapter 110
The Moon Had Set
July 13, 1881—Before Midnight

He had heard Petey Ray Maxwell ride off at a gallop and now he stood alone in the kitchen. The stove had been stoked and a fire was going in the firebox. He thought of the butchered doe but he decided not to eat, and instead went out the kitchen door to the weedy yard where the Appaloosa was waiting.

He unsaddled the Appaloosa and set her loose to graze in a grassy patch beside the trough. He shook the dust from the saddle blanket and he unfastened his kit and canteen and his bedroll and started for the house but stopped just short of the door. He turned and looked back at the Appaloosa. She was pulling at the summer grass, and he stood a moment and watched the workings of her jaw and the rhythmic motion of the muscles in her face. He could smell the raw and green smell of the newly cropped grass and the smell of the desert hardpan as it began to cool with the dusk. He heard the final calls of birds as they settled on their perches and a low yip yip he took to be an owl or a coyote. Cricket song was just starting up from somewhere near and he heard that too, and the sound of the grass being shorn from its root-holds and the Appaloosa's teeth grinding the grass. I never did name you, he told her. Never did, he said. He hoisted up the blankets and saddle and his gear and carried them into the house.

By now there was early starlight. By now a bright gibbous moon had risen.

The room off the kitchen was dimly lit by a lantern that was nothing more than a flayed tin can stuck with a candle, and by moonlight coming in the only window. The glass stood upright in shards held by the last bits of broken molding and the rotted sash. He stood for a moment and looked out to the silvery plain and the darker band of trees on the banks of the river. He set his saddle on the floor. He unbuckled his holster and his pistol and set them on the old plank bed. He took off his hat and folded it over for a pillow. He took off his boots and held one in his lap. He pulled the nail from its fittings, swiveled the boot-heel open, and worked the paper out of the hollow with his finger. He held it against his knee and took his pencil stub from his pocket and proceeded to write. After a while he refolded the paper into the boot-heel and swiveled it back into position and smacked the heel to the floor to set the nail. And he set both boots soles down and side by side just under the bed. He uncorked the canteen and tipped it up and took the last of the water. He covered himself with the bedroll blanket and stretched out listening to the sounds of the house.

The call of the short-eared owl (Asio flammeus) resembles the bark or yip of a coyote.

When he woke, the moon had set. The candle in the tin can lantern was a smoking wick in a spill of wax. He felt for his pistol beside him on the bed. It was there. He lay still for a moment, peering about, recalling his ride north along the Pecos, remembering that Petey Ray had offered him this small room off the kitchen. The moon had set. The Appaloosa was nickering. He threw off the blanket and stood. There were shards in the window. A sprinkling of stars. The moon had set. The plain beyond the house had lost its silver. He could not see the river. The dark band of trees. The moon had set. Shadows seemed to shift amid the clumps of sage and he thought they might be the shapes of men or horses. He gazed out at the terrain for a while until he thought they were neither and though he had slept he was too weary to keep watch, and he decided that there was nothing moving at all. The moon had set. The shards in the window. He reached for the uncorked canteen and put his mouth to the rim. Nary a drop. He did not pick up his pistol. He did not put on his boots. The smell of candlewax and smoke. The shed out back. The meat in the shed. Them buzzards, them buzzards, Petey said. That's a doe that they're smelling. Already skinned. Hung. Partway butchered. Help yourself, Billyboy. Go cut yourself a steak. The stove's still hot. A greased pan on the grate. Help yourself. Cut a steak. There's a knife on my list. In my kit:

knife
tinderbox
tinder
matches
salt

Go ahead there Billyboy. Help yourself, Billyboy. The stove in the kitchen. Gone cold by now. Ash in the firebox. Matches. Tinder. The greased pan. On the stove. On the grate. The trough. The Appaloosa by the grassy patch. Meat shed. Matches. Knife. Kitchen. The moon had set. There are shards in the window. The moon had set. He stood in the dark in the small room off the kitchen. The Appaloosa was nickering. Another sound now. Footfall or floorboard, he wondered. Quien es? he said. He waited. He listened for an answer. Did he know there was no need to ask who is it? Or for anyone of us ask who or what it is that in shadow or in sunlight? He did not ask again.

He started for the door.

Chapter 111
The Colt
1966

Historic Gun Sells for Undisclosed Amount

The Colt revolver used by Sheriff Patrick Garrett to shoot Billy the Kid over 140 years ago was recently sold at public auction, fetching more than several times the anticipated amount. Nigel Lloyd, director of Atkinson & Lloyd Auctions, Inc. was not surprised at the winning bid which came from an unidentified collector, stating that the firearm is "the most important and fabled relic of the American West, with an unusually well-authenticated provenance."

—*Firearm Quarterly Review. Vol. 27, Feb. 10, 1966*

Chapter 112
What Must Be Remembered When Putting Him Down
July 14, 1881—The Early Morning Hours Before Sunrise

The moon has set. Billy stands in the dark in the small room off the kitchen. The Appaloosa is nickering.

The stove is in the kitchen. The kitchen is beyond the door. The pan is on the stove. The meat is in the shed. The knife is in his hand. The moon has set. There are shards in the window.

He starts for the door.

A man waits on the other side of the door. He is tall and straight with the stance and the look of a lawman. A thick mustache, but trimmed and dapper. Low-crowed hat set level on his head. Narrow brim and uncreased crown. Tweed coat. Tin star. He reaches for his six-shooter. Colt revolver, single action. He considers the height of the man in the room behind the door in front of him. The room just off the kitchen. The small room with one window. He lifts his pistol. He imagines the figure stepping into the doorway. Where to aim? A chest hit will do. And slightly to the left for the heart. But perhaps a little lower. After all, the one he's been hunting is smaller than a man. But hardly a kid. A runt of a man. That must be understood, must be remembered when putting him down. He's a man, after all. Nineteen is full-grown. Remember nineteen? Remember how it was. Knowing right from wrong. Knowing what was what. Behind that door is a killer, not a kid. Rustler, thief, murderer, assassin, felon, criminal, killer. Toting his gun. Always ready to kill and this time kill me, right here in this house, in this doorway, in the dark. But it will be me that's doing the killing with my one chance, one shot. I must be ready. I am ready. I am watching. I am breathing. I am ready. I am a patient man. I wait. The moon has set and I wait in the dark.

He waits for a sound. A rustling. A breath. The click of a hammer. Anything. He watches the door. A patient man. Standing still in the kitchen in the dark with his Colt Single Action pointed at the door. The knob turns. Or seems to turn. Too dark to see. But now, yes. Now it comes. A squeak. A hinge. Ready now. Ready now. The door is opened. There. The boy. The kid. The killer. He adjusts his aim and cocks the hammer.

A single sound and all is set in motion.

A canyon is fully carved with the first tick of the geologic clock.

The trigger drops the hammer. The hammer strikes the firing pin. The firing pin strikes the primer. The primer sparks. The spark ignites the gunpower. Fire, flash. Explosion, propulsion. The bullet spirals down the barrel. Exits the muzzle. Thunderclap report. Thread of smoke. Bullet moving through the air. Through the vest. Through the shirt. Through Billy: left chest, third rib, heart.

The crust of the earth is buckled by a single seismic beat.

A meteor descends, strikes, but leaves no trace of the trail that burned in its wake.

The lead projectile moves imperceptibly through the air, faster than the fracturing of a scarp. Faster than the onset of pain or knowing. Slower than the speed of light that leaves a dying star.

And in that instant, she is there. Jacinta the little señorita. She stands before him, saying what she once had said. Tómame, she tells Billy. Take me. He pulls her to him. Her hair spills over. The scent of a cactus flower. Now his turn to tell her. Tómame, he says. Take me.

Outside, the short-eared owl has ceased its hooting. The crickets have gone silent. A light wind rustles the summer grass that grows around the trough. The Appaloosa briefly paws and snorts and then is still.

In a moment the owl resumes its calling. Bark-like, it is said. As if from a coyote or dog. Yip yip. The last bird. Yip yip yip.

Chapter 113
Cottonwood Being Easier to Chisel
July 14, 1881—Later in the Day

The coffin bearing the corpse was carried from the porch by four men and placed in the bed of a buckboard. The Appaloosa mare had been found wandering beyond the weedy yard of the sheepherder's house, but not far from where Billy had left her, and they attempted to hitch her to the buckboard. She had never pulled a wagon or carriage or cart, and she reared up wildly when the driving halter was looped over her withers and the breast strap touched her neck and she then stood trembling in the tracing, rolling her eyes to the whites. Alejandro Palacios, the milkgoat rancher, stepped out from the small group of remaining onlookers and came forward. He stood before the Appaloosa, speaking to her softly. Chica bonita, muy bonita. He patted her forehead and stroked her nose and when she was quieted, he climbed up into the driving seat of the buckboard and urged her on to the old fort boneyard where the grave had been dug.

The coffin was lowered by ropes. The hole was filled in. The soil was tamped. A trench was made and the marker-plank of cottonwood set in place. Cottonwood had been selected, being a softer wood, free of knots and easier to chisel. Stove soot was rubbed into the words. Here Lies Billy the Kid. No dates had been engraved. No surname had been written. The few in attendance did not linger graveside. It was July, after all. The Moon of Long Day Heat. The afternoon sun was hot and there was no shade.

The sun sets. The western sky glows red. The hardpan quickly cools.

Travelers in the high desert always hurry along through these wide and wild unsheltered places. Some may notice the rising sound of birds calling in the hour before dark. The soft hooting of doves. The warbling of a golden-crowned kinglet. The buzz of a clay-colored sparrow.

Some may hear them in the hour before dawn when their voices fill the cool desert air.

Some may be listening to those early chirps and whistles.

But he will not be listening. And daybreak birdsong will not wake him.

The raspy chatter of a black-billed magpie will be mistaken for the trill of the sagebrush sparrow, or the call-note of the least flycatcher in the chaparral, or even for the voice of the spadefoot toad after an evening rain when it emerges from its burrow.

Any day now Apache plume will be seen blooming along the roadside.

Prickly pear will blossom amid the sage and chamisa.

Desert marigold will fill the gullies.

A trio of coyote pups will emerge from their den in a rocky outcrop. Soon enough they will set out on their own, trotting along the hardpan. Sometime soon, as the cooler weather sets in, in the month the Apache call the Moon of Leaving Geese.

Chapter 114
Personal Effects

LINCOLN COUNTY HISTORICAL SOCIETY

Exhibit 7: List and Display of Personal Effects
of William Henry Bonney, Known as Billy the Kid
Gift to Lincoln County Historical Society
from the estate of Mildred Rudolph-Rotenmeyer, great-great
granddaughter of Milnor Rudolph

In the early morning hours of July 14, 1881, District Coroner Milnor Rudolph was notified of William Bonney's death. Rudolph examined the body, arranged the inquest, and retrieved the boots of the deceased as well as the contents of his saddlebag and kit (Items a. through c. below). After a public viewing, Billy the Kid was interred in the old military cemetery of Fort Sumner. Decades later, an attempt was made to locate the grave but all traces had been washed away by flash flooding in the area.

a. Yellow canary, mounted specimen: The irregular stitching and use of peppercorns for eyes suggest that the taxidermy was not done by a professional.

b. Blue feather, frayed: Given the length and deep blue coloration, it is likely the tail feather of a large domesticated parrot, such as a blue macaw.

c. Leather boots, badly scuffed with worn soles: The left heel opens to a hollow interior which holds a folded square of paper bearing a list of bird species that appear to be in Billy's handwriting. However, discrepancies were found in the formation of the "a" in buzzard, the "m" in magpie, and the "p" in pintail duck.

THE END

Permissions

Excerpts have been published in the following literary journals:

"Nary a Moon for the Mother of Billy the Kid" in *Propagule*;

"The Tintype of Billy the Kid" in *Fence*;

"The Kid's First Kill" and "Tribulations" in *Fictive Dream*;

"The Apache Ponies Do Not Answer" and "With Two Rivers Behind Me" in *The Rupture*;

"As Blades Are Honed" in *Epiphany*;

"The Livery is Short a Horse" in *Frontier Tales*;

"The Turtles of Tortuga" (appeared as "Tortuga") in *Big Other*;

"As The People So Sit" and "The First Cold Winds Coming" in *Socrates on the Beach*;

"Abilene" in *Exacting Clam*;

"Biddy Doro Foraging Flora and Fauna" (which appeared as "Elixirs, Medicinals, and Reliable Remedies for the Mother of Billy the Kid") in *New World Writing*;

"A Dab on the Dummy Teat," "Mrs. Catherine McCarty Hunts the Solitary Stone," "Parchment Note," "Baptism of a Changeling," "Historical Artifact Stolen," "Dr. Arthur Broadwater's Guide to Pregnancy and Birth," and "Preparation for a Hanging in the High Desert" (which appeared as "Before the Hanging") in *The Brooklyn Rail*;

"My First Arrest and Swift Departure," "Silver City Sentinel," and "First Light, Last Look" in *Unsaid*.

www.ingramcontent.com/pod-product-compliance
Lightning Source LLC
LaVergne TN
LVHW010555100826
845148LV00014B/2722